BLACK AND WHITE AND
DEAD ALL OVER

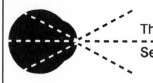

BLACK AND WHITE AND DEAD ALL OVER

JOHN DARNTON

THORNDIKE PRESS
A part of Gale, Cengage Learning

GALE
CENGAGE Learning™

Detroit • New York • San Francisco • New Haven, Conn • Waterville, Maine • London

GALE
CENGAGE Learning™

LIBRARY OF CONGRESS CATALOGING-IN-PUBLICATION DATA

Darnton, John.
  Black and white and dead all over / by John Darnton.
    p. cm.
  ISBN-13: 978-1-4104-1093-1 (hardcover : alk. paper)
  ISBN-10: 1-4104-1093-5 (hardcover : alk. paper)
  1. Newspapers—Fiction. 2. New York (N.Y.)—Fiction. 3. Murder—Fiction. 4. Large type books. I. Title.
PS3554.A727B55 2008b
813'.54—dc22   2008032340

Published in 2008 by arrangement with Alfred A. Knopf, Inc.

To the memory of:

Homer Bigart, Peter Kihss,
Murray Schumach,
Gloria Emerson, Bill Farrell,
Tony Lukas,
Joe Schroeder, Flora Lewis,
Abe Rosenthal,
Dick Shepard, Shelly Binn, and
Johnny Apple

He had once seen . . . a barely intelligible film about newspaper life in New York where neurotic men in shirt sleeves and eye-shades had rushed from telephone to tape machine, insulting and betraying one another in surroundings of unredeemed squalor.

Evelyn Waugh, *Scoop*

1

Ellen Butterby had never before seen a dead body. So she was not at all prepared for what she found on that mid-September morning.

It was a chilly day, mist turning to rain. She emerged still groggy from New York's Port Authority bus terminal on Eighth Avenue — she had napped on the bus from Montclair — and angry that she had left her umbrella at home. To be unprepared ran against her character. Her gray hair was already covered with tiny droplets, a spider's web glistening with morning dew.

She walked to the open-air coffee wagon on West Forty-fifth Street and joined the line behind five people. She seethed that it was moving so slowly, depriving her of the shelter of the wagon's metal sideboard, propped up to provide a roof for only the first two or three customers.

Finally she reached the service window.

From inside, Bashir flashed a smile.

"Some day, isn't it?" he remarked.

She nodded curtly by way of reply.

He had anticipated her order, one hand holding the container with the Lipton tea bag, the other bent at the wrist, pulling back the hot-water tap. On days like this, when the windows of his wagon steamed over and he hunched down to make change from the coins scattered on a towel beside the window, the Afghan struck her as a troll in his lair.

She picked up the container and set off down the block, leaning into the now-quickening rain. She reflected on the fact that she was rarely pleasant to Bashir. Perhaps, she mused, she was something of a snob. She felt a vague stab of emptiness. What did she have to be snobbish about? Childless, unmarried, fifty-seven years old, and living with her bedridden mother, she had not drunk deeply from life. As a young woman fresh out of secretarial school, she had answered a help wanted ad, appeared in the cavernous lobby of the *New York Globe,* and was hired at ninety dollars a week. That was thirty-six years ago, and she had been there ever since. What had she accomplished? Like everyone else, she had given everything to the paper, that bottomless pit. She was aware, on days when she scanned the obits, that she wouldn't merit a single paragraph.

But lately, it seemed, the newspaper was beginning to repay her. She had risen through the ranks to a respectable position, administrative assistant to none other than Theodore S. Ratnoff, the *Globe*'s much-feared assistant managing editor. Ratnoff was famous for the dressing-downs meted out to subordinates, especially copy editors, who labored in suffering obscurity like half-blind medieval monks churning out illuminated manuscripts. He was in charge of style, standards, and usage — the coin of the realm — and he enforced his edicts with Torquemadan unrestraint. A dangling modifier led to a verbal lash of the whip, a pejorative anonymous quote to a figurative stab with a red-hot poker. Headlines of unintentional ambiguity — so-called two-faced heads — brought out the rack. But on substantive issues — like pandering to the reader with puff pieces — he was among the worst.

Two things were notable about Ratnoff. One was his intelligence, which made his remarks all the more cutting; he was rarely wrong, and on those rare occasions when he was, no one below the masthead called

11

him on it. The other was his imposing demeanor and fastidious dress. He was tall and blond, of German extraction on his mother's side and Hungarian on his father's, with a crew cut like a ship's prow and cold blue eyes. His black pinstriped suits were bespoke and the white cuffs of his Turnbull & Asser shirts were clasped by diamond-chipped links. His shoes were polished to the patina of a black tulip. Such an outfit might turn a smaller man into a dandy, but in Ratnoff's case it accentuated his naturally dominating presence. When he walked into a room, other men sometimes felt a tingling in their gonads.

Among all the reporters and editors, only Ratnoff was permitted to use a purple flow pen. How this corporate crotchet came about, no one remembered, but it had become a law of its own, enforced when necessary by Ratnoff himself. A cocky young editor who bucked the sanction in his first week — he used a purple pen to fill out an overtime form — was shortly afterward banished to real estate news. This coup de grâce spread Ratnoff's notoriety to newsrooms all the way to the West Coast.

Ratnoff wielded his purple pen liberally, dispensing critical notes of Teutonic exactitude with such abandon that copy editors reporting for work developed the habit of gravitating toward their mailboxes to see if the walnut interior reflected a lavender glow. Every few weeks, Ratnoff's messages — he kept dupes, naturally — were collated into a bundle the size of a suburban phone directory and distributed to the staff. These became known as "poison plums." The public humiliation from the plums took such a toll on morale that senior management eventually prevailed on Ratnoff to leaven the dough with an occasional compliment. He complied. Thereafter, he trolled through each day's paper with one eyebrow raised, turning the pages at arm's length, as if they were radioactive, looking for bright news stories and clever turns of phrase to praise. Whenever he came upon a felicitous headline, along the lines of WAL-MART CASH REGISTERS RINGING UP A GREEN CHRISTMAS or ST. PAT'S PARADE TURNS IRISH EYES TO SMILING, he would fire off a note to "the slot" — the person in charge of the appropriate copy desk — demanding the name of the author. These notes invariably consisted of two words whose brevity was peremptory: "Nice. Who?"

Butterby came to the revolving door and pushed. The brushed edges gave way with customary reluctance. The lobby floor was

13

slippery. She noticed with approbation that the guards, seated behind their pale consoles, were chatting amiably. They had not yet laid the trail of thick green carpeting that grew so soggy that a trip to the elevator bank was like wading through the Everglades. She pulled out her ID card, swiped it, and gave the turnstile arm a sideways pelvic thrust. She skirted the massive five-foot globe of the earth suspended by wires over an upside-down dome in the floor — the paper's symbol, also printed on its front-page nameplate — that had so impressed her during that long-ago job interview and that the reporters, cynical souls all, called "the barbecue pit."

She rode the elevator to the fifth floor, still thinking about Ratnoff. If she were honest with herself, she'd have to admit that she drew a certain satisfaction from his tyrannical reputation because some of it rubbed off on her. With self-satisfied magnanimity, she pretended not to notice the kowtowing of other secretaries who hurried to make space for her in the company cafeteria, or the catch in the voice of a backfield editor who languidly picked up a phone receiver and learned who was calling.

The receptionist's desk on the fifth floor

was unoccupied. Behind it lay the vast newsroom, now dormant. It was an entire block long, from Forty-fifth Street to Forty-sixth Street, with windows on either end. Clocks affixed to pillars ticked off seconds noiselessly and computers glowed, their screen savers floating eerily, as if they were signaling one another. Butterby loved it like this, deserted and peaceful, a battlefield after the slaughter. Page proofs and notes and photos cluttered the editors' desks like spent bandages and cartridge belts. The reporters' cubicles were darkened, burned-out pillboxes. Their desks were stacked with debris — yellowing newspapers, thick bound reports, legal pads, loose notes, books, food containers, coffee cups. Inside, the fabric walls were plastered over with clipped cartoons, yellow Post-its, vacation photos, and clever sayings about deadlines: "What dead lion? I don't know anything about a dead lion."

She looked at a clock. Eight-thirty. In another half hour, the place would begin to come alive, at first gradually as the copy people came in to clean up, then more quickly as the news clerks arrived to check the wires and look for messages, and then rapidly as the assistant editors rushed in to review assignments and draw up news schedules, and finally frantically as the desk heads and senior editors strode in to check the overnight reports and phone the foreign, national, and metro desks to ask what was going on.

It was a ballet she had seen hundreds of times, thousands.

Except that today it was different.

For today, as she rounded the central aisle of the newsroom, not far from Ratnoff's glassed-in office, she saw something lying in the middle of an open space near the page-one conference room. It was large, indistinct, and definitely out of place — a pile of something, perhaps, or an overturned piece of furniture or — was this possible? — an animal of some sort. A Great Dane? A beached shark?

She strode closer and gasped, her hand rising involuntarily to her mouth, ready to stifle a scream.

It was a body, a lifeless body, and not just any body. It was Ratnoff. On his back, his arms outstretched as if ready to hug the air, lying in a pool of blood that had almost reached the glass doors of the conference room, turning the heavy-wear carpet a rusted brown. She tiptoed closer and looked down.

Ratnoff's eyes were closed. His face looked

peaceful. But there, in the center of his chest, was a four-inch-wide green hunk of metal. She recognized it immediately. It was the base of an editor's spike, used in the old days to kill stories. The metal shaft protruding from it was sunk into Ratnoff's blue-and-red-striped shirt, hammered in so hard that it had created a tiny cavity filled with bright blood. The end of his red tie dipped into it, like a tongue into a martini glass. Fixed to the spike was a note.

She leaned over the body to read it. It was in purple ink.

It said simply: "Nice. Who?"

2

"You see," said Skeeter Diamond, clearing his throat with a guttural cough that he hoped would lend a touch of gravitas to his words, "we're looking for . . . ah . . . heft in our classical music coverage."

Was that the right word — *heft?* He wasn't sure. And in talking about concert reviews, was it proper to speak of *coverage?* That didn't sound quite right, either. He continued.

"We are, as perhaps you're aware, about to broaden our . . . coverage of rock music and rap. And so naturally this seems to be a propitious time to . . . ah . . . take a hard look at our classical music department and perhaps consolidate it."

Consolidate was perhaps an understatement. The paper had five classical music critics (who were always feuding — something about "uptown" music versus "downtown," a distinction that escaped him).

18

Given the paper's need for economy and its quest for ever-younger readers, he had concluded that the time had come to whittle their number down somewhat . . . in fact, to one. And to fill that slot with someone from the outside. So here he was, the executive editor, wooing a potential critic over a breakfast of scrambled eggs and croissants at the Millennium Hotel. The wooing was not going very well, in part because Diamond felt out of his depth when it came to culture. That was not where he had earned his spurs. At a meeting just the other day, Suzanne Preston, the culture editor, had seemed to confuse Pavarotti with Placido Domingo, but he wasn't certain enough to call her on it.

And in fact, Suzanne Preston, by remarkable coincidence, was at that very moment seated across the room, entertaining one of the current music critics, Donald Yeagum, who hadn't yet been sacked but who looked as if his dog had just died. Every so often, one or the other glanced his way, which cramped Diamond's style. He had initially tried to pretend that his dining partner was merely a friend, draping his arm casually over the back of his chair and smiling often, but the pale young man with spiked hair sitting across from him, taciturn and tight as a clam, refused to cooperate. No matter what restaurant Diamond chose lately, he seemed to run into someone from the *Globe.* Maybe his secretary was e-mailing his schedule around.

He had set his cell phone on vibrate, and it went off in his right trouser pocket, producing what felt like an electric current to the groin. He jerked his knee upward, banging the bottom of the table and spilling his coffee into the saucer and onto the white cloth.

"Shit," he said. He quickly apologized. The critic, who came from an effete Web magazine called *Artz Tzar,* didn't look like someone who spent much time in the trenches.

"I think I've got to take this," Diamond said. He stood up, one finger in his ear, trying to decipher an indistinct, somewhat hysterical voice in the other ear, and walked toward the lobby.

Diamond still retained a bit of the swagger of a foreign correspondent, but it was covered over now with Armani suits and a weight of corporate concerns. His jaw was square and his eyes an alluring hazel, which was advantageous for an executive. His ears were pinned close to his head and his hair was speckled with gray except for his white-tufted temples. But his features were slightly marred by a perverse facial tic. It had begun some time ago in the left eye, a sort of squinting. Initially, it could be passed off as an assertive blink, but then it had spread, so that the entire side of his face scrunched up, and recently it had jumped to the other eye, as well. At critical moments, he felt like a goddamned owl.

Things had been rough lately. The *Globe*'s stock had been declining — it was almost in free fall — and so the damn publisher was on his back, demanding that he do something . . . anything. The bean counters were on him, too, and now they'd been joined by the cost cutters. He detested them — humorless types in starched white shirts, whose idea of excitement was a golf game at the local country club. They wouldn't know a good newspaper if it kicked them in the balls. Negotiations with the business side were an orgy of hypocrisy. The pretense was, We're all in this together, but that wasn't true: *He* was in it and they were sitting on the sidelines. He had already given up a correspondent's slot in Tokyo and agreed to close the Abidjan bureau — he, a onetime foreign correspondent who had cut his milk teeth in Africa! And they still weren't satisfied. They wanted more! They demand cuts and then circulation goes down and then they're surprised and up in arms. What do they expect? And the old-time reporters and editors — "the dinosaur brigade," he called them — were whining. He knew they denigrated him, just because he tried to liven up the paper with imaginative features and soft news. You'd think they'd wake up and see that meteor spinning though space right at them. You'd think they'd want to avoid extinction.

Diamond hadn't gotten much sleep last night. He awoke at 3:00 a.m., tossed the blankets off, and retreated to his newly reconstructed kitchen with its travertine marble island, recessed lighting, and purring Sub-Zero. He poured a glass of milk and opened a box of Oreos, a combination that used to soothe him as a child. He looked out the window: deserted Central Park West, traffic lights turning red, a bit of fog, steam rising from the manhole covers. He felt his diaphragm contract, a catch in his breathing. A spreading sense of loss suffused his limbs and brain. Where had it all gone? Those years of adventure and confidence. And hope. Interviewing Yeltsin over a bottle of vodka in his private Tupolev. Chewing khat with Somali guerrillas in the Ogaden while Ethiopian jets scoured the skies above. Watching the Berlin Wall come down and, briefly, throwing his objectivity to the winds, dancing on it with those chanting students. Riding into Kampala for the downfall of Idi Amin — he was the guy who had opened Amin's basement freezer to see if it actually contained human hearts (it didn't). He had even gone into Uganda two years before and played basketball with the man! In a moment of bravado, he had blocked Amin's jump shot, a feat that went zooming over telexes all across Africa and made him the hero of the press corps. No question about it: He had been the best hack going. Even that word *hack,* the self-deprecating term that was all part of the pose (We're no big deal, just guys out here doing a job) — you don't hear it anymore. Now they call themselves *journalists,* for Christ sake.

And so . . . no more dictators, no more coups or earthquakes. Just bean counters and a shrinking news hole and ambitious underlings. He dunked the last Oreo, finished it, turned out the lights, and returned to bed. His wife, Adele, was still asleep, snoring demurely, and his cocker spaniel had taken his place. He pushed the dog down, stripped off his satin pajamas, and went to sleep buck naked, the way he used to in the tropics, like a true hack. In the morning, he had hit the snooze button three times and groaned when he remembered the breakfast meeting. Classical music, of all things . . .

"Wait a minute. I think something's up," said Suzanne Preston, watching Diamond as he took the call outside the hotel, standing close to the building to avoid the downpour. He was framed by the restaurant window and she had a perfect view. Across from her, Yeagum, pouring himself another coffee, was droning on about a recent review that had gone wrong.

"How was I to know the tenor had a cold? It's not like it was common knowledge. I mean, okay, so they announced it from the stage. I was busy studying the sheet music. He sounded just fine to me."

Preston tuned him out and continued to stare at Diamond, trying to read his body language. She liked Skeeter, sort of, no matter what the others said. She supposed she was one of "his people," since he had been the one to appoint her culture editor. It had happened two years earlier, following his visit to London, where she'd been number two in the *Globe*'s bureau. By chance, he saw her leaving the National Gallery (she had actually just dashed in to use the toilet). They strolled up the Strand, stopped for coffee, and she mentioned that she had a soft spot for art, which was to some degree true. An undercurrent of flirtation circled their talk that day and it had continued more or less ever since, though neither acted upon it. He wasn't as bad as some of the bosses. Still, he seemed different lately, less spontaneous, less vital. That happened to all of them when they got way up there. She remembered hearing a metro reporter recently proclaim, "The publisher's been pissing so much on Skeeter, his fire's gone out."

"And you remember my review of Bartoli in *Cenerentola*?" Yeagum continued. "Okay, so maybe I got one thing wrong — maybe she wasn't miked. But she sure as hell sounded like it. And it's the rotund bouquet of the sound that matters, after all. I think Diamond dropped the ball on that one. He should've stood behind me."

But Preston wasn't listening. She was transfixed by what she saw.

"Jesus," she muttered. "This looks big."

Diamond's jaw had dropped. She had always assumed that was just an expression, but there he stood, mouth wide open, chin touching his collar, gaping in the rain. Then

25

he pocketed his phone, spun around, came in to grab his coat, and, mumbling a few words, ran out, leaving the poor young critic alone — and stiffing him with the bill.

"I'm out of here," she said.

Outside, she caught up with Diamond and offered him half of her umbrella. He ducked under, walking so fast, she had to practically run in her high heels to keep up.

She thought of using a line like "Where's the fire?" but it sounded corny.

"What's up?" she asked.

"Ratnoff."

"Ratnoff?"

"He's dead."

"What? When? How?"

"Sounds like he's been murdered."

"Murdered!"

She stopped in her tracks and he grabbed her arm and pulled her.

"Who did it?"

"I don't know. But it happened in the newsroom."

"Jesus Christ! You mean —"

"— an inside job, as they say."

She looked over at Diamond. His face was contorted as if in pain, but she realized it was his tic, working overtime.

"Someone we know?" Her voice had dropped almost to a whisper.

"No doubt."

"Any suspects?"

"Let's see. How many people are there in editorial? I'd say about twelve hundred." He halted, looking ahead along the block. "Shit."

There, in front of the *Globe*'s revolving door, two police cars were parked at angles to the sidewalk, the doors hanging open. The whirling beams on top bathed a crowd and the slick sidewalk in flickering red. Another cop car came down the street, siren blaring.

Suzanne and Skeeter approached. The crowd was milling about and growing like a pinwheel. The police had strung yellow tape around the entrance, winding it around a NO PARKING sign. A line had formed to one side and two cops were checking IDs and letting people in one by one. Diamond approached a sergeant, pulled out his wallet with his ID, and showed it to him.

"Officer, I need to pass," he said in a voice that had overcome countless African road-blocks.

"Oh yeah? And why is that?"

Diamond raised his hand and waved it at the building. "I'm in charge of this place."

The sergeant gestured at the crowd and the street. "Well, I'm in charge of *this* place.

27

And you're gonna stand in line like everyone else."

3

The publisher of the *Globe,* Elisha R. Hagenbuckle, moved from pacing around his office on the thirteenth floor to pacing around the thick mahogany conference table in the adjoining boardroom. His nervous legs demanded greater range. He was like a rhino with cage fever. He felt like smoking — for the first time in ten years — and he was muttering to himself. He walked quickly, holding his hands behind him, palms outward as if wearing invisible handcuffs, a parody of a man in animated concentration. Thinking was not his forte, but he had a certain cunning.

The boardroom's cream-colored walls were covered top to bottom with blackframed photos, signed in black ink, of eminent visitors down through the decades, everyone from Chiang Kai-shek to Houdini ("You had me tied up in knots. Warmly, Harry") and from Douglas Fairbanks to

Molotov ("Enjoyed the cocktails. Best wishes always, Slava"). Usually, Hagenbuckle derived comfort in contemplating them, evoking as they did the paper's storied past, but this time he gave them not a single glance.

Today had begun normally. The most vexing item on his calendar was an afternoon appointment with a rabbinical council from Williamsburg, protesting, no doubt, yesterday's front-page story about the Israelis bulldozing Palestinian houses on the West Bank. He had planned to summon Skeeter Diamond to handle it, maybe even the foreign editor, too (whoever that was), while he sat back behind his desk and remained silent, occasionally frowning or nodding.

But this . . . this business! A murder right in the newsroom! It was bound to push the stock even deeper down the toilet. A scandal like this was unheard of. Nothing like this had happened since . . . He stopped pacing for a moment, thought back. The name came to him out of the ether: Charles E. Chapin, the much-hated city editor of the *Evening World.* He murdered his wife in a hotel room and left a DO NOT DISTURB sign on the door. As Hagenbuckle remembered reading somewhere, Chapin, on the way to his execution at Sing Sing in 1930, had criticized how the papers, especially his own, were handling his story. True to the end. You almost had to admire it.

Hagenbuckle walked back into his office. If you didn't know that he was a big-game hunter, you knew it the moment you stepped inside. The walls were adorned with a wide array of hoofed fauna, mostly of the horned variety: elk, stag, antelope, and, his pièce de résistance, a menacing water buffalo that he had brought down in Masai Mara with the aid, he rarely admitted, of a sharp-shooting white hunter from Governors' Camp. If a guest came to visit with an ulterior agenda — say, a union leader or a liberal politician — Hagenbuckle usually sat him directly under the buffalo's jaw. "You can almost feel him drooling on you," he liked to say when beginning the conversation.

Not that Hagenbuckle needed a prop to be intimidating. Six three, big-chested, a head of hair like a lion, ruddy-faced, with tiny squiggles of red-purple spider veins in his cheeks that might lead one to think, erroneously, he was a problem drinker, he dominated those around him as a given right. He was a man of action, but he liked to imagine — incorrectly — that he had more than a passing acquaintance with

Shakespeare. In his sixty-six years, he had done it all: skydiving, Formula One racing, Jackie Kennedy escorting, flying a shuttle simulator with Carl Sagan, and playing checkers underwater with Jacques Cousteau (the pieces were magnetized to the board). He kept a fireman's helmet in his closet and a pilot's license in his wallet, which he had once handed over to a trooper who caught him doing 110 on the New York State Thruway. "He just shook his head and let me go," he'd add in a deep basso as he recounted the story over cigars.

Hagenbuckle had married into his position (his wife was the only child of the paper's renowned founder, now deceased). First the old man and then he himself had presided with majesty during the paper's glory days. The countless scoops, going toe-to-toe with Richard Nixon, refusing to buckle before the White House or City Hall, the Knapp Commission, New York City's fiscal crisis, Soviet dissidents, the moon landing, Clinton's impeachment, 9/11 — all of it seeming to happen so effortlessly. In the morning, you picked up the newspaper and there it was, neatly laid out with head-lines whose size and placement told you what was important. The prizes and revenue poured in. It was like standing on the bridge of an aircraft carrier and believing that you, not the ocean, were actually keeping the damn thing afloat. But now, with the Internet, the blogs, MSNBC, fifteen-minute news cycles, giveaway papers in the subway — Christ, you turn around for a moment and the whole damn world is different. A cliché, maybe, but it's true. Just two days ago, he had asked Rosen, one of his two sons, a computer geek, to introduce him to some sites; he read a smattering of them (superficial.com, gawker.com, defamer .com) and he was aghast. Where the hell did it come from, this abiding compulsion to read about the breakups and breakdowns of third-rate celebrities? To pursue them into restaurants and nightclubs as they turned bulimic or cheated on their partners or adopted African babies? And written in a spirit of such spite (he didn't know the word *schadenfreude*). "That's the whole point, Dad," his son had said, laughing condescendingly. "You've got to be snarky."

He should have seen the end of the world coming when the circulation of *People* magazine surpassed that of *Time.* What was a man to do? The editors assured him the public appetite for "personality" stories was driving the news these days. In his darker moments, which seemed to be coming more frequently lately, he thought maybe it was time to give it all up, to step off the bridge and hand the USS *Globe* over to someone younger. But who? That was the question that always stumped him. Not to put too fine a point on it, his twin sons were dolts. Sharper than a serpent's tooth is an idiotic child.

If he were still smoking, this would be the moment to light up. He made a pass at the desk and swiped at the intercom.

"Miss Overton, where the blazes are they?"

"Here, sir. In the anteroom. Waiting for you."

"Well, damn it, send them in."

He prepared himself to deal with his editorial underlings. No one was better at speaking power to truth.

Diamond entered, looking stricken, and behind him came Bernie Grabble, whose expression was indecipherable. Grabble was the metro editor, an energetic, overheated, lanky windmill of a man with a boundless imagination — he could tilt back his chair, look up at the ceiling's acoustical tiles, and spot a heartrending story in the dots. But in selling it to a reporter, he could be as crafty as a used-car salesman.

Hagenbuckle sat down and gave them

both tough stares. "What do we know and what do we know about it?" he asked, his customary way of leading subordinates to tackle a tough problem.

"Not a helluva lot," said Diamond. "Ratnoff was killed sometime overnight. Probably in the building. No one saw it — or no one we know of. It looks pretty brutal. A spike was . . . ah . . . hammered into his chest."

"A spike?"

"An editor's spike," put in Grabble.

"Good God, I thought we did away with those when we went to computers."

"The old-timers keep them around. It makes them feel safe — dealing with paper and all that."

"But that was the whole point of computers — get rid of the paper. Wasn't it?"

"Yes, it may still happen . . . someday."

Hagenbuckle fell silent, and so did the two editors. There was a moment's silence — everyone thinking. Then suddenly he smacked the top of his desk with his palm, causing Grabble, sitting on the edge of his seat, to jump. Diamond, slumped in his chair, sat immobile.

"We're up shit's creek without a paddle," said the publisher. "Once the tabs get hold of this, there'll be no stopping them. There's

35

gotta be some explanation that's halfway . . . you know . . . believable. Maybe he was killed by an outsider. A freak occurrence — could have happened anywhere. He was working late; an intruder comes in. He finds his way to the fifth floor. Maybe had a grudge against the paper. He's angry over one of our exposés. . . ."

"Um . . . we could try that," said Diamond.

"There's a problem," said Grabble. He told them about the note.

"Jesus," said Hagenbuckle. "That makes it sound like somebody who works here." He paused, grasping at straws. "Maybe it's a serial intruder. He goes to the cafeteria a lot, overhears conversations. He comes in so often, he gets to know the place — the personalities."

Diamond looked at the carpet. Grabble began shaking his head dubiously. They kicked around a few other scenarios, none of them convincing.

"How's the newsroom taking it?" Hagenbuckle asked. He somehow felt he should inquire.

Grabble piped up. "Pretty good, better than you'd expect."

"Maybe it hasn't hit them yet," the publisher ventured.

"They're crowding around the body — those who can get in," said Diamond.

"I arrived early, so I wasn't stopped by the police," added Grabble. "They stopped Skeeter, but I called down and managed to get him through." At this, Diamond's brow furrowed into a frown, which began a slow conversion into a tic. Grabble continued: "They're checking IDs but slowly letting people in, so at some point all the reporters will be here. I'm tackling the morale problem. I've ordered bagels and cream cheese."

"Good idea," said Hagenbuckle. "Maybe throw in some Nova. And don't charge them this time. By the way, where's the body?"

Both editors answered at once, but Diamond kept talking and overrode the metro editor. "It's still lying there next to the conference room. There's nothing we can do about that. We can't move it till the cops give the okay. The police will be . . . ah . . . asking a lot of questions."

"Hmmm," replied Hagenbuckle. "And how about our own coverage?"

"I've assigned Jude Hurley," said Grabble.

Diamond shot him a hard look. "Hurley. Why Hurley? We should have talked about this."

Hagenbuckle frowned. He seemed to

recall the man's name — something about a scandal he uncovered down at police headquarters. "What's wrong with him?" he asked.

"He's a little young," said Diamond. "I mean, he's a good investigative reporter and all that, but this is sensitive stuff. An in-house story. I'd have preferred someone we can trust — you know, someone like Riddleton."

Steven R. Riddleton, a veteran reporter approaching retirement, had never set the world on fire, but he was a solid company man, with what the British would call "good hands." He had written all the recent sensitive stories about the *Globe*'s plummeting stock, which were light on specifics and heavy on historical context.

"It's a little late to change it now," said Grabble, a thin smile pursing his lips. "We take Hurley off it and you'll be reading about it in the *Observer*. In fact, they've already called a couple of times to find out what's going on."

"We could add Riddleton. Double-team it."

Grabble shook his head, not too vehemently — he was, after all, Diamond's subordinate — but enough to register thoughtful dissent. "I don't know . . . that might make it into a bigger deal. We ought to downplay it, as much as we can. Treat it just like another story — not routine, of course, but hardly the Second Coming. Play it inside." He looked at Hagenbuckle. "Don't you think?"

"Damn right. You're in the shit, you don't advertise it." He stood up, a sign that the meeting was over. "I want you to watch this closely." He looked at Diamond. "What's the matter with your eye?"

"Nothing. Little cold I picked up."

The editors filed out. Just at that moment, his secretary buzzed and announced over an intercom, "The police are on their way up."

"As if my day wasn't bad enough," Hagenbuckle snapped back. "Go out and get me a pack of Trues."

In the elevator, Diamond turned to Grabble, ready to give him a piece of his mind. But the car stopped one floor down at the cafeteria level, and three members of the art department got in, buzzing about the murder. The moment they saw who was inside, they stopped. Everyone rode in silence to the fifth floor.

In the newsroom, Grabble consciously turned his back on the knot of people crowded around the body. He was squeamish. He motioned for his deputy, Bridget Bates, to follow him into his private office, leading the way in long strides. He closed the door and spoke softly but firmly.

"I want you to find Jude Hurley the moment he comes in. Use his cell if you have to. Get him here. I want to assign him to the Ratnoff murder."

"Okay," she replied. She paused. "But . . . why Hurley? Isn't he — you know — sort of a loose cannon?"

"He's one damn fine reporter. He's a digger. Relentless — a goddamned terrier. He sinks his teeth in, he won't let go. At times like this, you need to get to the bottom of it. Find out what happened. That's what you want. That's what you need. Get it?"

"Got it," she said, her voice filled with genuine admiration.

4

Riding the shuttle from Grand Central to Times Square, Jude only half listened to the panhandler collecting donations for the homeless — and holding up a plastic garbage bag of "sandwiches" to bolster the claim. He had heard the man's spiel before. And anyway, he had other things on his mind.

He was feeling restless and he didn't know why. Things were going okay at the *Globe*, though a wisecrack had cut short a recent stint in the Albany bureau. The governor had held a long and incomprehensible news conference to explain why the state budget was six months late; the press corps was confused and bored, and Jude raised his hand to ask, "Is it too late to drop this course?" It brought a huge laugh, also an official complaint, and he had found himself on a train back to the city, gazing at the autumnal Hudson.

Still, the thrill of the job hadn't worn off, even after nine years as a reporter and before that, three as a copyboy. He had found his calling following a parade of dead-end jobs after graduating from the University of Wisconsin. Reporting was a good fit and he was good at it. He liked the adrenaline rush of working on deadline and nailing a story just right. He liked being at the center of the action and tilting at the citadels of power. He exulted in the old newspaper battle cry: "To afflict the comfortable and comfort the afflicted."

But he couldn't shake the feeling that he should move on to the next stage, whatever that might be. He was hungry for something big to happen in his life. He was thirty-five years old and living in a walk-up on Avenue B, alone unless you counted his dog, a mix of German shepherd and Irish setter named TK. He liked New York and knew where the good bars and jazz clubs were and had a close circle of friends, though they were all busy with their own careers and didn't see one another as often as they used to.

And then there was Elaine, his almost live-in girlfriend. They had been going out for more than a year, and the thrill of mutual discovery was steadily giving way to routine. Perversely, as things cooled, she had begun pressuring him to marry her. He vacillated between moments of weakness, usually after sex, in which he came within a hairsbreadth of inviting her to move in with him, and reveries of independence, brought about by their arguments. She accused him of giving more of himself to his job than to her.

Two nights ago, in a coffeehouse, she had called him a "work-obsessed, irresponsible, selfish bastard." He told her that he objected to the "bastard" part, which led to a further charge that he never took her seriously. Throughout, the waitress stood against a wall and watched with a tight smile. When she passed him the check, she had written on it, "I'm a lot less high-maintenance," followed by her phone number. He had slipped it into his pocket, following the reporter's doctrine that any check anywhere might someday prove reimbursable, and he promptly forgot about it — that is, until he poured it out with his change and keys onto his bureau right in front of Elaine. More grist for her mill. So okay — if he hadn't been flirting with her, why had she written that down? And once she'd written it down, why had he kept it? Explain that one. He gave up. She had gone home.

Was that why he was feeling these currents of dissatisfaction? All because of her? But if so, then why was he daydreaming of something else — of ways to inject more juice into his life? Avoidance of boredom had been his life credo for years. That was why he had become a reporter.

The subway lurched to a stop. Jude took out a crumpled dollar and placed it in the palm of the panhandler, who recognized him and whispered low: "Thanks, my man." Jude mounted the stairs two at a time and took the underground passageway, past stores selling shirts, DVDs, and newspapers. His reflection dogged him in the plate-glass windows. Jude had a thin, angular face, with hair that tended toward the unruly and a wise-guy smile that could open doors. His looks were protean, a lover had once told him in bed: One minute he looked almost ordinary, but the next — looking serious after a movie, telling a joke at a bar, walking hunched with his hands in his pockets in the cold — he could be devastating. He had liked her saying that.

He mounted another set of stairs and was greeted by rain. He pulled his collar up and walked two blocks uptown, threading his way through the tourists who meandered along slowly and blocked the sidewalk with their umbrellas. Sometimes he felt like plowing right through them. He was put off by the new Times Square, so Disneyfied and commercially bland, not that he openly longed for the old days of the pimps and the pushers.

He stopped at Bashir's wagon for a black coffee.

"Jude," said Bashir, "did you hear the news?"

He shook his head, waiting. Bashir, who often provided intricate descriptions of military campaigns in Afghanistan weeks before correspondents there cottoned on to them, was nothing if not reliable.

"Ratnoff — he's dead. His body is still there on the floor of the newsroom."

Jude was struck dumb. His eyes said it all, opened wide in disbelief.

"It's so. He has been murdered. The police are there. Everyone's looking. As we say in my homeland, 'A donkey that dies on the riverbank brings many flies.' "

Jude abandoned his coffee and ran down the street. The news was too sensational, too far-fetched, not to be true. Still, it was hard to take it on board. Not until he came near the *Globe* building and saw the burgeoning crowd and the police tape and the cops and the TV cameras, whose lights turned the raindrops a golden yellow, did it seem real.

Ratnoff dead. He couldn't believe it. He felt sorry for the guy even though most others undoubtedly wouldn't. Just yesterday, he had passed him in the hallway, stepping to one side to let the big man pass. Ratnoff had corked a lot of careers in his time, but he had never done Jude dirt. He had even praised some of his scoops. Once, he had excoriated him for starting a story with the word *it,* arguing that the use of the third-person singular pronoun at the beginning of a news article was sophomoric. In half an hour's research, Jude had found ten major novels, including *Pride and Prejudice,* that employed the device; he had sent Xeroxes of the opening pages to Ratnoff and heard not a word back, interpreting the silence to mean point taken.

"Why not let us in?" a reporter yelled out to the police.

"One by one," a cop said. "It's a crime scene."

"Whaddaya expect?" the reporter replied. "It's a newspaper."

Jude passed by the entrance, turned onto Eighth Avenue, pulled out his cell phone, and punched in the metro desk. The call was answered by Clive Small, a news assistant, who was his friend. Clive reminded him of himself at a younger age. Jude had helped him compose ledes on his feature stories, and Clive, in turn, kept Jude up-to-date on newsroom rumors.

"Clive. What's going on? Any idea who killed Ratnoff?"

"No. And it's a madhouse, dude. I mean, even more than usual."

"Anyone assigned to the story?"

"Not yet."

Jude hung up and took a narrow alley to a back door. He felt in his pocket for his keys and pulled them out. Years ago, the Istanbul bureau chief, on home leave, had filched a master key from a senior editor during a night of heavy drinking, duplicating it and sending copies to a dozen friends on staff, who reproduced them. Typical, Jude thought: a world-famous newspaper, a building listed as a possible terrorist target, a lockdown because of a murder — and all you need to get in is one of about fifty keys floating around. He opened the door and climbed five flights in a dimly lighted stairwell, almost slipping on the fresh carpet of cigarette butts. That, too, was typical — smoking anywhere in the building had been outlawed three years ago.

As soon as he stepped into the newsroom, Bridget Bates, the deputy metro editor, was on him like an attack dog. She led him to Grabble's private office and told him to sit down.

"Don't move a muscle," she warned, a bead of sweat on her upper lip revealing a darkening trace. She left, closing the door, as if to keep him prisoner. Sitting in a hard-backed wooden chair, he scanned the walls. They were covered with metal press plates of page-one metro stories (JERSEY FLOODED, THOUSANDS FLEE, OTHERS DROWN; BLACKOUT PLUNGES CITY INTO DARKNESS; and MAYORAL CANDIDATE UNDERGOES SURGERY — with a subhead: "Denies Sex Change").

Jude's palms were beginning to sweat. He hardly dared voice his hope. Usually, metro editors summoned reporters to the city desk to dole out assignments from a pile of notes and the Associated Press daybook or patrolled the aisles like muggers. But every once in a while, if the assignment was truly special, the reporter would be herded into Grabble's office, where . . .

At that moment, Bernie Grabble bounded in, opening the door and shutting it so quickly behind him that he was like an actor rushing onstage.

"Where've you been?" he demanded. "I've been looking all over for you. What's with

you anyway? Don't you know, a good reporter, something happens . . . tragedy
strikes . . . he's right there. Like a bloodhound. Faster than a bloodhound."

Jude respected Grabble. The editor prodded and conned and snookered his reporters to get the best out of them, and in their
honest moments, after a few drinks, they
gave him credit for it, saying so quietly, as if
it were an unseemly confession. But Jude
often felt off balance dealing with him —
the man talked so damned fast.

"The cops — outside," Jude said. "They
wouldn't let anyone in. Not right away."

"No excuses. You're lucky. I almost gave
the assignment away. But I saved it for you.
You owe me."

"The assignment?"

"Yes, damn it, Ratnoff. I want you to cover
the Ratnoff murder."

Jude knew enough to remain quiet while
Grabble bent over and paced the room in
looping strides, like an outsized Groucho
Marx.

"I don't need to tell you how important
this story is — and how sensitive."

Jude nodded. No, he did not need to tell
him, but Jude bet he would.

"It's *extremely* important and *extremely*
sensitive. There's a lot of interest. It's not

49

every day that a murder turns up like this on our own doorstep." He gestured toward the door. "Not even our doorstep . . . our —"

"Newsroom," prompted Jude.

"Right." Grabble spun around. A thought struck him. "What's the matter. Aren't you excited? You don't seem very excited."

"No, I am. I am."

"You better be. It's not too late to take this away from you. It's sensitive. I trust you'll check in with me as you go along. And if your reporting turns up something . . . you know, *significant,* you'll let me know, right away. I don't want to have to go reading it in the goddamned paper. I'm the editor."

Amazing, thought Jude, how newspapers, so quick to pry into other people's business, were always so paranoid about their own.

"Got that?" asked Grabble.

"Yes, sure. We can talk during the day. I don't think I'm going to dig up any deep, dark secrets, but if I did . . . I mean, I'll write them. I'm not, you know, some kind of in-house spy."

"No one's asking you to be a spy. Of course not. I just want to know everything you know — ahead of time. To guide you. We wouldn't want to blacken anyone's name prematurely."

"No, certainly not prematurely." Jude felt the time had come to end the conversation. "Don't worry, if I solve the murder, you'll be the second to know."

"The *second?*"

"Right after the murderer, of course. We'll need comment from him."

"Wiseass. Here I give you the dream assignment and you turn into a goddamned wiseass."

But Grabble had the grace to let it go at that. He headed toward the door and patted Jude on the back.

"By the way . . . ," began Jude. He needed to know the name to slap on top of the story, which would track it through production. "What's the slug?"

Grabble didn't pause. " '*Slay,*' " he said. "Slug it '*slay.*' "

Jude felt a flutter in his abdomen. "*Slay*" was reserved for only the most newsworthy of homicides. Many years ago, when a World War I veteran went berserk and killed twelve people in a rampage in Camden, the reporter who followed his bloody trail — and who won a Pulitzer — had slugged his story "*slay.*" When the Lindbergh baby was missing, the slug on the running story was "*kidnap,*" but as soon as the baby was found dead, it became *"slay."* The Ted Bundy stories had been slugged *"slay."* So had the O.J. stories. A line of mayhem and murder stretched back through generations and thousands of reporters had looped themselves to it with that pithy four-letter word.

On the way out, Jude looked again at the press plates on the wall. Grabble saw him and waved his long arms through the air in circles like a conductor calling for more oomph from the brass section.

"The wall of honor," he said. "The immortals — stories that never grow old and never die. Who knows? Handle this thing right and maybe one day you'll be up there. I can't guarantee it. But who knows?"

5

Jude hurried to his cubicle. It was messy, but hardly the worst in the room. Manila folders and books were piled on the floor, but the walls were relatively bare. Next to the computer was pinned a photo of Elaine that he had taken during a week in Scotland eight months ago. She was standing straddling a bike, her hair blowsy in the wind against a backdrop of heather and wildflowers. Sexy-looking.

He opened a drawer and pulled out a notebook slim enough to fit into his back pocket. On the cover he printed "SLAY" and the date, September 16. He attached his police card to a lanyard and hung it around his neck. His message light was blinking, so he retrieved his voice mail. The first message was from Clive, the news assistant.

"So, you got the assignment. I'm impressed. I admire your footwork. Good luck. I hear

anything, I'll let you know."

The second message was from Edith Sawyer, the first reporter on the fifth floor and maybe the whole city to come up with a juicy bit of gossip:

"Sweetheart, I hear you've been given the big one. Aren't you the lucky one! Or could it be your talent? Just make sure you don't fuck it up. And congratulations — I think."

He was instantly wary. He imagined that she had lobbied for his story, as she sometimes did, working the phones to come up with a compelling factoid that she could take to an editor as proof that she was indispensable and should share the byline. But maybe this one was too hot even for her.

In the old days, he had heard, reporters were given their assignments in a more brutal way. Their names were boomed out over a loudspeaker and they had to march up to the metro desk past rows of other reporters, who hoped that the story was chickenshit or that it would be flubbed, or, ideally, both. Time had changed the dance but not the tune.

He looked up and there was Edith Sawyer in the flesh, leaning one arm on top of the partition.

"Got anything yet?" she asked.

54

Sawyer was fifty-two years old but still wore her red hair in a cutesy ponytail. Depending on whether she liked you or detested you, she could be a Labrador retriever or a pit bull. As a reporter, she was relentless and indefatigable. In the newsroom, reporters who liked to deal gently with their sources on the telephone, feeding out the line and reeling them in slowly, covered the receiver when she was on a nearby phone. She smashed her sources on the head with an oar. She was smart, gossipy, and given to hanging out in power circles. She loved the idea of being on the inside and knew not only the power players at the Four Seasons but also the names of their wives, dogs, and divorce lawyers.

Sawyer collected exclusives the way early American fur trappers collected pelts. She had had a stint in Latin America, where, rumor had it, she bedded an array of dictators and banana magnates, emerging pregnant with stories. The rumor raised ugly charges of sexism from female colleagues, especially those who suspected it to be true. She was loathed by Virgil Bogart, the legendary, now retired, foreign correspondent. When told, in a bar in Buenos Aires, that she had just had a baby, Bogart had stuttered, "Wh . . . wh . . . who's the mother?"

55

Jude stared at her. "I got you hanging around my desk. That tells me I got an important story."

"Don't get snide. I'm just being friendly. You seen the body?"

"Not yet. I'm waiting for the ghouls to leave."

"You better hurry, before it melts. People are standing around warming themselves in the glow. It's like a picnic around a campfire." She glanced down toward his computer. "I see you still have a picture of what's-her-name. So — you two haven't broken up yet, huh?"

"No."

"Too bad." She shrugged. "Let me know if you need some help on the story. I've got a new contact at the DA's office. Unlike you, he can't say no to me. And let me know if you do break up." She strolled off, waggling her behind.

A head suddenly appeared above the partition next door. It was his neighbor Fred Bradshaw. Jude disliked it when Fred popped up like that — it made him think of that commercial in which the workers bounced up like prairie dogs — and he had complained about it once, but Fred was such a sad case, he didn't want to hurt his feelings. That is, assuming Fred had any feelings left after the way the paper had treated him all these years. Poor, gullible, well-meaning Fred, temperamentally unsuited to be a reporter. As an aspiring beginner, he'd been handed a big news break — a rip-roaring three-alarm fire that destroyed a family in Brooklyn — and he wrote a lede so egregious and insensitive that even though it was killed before it saw print, it sent his career into a tailspin. That was more than ten years ago, during which time fading Xeroxes of the lede were kept in the desk drawers of rewrite men, to be pulled out for amusement during downtime. He was assigned to graveyard beats and frivolous features. Reporters accepted him as one of their own, as a mascot and a martyr.

"I couldn't help overhearing," he said, lowering his eyes quickly like a beaten dog. "Sounds like you've got the Ratnoff murder. You should probably be congratulated. That's quite a testament to . . . to what they think of you." He wore a smile that was hard to read — half sincere, half envious.

"Yeah," piped in a voice from another nearby cubicle. "More testaments like that and you're toast. Whose shit list are you on?"

The voice belonged to Charlie Stengler, his other neighbor. Charlie was the antithesis of Fred, a slick talker who cut corners. The old expression "too good to check" — for a delicious fact that might not hold up — was coined for him. He devoted most of his energy to ducking assignments. More than once, Jude had seen him hide under his desk when Grabble was prowling around with that predatory look. On the rare occasion when he did write a story, he tended to leave out the best parts, which he then retailed at the few dinner tables that would still have him. He was a world-class rumormonger.

"I hear Grabble's sending down some food," he said, standing up. "Maybe if we get a double homicide, we'll score a three-course meal."

The heads popped down. Jude left. He walked down the corridor and around the corner, heading toward the conference room. On the way, he spotted Grabble, who was standing tall behind his desk, holding a piece of paper and turning his hawklike gaze upon the newsroom. Grabble saw him and waved — an ambiguous wave, a sort of knowing, threatening, "Good-luck-but-I'm-not-to-blame-if-this-goes-wrong" kind of wave.

In front of the glass doors of the page-one room, Jude stopped and stared. Ratnoff's body was still there. The blood on his striped shirt was halfway dry now and the spike looked like it was there for keeps. His skin was grayish and his large form seemed to have settled into the floor as if it belonged. Jude had seen dead bodies before, but outside of a funeral home, never someone he'd known as well as he'd known Ratnoff, and he paused momentarily, uncertain.

By now, the cops had shooed most of the onlookers away. They were dusting the area for prints. A police photographer was snapping stills, and forensic specialists were on their hands and knees, putting scraps in plastic bags and vacuuming the carpet — presumably for fibers. Other cops were standing around. The *Globe's* security man — Jude thought his name was Engleheart or Engleberg, something like that — was leaning against a pillar with his hands in his pockets.

A woman detective in a blue pinstriped suit came out of a nearby office. Behind her, seated at a desk, was Ellen Butterby, Ratnoff's assistant, holding a handkerchief to her forehead and sniffling quietly. She had just been interviewed.

The detective seemed to be in charge. She was a dark-haired woman in her midthirties. She had an oval face with dark,

59

penetrating eyes set wide apart, high cheek-bones, and a strong nose. Her complexion was olive. She had an intimidating, no-nonsense manner.

"And who might you be?" she asked Jude, who had begun taking notes.

He introduced himself, offered his hand, which was not accepted, and said he was covering it for the *Globe.*

"Got it all to yourself, huh?" she said.

He smiled and shrugged.

"I can't give you anything," she said. "It'll all have to come from headquarters."

"Understood. You don't mind if I just watch." It was a statement, not a question.

"Depends. Maybe you can help out." She looked him in the eye, dead straight, and lifted one foot toward the spike. "What can you tell me about that?"

"It's an editor's spike."

"So I gather. But what's it mean?"

"What do you mean, 'mean'?"

"It's a strange thing to use as a murder weapon. Your security chief here, Mr. Engle-heart, says he's never seen one. I don't see a whole bunch of others around. So what's it mean?"

"They used to be all over the newsroom. In the old days, when reporters used type-writers and editors went over their stories on paper before sending them up to the composing room, there'd be one next to every editor. He'd use it to kill stories, to *spike* them. He'd slap the copy down right through the spike. The command *spike* still lives on in our computers."

"I see. And our friend here" — now the foot pointed toward Ratnoff — "did he kill many stories?"

"Yes, he did."

"Well, probably no more than any other editor — right?" interjected Engleheart.

"That true?" asked the detective.

"No. He killed a lot of stories. He was in charge of standards and libel. I'd say killing stories was something of a specialty for him."

"I see." She pointed to the note. "And what's that mean? — 'Nice. Who?' "

"That was another one of his specialties. He'd send notes to copy desks. Most of them were critical, but when he liked a headline or something else, he'd send that note, asking who wrote it."

"I see. So what we have here is a bit of mockery."

"I guess so," replied Jude. "And he always wrote in purple."

"Ah. More mockery."

Jude shrugged. But he was impressed —

61

she was on to something. Perhaps the spike *was* a symbol. But if so, it wasn't a symbol for decisiveness. It was the opposite — it symbolized indecision and vacillation. When an editor spiked a story, he didn't make it disappear. He kept it at hand so that it could be retrieved if the reporter screamed bloody murder or a higher-up countermanded the decision. It was a device for the pusillanimous. And come to think of it, the spike *did* seem an appropriate weapon to dispatch Ratnoff. He'd given the impression of being a man of decisive action, but in reality he hadn't been. He'd always tested the waters before wading in. And as standards enforcer, he more than anyone else had acceded to the dumbing down of the paper, the drip-by-drip deterioration in standards, what the old-timers called "death by a thousand cuts." Recently, the guys on rewrite, who watched everything from their privileged perch close to the metro desk, had come up with a new game, using editors' names as verbs — *to Ratnoff* was defined as "to cling steadfastly to an ever-changing set of principles."

The police detective turned to the fingerprint men. "Dust the note. Don't bother with the spike now. We can do it later in the lab — there probably won't be anything on it. The surface is too rough. Anyway, I doubt it's the murder weapon."

"What?" said Engleheart, surprised. "How do you know?"

"Not enough blood. There'll be another wound somewhere, maybe his back. He was killed with something else. This was hammered into him afterward, which is why I find it interesting. He wasn't killed here, either. He was brought here." She turned to the forensics man. "Find anything?"

"Bits of rubber, some kind of tire marks. He wasn't dragged here — that's for sure. Nobody could lift that carcass."

"Any kind of cart around, a hand trolley, something like that?" She was looking at Engleheart, who scratched his head and shook it no.

She looked at Jude. "How about you? What do you say?"

"There's a cart for the newspapers. It used to bring them up from the basement when the presses were there. Now it brings them up from the outdoor decks, where they're delivered from the plant in Queens. It has rubber wheels."

"Where is it?"

"In the basement, I think."

"Good. Would you show my partner here where it is, please?"

63

As Jude turned to leave, she called him back. "What'd you say your name was?"

"Hurley. Jude Hurley."

She handed him a card. "Thanks for your help. Sorry I can't reciprocate." Something about the remark bothered Jude. She wasn't all that much older than he, really, and she certainly didn't mind showing who was in charge. Her sidekick followed him silently to the elevator bank.

Jude looked at her card. It was from the Eighteenth Precinct. Her name was in bold letters: Priscilla Bollingsworth.

Funny name for a cop, he thought.

6

An hour later, on his way to the upstairs cafeteria for a coffee fix, Jude found himself sharing the elevator with Slim Jim Cutler, a reporter widely believed to have gone off the deep end. Slim Jim had a tendency to over-immerse himself in his beats, and some time back, working in the cluster of religious reporters, the "God pod," he had converted to Pentecostalism. Imbued with apocalyptic zeal, he spent a fair number of hours on his knees next to the poker game in the sports department, praying for the souls of the participants. Some of them liked having him there; they thought he brought good luck.

Slim Jim could still write a beautiful story, sharp and concise, as long as it in no way touched upon religion. He did, however, talk with God about the Bible, sequentially, and his recent mumblings suggested that he had now arrived at the Book of Revelation. In idle moments, reporters on the rewrite bank laid odds on precisely when he might burst into the newsroom with an AK-47 and, in the name of the Lord, clean the place out.

This morning, Slim Jim seemed especially agitated. He was staring down at the elevator's console, trying to debate with it the numerology of plagues, angels, and trumpets. Jude decided on the spur of the moment to step out at the eighth floor and visit his friend Francis O'Donnell. Glancing back at Slim Jim, he wondered if the Ratnoff business wasn't getting to everybody, the unhinged and hinged alike. It would be good to get O'Donnell's take on it.

Going on fifty-eight, O'Donnell was only twelve years shy of being twice Jude's age, but the two were close. He was a good-sized man with a handsome weather-beaten face, a wide mustache, and an expansive belly covered almost always with slacks that needed pressing, a blue-and-white-striped shirt, and bright red suspenders. To Jude, he was the quintessence of a newspaperman — a quick mind and a tough exterior. His credo was: If your mother says she loves you, demand a second source.

Jude turned down the corridor toward O'Donnell's cubicle. It was a small windowless spot at the end of a rabbit warren of corridors and storage areas. What O'Donnell did was not entirely clear — he was involved in projects of some kind that rarely saw print. In his day, he had been a fine reporter. He'd come close to winning a Pulitzer three or four times; had he gained that little piece of paper, it might have provided a happier landing for his middle age. At one time, he had been an editor on the national desk, but he had been cast aside in one of those periodic power struggles that seized high management with the frenzy of the Communist Kremlin.

One reason that Jude was drawn to him was that he liked hearing stories about the old days, when there were six or seven papers in town and reporters were no big deal, just average Joes doing their job and finding a lot of laughter in it. And O'Donnell, Irish to his marrow, was a raconteur par excellence, especially after a couple of beers.

"Don't you want to hear about the rabbits again, Lennie?" he'd say, playing off the line from *Of Mice and Men*. And he'd start off.

He had begun as a cub reporter in the old shack across from police headquarters on Mulberry Street. The shack had no air-conditioning or, for that matter, furniture of any kind, other than chewed-up wooden desks. A fire bell sounded once every ten minutes or so, an irregular series of muffled thuds that only the regulars could decipher. They would pause, listen, and say something along the lines of "Two alarms, Grand Concourse and East 161st." An arrangement of colored lightbulbs was installed outside on the street to tell whose phone was ringing: Yellow meant the *World,* purple meant the *Journal,* and so on. That way, reporters could keep the poker game going at the sidewalk table during summer evenings. Most of the staffers could barely write an intelligible sentence. They were there to monitor the pulse of the city and alert their superiors to any crime or disaster that rose above the normal toxic throb. It was hard to tell the reporters from the cops or, for that matter, sometimes from the criminals.

O'Donnell had eight different verbs for suicide, depending on such nuances as whether the jumper had landed on the sidewalk or in the river. He loved to tell stories of the petty crooks who wandered in from the bail bondsman next door or of the reporters caught pulling a fast one.

"There was this guy, Halloran, from the *Post.* He thought he would take a little trip to Bermuda on the q.t. He figured the desk would never know. So he calls in as soon as he arrives from a phone booth in the harbor, and the editor asks him if he's going to file on the flood. 'What flood?' he says. 'The one you're standing in. I can hear the waves crashing around you.' " Then O'Donnell would throw his head back and laugh.

Listening to him, Jude felt like a throwback. He wished he could have experienced those times himself.

"You woulda loved it, kiddo. The newsroom was hopping. A lot of breaking news in those days, none of these so-called trend stories. So everyone's on deadline. Around three o'clock, the trucks pull in to deliver the newsprint. These fourteen-hundred-pound rolls come barrel-assing down and smack the back of the bays, shaking the building like an earthquake. You felt that and you knew it was time to start writing. You'd pound out your lede and yell 'Copy' and rip it out of the typewriter, and some kid would come running and grab it. You'd start on your next page. By the time you'd reached the third page, your lede was already punched out on the linotype machine. The place'd get louder and louder. Just before deadline, around six o'clock, with all the typewriters pounding, the din was deafening. You couldn't hear yourself think. If you didn't know how to spell a word, you shouted it out and somebody would shout back the answer — you didn't even know who. Then you'd wrap it up. You felt like you crossed a finish line. You'd look around; everyone was feeling the same. Then you'd wait for the night city editor to dismiss you with a 'good night.' And you'd all go out for a drink. Or ten.

"These days, with those damned computers, the place is too quiet. It's like a goddamned insurance office. No one has to get a 'good night' before they can leave. And everyone runs to catch a train to go home to a house with a lawn in the suburbs."

O'Donnell's cubicle was vacant, but Jude could tell he had been there recently. The signs of a morning's work were spread out on the desk — files and folders and memos. Jude couldn't help but look. Surprisingly, the material was about Ratnoff. For some reason, O'Donnell had obtained Ratnoff's personnel file, some clippings from his early days when he'd tried his hand at reporting, stacks of "poison plums," even evaluations written by his superiors. Jude tapped a key on the computer and the screen popped to life; on it was what looked like notes lifted from Ratnoff's computer. For all his anti-computer talk, O'Donnell was crafty when

70

it came to using one. Had he hacked into Ratnoff's computer?

Maybe he had pulled the material this morning to write something about Ratnoff for the paper or maybe — unlikely as it seemed — to compose an appreciation for a memorial service or for the house organ, the *Globe Trotter.* Then Jude spotted the date stamped on some of the morgue folders. O'Donnell had taken them out three weeks earlier. For some reason, long before Ratnoff's death, he had been compiling a dossier of information about the man.

Jude caught the elevator to the cafeteria. As he carried his coffee from the cashier's, he spotted O'Donnell seated near a window table, at the center of a dozen reporters and copy editors. He walked over to join them.

"Pull up a chair, kiddo," the Irishman greeted him. "Bet you can't guess what we're talking about."

"I don't need to guess and I won't take your money."

Alston Wickham Howard had the floor. Howard — who was usually called by all three names, like an assassin — was the advance obituary writer. He was nicknamed "the Angel of Death," and if you were well known and he phoned you for biographical details, you had trouble sleeping that night.

Sometimes he called up top editors, saying, "Just want to keep in touch."

"So we got word that the bishop died, right on deadline. This guy called up and said he was his son. Cancer, he said. We shoved the obit in at the last moment. And then, of course, it turns out that he was very much alive — and very pissed off. We had to print that bootlicking retraction. Ratnoff was a real shit about it . . . said I should have been able to figure out it was a hoax. Just 'cause he was Catholic."

"I remember," said O'Donnell. "I thought you used Wikipedia."

"I did. It mentioned the son, too. It also said the bishop was a bigamist, but I left that out. I was suspicious because it said he had been excommunicated in 1912, which was before he was born."

"Good move."

"Anyway, Ratnoff bored me a new asshole. I would've been fired, except they couldn't find anyone else to take my job."

Howard shook his head, stood up, and left.

O'Donnell finished his coffee and leaned back. "I don't mind saying, a lot of people aren't sad that he bought the farm. And I'm at the head of the list. I never said this before, but I'll say it now: He was the bastard who did me in. We never got along.

He used to say I was crossing him at every turn. He was just waiting for a chance to get me. It came when I was on the national desk and I let that story get into the paper — you remember the one, saying that Reagan had Alzheimer's at the Reykjavik summit? The sourcing was poor, okay — though I believe it to this day. Rushing it into the paper was a mistake and I admitted it. He said I had no judgment; he hounded me to the ends of the earth, even went to the executive editor. He used that one slipup as a stick to beat me down, and I never recovered.

"So I say, Good riddance." He looked around the table. "Let's have a show of hands. Who here had a compelling reason to kill Ratnoff? You can't vote, Jude, 'cause you're doing the story — you have to remain objective."

Almost all the hands went up. The holdouts were scoffed at. "C'mon, Fred," O'Donnell yelled over at Bradshaw, Jude's cubicle neighbor, who was sitting quietly on the fringes. Blushing, Bradshaw raised his hand halfway.

"All right," continued O'Donnell, "I rest my case. I say we catch the murderer, we have to turn him in, but they want character witnesses for the defense, we all show up."

"I remember once covering a shooting in the South Bronx," said a reporter named Simon Besserman. "The dead man was a drug dealer. Nobody on the block wanted to cross him. I interviewed one young guy who said, 'You know, he wasn't really such a bad guy. He was just a guy who needed killing.' That's what we have here."

Just then, a shadow fell over the table. Up loomed Slim Jim Cutler, and he smiled broadly at them — it was more of a leer — and then sat down with a bowl of yogurt. He observed, apropos of nothing, that he had just counted the former masthead editors who had died over the past ten years and — "Lord help me!" — they were the same number as the kings in Revelation. "Ratnoff was the seventh," he said, "so you can see that his death assumes special significance in apocalyptic terms."

"Yes, well," said O'Donnell. "On that note, I must be going."

Slim Jim looked upset. O'Donnell put his empty cup on a tray and walked off. Slim Jim looked after him and said, "I don't know why that man never listens. Seven seals, seven trumpets, seven angles, it all falls into place. . . . Man, am I sorry I have to work today. My head's not too clear. And I have to write Ratnoff's obit."

"Why doesn't Alston Wickham Howard write it?" asked Fred.

"He says he only does advance obits. He refuses to write about people once they're dead."

This is going to be one crazy day, thought Jude. Maybe that's what happens when a guy who needs killing is murdered.

7

Priscilla Bollingsworth had insisted that she sit in on the page-one meeting of editors at noon. She needed to familiarize herself with the place and get to know the main players, which was crucial, since the murder looked to be an inside job. Also, she was curious — she wanted to observe the inner sanctum of one of the world's most prestigious newspapers.

To baby-sit her, the publisher had assigned the paper's PR manager, Gulliam Toothy. After offering a rather limp handshake, Toothy took her aside and explained the procedure: each desk editor — foreign, national, metro, business, sports, culture, and style — would pitch possible page-one stories to the top editors. They would begin by reciting the story's slug, then provide a brief description. Some of the pitches were bound to be sketchy, since most of the stories weren't yet written, except for some of those from the foreign desk, where Europe's six-hour time difference conferred an advantage. A second meeting would be held at 4:00 p.m., crisper and better organized, since by then the top editors would have read summaries of the unfolding stories and the desk heads would have had the opportunity to memorize the facts and hone their deliveries.

"Oh, and I must say at the outset, all of this is totally off the record."

"I'm a cop," she replied, "not a reporter." Toothy was a skittish young man and his officious manner grated on her. He had begun by confessing that this was by far the most dreadful day in his seven-year career, the unspoken suggestion being that he hoped she wouldn't make it worse. She tried to think of how to do that.

Bollingsworth seated herself in a corner, where she'd have a good view of everyone and where she'd be less conspicuous, though she could tell by the furtive looks cast her way, and the whispering that followed them, that the participants knew who she was and why she was there.

Things seemed strange at the outset. For one thing, Ratnoff was still lying just outside the conference room's double glass doors. Forensics had finished only ten minutes before and she had given instructions to send the body to the medical examiner, but the ambulance was unaccountably missing its gurney. In the meantime, the corpse was draped in a large gray coverlet. It could have passed for, say, a hassock under a painter's drop cloth were it not for the two immaculately polished black shoes that peeked out under one edge. Still, to enter the room, the editors had been obliged to tread around the heap, taking care not to get blood on their loafers and high heels.

And then there was that mysterious smell of bagels and Nova. For some reason, someone had placed a breakfast spread not ten feet away from the dead man. None of it had been touched. Was this, Bollingsworth half wondered, some arcane newsroom ritual to help a deceased colleague on the journey to the spirit world? Like the Choctaws, who elevate their dead on platforms in the sky with a dead dog?

She looked around the conference room. It was a cross between something you'd find in a Park Avenue law office and the basement of Madison Square Garden. It was windowless and stuffy and the walls were flaked and sullied. In the center was a large table that was neither round nor rectangular — that is, neither egalitarian nor authoritarian — but a perfect oval. Around it were a dozen stuffed chairs on wheels, occupied by men and women whose dress she found surprisingly casual until she thought about it: Editors don't go out of the building — that falls to the reporters.

Others sat on hard-backed chairs that lined the walls. Among them were six stern-looking young people in blue jeans and T-shirts. They wore designer stainless steel water bottles attached to one side of their belts and cell phones in Velcro-fastened pouches on the other side, like six-shooters in the Old West. "They're from the Web site," whispered Toothy, who was on her left, sitting uncomfortably close to her elbow.

Attached to the ceiling above the table was a projector of some sort with a lens that faced a wall screen, a device, she assumed, for exhibiting blown-up photographs when it came time to choose among them. A woman she took to be the picture editor was anxiously fiddling with a computer keyboard.

The meeting began. A man with Coke-bottle glasses and curly hair cleared his throat to speak from his position at the table near them. He had an aristocratic mien but a distracted, absentminded air.

"The foreign editor," whispered Toothy,

providing play-by-play commentary in hushed tones, as if he were narrating the U.S. Open. "Heaton Squire."

"Iraq," Squire said. "Same old, same old. Some more bombs — one in a market killed . . . let me see . . . forty-eight people. More U.S. troops killed, a number of suicides. The Pentagon's worried, say they don't know if they can hold back the insurgents. The president says everything's fine."

Skeeter Diamond interjected: "Why don't we start the story with the military worries, if the ground action isn't so hot? Lead with the Washington stuff, plug in reaction up high."

A disembodied voice boomed down from the ceiling. "We could do that."

Squire frowned, made a point of jotting a note on a pad held by a clipboard.

"Good," replied Diamond, lifting his head to the ceiling.

"Up there is the Washington bureau," whispered Toothy in his tennis announcer's voice. "They participate electronically. That was the bureau chief, Brisley Townsend — he's a rising star."

Squire continued: "*Iran.* There's been another letter to the American people from the Iranian president." He glanced down at his pad. Bollingsworth, peering over his shoulder, saw what he had written on it: Maeh-mood Ach-mah-dean-new-jad. "As you know," he went on, "the president is Mahmoud Ahmadinejad."

"What's it mean?" asked Diamond.

Squire looked alarmed. "I have no idea. It's just a common name, I think."

"I mean the story."

"Oh. Well, our analysis is that he wants to speak directly to the American people. That's why he wrote to them . . . us."

Bollingsworth whispered to Toothy, "I'm not sure he's making the most out of his time advantage." Toothy grimaced.

The foreign editor ran through a couple of other stories, beginning each with its slug — *"Mideast," "India," "Japan"* — followed by a perfunctory description. He perked up when he came to one slugged *"mercy."* "This is a neat little story. I could see it at the bottom of the page. It seems the Netherlands has passed a 'mercy killing' law. All you need for legalized euthanasia is a doctor's note and two affidavits from relatives or close friends."

The editors broke out in smiles and titters. "Better not try that here," whispered one, covering his mouth.

"With my family, I get a cold and I'm toast," said Diamond. They all roared.

"If we had that law in this building, there'd be no one left to put out the paper," declared Grabble. They laughed again, even more uproariously.

A stocky woman whose sharp elbows took more than her fair share of table space spoke up. ("Vickie Gimmy, national editor," whispered Toothy in awe, as if Maria Sharapova had just stepped onto the court.)

Gimmy had not joined in the joviality. "Wait a minute. We have a story on Kevorkian," she protested. "The *'mercy'* story should be packaged with ours."

Squire objected — "Oh no, you don't" — and held up his clipboard as if to fend off an attack. The titters continued.

"This is the kind of dispute that Ratnoff would have settled," whispered Toothy wistfully.

"What's yours about?" Diamond asked Gimmy.

"Let's see" — she was looking down at her notes — "Kevorkian's been out of prison for over a year now, more or less behaving himself . . . but there are reports he wants to fire up his Thanatron again."

"See if you can definitely say he wants to resume using it and . . . ah . . . Michigan won't let him. Do that and it goes on page one."

"You got it," she said.

"Why don't you take it from here," Diamond replied.

"We've got one slugged *'priest,'*" she said. "It's about a hardworking priest in the slums of Boston, going about doing good works. He's upset, you know, about all the sexual-abuse stuff."

"No," interjected Diamond. "It's not the time for a positive story. We've got a fine scandal rolling along here — you don't want to . . . ah . . . throw rocks in its path."

Grabble looked shocked. ("He's the metro editor," whispered Toothy.) "Since when do we manipulate the news like this?"

"Since now," replied Diamond. "We got a good thing going. Let's not slow it down."

Grabble frowned.

Gimmy crossed the slug off her pad and went on to describe a number of other stories. Then she said, "I'm saving the best for last. It's slugged *'license'* and it's perfect for that spot on page one where *'mercy'* is *not* going to appear. It seems there's a grass-roots movement all over the country for cross-dressers to be allowed two photo IDs on their licenses. They want one of each gender so they won't be hassled if cops stop them."

"Is that for real?" asked Diamond. He

sounded interested.

"Yes. There're signs the movement's growing."

"Like what?"

"Well, somewhere there's a rally. I think it's in some neighborhood in San Francisco. Next week — or maybe it happened already."

Diamond wrote the slug on his pad. "Sounds good," he said. "Make sure you include the sociological significance." Gimmy smiled.

The dining editor was next, a thin-boned woman in a narrow chemise. "This may be a busy news day," she began, with a halting look at the gray hulk outside, "but you might want a change of pace. We have a delightful little story by our food critic Outsalot on the rise of the lowly olive. It's now being stuffed with anchovies. She calls it 'the court jester of the hors d'oeuvre tray.' "

"What the hell does *that* mean?" asked Gimmy.

The dining editor shrunk down in her chair. "Ummm . . . saucy," she said. "Sort of piquant." She looked directly at Gimmy. "Tart."

Bollingsworth heard a chuckle coming from the ceiling — the Washington bureau.

"Let's . . . ah . . . move on," said Diamond.

84

The culture editor, Suzanne Preston, spoke up. She was wearing, Bollingsworth noted, a low-cut blouse that invited darting glances from the man next to her ("Haggart Thomas, sports editor"). Haggart was, she noted further, the only African-American at the main table.

"We don't have anything for the front," Preston said. "But we have a good story on our dress page. You might want a reefer." (Bollingsworth raised an eyebrow and Toothy quickly explained: "A reefer's a mention in that little page-one box. It *refers* to a story that's inside.") "It's about a new rapper who infuses his lyrics with his story of growing up middle-class in the suburbs."

"What's the slug?" asked Diamond.

" *'Scarsdale.'* "

"God. Not another story on rap," put in Grabble. "You're really going after our core audience."

"These are white kids," said Preston. "That's our demographic."

"But it's a *black* art form," said Thomas.

Gimmy opened her mouth and inserted her finger, making gagging sounds.

"Okay, cut it out," said Diamond. He turned to the culture editor. "Put another white suburb in there somewhere and you're in business."

"You got it."

The meeting was almost over. Only a few speakers remained. Bollingsworth was astounded. Beneath the jumbled accounts of the world's goings-on ran a current of adolescent one-upmanship. Notes were passed, meaningful looks shared, animosities laid bare. The desk editors promoted their stories by dropping an obscure but arresting fact and sabotaged those of their colleagues by yawning or holding their temples in a viselike grip. They broke out with an occasional "Didn't we already know that?" or "Didn't somebody else print that somewhere?"

And Diamond seemed to have no compunctions about sticking his hand in and shaping a story to his liking. The editors' body language spoke volumes about the power vectors. At the beginning most were focused on Diamond, but by the end some had shifted toward Grabble; others swiveled their heads back and forth in a way that made Toothy's tennis narration seem apt. The only person she had met all morning who seemed to have his head screwed on right was that reporter Jude Hurley.

The maneuvering and politicking struck her as especially surprising given that a very dead Ratnoff lay not twenty feet away. Unless, thought Bollingsworth, it's *because* Ratnoff is there. A classic case of a vacuum of authority. The hall monitor is dead; long live the hall monitor.

Then came the moment she had been waiting for. It was Grabble's turn, and he pronounced, in a stentorian tone, the slug *"slay."* The room fell silent as he laid out the few facts that were known: the discovery of the body, the missing murder weapon, the note, Ratnoff's long service to the paper. It was as if a curtain had fallen. No one allowed a reaction. And by now, after seeing this group in action, Bollingsworth thought she knew why: Ratnoff was indeed widely detested. It was not going to be easy to whittle down the list of enemies he had made over a long and bruising career.

After a moment of silence, it was the turn of the style editor and gossip columnist, Peregrin Whibbleby. She was wearing dark glasses and looked a bit ashen. Her stiff demeanor had not changed one iota and up to now she hadn't said a word.

Bollingsworth saw through the glass doors that the paramedics had finally arrived. They lowered the gurney and were grimacing as they tried to roll Ratnoff's heavy body onto it. Whibbleby, looking up skittishly from a notepad and then back down, seemed aware of the movement, too.

"We have a story slugged *'scandal,'*" she said softly. Her voice sounded like that of a frightened little girl. "The First Lady wore a designer gown to a White House function and, unbeknownst to her, two other women turned up in the same dress, and now all of Washington is in a dither."

"Do you get into the deeper meaning, the sociology and so on?" asked Diamond hopefully.

"Oh yes, the story goes on to —" But the words never came out. In their place came a scream, high and rising higher. The body bearers, in struggling with Ratnoff's corpse, had let the cloth rise up. Hanging upside down, his face was gray, and his eyes, now wide open, seemed to be staring — right at Peregrin Whibbleby. She stopped in horror and couldn't go on.

Diamond sighed. "Let's not run through the pictures," he said. "We can . . . ah . . . do that at four o'clock."

8

Jude descended to the lobby, raised his jacket collar, and stepped outside. The rain had stopped, but a chill wind blew down the canyon from Broadway.

He was wrung out. He had had to write fifteen hundred words — with Grabble interrupting him every ten minutes with questions. Also, he'd had to dash off a summary and feed the Web site and record a podcast and make a radio broadcast and wrestle with the copy editor. Then at the last minute, it had dawned on someone that Slim Jim couldn't deliver Ratnoff's obit, and so he'd had to help rewrite do a quick and dirty job. It was like being nibbled to death by ducks.

He looked at his watch: a little after 7:00 p.m. His legs seemed to know where he wanted to go and they guided him on their own, like a milkman's horse, across the street and into Slough's, the low-rent bar that was a *Globe* hangout.

Surprisingly, he could hear laughter and the clinking of glasses even before he entered. Once inside, he pushed his way to the bar, where he caught the eye of Woody, the owner, and ordered a J&B neat.

"What's going on?" he asked. "Some kind of celebration?"

"You got that right," said Woody, pouring him a stiff one to the top of the glass. "Almost like the old days — isn't it?"

Jude had to agree. The place was as packed as it had been when he first ventured in a dozen years ago, a nervous copyboy. In that long-ago era, he had formed an attachment to Slough's, in contrast to Sardi's, where the high-priced editorial talent hung out. This was the watering hole for reporters, copy editors, and pressmen out on break, ink on their hands and their heads covered with jaunty caps made by folding, origami-like, sheets of newsprint. Since the presses moved out of the basement, the dive hadn't been the same.

Jude looked around. The decor — if that was the word — hadn't changed. On a side wall was the painting of Joe Louis landing his first-round KO punch on Max Schmeling's jaw, the canvas so covered with grit that the Brown Bomber was a mere shadow.

The wall behind the bar was still a shrine to baseball, with dated, nondenominational relics: photos of Mantle, Campanella, and Mays, faded pennants, a framed yearbook of "Da Bums," a sign from the Polo Grounds, a splinter from Abe Stark's billboard in Ebbets Field, and old baseball cards immured in plastic like aspic. House policy was that if you brought a bit of memorabilia, you got a night's worth of free drinks, which might explain the many famous homerun balls, including four of Bobby Thomson's against poor Ralph Branca. "Who knows?" Woody was reported to have said, shrugging. "Maybe one of them really is."

Jude looked at the twenty-gallon fish tank behind the bar. Swimming in circles, a few inches longer now, was the ferocious red tiger oscar. The reporters who used to raise a glass to it at feeding time (two goldfish, two guppies) had named it "Schwartzbaum" after the then executive editor, Max Schwartzbaum, who had since been bounced upstairs with a column. The hallways and bathrooms of the *Globe* still echoed with stories about the "Max days" — stories, the reporters swore, that they told their naughty children to frighten them at bedtime.

Woody brought him another scotch. "It's from them," he said, gesturing with his bartender's towel toward a table in the rear, where two dozen reporters were whooping it up.

"Man of the hour!" shouted Van Wessel, the *Globe*'s court reporter, who had come uptown to partake in the excitement. They waved him over. Jude felt in his pocket — he had two twenties — and told Woody to send over another round, and then he joined them.

Jude's cubicle neighbor Fred Bradshaw was there. So were Charlie Stengler, his other neighbor, who was already in his cups, and Alston Wickham Howard and many others. Smack in the center was Edith Sawyer, looking like a homecoming queen at her thirtieth reunion. She pushed another reporter out of a seat next to her and motioned to Jude to sit; he pretended not to notice and took a chair on the other side of the table.

"Spill," she commanded. "As you-know-who would say, 'What do we know and what do we know about it?' "

"It's more a matter of what we don't know," he said.

"C'mon, did you dig up anything?"

"Not much," he said. And that was the

truth. His story covered most of the bases — the *who, what, where,* and *when,* a little bit of the *how,* but nothing of the *why.* There *was* nothing. He had included some interesting background stuff, some quotes from members of the staff expressing shock and surprise, a bit of history about the paper and about the three-ring circus called the newsroom, and he'd spiced it up with some anecdotes about Ratnoff, including two or three that showed his darker side and that Jude suspected wouldn't see print. But there was a plethora of unanswered questions.

"Here," he said, "read it yourself." He pulled a sheaf of paper from his inside jacket pocket. (The old-timers had taught him to print out a copy and carry it home, the better to fend off late-night queries from the city desk.)

Edith snatched it in midair, put on her glasses, and began to read it aloud.

In a baffling and grisly scene that could have leapt straight out of a dime-store detective novel, Theodore S. Ratnoff, assistant managing editor of the *New York Globe,* was found murdered this morning in the center of the newsroom at the paper's Forty-fifth Street headquarters, where he had become a power behind the scenes and a force for studied change at a time of crisis in the industry.

His body, spread-eagled, was lying on the floor near the main conference room with an editor's spike pounded in his chest and a note attached. The note consisted of only two words: "Nice. Who?" — identical to words of praise that the editor sometimes fired off, along with critical comments, to copy desks under his command. The corpse was discovered at 8:30 a.m. by Ms. Ellen Butterby, Mr. Ratnoff's administrative assistant. . . .

Edith read most of the article but abruptly stopped before the end. The others had been listening closely, nodding here and there or shaking their heads, some up and down, others sideways — whether in agreement or disbelief that the whole thing had happened was hard to tell.

"No murder weapon, huh?" she said.

"Nope."

"You'll have trouble with that 'dime-store detective novel' in the lede, kiddo," said a familiar voice over Jude's shoulder. It was O'Donnell, who had gone off to the men's room and slipped back unnoticed, a glass of Guinness in his hand. He pulled up a chair and the others quickly made room for him.

He was right. The subordinate clause leading off the story had been flagged by a peon on the copy desk. Jude suspected the editor had found the pulp-magazine metaphor unseemly, but that wasn't what she'd said. She'd argued that dime stores no longer existed and consequently that dime-store novels were an anachronism, then suggested Jude begin instead with the phrase "In a surprising development . . ." Jude had knocked that down and proposed one even more graphic: "In a baffling and grisly scene that could have leapt from the screen of a slasher movie . . ." The gambit had worked; he was allowed to keep "dime-store detective novel" — a small victory, but even small victories over copy editors were to be celebrated.

Jude, however, didn't mention it. Something bothered him, a tiny itch in his brain. Edith had stopped reading aloud before the one paragraph that had a nugget of exclusive information — the fact that Ratnoff was killed somewhere other than the newsroom. Bollingsworth's partner, in examining the cart used to transport the papers, had found bloodstains on it and had also theorized that the basement was the likely scene of the crime, though he asked Jude to omit those particular details, arguing that they needed to hold back some information known only to the killer. "But don't worry," he had said. "I'll tell Bollocks — I mean, Detective Bollingsworth. She'll owe you. Tell her to throw you a bone." Jude had, in fact, tried retrieving the bone. He had telephoned Bollingsworth twice, but the cop who answered said she was out, and she hadn't returned his call.

Finding the cart had only compounded the mystery. It might explain how the killer had gotten Ratnoff six flights up, but it didn't explain how he — or she — had managed to hoist the body into the cart to begin with. A person would have to be strong to do that; at deadweight, the body had to rack up at close to 220 pounds.

The question that nagged at him was why Edith had stopped reading when she did. Was it that she didn't want to start a round of speculation? Everyone knew there was no love lost between her and Ratnoff. She had often complained that he had a vendetta against her, without explaining what it might be. Jude found his eyes surveying Edith's body. It was, for someone of her age, surprisingly muscular. Her shoulders were broad and, now that her jacket was hanging on the back of her chair, her biceps appeared nicely rounded. She looked as if she worked out.

"Hey, Edith," said Fred Bradshaw, suddenly speaking up, "let me ask you something. Everybody else has stepped up to the plate as a candidate for the murderer — except you. And you're one who's known to hate his guts. How do you explain that?"

The crowd fell silent, partly to hear her answer and partly out of surprise because Bradshaw's blunt question was so uncharacteristic.

"I don't owe anyone an explanation," she said. "Least of all you, deadbeat. But if you must know, I'm Catholic. So chalk it up to my innate respect for the dead." She narrowed her eyes. "And while you're at it, you might want to lay off whatever it is you're drinking."

The remark drew a chorus of boos.

"Come, come," said O'Donnell, "it's not the time for bickering." He rose, none too steadily, and extended his glass at chest level. "I'd like to propose a toast." Everyone stood, except Stengler, who was lying on the floor. "Today, the Angel of Death" — here he tipped an imaginary cap in the direction of Alston Wickham Howard — "has seen fit to fly down and brush one of our colleagues with his heavy wing. As he was one of God's creatures, we should mark the occasion with solemnity. As a person . . . that's another matter. I'm not a man to speak ill of the dead, so I'll bring my toast to a close with a simple thought: There's a lesson to be drawn . . ."

They began drinking.

". . . and that lesson is to live life to the fullest." He drained his glass. "In other words, carpe diem."

"Whazzat mean?" said Stengler from the floor. "Shpeak Englis fer Chrissakes."

"Carpe diem," said Jude. "It means 'complain every day.' "

More boos — and more booze. Theories began shooting across the tables. They didn't notice that there were hangers-on in the periphery, people who looked like reporters but weren't known to them. The strangers cocked their ears and sometimes went to the toilets, where they entered stalls to scribble into notebooks.

"You hear the damn bloggers?" said Van Wessel. "They're in overdrive. The latest rumor is that Ratnoff had a twin brother who needed a kidney transplant. Ratnoff refused him, so his brother stabbed him and took the kidney. . . ." He paused, caught in thought. "Of course, the notion of Ratnoff refusing a brother does lend it a certain plausibility."

"I hear," said Bradshaw, again speaking more loudly than was his wont, "that Ratnoff was editing some big piece on police corruption. Maybe that's why he was killed."

And so it went, for more than an hour.

Jude's cell phone rang. He checked the caller ID and was hardly surprised: It was "the desk." "The desk" always called at inconvenient times. He remembered Elaine saying, "If you ever drive me to a shrink, he'll wonder why it is I keep talking about a goddamned piece of furniture."

He walked outside to take the call. On the way, he checked his watch — ten o'clock. Of course, the tabloids were up. He was getting a call to match them. Maybe the *Maul* — which is what reporters called the *Daily Mail* — had something he didn't. Or maybe the *Grifter,* which is what they called the *New York Graphic.* On a good murder, they usually led the pack.

It was Shirley, the night city editor. She didn't beat around the bush. "We got a call from a reporter at the *Maul.* He said he had heard that Ratnoff was editing some big piece on police corruption, wanted to know if it's true. I said I didn't know. I mean, I was honest — nobody around here tells me anything. But I thought you should know."

She paused. "Why are you laughing?"

"Nothing, never mind. I'll check, and if there's anything to it, I'll get back to you. And Shirley —"

"Yes."

"If you hear a story about Ratnoff and his twin brother, you don't have to call."

As he hung up, Jude saw Edith leaving the bar with a mountain of a man. She waved as they walked off down the street. He had forgotten how big her husband was. Now, *there's* someone who could have moved Ratnoff all by himself, Jude thought.

Back inside, the group had broken up. O'Donnell was holding forth, explaining to a tipsy Fred Bradshaw why the Internet would never replace newspapers.

"Do you have any idea how many newspapers line the bottom of parakeet cages?" he asked. "And how many other newspapers are used to wrap fish? That's something the Internet can never do. What's going to happen to all that parakeet shit? And all the fish guts? They'll still need us, don't you see? We're eternal! We're golden!"

Jude had to wait another forty minutes — his stomach groaning with hunger — to pose the question that had been bothering him ever since he'd visited O'Donnell's cubicle that morning. As the three of them were putting on their jackets, he finally asked him what he was doing with all that material on Ratnoff.

O'Donnell drew back, seemingly in confusion. Then he said, "Oh, that. I was just curious about the man . . . going over old times. You know — a stroll down memory lane." He paused, his voice turning angry. "And incidentally, I'd like to quibble with that phrase of yours in your lede — you call him 'a force for studied change.' What the fuck does that mean? *Studied change,* my ass. Yes — if *studied change* means editing the paper for teenyboppers with the attention span of mosquitoes. If *studied change* means diving straight into the shithouse to pick up pieces of silver." He walked out, then turned back and glared at Jude.

"So think about what you write and about what you say — before you go around accusing people."

Jude was too stunned to reply, and O'Donnell walked off.

On the subway home, Jude realized he hadn't thought about Elaine once since hearing of Ratnoff's murder. He had wanted to phone her to make up, maybe take her out to dinner. It was too late now. He felt a familiar ache, a churning in his esophagus,

which one doctor had warned him could
well signal the birth of an ulcer.

9

Elisha Hagenbuckle had heard somewhere that John D. Rockefeller used to have his butler wake him half an hour early to tell him he had more time to sleep, which prompted a change in his own morning ritual. Nowadays, he had his Ecuadorian maid, Concepción, rouse him gently and return half an hour later with a white wicker breakfast tray of steaming coffee and fat-free half-and-half in silver pitchers. The tray had two pockets, one on either side; into the left was placed the *Globe,* into the right — as if to avoid contamination — the two city tabloids. Normally, Hagenbuckle read the *Globe* first, but today he reached for the tabs. He did so with dread.

The dread was well founded. As he had feared, the Ratnoff story had made the wood in both papers. DEATH STALKS NEWSROOM, screamed the front page of the *Daily Mail.* NEWS BIGGIE GOES DOWN, yelled the *New York Graphic.* Somehow, the *Graphic* had obtained a picture of Ratnoff's body — or a mound of something that looked suspiciously like it, the face hidden under some kind of tarpaulin. A caption suggested that it was being carried outside through the *Globe*'s back entrance. Lester Moloch, the New Zealand mogul who owned the *Graphic,* had probably been tipped off by a spy in the newsroom, someone on his secret payroll. That sort of intrigue was right up Moloch's alley.

Hagenbuckle sighed and picked up his own paper. The lead story was about Iraq — written, for some unknown reason, under a Washington dateline. He picked up a pad and jotted a note to himself: "Talk to Diamond. Re: Iraq. Why Washington?" He scanned the rest of the page. Above the fold were two stories twinned under a single headline: one about a "mercy killing" law in the Netherlands, the other about Dr. Kevorkian. Below the fold was a headline, NO LONGER JUST THE PITS; it seemed to be saying something about olives. There was a single-column headline over yet another story about sexual abuse by priests. At the bottom were three pictures — of the First Lady and two other women, each wearing the same dress. "Triple Play," read the cheerful kicker on the caption underneath.

He turned to the front pages of the back sections. Science had a story about the predicted end of the earth, when galaxies would collide in two billion years (NOT WITH A WHIMPER BUT A BANG). Food ran a piece about new vineyards in southern Alaska producing surprisingly good Beaujolais (THIS BREW LIKES THE COLD SHOULDER). Culture had one on rap music in Scarsdale (BLACK ROOTS SINK DEEP IN WHITE SOIL). The top headline on the Metro section read: ALONE, SICK, SCORNED, AND PENNILESS, over a picture of a man in a bedraggled cardigan sifting through a mound of garbage. The story was an account of the plight of homeless, HIV-positive, gay evangelical priests.

Abigail wouldn't like that one. He looked over at his wife, still sleeping, a tuft of auburn-dyed hair sticking out of a mound of blankets. He fingered the index and found the reference he was looking for: "Assistant managing editor expires in newsroom. Page 32." He turned to the page. The story was given discreet play under a Bloomingdale's ad for black lace Wonderbras. It was accompanied by an airbrushed photo of Ratnoff in a suit jacket, his hair slicked down as if he were off to a wedding; his face bore an uncharacteristically pleasant smile that looked computer-generated.

He jotted another note: "Query Diamond. Folo-up Ratnoff story?" He paused a moment, scratched out "Diamond" and wrote "Grabble."

The byline, Jude Hurley, again prompted a distant memory, just out of reach — some vague business to do with the police. Another note: "Query Grabble. Hurley's background?"

Ratnoff — what a nuisance, getting himself killed like that. Questions poured in from all sides. Would the editor qualify for some sort of extra payment, dying on the job? Would there be a service with — God forbid — an open casket? A weeping widow? Would he himself have to speak? What in heaven's name would he say? After all, he barely knew the man. He shuddered. And when would this murder story end? He had had enough experience with the vicissitudes of news to know that something like this could keep going day after day — there'd be the search for the weapon, the leak from police, the arrest, the so-called perp walk. The story had legs, as they said on the fifth floor. And even if it hadn't, Moloch wouldn't let go — he'd prop it up and put it in a goddamn electronic wheelchair to keep it going. Hagenbuckle's coffee seemed suddenly tepid.

He'd never dreamed there'd be times like this, certainly not twenty-five years ago, when he married Abby. He thought back to her father, Tassius Appleby. What a tough son of a bitch he'd been! His was quite a story, typical Horatio Alger. Raised in a poor mountain village in Cyprus, sent by the elders to make his way in the world, learning the olive oil trade in Athens, arriving in New York as a ruthlessly ambitious immigrant. Then the hard years — working in the Fur District, husbanding his money, eventually investing and diversifying. Finally the successful years — owning ships, food wholesalers, and buying the *Globe* for a song and making it profitable and powerful. He had changed his name from Appinopoulis to Appleby, bulldozed his way into society, which had already lowered its walls to embrace him, and married a wealthy widow, who promptly passed away after producing the precious Abigail, lying no more than two feet away on the bed.

Hagenbuckle thought back to their courtship — how the old man had checked him out with three private detectives, weighed his intentions over countless rounds of brandy, and eventually came around to accepting him, a Yale boy with family connections but not much money. Appleby made no secret of his aspiration to hand the reins of the *Globe* over to his son-in-law and put Hagenbuckle through all the Stations of the Cross: He worked as a sorter in the mail room, a news clerk in City Hall, a cub reporter in the Detroit bureau, a flak in promotion, a manager in marketing, ad sales, and even forestry products — all to prepare him for the glorious day when he would step onto the bridge of the aircraft carrier and don the admiral's cap.

But nothing . . . nothing could have prepared him for this. Worries assailed him from all quarters. He felt like King Lear. Was it Lear? *When sorrows come, they come not single spies, but in whole big groups.* He got out of bed and began pacing. He caught sight of himself in a full-length mirror, striding in his navy-blue-purple-and-white-striped Bergdorf Goodman bathrobe. Well, at least he still cut a pretty good figure.

The thought brought him to his senses. He decided to enumerate his problems, make a mental list. He believed in doing that — it somehow made the problems seem less daunting, as if listing them was the first step in vanquishing them.

One. The *Globe* stock. It had indeed gone

south, twelve points, in response to the Rat-noff killing. What could be done to counter-act this? Maybe have Toothy put out a press release on something positive . . . but what? How do you counteract murder? Issue a press release on all the employees who've not been killed?

His thoughts drifted back to Appleby. Luckily, the clever old man had arranged for a dual-class structure to keep the paper in family hands. The stock was split into two groups: voting shares for the Appleby-Hagenbuckle members, which provided total control of the company, and general shares for the public ("the great unwashed," Appleby used to call them). That meant the company was practically invulnerable to takeover. Still, these were worrisome times; other newspapers with similar arrangements had not been able to fend off suitors. When the waters recede, all boats go down, luxury yachts as well as the rowboats.

Two. The paper's morale. Things seemed to be a mess down there. He didn't know this firsthand, because he didn't have many acquaintances on the fifth floor, but he had heard — from editors who had been pushed aside or were straining at the bit for promo-tion — that a lot of workers were unhappy. Ordinarily, it wouldn't matter, but if dissatisfaction grew, it might soon hurt productivity. Why were reporters and editors such children? Diamond and Grabble were always quibbling. What to do? Create a Bring Your Daughter to Work Day? Hand out cut-rate coupons for an exercise club? Better food in the cafeteria?

Three. Lester Moloch. The global tycoon was definitely up to something. Hagenbuckle had run into him twice last year, once at a session of the publishers' ecological forum, CUT (Conference to Underwrite Trees), and once at the annual meeting of NOPE (Newspaper Owners, Publishers, and Executives). Both times, the weaselly New Zealander couldn't suppress his little shit-eating grin. It wasn't enough that he'd cornered the satellite market over Asia. His appetite demanded something big closer to home.

Four. Max Schwartzbaum. The former executive editor was restive. Giving him that column, "Under My Thumb," had seemed a brilliant stroke at the time, but it hadn't dulled his ambition. Old executive editors never die — they don't even fade away. Hagenbuckle had passed Schwartzbaum in the hall the other day and said an upbeat hello, and the man practically growled back.

Five (and this was the one that really got

to him). His wife had never learned the complete story of old man Appleby: how he had sown his oats as a young man in that Greek mountain village. For reasons of delicacy, the episode had been omitted from his biographies and even, somehow, from family lore. Suffice it to say that the drive that fueled his rise to power had a libidinal side and that during a fling with a village maiden long ago he had fathered an illegitimate daughter. Years later, he had quietly brought the daughter to America and set her up in a house in Greenwich, where she married and bore a son. Tragically, she and her husband were killed in a car accident, leaving the boy an orphan. Appleby had found a place for his grandson and sent money to raise him but never saw him.

When the old coot died, the skeleton threatened to come clattering out of the closet. Papers from a vault behind a painting (a Rembrandt, later found to be "of the school of Rembrandt") revealed all. In his will, Appleby had wanted to do the decent thing, up to a point. He granted posthumous recognition of his paternity of the boy's mother, but quietly and in legal chambers only. The boy would be told who his grandfather was when he reached the age of twenty-five. He'd be given a job for life at the paper if he wanted it but would not be entitled to a piece of the pie: He would not be granted any voting shares. Hagenbuckle had dutifully obeyed the letter of the injunction and hushed up the entire episode. But now things were about to come to a head. The boy, working in a low position at the paper, was twenty-four years, eleven months, and sixteen days old. In another two weeks, he would learn about his lineage.

The publisher looked over at Abby. Her heart would break if she knew any of this. She had always put her father on a pedestal, and if anything could topple him, it would be the knowledge of this out-of-wedlock progeny. On one level, that might not be so bad, he thought, since he was a bit fed up trying to compete with a ghost. But their marriage would suffer if she thought he had been instrumental in bringing it about. The damned orphan was always there in the back of his mind, a shadowy figure threatening by his mere existence to blow the happy Hagenbuckle household to smithereens.

He scribbled a reminder to himself in his diary, the black book always at his side: October 1 was the day the lad would reach the age set down in the will and the lawyers would call him in. He wrote the note in code, using the boy's initials.

Almost as if she could divine his thoughts, Abigail began to stir. The auburn crown rose out of the blankets, revealing her face, puffed up from sleep. She opened her eyes and fixed them on her husband.

"Coffee, my poppet?" he asked.

"Yes, please." She sat up, leaned her pillow against the headboard. "How long have you been awake? Oh, I do hope you haven't been worrying again." She smiled at him and took his hand.

"No, not really," he replied, squeezing hers in turn. "Well, perhaps a bit. But nothing serious . . . nothing that need concern you."

10

Jude checked his watch: 11:00 a.m. He paced in front of the *Globe*'s elevators, which were notoriously slow. (It wasn't unusual to return from lunch and find a score of people milling about like stranded airline passengers, three or four of them — reporters facing deadline — punching the buttons with mounting ferocity.) Now Jude expected an even longer wait; only two of the eight elevators descended to the basement, where he was going.

He stopped before the brass doors, caught sight of his jaundiced reflection and the bags under his eyes. Jesus, I look beat, he thought. What did he expect? He had scarcely slept. First, he had consumed all that coffee while writing the story, then all those scotches at Slough's. Once in bed had come the obligatory noise from the club crawlers under his window on Avenue B, prompting TK to fall into a barking fit.

He had also been roused by second- and third-edition phone calls from Chuck, the late man. As a rule Chuck, a feckless soul, reported for work at 6:00 p.m. and sat unobtrusively at his desk until all the bosses left. But once in charge, he turned into a monstrous, demanding Stakhonovite. He dug into the wires and blogs to turn up scoops and rumors to be matched or shot down. He delighted in tracking down a reporter to interrupt dinner with a long-suffering spouse, a candlelit assignation, or, worst of all, sweet slumber.

With Jude, at least, he was unabashedly craven. "Here's another COMA," he'd told him the night before, using his own personal acronym for "cover my ass." "City news is saying Ratnoff had huge amounts of alcohol in his blood, that he may have committed suicide by diving onto the spike from his desk. Thought I should pass it along. I dunno. Maybe there's something to it. Whaddaya think? Ball's in your court."

Jude had answered as he always did: He'd check it out and call back if it held up. Then he had gone back to sleep — until the next COMA. He had made it a policy never to yell at the late guys, whose jobs made them easy scapegoats for the top editors.

Finally, the elevator arrived. Jude pressed

the button for the basement, where the presses used to be. As he sank down into the bowels of the building, he thought back to the club crawlers. Not that long ago, he might have been among them, he and Elaine. In fact, he had a memory of her one winter night, laughing as they emerged from that very same basement club into a blizzard. She had opened her mouth to let the snowflakes melt on her tongue. At the time, he predicted that if they ever broke up, the image would stay with him, along with a dozen others, like scenes from a movie he couldn't forget. And now a breakup was clearly imminent. He had tried several times this morning to phone her. He figured he might as well apologize, though for what, he wasn't entirely sure. But she hadn't picked up the phone. It was before she usually left for work. She had caller ID. You didn't have to be a genius to add it up.

He stepped out of the elevator into the Stygian gloom. The passageway leading to the cavernous pressroom was darker than usual. He glanced up at the ceiling — the lightbulb wasn't working. He stretched and couldn't touch it. From his back pocket he pulled out his notebook, grasped it by the spiral binding, and leapt up, tapping the bulb gently. It flickered on, then off again.

So it had managed to work itself loose and no one had bothered to tighten it. That figured: With all the budget cuts, the janitorial staff was almost nonexistent these days.

He found a small wooden crate in a corner, dragged it over, and climbed up to tighten the bulb. It flashed on, blinding him. By the time he returned the crate to the corner, he could see again. The passageway's concrete walls, painted an institutional dark green, were coated with grit from generations of ink-sprayed fingers. A punch clock was mounted on a wall near the elevators, along with a metal rack holding about a dozen cards. Most were for phantom pressmen, holdovers from the union's last contract, who still reported for work as if they had real jobs. Jude checked one of the cards; it was stamped three days before.

He walked through the passageway into the pressroom. The floor, lined with metal tiles and tracks once used for carrying lead plates to the presses, extended forty feet ahead and then dropped off into nothingness. Crude sawhorses lined the edge of the precipice. The view took his breath away. It was like stepping from a sacristy into the soaring space of a cathedral, except that the interior of this cathedral had been gouged out as if it had been bombed. He walked over to the sawhorses and peered down. He was staring into a crater three floors deep, disappearing into shadows at the bottom. The levels were lined with pillars flaked with paint blisters and black with ink. Running horizontally were catwalks for the pressmen. Conveyor belts that once carried a ribbon of newspapers extended up the walls and crisscrossed in the void overhead.

He wasn't sure what he was looking for in the basement. His reporter's instinct had brought him here, since it was the likely scene of the murder. He had not really had time to examine it yesterday when he and Bollingsworth's partner discovered the newspaper cart that apparently carried Ratnoff's body to the newsroom. He didn't expect to find any clues overlooked by the police, but still, it was important to be able to visualize the place he would be writing about.

The floor was largely empty. The cart, of course, was gone, and he thought one or two pieces of equipment were missing, too, undoubtedly taken by the police. Here and there he spotted the telltale white residue from fingerprinting. He imagined it would be hard to lift any good prints in a place that had once been so busy and hadn't been cleaned for years.

If Ratnoff had indeed been killed here, what in God's name was he doing?

Jude walked around the elevator shaft to the back, where there was a door to the freight elevator. It was closed. That was a logical way for the killer to have transported the cart with the body — presuming that cold-blooded logic played a role in the killing. He examined the threshold for spots of blood or other telltale traces but found nothing.

He moved around the basement methodically, checking the nooks and walkways and even the air ducts overhead. One passageway led to a glassed-in rectangular room, the workers' canteen. He entered through a thick metal door, solid enough, he figured, to muffle the pounding from the presses. The room contained a single piece of furniture, a scarred wooden table, apparently abandoned because it was too wide to fit through the doorway. The walls must have been built after it was installed. The sullied outlines of Coke and candy machines were visible against the pale yellow paint on the far side. A blanket of dust coated the narrow windowsills and the floor. He could see trails of shoe prints in it. All in all, the room was a claustrophobic horror. No wonder the pressmen had fled in droves to

Slough's.

Outside the room, he followed another passage to where the paper's morgue — what was left of it — was housed. Up until fifteen years ago, when it was replaced by an electronic data-retrieval system, the morgue containing old newspaper articles had been on the fifth floor. It had been the *Globe*'s pride, the accumulation of 150 years of painstaking clipping and classifying by a succession of obsessive, anal-retentive archivists. Now it had been reduced to one-tenth its size; only the files of major subjects and important people remained, along with the byline folders of reporters. These had been combined with the publishers' and executive editors' papers to fill twenty rows of metal filing cabinets that marched off into the shadows like a maze.

That could have been Ratnoff's destination, Jude thought. He might have been researching something in the morgue, trying to track down something or other of interest in the archives or clips. But what could it have been? And why did he want to know it? Getting yourself killed in the morgue, he mused — how's that for an ironic ending?

It was just as he was about to leave that he heard the distant rumble of the elevator.

It was being summoned by someone on the ground floor. Moving quickly, he hid in a darkened cranny at the end of the passageway. There he waited, his breathing quickening. The rumble stopped momentarily and then resumed as the elevator descended. The doors opened and someone stepped out. A woman. He couldn't make out who it was until she had walked right past him.

"Edith!" he exclaimed. She jumped a full two inches into the air and turned toward him, ashen-faced. Her ponytail quivered like an air sock.

"Jesus Christ. You scared the shit out of me." She collected herself, leaned her butt against a wall, placed one hand theatrically against her chest, bent down a bit to take deep breaths, and looked up at him through long eyelashes.

"What are you doing here?" he demanded.

"I could ask you the same thing."

"I came here to look around . . . to see what I could see. I'm covering the story, you know. But you — what's your excuse? Why are *you* here?"

"Same reason. To look around. You're not the only one who's got a right to be nosy."

"You came here to check out the murder scene?"

"Damned straight."

"But how did you know that? It wasn't in my story."

"Oh, c'mon. It's all over the damn building. You think you're the only reporter around here?"

Typical Edith — when football coaches were still in britches, she had invented the maxim that the best defense was a strong offense. She moved closer to him and cast him a conspiratorial, slightly flirtatious look. Years before, he abruptly recalled, when it looked as though he might be a rising star at the paper, she had come on to him after several martinis on the last night of the Democratic National Convention in Boston. He had shuddered when he repelled her advance and he shuddered whenever he relived it.

"It's creepy down here. Why don't we look around together?" she whispered huskily. "Two heads are better than one." Something about the way she said it made it sound obscene. He remembered Virgil Bogart's second famous line when told Edith had mothered a child: "What's she going to do with the baby? Eat it?"

Her hand slipped into the crook of his arm.

At that precise moment, her fingers tightened. She had heard something, and in a moment so did he. That same distant sound, the rumbling. The elevator was on the move again. Now they both hid in the cranny — she stood close to him and he felt her breath warming his neck — and waited for the car to descend. The doors opened slowly. Out stepped a figure, someone familiar, another woman. High heels and a tight leather skirt.

Of all people! It was the style editor and gossip columnist, Peregrin Whibbleby.

Edith whispered into his ear, "Please, let me be the one to scare the shit out of her."

11

Jude sat in front of his computer and typed in his password, L-U-D-D-I-T-E. Then he stared at the blank screen. Second-day stories on big murders were often difficult. Expectations tended to run high and information low. That is, unless there was a major news break, which in this case showed no sign of happening. He had been beating the bushes like an African poacher.

Every half hour or so, Grabble called him and insisted on seeing him right away in his private office. There the metro editor would pace, peppering him with questions. "How about suspects? Any suspects yet?"

Jude would shake his head, look at his watch, and set his foot to wiggling. He couldn't wait to get back to his desk, and once there, thirty minutes later, his phone would ring and Grabble would summon him again. "Motive. How about a motive?

They must be working on some kind of motive."

Jude finally blew up and said he couldn't answer any questions if he didn't get a chance to work the phones. Grabble was stunned at the outburst and left him alone for a full forty-five minutes.

The shuttling back and forth to Grabble's office did not go unnoticed by the other reporters. Jude felt them smirking. On his fourth trip, he found the path marked by scribbled arrows taped up on walls, pointing the way, under a scrawled sign: TRAIL OF TEARS. He looked in at Charlie Stengler, who was leaning back with his feet on his desk and reading *Maxim.* His smile said it all: He had done it.

Jude figured it was time to teach him a lesson, but just at that moment in stepped Fred Bradshaw, the arrow signs bunched in his fist. "That's not funny," he said. "How'd you like it if somebody did that to you?"

"No chance," replied Stengler, looking back at his magazine. "I'd never get an assignment like that. If I did, I'd give up trying to report it. If I reported it, I'd give up trying to write it."

"There's no arguing with incompetence," said Fred, turning on his heel.

Jude's anger drained away. Good old

Bradshaw, he thought. The man's capacity for empathy had been enhanced by long-term suffering. Jude asked him what story he was working on. Bradshaw said he had been sent to the Children's Zoo to cover the birth of an albino hamster.

"I've written the lede," he said. "But I can't think of anything for the second graph." Still, he observed, it was an improvement over his last assignment, which was to interview a farmer in Cape May County who had grown a squash with a face that was, the farmer insisted, a dead ringer for French president Nicholas Sarkozy.

Bradshaw was not a dunce. He had gone to Princeton at the insistence of his father, a stuffed shirt of a lawyer in a white-shoe firm downtown, who assumed his son would follow in his footsteps. He majored in comp lit, but in his sophomore year he had taken a course on constitutional law that was heavy on the First Amendment, John Peter Zenger, and the glory of a free press. He was bitten by the bug, became a campus stringer, and was hired after graduation by an assistant managing editor in charge of personnel, who then asked if he could use Bradshaw's ID card to play squash at the Princeton Club.

He was a thoughtful type, secretive and

reserved. His quiet exterior hid a wellspring of ambition. He might have gone into law, maybe on the corporate side, and made a better living, despite the fact that it didn't measure up to his ideal of fame. Big bucks would at least have been compensation. Ever since his career went down the toilet, because of that unfortunate lede on the three-alarm fire in Brooklyn, he tortured himself with the thought that his father was right, that he had chosen the wrong career and that it was too late to switch. This profession was wrong for him. He just didn't seem able to get the moves down.

Jude's phone rang and he ducked back into his cubicle to take the call. It was the *Globe's* Web site asking for a quick précis of his story to send out on the wire. He told them he'd get back to them.

He tried calling Bollingsworth, but she was still avoiding him. He had her card pinned up next to his computer, and as he looked at the blank screen, he felt a wave of anger. It was so typical of cops — you give them a hand and then when you're drowning, they don't even turn around to toss you a life preserver.

He put in a call to Hank Higgle, the *Globe's* man down at police headquarters. He asked him if he could help out, maybe ask around to see if anyone there knew anything about the case. Higgle was usually very protective of his beat, but he must have picked up the desperation in Jude's voice, because he said he would try.

The phone rang again. It wasn't Bollingsworth or Hank Higgle. It was a subeditor on the metro desk who wanted a summary of his story for the 4:00 p.m. meeting. Jude told him he'd send it as soon as he had the vaguest idea about what he was going to write. His screen was still blank.

Grabble rang back.

"What's the problem? You can't even write a goddamned summary?"

"I'm working on it!" Jude shouted into the receiver. He hung up.

The phone rang again.

"What now?" he yelled.

It was Elaine.

"Jude. We've got to talk."

He could tell by the hollow coldness of her tone that the lines were rehearsed. That could mean only one thing: She was finally fed up and was going to call it all off. This would require nimble footwork. He typed the slug: S-L-A-Y. Sure enough, just as he was trying to pull together the words for his lede sentence, he caught the tail end of her sentence: ". . . we've reached the end of the road." She recited a litany of grievances: that he spent too much time at work, that he didn't pay enough attention to her, that he never had enough money, and that she had other needs that required tending to.

"But we had some great times," he replied. "We laugh a lot. And the sex is great."

"Jude, are you typing? I hear typing. Is that you?"

He had to own up that he was. He explained that he was on deadline — a word he knew, the moment it crossed his lips, would send her over the edge. It did.

"That is so typical. Here I try to tell you that you're too tied up with work and that you ignore me, and you can't even listen to me because you're on deadline."

He explained that he had been given a big story and that he was trying to write it.

"You're always talking about some big story. I'm talking about us. Don't you see?" She said that they were through and asked him not to call her anymore. She also added, by way of a coda, that she had met a man named Harry, a business consultant who happened to be independently wealthy, and that he cared for her and that they had "clicked."

" 'Clicked'? What the fuck does that mean?"

"No need to swear."

Those were the last words he heard from her. The line went dead. In the rush of emotions, he couldn't tell exactly what he felt, though as he listened to the empty stillness on the line, he thought he detected somewhere in the gloom a gleam of relief. He imagined the full impact would hit him later, once he was through struggling with the damn story.

He looked at the screen. The few phrases he had typed didn't say anything. He deleted them and stood up. He decided to visit O'Donnell. Maybe he'd have some ideas.

In the elevator en route to the eighth floor, he thought about Peregrin Whibbleby and their confrontation in the pressroom basement. She had seemed so fragile. When Edith leapt out at her, she had collapsed on the concrete floor in a veritable faint. And then when she recovered, she sputtered and stammered and finally came up with the same lame response that Edith had used: that she wanted to visit the scene of the murder. Except she put it differently: She wanted to see "where Teddy had drawn his last breath." He had seen Edith's eyebrows rise up at that one.

Whibbleby had always been a puzzle to him with her high-class manners and her lowbrow interests. She was ethereal and spacey, like a being who'd dropped in from a planet where the air was thinner and the gravity weaker. If you met her, you would think she was a ballet dancer. Yet she had to have a nasty side, because she wrote that god-awful gossip column. She'd been doing it for years, first for the tabloids and now for the *Globe.* And how could she take her job as style editor seriously? All those stories about the American *lifestyle,* a term that Jude despised.

Upstairs, O'Donnell was in his cubicle. One look at Jude and he pulled over a second chair, pushed aside the papers on his desk, and put his feet up.

"You look like shit," he said helpfully.

"I feel like shit."

"It's not coming together?"

"Not at all."

"Got anything?"

"Nothing worth a damn. The cops aren't returning my calls."

O'Donnell leaned back in his chair. "It happens to most big stories sooner or later. In your case just sooner, that's all. It's the lull after the page-one headline. I call it the 'horse latitudes' — which, in case you're scientifically inclined, are subtropical, between thirty and thirty-five degrees.

Muggy heat, no wind, waves that roll softly. A sailing ship slows to a crawl; sometimes she's stalled for weeks on end. In the old days, the sailors used to catch the faint breeze by lightening the load. They tossed the horses and cattle overboard . . . that's where the name comes from.

"The same thing can happen to a breaking story. After a certain point, nothing much occurs. Sources clam up; newsworthy developments unaccountably tail off. The wind dies down and you're in a trough. You're left there stranded."

"What do you do?"

O'Donnell reached into his bottom drawer, pulled out a bottle of scotch and two plastic cups, and filled them, handing one to Jude and tilting back the other.

"It can be treacherous. Airtime has to be filled. The presses have to run. Ink has to be spilled. It's a time when rumors and false leads raise their ugly heads. Especially with the Internet, which creates ill winds and artificial waves."

"Maybe you should get off this metaphor before we both drown."

O'Donnell smiled. "The main thing is just to avoid doing anything wrong. Writing something that's not true."

Jude had to admit it: The liquor certainly

went down smooth. It felt as if it were zapping out his esophagus.

"Did I ever tell you about the downfall of Big Bill McElroy?"

"No — but I've a feeling you're going to."

"C'mon, Lennie. Don't you want to hear about the rabbits?"

"Sure, George."

"Well, Big Bill McElroy was the star rewrite man for the *Journal-American,* a Hearst paper. It was a scrappy paper, put out without an overly high regard for what you might call truth. In those days, you know, a propensity for exaggeration came with the territory — it was called 'piping.' A certain amount was even expected, but it had to be kept within some indefinable limit. Each paper had its own version of the limit, of course, and the *Journal* was perhaps the most flexible in this regard.

"Anyway, Big Bill was such a star that he was eventually given his own column. It was called 'The Dial-Up Interview' and the idea was that Big Bill would sit at his desk and call some person in a big news story and get the scoop over the phone — there was even a little logo of a stand-up telephone. This caught on and it became a big hit. He's riding high. Then one day there's a bad fire on Staten Island, single-family residence

133

burned to the ground. But luckily no one was killed, thanks to a heroic thirteen-year-old boy who saved his entire family.

"Big Bill calls up the boy. Gets it all down — how he saved his mother, then his father, then his sister. Each time, he heads back into the inferno. Bill quotes him describing the smoke blinding his sight, searing his lungs, scorching his clothes. By the end, so help me, the boy's crawling back in to save the family dog, then the cat. The interview's written up. It's a triumph. The paper's printed. Then half an hour later, up pops the rival paper, the *World-Telegram and Sun.* It's got a ribbon headline across the front page: DEAF-MUTE SAVES THREE ON STATEN ISLAND."

Here, O'Donnell couldn't help but chuckle.

"Well, naturally, the editors are livid. They're ready to take Big Bill out to the woodshed. They call him up to the desk and demand an explanation. In a reply that became instant legend, he hitched himself up to his full height and thundered, 'Well, he didn't tell *me* that!' "

Jude laughed. O'Donnell laughed. They drained their cups, still laughing.

"I think I get the message," said Jude. "So I know what not to do. But what the hell *do*

I do to get out of the horse latitudes?"

"You got anything you're holding back?"

"One thing. The cops think Ratnoff was killed in the basement, dumped in a newspaper cart, and taken up the back elevator to the newsroom, where his body was dropped in front of the conference room."

"Sounds good to me. Why didn't you use it yesterday?"

"A cop asked me not to. Said it would be smart to hold back something only the murderer knew. So all I said was that he wasn't killed in the newsroom, but somewhere else."

"There're a lot of things only the murderer knows. Besides, you've been trying to call the cops all afternoon — to tell them you've got to go with it unless they give you something else, right?"

Jude smiled. "Right."

O'Donnell cleared his computer screen and started banging out a paragraph:

Confronted with a deepening mystery over the murder of an assistant managing editor at the *Globe,* police are working on the theory that the news executive was ambushed and killed in the basement and that his body was then secretly carried to the newsroom in a metal-rimmed canvas container that used to transport countless copies of the newspaper he once edited.

He printed out a copy and handed it to Jude, who accepted it gratefully, stuffed it into his back pocket, and took a final swig of scotch.

"Now," said O'Donnell. "You may want to add something about what's in the basement and maybe even some thoughts about what he may have been doing down there — all within the acceptable limit, of course."

Jude thanked him.

Back downstairs, Grabble was prowling around Jude's cubicle. He straightened up when he saw him. "Got anything?" he demanded.

"Enough to catch the wind and move us forward," Jude replied.

12

The next morning, Jude went to Ratnoff's funeral at Christ Church United Methodist on Park Avenue. He walked halfway up the right aisle, slid into a pew, and found himself seated next to Outsalot, the *Globe's* inestimable food critic. O'Donnell, who slid in behind Jude, grunted when he saw her. He didn't approve of celebrity journalists. Fred, bringing up the rear, moved to a different pew. He couldn't stand the woman.

Outsalot's first name was Judith, but the reporters called her Dinah. She was a big woman in more ways than one. Born in Dallas and raised on Texas barbecue, she was over six feet tall and had never tried to hide her height, on the principle that anything that distinguished her from the run-of-the-mill was to the good. Around the office, she wore custom-made cowboy boots with longhorns emblazoned in leather on the sides. When she reviewed restaurants, marching in like an executioner, she wore designer frocks and a long blond wig — the latter to remain, in principle, incognito. But the wig had become such an identifiable trademark — she wore it on her TV cooking show, *Someone's in the Kitchen with Dinah* — that she risked being missed without it. In any event, she was so superfamous that chefs didn't bother to post a "watch for this one" photo of her in the serving sections of their kitchens.

Early on, Dinah Outsalot had lost a parent and three grandparents to exotic diseases that were just moving into the mainstream. She had composed moving firstperson accounts of caring for all of them at their bedsides. In the last case, that of her paternal grandmother, she combined the account of the disease with a smattering of her grandmother's favorite recipes, which she cooked throughout the mourning period. The book, *Eating Your Way Through Grief,* had topped the "How To" best-seller list for five months. It was being made into a movie starring Meryl Streep.

"How are you?" asked Jude.

"So-so. I don't know if you heard, but my second cousin has come down with a motorneuron disease. He's wasting away and they haven't been able to identify it yet."

"Lord Jesus," muttered O'Donnell. "Where does she come up with this? She must have a contact at the CDC who slips her vials of the stuff."

"Shhh," said Jude.

Outsalot didn't hear him. "Too bad Ratnoff wasn't Irish," she growled. "Instead of a Methodist funeral, we'd have a wake. Everyone gets hammered, curses him out, and ends up singing sentimental ballads and lying — saying things like 'You know, he wasn't really such a bad-ass motherfucker.' But this . . ."

"You're not Irish — are you?"

"Me? Well, not personally, no."

"Thank God," put in O'Donnell.

Jude turned and looked over the heads and shoulders in the wooden pews behind him, past the stone pillars to the vestibule. The vast interior was filling up rapidly. It was startling to see one's *Globe* colleagues in black suits and sedate dark dresses, as if they were ordinary people who went to funeral services and therefore possibly also did everyday things, normal Americans who actually led lives outside the paper.

He felt an elbow dig into his ribs. "See that coffin?" said Outsalot. He turned back. She was waving a large hand at the funeral tableau, a dais of blue high-pile carpet on

139

which stood a marble-topped stand holding a vase of lilies. An immense gray casket rested on a bier of blue velvet. "That set them back a cool twenty g's. I know these things. I don't know if you're aware of it, but I've buried several members of my family."

"Yes, I know," said Jude.

"Do tell," whispered O'Donnell.

"Keep it down," Jude whispered back.

"Too bad he wasn't cremated," Outsalot continued. "He could have supplied a lot of oil for the lamps back in his native land."

She shifted her considerable weight to crane her neck in the other direction, and Jude could tell she was trying to read power struggles and shifts in the seating selection. Ratnoff's family — his wife and three children, two boys and a girl — sat in the first row on the left, staring stoically straight ahead. Next to them sat Ellen Butterby, Ratnoff's administrative assistant, holding a handkerchief to her mouth as if to contain the grief that might otherwise convulse her thin body in racking sobs. Across the aisle sat the publisher, Hagenbuckle, nervously poring over his speaking notes. To his right sat Elmer Boxby, the publisher's assistant and bagman, his baby face inscrutable behind thick-lensed glasses. And next to

Boxby was Skeeter Diamond. His head was mostly immobile, but once or twice he turned to look at the crowd; Jude noticed that his tic was mysteriously in abeyance.

Scattered in the rows behind the top brass was a retinue of desk heads and lesser editors: Suzanne Preston, culture editor, looking sexy in a black blouse; Vickie Gimmy, national editor, slunk down in her chair; and Heaton Squire, foreign editor, gazing distractedly at the vaulted ceiling. Brisley Townsend, looking resplendent in a double-breasted pinstriped suit, had come up from Washington and sat on the aisle, one arm draped along the back of the pew. Bernie Grabble, the metro editor, had arrived too late for the first three rows and seemed to resent being consigned to the fourth. His towering figure cast a shadow across Haggart Thomas, sports editor.

"Look at that," said Outsalot. "Brisley Townsend's been bumped. Usually, he sits next to Skeeter. The fact that they're apart leads me to suspect that they're on the skids. Either that or they're conspiring. That's the trouble. You never know which it is. I call it 'the law of the excluded middle.' "

Funeral services of high-ranking figures at the *Globe,* which brought all sorts of people from their customary haunts to heap praise

141

on the deceased, often had titillating under-currents. What would the speakers say about the departed? How far would they venture onto truth's thin ice? Among the grieving congregants, what former lovers would risk sitting side by side, their thighs possibly touching? What office enemies might find themselves in proximity and dis each other, bringing a simmering feud to a long-promised boil?

This one looked to be right up there with the best of them. Given Ratnoff's stature, all three former executive editors were expected to appear. Since not one of them was on speaking terms with the other two, that made the seating configuration interest-ing, in the way that an automobile accident can be said to be interesting to an insurance investigator.

"Okay," said Outsalot, a little too loudly for Jude's liking. "Two o'clock — here comes Richard the Third." Jude turned and looked at the back of the right aisle. There was Max Schwartzbaum. He wandered slowly up the aisle, stopped ten rows in — conspicuously far back — and sat down, his body hunched and his eyes narrowed in defensive vigilance.

"Twelve o'clock," declared Outsalot. "It's Prince Hal. Damn it, he's taking a different aisle. Not much chance for an encounter." Jude swung his gaze to the rear of the left aisle and saw Herman Althorpe, the man who had dethroned Schwartzbaum, a genial, pipe-smoking executive editor whose reign had been benign but ineffectual.

"Where the hell's Coriolanus?" she asked, in her excitement speaking so loudly that people in three nearby rows turned, frowning. She was referring, Jude deduced, to Hickory Bosch, the worst executive editor of them all. His bloodied kingdom had collapsed in scandal ten years before. "Aha! There he is! Bringing up the rear." This time, almost everyone turned, the backs of their heads directed at the funeral party. Sure enough, in came a small man who slipped into the back row, removing a brown Panama hat and sinking deep in his seat.

Jude scanned the rest of the crowd. Halfway back was Peregrin Whibbleby, sitting erect and motionless next to her husband, a handsome, well-built man, muscles bulging under his jacket. Jude remembered hearing that he was a personal trainer; he definitely worked out with weights.

His eyes turned to the far rear. There in the last row, conspicuous as a band of skunks at a garden party, sat a contingent of police. They were clustered around that elusive detective, Priscilla Bollingsworth. He was surprised to find, when he zeroed in on her, that she returned his stare.

A minister in a black-and-white robe walked to a wooden lectern and began the service. He spoke of Ratnoff's warmth and humanity and said he would be missed by everybody. He kept referring to Ratnoff's "loved ones," a reference that proved initially confusing. Jude looked at the backs of his children and his wife, all of them with their heads bowed and barely moving. Sure enough, they appeared to be in mourning. Had Ratnoff been a good husband and father? Had he turned into a different person at home — called "Hello" when he opened the door, unwound with a shot of vodka, regaled them with stories of his day at the office? Given them presents on their birthdays?

Hymns were sung; psalms were read. Three or four speakers took the floor. Ellen Butterby spoke briefly, her handkerchief at the ready. In a voice surprisingly strong, she told an anecdote about the time Ratnoff had remembered Secretary's Day and brought her a bouquet of flowers — "Daisies, I think they were."

Then Hagenbuckle rose to deliver the eulogy. He cleared his throat two or three times before speaking, looking out over the assembled congregation as if they were indeed his flock and he were their shepherd. He began by saying that no one on the paper was closer to him than Theodore S. Ratnoff. He enumerated Ratnoff's accomplishments: his role in dropping the period after the *Globe* on the page-one nameplate, the many decisions over the use of profanity, the day that a felon was first referred to as "Mr."

Jude's attention began to wander. He must have daydreamed, for it seemed that almost no time had passed before Hagenbuckle was winding up. He was saying something about a steady hand on the tiller and rough seas and standing all alone on the bridge of an aircraft carrier. Finally, he brought up the editor's spike that had pierced the dead man's chest and insisted that it was a perfect metaphor for Ratnoff's decisiveness and leadership. In a booming voice that seemed to echo off the walls, he asserted that it symbolized the man's commitment to the paper, his willingness to give his all, to the point — and here Hagenbuckle blushed a bit, as if even he realized the danger of going over the top — of sacrificing his heart and very lifeblood for the *Globe.*

Jude felt his cheeks redden as well, but in irritation at the fatuous words.

"Jesus," said Outsalot. "How is it possible for a man to be so absolutely wrong about everything?"

Next to him, Jude could feel O'Donnell bristling with anger. He looked over and the old newspaperman was gripping the back of the pew ahead of him. His knuckles were white.

"Ratnoff as a hero, upholding standards — that's so perverse, it's not even funny," said O'Donnell. "Hell, he was the worst of the lot. He could tell which way the wind was blowing inside a locked vault."

The congregation shifted forward to place knees on the prayer benches, and the minister intoned a final prayer for Ratnoff's soul. There was a moment of silence. A cry erupted from the rear — it was Slim Jim Cutler shouting out "Hallelujah!" — and at the same time an organ blasted what sounded like a Bach fugue. People stood and looked around. From the front, the procession moved down the center aisle toward the rear doors, led by Ratnoff's widow, steady and calm, progressing slowly, and beside her the three children, looking stricken. Jude felt his throat constrict. He glanced over at O'Donnell, once again gripping the pew, unrelenting in his resentment.

Then another sound rose over the notes of the organ and the shouts of "Hallelujah" and it froze everyone in place. Jude turned. It was Peregrin Whibbleby, sobbing uncontrollably, her body shaking so violently it looked as if it might snap. Next to her, standing at a remove and pretending to ignore her, his face set in barely repressed rage, was her husband.

"Well, well," murmured Outsalot. "And what do we have here?"

The crowd moved slowly down the aisle, gathering in the vestibule, where some had stopped to sign the condolence book. At one point, it looked as if Schwartzbaum was headed for his nemesis, Herman Althorpe, who was lighting his pipe on the steps outside, but a quick-thinking usher headed him off with a question about his health — to the obvious disappointment of the crowd. Hickory Bosch slipped into a black Town Car and disappeared. It took a long time for people to reach the street, and once there, they milled about in a mood of anticlimax, as if waiting for something earth-shaking to happen.

Jude was surprised to find that it had turned into a good day. The sun warmed him and he lifted his face toward it. There was a scrum of media people and cameras from the tabloids on the sidewalk, but he sidestepped it and decided to walk to the paper.

Then he felt someone approach. It was Detective Bollingsworth, walking briskly. She reintroduced herself, and he replied that he remembered very well who she was: the woman who didn't return his calls.

"Sorry about that," she said. "I've been preoccupied — a little thing called murder." She was silent for a moment and seemed to want something from him.

"What can I do for you?" he asked.

"I wonder if you might accompany us down to the station house," she said, in a tone more commanding than polite.

"I guess. Sure. When?"

"How about now?" she said firmly.

13

Bollingsworth's driver, a burly cop with a shaved head and plenty of muscle, opened the rear door of the unmarked car and, in a move that struck Jude as ridiculous, placed a heavy hand on his head to push him into the backseat. But then he bent over, leaned his thick lips so close that Jude could smell his sour breath, and said, "I know who you are. I know all about you." He slammed the door shut — hard.

Bollingsworth took the seat behind the driver. She said they were going to the Eighteenth Precinct on West Fifty-fourth Street and fell silent.

They sped down Park Avenue and then went west on Fifty-seventh Street. Jude stared out the window at familiar sights: kids on Rollerblades and shoppers, trees getting ready to lose their leaves. A hot dog vendor leaned against his cart, smoking and gazing into the distance. Everyday things appeared slightly different, more vivid. He realized his heart was speeding.

He glanced over at Bollingsworth. Today, she looked a little older, but still close to him in age. Her hair was pulled straight back off her forehead and wound in a bun. Her eyes were dark and he noticed with a flicker of satisfaction that they had circles underneath. She, too, was probably missing out on sleep. She sensed his gaze and turned to give him a hard stare, so he looked away.

The station house was a four-story fortress dating back to La Guardia's day. A sullied American flag hung on a pole in the center, and to the right the front stoop was flanked by stanchions holding green lanterns. Inside, thousands of police badges from across the country plastered the entryway, and a framed Rangers jersey, autographed by a dozen players, crowded out the wanted posters. A shoulder-high wood partition surrounded the desk officers, who faced a wall of closed-circuit screens. Bollingsworth did not take him to an interrogation room — though she seemed to make a point of passing by one — but instead threaded her way through a room packed with men and women pecking at computers, talking on the phones, and shooting the breeze. They glanced up with interest as he passed. She

150

led him into a side office, cluttered but unoccupied, and gestured toward a wooden chair. She sat behind a desk, facing him.

"Want some coffee?"

He shook his head. "You sure? I'm having herbal tea myself." He relented and she pressed an intercom button and placed the order.

"Herbal tea — that seems strange . . ."

"For a cop, you mean. We're like regular people. Some of us drink coffee, others tea. Then again, maybe I'm a strange cop."

She gave him a half smile. "You're famous around here, you know. Or maybe *infamous* is the right word for it."

He looked at her quizzically. She was no longer smiling. "Your stories on cooping. When was that exactly — three years ago?"

So that was it. Of course. And that explained the pugnacious driver. Policemen sleeping in patrol cars when they should have been out patrolling the streets. The headline was POLICE SNOOZING WHEN THEY SHOULD BE CRUISING. It had taken him almost two months to nail down the story and ferret out their hiding places. What really rankled the cops were the photos — some with license plates visible — of squad cars tucked away under bridges and in leafy groves; the pictures carried digital time notations in the upper corners, showing how long they had been there. For months afterward, cops had splattered parking tickets on cars with press plates anywhere in the city. Still, most cops seemed to have forgotten about it some time ago.

"Three years last month," he replied.

"Six of those cops came from here."

"Oh. I forgot."

"They haven't. They're still here. And you know what?"

"What?"

"They're still cooping."

He couldn't quite tell — had the half smile returned? The drinks came in, brought by an assistant. His coffee had splashed onto the cardboard tray. When the door closed, Bollingsworth blew on her tea and gave him another one of those piercing stares.

"Look. You've got some questions and I've got some questions. Let's make a deal."

"What kind of deal?"

"A swap."

"Maybe."

"You're hesitant."

"I'd like to add some . . . some caveats."

"Like what?"

He explained: He didn't like people going off the record unless it was absolutely necessary, he didn't want to print anything untrue, he didn't want to float any trial balloons, he didn't want to be used — and in general, he wasn't crazy about working too closely with authorities who had a vested interest in what he wrote.

"Quite a little speech. You take yourself seriously."

"No, it's my job. I take *that* seriously."

"Good, I can respect that. Maybe I shouldn't have said *deal.* What I mean is a mutually advantageous arrangement. Nothing underhanded. Nothing secret. You've got some information. I've got some information. Let's exchange notes."

"Okay."

"Here's how it goes. You ever play Twenty Questions? It's just like that. Except this is Two Questions. We each get two. And you go first. Ready?"

He found the conversation increasingly bizarre, but he was intrigued. "Yes," he said.

"Go ahead. Ask your first question."

He didn't have to think long. "The murder weapon — do you have it? Do you know what it is?"

"That's two questions."

"Okay. What was the murder weapon?"

"We haven't recovered it. We don't know where it is, but we know what it is. It's an ice pick. We know this from an analysis of the wound. It was plunged into the victim's neck from behind, upward into the back of his brain stem. That's why you couldn't see the wound when he was lying spread-eagled on his back." She paused. "How's that for an answer?"

Jude pulled out his notebook and scribbled some words. "Very thorough," he said. He felt honestly grateful.

"Ask your second."

This time, he didn't hesitate. "Do you have a suspect?"

"No."

"*No* — that's it?"

"No, that's it. I might add that in terms of potential suspects, there seems to be an ample field. That's some zoo you work in."

"Tell me about it."

"No, now I want *you* to tell *me* about it."

"Okay, shoot."

"First question. Engleheart, your security chief. What can you tell me about him?"

Jude was surprised. How would he figure in all this?

"Not much, I'm afraid. We don't cross paths that much. He's been there . . . I'm not sure, maybe about five, six years."

"What's he do?"

"Mostly, he's in charge of building security, I guess. He's got a staff of six, seven people. They keep some of the crazies out. If we get a demonstration outside or a bomb scare, he takes over. Blocks off the street. Clears the building. That sort of thing."

"What sort of reputation does he have?"

"I don't know. I haven't heard anything one way or the other. Why — if I may ask — do you want to know?"

"I'm interested in him. You know five years ago he used to be a cop?"

"No, but I assumed it. A lot of security guys are former cops. So what?"

"He ran with a fast crowd. They're not my favorite people. Anything else you can tell me?"

"Not really. He doesn't seem to like me very much."

"That probably goes back to the cooping business. Or maybe it's your reputation as an investigative reporter."

Bollingsworth finished her tea, so Jude swallowed the last of his coffee. He was eager to write a story about the murder weapon and thought of bringing their talk to an end.

"You've used up your two questions."

"No. All that was just one. My second one is about Ms. Whibbleby. She seemed more upset than anyone else this morning. I take it there's a reason for that."

"I saw that too, obviously. But I can't say why."

"So you mean to tell me you never heard any gossip about the two of them?"

"No, I never heard anything. I was as surprised as you were."

"I didn't say I was surprised. I wondered if you were."

"Well, yes — to answer your question — I was."

"Okay, now the game is over. I've got one more question." She looked dead serious.

"Go ahead."

"Where were you on the night of September fifteenth between the hours of six p.m. and two a.m.?"

"You're joking."

"On the contrary. I've never been more serious."

Jude's chest tightened. His mouth went dry. He tried to recall. "Let me think . . ." He seemed to be hitting a blind spot. ". . . six p.m. . . ."

"That was only four nights ago."

He played for time. "I suppose you have to ask that of everyone. . . ."

She didn't answer. He saw she was looking at his hands and neck, probably checking him out for scratches.

Slowly, it came to him. The night of Ratnoff's murder. The night after that argument with Elaine. He had been at work. He was reporting a story — two, in fact. An assistant metro editor had assigned him to do a feature on the latest fad — young upscale mothers hiring Tibetan nannies — and he was resisting that in favor of one about a city councilman who seemed to have his hand in the till of an antipoverty program in the South Bronx. He managed to get out of the first story and wrote the second, he told Bollingsworth.

"Then what?"

"I left work about seven, came home, ate alone, and walked my dog, TK."

"TK?"

"It's a printer's term. It means 'to come.' You put it in your copy when you're going to fill in the blank later. I couldn't think of a good name for my dog, so —"

"And then what did you do?"

"I went out to a movie — again alone."

"What was the movie?"

"His Girl Friday."

"What's it about?"

"It's Ben Hecht's *Front Page* made over for the screen. An old movie."

"Who's in it?"

"Cary Grant and . . ." He went blank. Amazing how the moment an accusation hits the air, even if you're innocent, you start acting guilty. "The woman — she's a famous actress. I just can't remember her name."

"Rosalind Russell. Interesting that you came up with an old movie you could have seen anytime anywhere. Can you tell me the theater where it was playing and the showtime?"

"Yes."

He did.

"Anyone see you there?"

"No. No one I know."

"You do that a lot? Go to a movie alone."

"Sometimes. If I'm, you know, feeling low."

"And afterward?"

He felt a wave of relief. He had called up a friend from college, Ray, and they'd gone out for a couple of beers — more than a couple.

"That's checkable. You'll give me his name? The name of the bar."

He did. "Look, are you seriously accusing me? Do I need a lawyer?"

"It's your right, of course. But I don't think you need one — not at this stage."

Not at this stage!

"No. Now that takes us to . . . what time?"

"This is totally insane. I had nothing to

do with Ratnoff's death. I was assigned to cover it — that's all."

"You were telling me what you were doing . . . up until what time?"

"About midnight, maybe a little after."

"And then . . ."

He groaned inwardly at the recollection. Then he had gone home, more than a little drunk, and tried to call Elaine. She wasn't in — or she wasn't answering her phone — and he left a message. He called her a second time, maybe an hour later. She still wasn't in, and this time he had hung up moments after the answering machine came on.

"I made a few calls."

He explained the whole sorry mess to Bollingsworth, looking down more than he would have liked — who Elaine was, why he had suddenly felt a desperate need to talk to her. He gave her Elaine's number.

"Drunk dialing. This is good," she said. "This is checkable. The answering machine will have the time of the calls."

"Do you really have to contact her?"

Her tone softened, it seemed, for the first time.

"Afraid so."

14

Max Schwartzbaum sat behind his oak desk on the twelfth floor, picking through the *Globe* and fuming, as he did every day. All that fluff in the paper. Where did it come from? The nose as the latest fashion accessory (PROBING THE PROBOSCIS). The sixty-two-year-old pornography actress who adopted rescue dogs (PORN QUEEN HOLDS CANINE COURT). Two thousand words on how to eat an artichoke without gagging on the fuzz (THE ART OF EATING, NO CHOKE INTENDED). Each story was a wound. He felt like that painting of Saint Sebastian in the Met — he could never remember the name of the damned painter — with all those arrows sticking into his pale flesh.

He turned to the Metro front page and fumed some more. The lead story was respectable: Cops had gunned down a Somali street merchant in a hail of fire in Herald Square. At least the paper still covered news like that. But the off lead was a soft feature on the fad of hiring Tibetan nannies (THEY'RE BUDDHISTS, THEY'RE QUIET, THEY'RE NURTURING). It was written by a woman he'd never heard of. He scanned the article — sure enough, she had found a trend: three examples.

None of that crap would have made it through the front door during his day. It just goes to show, he thought: Mencken was right when he said no one ever went broke underestimating the taste of the American public.

Schwartzbaum walked over to his wall, covered with plaques and awards and photos of him in foreign countries and exotic garb. Surely his career was something to be proud of. He had been a strong executive editor. His underlings had jumped when he called. They nicknamed him "Max the Knife" — the first time he had heard that, he'd smiled. Interviewed once on the *Harry Thorn Show,* he was asked which world leader he admired most; he had answered Mandela, but Pinochet crossed his mind. Sure, he was a dictator, but he did more good than people realized.

Schwartzbaum had grown up on Chicago's South Side. As a boy, he sold newspapers on the street, ended up controlling

161

four square blocks and three newsstands, and made enough to put himself through the University of Chicago. His pride and shame over his childhood poverty and his love of newspapers never left him. He clawed his way to the top. He didn't have to read Sun Tzu's *The Art of War:* He was born knowing it.

Because power gravitated to him naturally, he thought it most unnatural when it was taken away. The day he was pushed upstairs to write his column, "Under My Thumb," was one of the darkest days in his life. He counted the number of people who came up to visit him in his new office, and he didn't need two hands to do it.

He walked over to the window and looked out on the blinking neon of Broadway and the towers beyond. Under a cloudy, late-afternoon sky, lights were already on. Sure, the column was something. It was satisfying to have your say three times a week and to have a million-plus readers cogitate on it while they munched their bagels and sipped their coffee. And he had used it to launch some campaigns for justice and human rights. But all the good causes, like the good diseases, were already taken, and it was hard to drum up that satisfying response of outrage. Recently, he had been reduced to decrying the Malian custom of pounding gold into women's earrings, on the grounds that it caused earlobe distortion.

And the column didn't give him the same visceral punch as sending reporters all around the world, parachuting them into trouble spots like the firefighters out west. He liked pulling the strings behind the scenes. He liked feeling the paper was his, part of him, like an arm. That's what he used to tell young reporters being called back to become editors: "Yes, you're losing your byline. But think of it this way: Now you'll have your stamp on the whole paper. You'll have fifty bylines every day!" Their eyes would glow with ambition — he could read that glow like no one else — and they would tackle the job enthusiastically until the day inevitably came when they failed and had to be cut down. He had been clever: He had picked successors with fatal flaws and groomed them until the flaws showed. All except that pipe-smoking idiot who succeeded him, Herman Althorpe — he hadn't seen that one coming (any more than Althorpe had seen him coming at the funeral earlier; if he himself hadn't been waylaid, there would have been a delicious confrontation).

He moved away from the window, back to

his desk. In his pessimistic moments, Schwartzbaum thought his career was winding down, that he'd have to content himself with the dinner parties in his new social set, where he regaled the other guests with anecdotes growing stale and tales of world leaders no longer in power. But in his optimistic moments . . . well, you never knew how things would turn out in this roulette wheel of a world. He had seen men who had been pushed aside come back with a vengeance; it happened all the time in movie studios and corporate TV. And he wasn't out of the game. He had his agents all over the paper.

Ratnoff's murder — it had crystallized the discontent in the newsroom. A murder! What a brilliant stroke. Not even in the depths of its doldrums had that Los Angeles paper managed to knock off a senior editor. The *Globe*'s stock was dropping and the board was reported to be unhappy. Sooner or later, there might be a call for a firm hand. That's what had happened in Chile.

Hagenbuckle no longer liked him, but Boxby seemed to be in his corner. Boxby, the vice president, with his corporatespeak and team spirit–building exercises, was the man of the future. And of course there was always the hope of a secret alliance with an up-and-comer. Maybe someone like that foreign editor — what was his name? No one would suspect the two of them teaming up. Maybe he could help him climb the greased pole. Then he himself would be the power behind the throne. The éminence greasy. He smiled at his pun. Or maybe he would just scamper up that pole himself.

The phone rang. He saw who it was on the caller ID, an internal line, one of his informants. He let it ring four times, then picked it up and cradled the receiver with his neck. He hit some keys on the computer to sound busy.

"What's up?" he demanded.

The voice on the other end crackled. It had gossip to unload. But first small talk. The voice observed that Max had almost bowled right into Althorpe at the funeral.

"Althorpe?" replied Schwartzbaum. "Was he there?"

More crackling.

"No, I didn't see him — I was thinking about my column on the way out. It's my writing day, you know."

More crackling — a question.

"Peregrin Whibbleby?" said Schwartzbaum. "Of course I know her."

Still more crackling.

"Yes," said Schwartzbaum, warming to the

subject. "I saw her bawling in the back."

He paused, listened. His mouth dropped open.

"No," he said. "I don't believe it."

And he almost didn't. But by the time he hung up, he did. He had heard that Whibbleby's husband, the personal trainer, was gay. Their marriage was a sham. An affair between her and Ratnoff — it wasn't out of the question. The more he thought about it, the more he believed it. The man had power. Wasn't it Henry Kissinger who said that power is the ultimate aphrodisiac?

Savoring the moment, Schwartzbaum picked up the telephone. He thought it only decent to share such an interesting piece of information with the outside world. In the old days, it would have been Patti Lorn, the *Mail*'s gossip columnist. But nowadays it was Nat Dreck, the blogger who got four million hits a day and was not overly fastidious about his sources.

Schwartzbaum didn't have to look up the number. He knew it by heart.

I may be old-fashioned when it comes to the paper, he thought, but I'm up-to-date when it comes to the Internet.

15

Skeeter Diamond kept the door to the executive editor's office ajar between six and eight inches. That was just the right amount, enough to signal that he was always available and yet not enough to encourage anyone to actually enter. It was difficult, this business of being a leader, striking the proper balance between being too aloof and too familiar.

One editor, a brash young woman who had transferred from that Washington paper where people were said to actually enjoy their work, had encouraged him to roam around the newsroom from time to time — for the sake of morale. Showed what she knew. The few times he tried, it had been a dud: The moment he approached, reporters pretended to be talking about the Knicks or the Mets or slunk off. It had reminded him of those early-morning game runs in Nairobi, how the antelope and gazelles twitched their ears and loped away as soon as the hyena scuttled into view.

Thank God for e-mail. When it came to conducting business without all the feints and frills of face-to-face contact, there was nothing like it. Trouble was, you had to be so damned careful how you phrased things. You leave out a compliment or give a direct command without larding it with praise and you can send a sensitive soul into a tailspin. Plus, the messages had a way of ending up in the wrong hands. He winced as he re-called how one of his had made the rounds and had come back with snide notations pointing up his fondness for telexese — just because he had used compacted phrases like "proceed Cairoward" and "onpass soonest" and signed off with that bright little Briti-cism *cheers* — "as if," the scoffer put it, "he thinks he's wearing a trench coat and send-ing home a dispatch from Addis Ababa."

Hitting the keyboard, Diamond heard the door open behind him. There was no knock, just a voice that said, "You want to see me?" He turned. It was Jude Hurley.

Diamond looked him over. Jude had on a tie with a knot that was loosened and lopsided, a white shirt with sleeves rolled up to the elbows, pants a bit mussed, and scuffed shoes — the clothes of a reporter, respectable and a touch seedy. Reminds me of the way I used to dress, Diamond thought. He didn't dislike Jude personally, but he had known it was a mistake to assign him to the *"slay"* story. He gave him a half smile and motioned toward his inner office. This was going to be delicate. Killing a reporter's lede was like reaching into the jaws of an alligator.

Jude had never been to the inner office before. It was a small, enclosed room with a couch, four chairs, a coffee table, and a bar set in what had once been a closet, with a three-sided mirror that multiplied the bottles of liquor. A punching bag was mounted on a small table — well used, by the look of it. A display of Russian nesting dolls was lined up on a shelf; the largest bore Diamond's likeness, the next largest that of the preceding executive editor, and so on, shrinking down to a one-inch-tall carving of a .32-caliber bullet. On another wall was a T-shirt with some kind of photograph on it, framed inside a glass case. Jude stared at it. The photo was of a huge black man in camouflage fatigues, being carried in a sedan chair by four white men. They were all laughing.

"What's that?" he inquired.

"Oh, just a bit of memorabilia." Diamond

settled onto the couch and stretched his legs out. "That's Idi Amin. He had it taken at a party in Kampala, back when he was showing his jovial side. We found crates of them in his basement. I don't know if you know it, but I . . . ah . . . covered his fall."

Jude nodded. Of course he knew. Everybody knew. Diamond was always reminding them.

"That was some story," Diamond continued. "Total chaos. No electricity. Looting. The capital in flames. Troops all over the place — Ugandan, Tanzanian, Libyan. Nobody in charge. Roadblocks everywhere. Guys with Kalashnikovs extorting money and valuables. I lost four watches in one week. Course they were knockoffs I bought for that purpose on Forty-second Street."

Jude looked at him. He couldn't imagine why he had been summoned. Also, he was beginning to feel a little sorry for Diamond, and he didn't like the feeling. He remembered the rewrite bank's initial definition of the verb *to Diamond:* "to gaze back nostalgically upon a world that never was."

"I wrote ten page-one stories in five days," Diamond continued. "Of course, no one remarked on it. In those days, you could get only one byline in the paper. Still, *I* knew it. And so did the other hacks. That's what counted, more than the awards or the kudos from the desk — though I got plenty of those — the respect of your colleagues, the way you were . . . ah . . . regarded in the field. We were a tight-knit press corps, let me tell you. The best I've ever seen."

Jude nodded again. He was at a loss as to how to respond. He stole a quick look at his watch. The afternoon was creeping away and he had some reporting left to do. He had that strong exclusive for his lede — that the police had concluded Ratnoff had been killed with an ice pick — and he wanted to get it out. An awkward silence descended.

Diamond cleared his throat. His tic started up, small and slow. Jude had a gathering sense of clouds on the horizon.

"So," Diamond resumed. "You've got a helluva story by the tail."

"Yes," replied Jude.

"It's like riding a tiger, isn't it? One slip and . . . ah . . . you end up in his belly."

"I guess. But I'm still on top."

"A murder right on our own doorstep. Not even our *doorstep*. Right inside our newsroom. I've never seen anything like it."

"There's probably never *been* anything like it."

Another throat clearing, another tic.

Jude could see that Diamond was under a

lot of pressure. One leg was still extended, but the other was bent at a right angle and was bouncing up and down almost as fast as the tic. He was like a one-man band.

"Are the police helpful?"

"Only halfway, I'm afraid."

That was accurate. After the interview earlier that day, Jude had run a number of rumors past Bollingsworth. They had a loose arrangement: She would wave him off false trails but wouldn't volunteer anything. Some rumors, he didn't even bother to check — all that crap from the blogs: that Ratnoff had indulged in child pornography and was murdered by a boy's father; that he was whacked by the Mob; and that he had ingested a tapeworm to lose weight and died trying to eradicate it. Bollingsworth's interrogation of him at the precinct — and the fact that technically he was still a suspect — bothered him. Whenever he'd asked her a question, it had sounded to him as if he was trying to clear his own name.

Diamond was still talking: "How about this . . . ah . . . business about Ratnoff and Peregrin Whibbleby being . . . you know, lovers. Think there's anything to that?"

"It's hard to say. That first surfaced with Nat Dreck, so I wouldn't go near it. Of course, it's all over the Web sites of the *Maul* and the *Grifter.* They picked it up from him."

Jude, in fact, *had* tracked the rumor down. Edith, naturally, had learned all about their affair, which had begun on an editors' retreat a year ago at a resort in Naples, Florida. The two got smashed in the bar and ended up in bed. A deputy society editor in the room below had heard the floorboards creaking. "Anyway," added Jude, "it's not our kind of story."

"No, of course not. I was just curious."

Diamond felt a sneaking respect for Ratnoff. Before, he had thought of him as a straight arrow who went in more for power than sex. And even though she wrote that racy gossip column under the pseudonym Toot Bavardez, Whibbleby had seemed a frigid little wisp of a thing. Somehow, Ratnoff had stormed her castle.

"So where do you think this whole thing is headed?" Diamond asked quietly.

"It's difficult to say. The police are working it hard; they've assigned more detectives. But I don't get the impression they're anywhere near solving it. It seems to be a process of whittling down a list of suspects, and that's taking a long time."

"Any names coming up?"

"Nothing solid. Everyone and no one."

"Hmmm. Not surprising. This place is a

snake pit under the best of circumstances. Never mind with a goddamned killer on the loose."

Another long pause. Jude felt he was seeing the other side of Diamond, one that he had heard about — the steely fist. How else to explain why so many people kowtowed before him and how he could manage to carry the paper down-market on his own back. He remembered rewrite's newest definition of *to Diamond:* "to pander to the lowest common denominator, even among prime numbers."

Diamond looked at a spot on the wall above him.

"Now . . . about the story you're working on today," he said softly. "That business with the ice pick . . . I don't think . . . ah . . . that really belongs in there."

Jude sat bolt upright. So that was it — the damned ice pick! How the hell did he know I was on to that? he wondered. A dark thought popped up — all those rumors that senior editors could tap into your computer without your knowing it. Then he remembered: He had mentioned the ice pick in the summary he had dictated in the cab from the station house. He had to think fast.

"There's a problem with that — leaving it out."

"Oh yes? And what might that be?"

"You see, I've already written it on the Web. It's out there now, and if we pull it and don't put it in the paper, it'll look fishy."

"Shit."

"And we'll lose our exclusive and —"

"All right. I get it." Diamond's voice was hard and his leg was pumping away. "I *see* the problem."

"What's wrong with it anyhow?" asked Jude.

"It's gruesome. It doesn't make the paper look good. I mean, an *ice pick,* for Christ sake. That's what they got Trotsky with in his villa in Mexico. It makes us look like a band of fucking Commie assassins."

"But that's what the police said. They're sure about it. It's true."

"Ah, yes. The truth." The tic was moving faster than the bouncing leg. They were out of sync. "Well, if it's on the Web, there's nothing to be done. You can leave it in."

"That's it, then?" Jude stood up.

"That's it. And . . . ah . . . you might as well just forget we had this conversation."

Mickey Spritz, Diamond's confidential secretary, poked her head in and announced that Hagenbuckle was on the line. "He still sounds pretty worked up," she added brightly. She knew what it was about. Only fifteen minutes earlier, eavesdropping, she had heard the publisher ordering Diamond to omit the ice pick from the story.

"Tell him I'm not here. Tell him I'm . . . at the gym."

She left.

"Fifth time today and it's not yet three o'clock," complained Diamond. "Even Idi Amin gave it a rest sometimes."

He stood up abruptly and walked Jude to the door, which, he observed, was always open to him.

Mickey Spritz was on the phone at her desk just outside. Jude could tell, from the way she looked at him, that she was gossiping, probably about their meeting, most certainly about the publisher's calls. She was the biggest rumormonger in the whole building and Diamond, the poor guy, didn't even realize it. One of the problems in reporting on your own shop was that you learned a lot more than you needed — or wanted — to know. Lately, he had picked up a number of reports that Diamond was in trouble upstairs.

He'd be in trouble, too, if he didn't hurry. He had to write his lede about the ice pick quickly. He hoped that Diamond wouldn't look for it immediately.

As he walked away, he heard a series of

thwacks coming from the inner office and it took him a moment to place the sound: Diamond's punching bag was getting a workout.

Back at his desk, he dialed Chris, the editor of the *Globe's* Web site.

"Chris," he said. "Do me a favor. I've got a story here that's got to go out right away."

16

Bollingsworth had decided to conduct this interview alone. It would require tact and sensitivity, traits she could employ if she put her mind to it. She practiced on the eagle-eyed doorman, politely asking for Peregrin Whibbleby and not identifying herself as a cop. Riding up in the elevator, she mused about the Upper East Side; she distrusted stereotypes, but still, she had just passed through an alternate universe of shih tzus and Labradoodles, young mothers in Prada pushing Bugaboo strollers, and tree-lined streets blocked by graffiti-free delivery vans from florists and antiques shops — everything, in short, that reminded her of her own upbringing, which she had fled years ago.

Most of the *Globe* reporters and editors, as far as she could tell, inhabited the West Side, where they blended in with the flora and fauna. But Ms. Whibbleby clearly hailed from the country called Wealth and kept her passport up-to-date. Co-ops in this building on East Seventieth Street had to go for a cool two million bucks, with twice that in reserve to get past the board. The 10021 zip code probably helped her in her dual positions at the paper — style editor and gossip columnist.

Peregrin herself answered the door, her eyes red and puffy. If she wanted to portray a cliché of a grief-stricken woman, she had hit it just right — or maybe, thought Bollingsworth, her radar antenna up, a little overdone. One hand on the doorknob, Peregrin invited her in, backpedaling and graciously helping her off with her coat. The smell of freshly brewed coffee filled the apartment.

"I'm glad you've come," said Peregrin, and oddly enough she sounded as if she meant it.

She had given the same impression when Bollingsworth phoned and was told to come right over. This is a woman, the radar said, locking on its target, with a big secret that she is dying to confess. Let me guess: adultery, regret, marital discord, shock, mourning — in that order.

Peregrin offered coffee and ushered Bollingsworth into a living room decorated in a riot of chintz sofas, early-twentieth-century handcrafted tables, and crystal lamps with black pinched-oval shades. She excused herself and went to the kitchen. On the way, she bumped her shoulder into the doorjamb.

For days now, since the murder, she had been discombobulated — that was the old-fashioned word she used to describe her state. Her husband, Alfred, was worried that her affair with Ratnoff would become public knowledge. "Why him, of all people?" he had bleated the night before the funeral, after two days of her weeping. Then he had left for the health club, slamming the door behind him.

How to explain her affair? How to describe that incredible first night at the corporate retreat when Ratnoff had seduced her and she succumbed to that glorious, scary feeling of being overwhelmed, almost smothered, by so much masculine flesh. Then the shock at what she had done, the tears of contrition and the painful pleasure of succumbing again and yet again. It was like hurling herself against a wall. And then gradually, she began to feel real affection for Ratnoff, and finally something close to love. Sex makes beasts of us all, she used to tell herself, buttoning her blouse in the top-floor room of the Sheraton, where they registered under the pseudonyms of Mr. and Mrs. Naples to commemorate the start of their affair in Florida.

What accounted for her attraction to him? Certainly, some of it had been his power. It was like having a large German shepherd that could tear you apart if it wanted to but never would. Some of it had undeniably been the sex, after years of sharing a bed with a gay man. And then some of it had been Ratnoff himself. He had had a sweet side — like a playful little boy — and she had loved that he'd showed it only to her. At 5:00 p.m., when the page-one dummy was drawn up with the display of the day's stories, he would send her a clandestine copy. They had gossiped about the paper; his position had made him privy to all kinds of secrets. She had liked the feeling of passing a crowd in the cafeteria and knowing which ones were about to get raises and which were about to be smacked down for fooling around with lovers or drugs. She was the insider's insider. It appealed to her bitchy side — which was, after all, the reason she had become a gossip hound.

She brought the coffee in on a tray. Bollingsworth crossed her legs demurely, the way she used to in her parents' living room.

"You know," she said, "I grew up just two

blocks from here — on Park and Seventy-second." She could tell, from Peregrin's raised eyebrow, that her words had cracked open a door. Shamelessly, she leaned against it: "I would have gone to school a block away, but Hunter moved when I was four, so I had to traipse all the way up to their building on Ninety-fourth Street."

"Oh, I see. Then how did you . . ."

"End up becoming a cop?" Bollingsworth had heard the question often. She elected to answer it seriously. "It was a late decision, after college, Sarah Lawrence. I guess I thought . . . having so many advantages given to me, being born with the proverbial silver spoon in my mouth and all that . . . that I had to do something different. I wanted to do something on my own . . . even if it meant dropping down a niche in society — *especially* if it meant that, if you know what I mean. My father nearly died when I told him."

Peregrin nodded somberly, taking the words to heart. She, too, had had a father who prodded her to make the right choices. On the Upper East Side, that was almost a given.

"Plus, I liked it. I was going to law school and I went out with a cop and started hanging out with all his buddies, and one day I thought, Hey, I can do that. So I switched to John Jay. Those were the days the force was beating the bushes for women."

"How did he like that? The cop," asked Peregrin.

Bollingsworth laughed. "At first he seemed to like it — until we got married. Then it didn't sit so well — the alternating day and night shifts, coming home smelling of sweat, riding in a patrol car with another guy — all that. He was jealous. By his code, only the man was entitled to play around." She looked over at Peregrin.

"So the marriage didn't last. Two years. Luckily, no kids. My father's happiest day — aside from the one he made his first million and bought his first sailboat — was the day I told him Jake and I were finished."

"And now?"

"You mean am I seeing anyone?"

Peregrin nodded.

"From time to time. But one thing I've learned: Keep it out of the workplace. That's just asking for trouble. You know what I mean?" She cast her a meaningful look.

Peregrin leapt up and ran to a table where there was a box of Kleenex. She grabbed a handful and began weeping before she made it back to the sofa. Bollingsworth sat next to her and put a hand on her arm, a gesture that unlocked the floodgates. Between sobs, Peregrin told her everything — the corporate retreat, the hot sex, Ratnoff's endearments, the fears of getting caught, and the horror of learning that he had been killed.

"And how *did* you learn about it?"

"As soon as I got to work. There were a whole bunch of people milling around the entrance. My secretary was there. She saw me and came over and told me. She's the only one in the building who knew about me and Teddy."

Somehow, Bollingsworth doubted this. "And Mr. Ratnoff . . . Teddy . . . did he have any enemies at work? Out of the ordinary, I mean. Did he talk about anyone out to get him or anything like that?" Peregrin sniffled and shook her head no. "Was he working on anything unusual? Any kind of special project?"

"He was in the basement a lot. He was doing research on some kind of book, but he didn't talk about it much. I kept asking him, but he was sort of mysterious about it."

"The basement — that's where the morgue is, right?"

"Yes."

"But he never told you what he was working on?"

"No. He could be pretty secretive."

Bollingsworth risked breaking the mood by pulling out a notebook and jotting something down. This actually seemed to bolster Peregrin, who sat upright, practically arching her back, and waited expectantly for more questions, like a cooperating witness. Bollingsworth brought the subject around to her husband, Alfred.

"And when did he learn you were having an affair?" she asked casually.

"About two weeks ago. Maybe longer. It wasn't a onetime thing, more of a process really. He didn't believe it at first. He found some cocktail napkins from the Sheraton and then some credit card receipts — I always insisted we should split the costs — and then some love notes, and some photos. By then, his doubts had disappeared. . . . He confronted me and I admitted it."

"How did he take the news?"

"Not so hot. He yelled a bit and stomped around. He kept talking about it, night after night." She looked pensive. "Sometimes I think he was more upset over *who* I was having an affair with than over the fact that I was having it. I think he felt threatened by Ratnoff . . . being a majordomo at the paper and all. And that he was married. In some way, it's as if Alfred thought all that reflected

185

badly on my choice — on my taste. And so on himself. Does that make any sense?"

"As much as anything else does."

"You know in some ways, with a gay man, you get the worst of both worlds."

"I can imagine." She lowered her pen, as if the conversation was nothing more than a friendly chat. "He's a big man, isn't he? I saw him at the funeral."

"Yes."

"Works out, does he?"

"Yes." Peregrin explained that he worked as a personal trainer at Equinox on Lexington Avenue.

Bollingsworth jotted another note. "And the night Ratnoff . . . ah, Teddy . . . was killed, where was Alfred?"

Her eyes grew large in disbelief. "Surely, you don't think . . . Oh, I couldn't bear to think that . . . He wouldn't hurt —"

"A flea. I know. It's a question we have to ask everyone. Purely routine."

Peregrin explained that Alfred had been with her most of the time, though there were some gaps — when he went out for salad, when he went to the basement gym, when he went to the video store. The answer came so quickly and precisely that Bollingsworth figured she had already asked herself the same question.

The conversation turned to work. They both complained about the hours.

"But tell me," said Bollingsworth. "You've got two jobs. You're the style editor and you're also the gossip columnist. How does that work?"

"I'm like Jekyll and Hyde." She giggled. "At meetings I'm me, Peregrin Whibbleby, talking about various lifestyle issues, like when should you stop your toddler from saying 'poop,' and online I'm Toot Bavardez, spreading the latest dirt. I get more hits than anyone at the paper except for a certain op-ed columnist, who shall remain nameless."

"Do you like it?"

"I do. It gives you a chance to expose what people are really like deep down and to . . . get even. Oh dear, that sounds dreadful, doesn't it?"

"A bit." Bollingsworth stopped writing. "Didn't you work at the *New York Graphic* years ago?"

"I was there for years. I helped write the 'TattleTale' column. I moved to the *Globe* eight years ago."

"Quite a step up. How do the old-timers at the paper like it?"

"Are you kidding? They think gossip is the lowest of the low. I try telling them that it's just a different kind of news and that people want to read it more than anything else, but they just don't get it."

"Did Teddy get it?"

"Yes, I think so. I think he was beginning to."

"And did that make people angry?"

"I suppose so, yes."

"Anyone in particular?"

"It's hard to say."

By now, Peregrin seemed to have left the Kleenex behind her. After finishing her second cup of coffee but before rising to retrieve her guest's coat, she said, "Can I ask you something? What it's like being a police officer — as a woman? Do you get — do the men treat you equally?"

Bollingsworth felt she owed her an honest answer. "It was the hardest thing I ever did. I used to find obscene notes in my mailbox. Condoms stuffed into my locker. Guys come on to you, and when you don't respond, they call you a dyke. Others don't want to be your partner. Even today there're certain guys who won't take orders from me."

Peregrin sighed. "And I thought *we* had it bad at the *Globe*." She brushed the collar of Bollingsworth's coat. "Men are scum — aren't they?"

17

When Danny Devlin worked the streets looking for a subject for his column, he moved with a slow but still graceful gait, his eyes alert and shining, like an old panther on the prowl. And now Danny was desperate. He had six hours to come up with something — and it had better be good. It was no secret that his column for the *Globe,* "On the Street," was slipping. The cynics said if it didn't liven up soon, it'd be called "Out on the Street," which is exactly where Danny would end up.

He walked along Eighth Avenue in the mid-Forties, drawn as always to the seedier side of Manhattan, though only a few remnants remained of its former glory days — two video porn shops and a live-action strip club called Puss 'N Boots. He turned west on Forty-sixth Street and passed the soup line at St. Luke's. Reflexively, he scanned the line of bedraggled men and women. In the old days, when the homeless were news, he used to find a good subject there — say the head of a corporation down on his luck or a Vietnam vet with a Purple Heart in his pocket. Danny had felt like a prospector coming across a gold nugget in a cold mountain stream.

He was, admittedly, a throwback. As a columnist, he was what used to be called "a shoe-leather man." He wore a disheveled raincoat. He smoked nearly a pack a day, though he had tried more than once, secretly, to give it up. ("Who wants to be a slave to their fucking willpower?" he had proclaimed after his last failure.) He drank a good amount every evening — only Jameson, neat. He made it a point not to start drinking before 6:00 p.m., but most days he began clock watching at 5:15. His face was puffy and creased with so many wrinkles, it looked like W. H. Auden's — though there, it must be said, the similarity ended.

He had grown up in Hell's Kitchen before it was called Clinton. He was beaten by the nuns in school, played stickball with kids who grew up to be Westies, and knew a lot of neighborhood families that produced both priests and second-story men. Sometimes, he would say, settled in a bar chair, he felt like a walking Martin Scorsese cliché. But at least, he would tell himself, unlike half a dozen people he could name, he didn't use his slum background as a passport to the good life, writing sentimental, gritty movie scripts and novels about the days of rats and winos.

Instead, he became a newspaperman. It happened by accident, after he had dropped out of high school in his senior year and spent some months running numbers. One of his clients was Brookford P. Smith, the dapper, cane-carrying managing editor of the *Clarion,* who took a shine to him, especially when he won. By pouring in the proceeds of others, Devlin made sure the man won almost every time. After eight months of this, he was put on staff at the paper. He discovered that reporting meant hanging out on stoops, talking to people, and gave you freedom to go to the races and ride around with Walter Winchell on police radio calls. He liked it and was good at it.

The tabloids were Devlin's Yale College and his Harvard. Writing a column, it turned out, was just telling stories — the way the old men used to do sitting on the folding chairs outside the Sons of Ireland Social Club on Eleventh Avenue. At the *Globe,* where he'd turned up six years ago,

191

choosing it because it was one of the last papers still standing, his column was appreciated for its "authentic" voice. But he never quite fitted in — his column looked strange in a broadsheet. He usually phoned it in from home and rarely went to the office. Now on the wrong side of sixty, he was doing something he had never done before: He was worrying about his future.

Devlin cruised the line, looking for someone he knew. If there was one thing he still had, it was his extensive network of sources, many of whom tended to frequent the city's lower echelons. Sure enough, there, behind a three-day growth of stubble and wearing a soiled ski parka, was a familiar figure — old Barney Roughen. Devlin had once written a column about Roughen, based on the man's uncanny ability always to lose while dealing out three-card monte. The column had brought in some contributions, and they had more or less remained friends ever since.

Barney spotted him but for some reason quickly looked away.

"How's it hanging?" asked Devlin. He knew, like most street columnists, that a friendly reference to genitals was a good conversation starter.

Barney seemed wary. He was grasping the

handles of a Bloomingdale's shopping bag, which looked heavy, and seemed to be trying to hold it out of sight, behind him.

"Whatcha got there?" asked Devlin.

"Nothing much . . . few old clothes."

"Why you hiding it?"

"I'm not hiding it."

"No?"

"No."

Devlin asked about three or four acquaintances and shot the breeze for a while, then came right out and asked Barney if he knew of anything interesting going on. Barney sucked his lips into his mouth while he thought, a habit that made his head, thin enough to begin with, look disconcertingly like a skull.

"You could go by Puss 'N Boots," he said finally. "They got a new exotic dancer there. She's moonlighting. During the day, she works as a dental hygienist."

Devlin thanked him and moved on. Barney was well-meaning but clearly hadn't yet developed a fine feel for the character of the *Globe.* Yet the tip did stir up a vague memory — he had heard somewhere that the strip joint was in trouble because of the new raft of city regulations devised to close down porn shops. Sixty percent of its floor space and inventory had to be set aside for so-called legitimate entertainment materials. The owner counted the stage in this category on Wednesday nights, when it was given over to The Razor's Edge, a neighborhood theater company. The company had mounted a version of *Waiting for Godot* in which Pozzo stripped naked. An undercover cop who happened to be in the audience busted them, and so now Puss 'N Boots was going to lose its license.

Maybe, he thought, I could do something with that — the juxtaposition of exotic dancing and modern drama, the irony of earnest, avant-garde artists inadvertently putting their theater out of business. He trundled off quickly down the avenue toward the marquee.

On the way, something nagged at him. Why was Barney acting so mysterious about that Bloomingdale's bag? All he had to do was show it to him.

18

Jude was desperate. Four days had passed since the murder and he had managed, somehow, to write each day. But now he was casting about, unsuccessfully, for another follow to the *"slay"* story.

He was preparing to go to lunch, standing in his cubicle with his coat on, when his phone rang.

"Oy, mate. Neville here. Got a minute?"

His heart sank. Neville Dumpster was the competition's heavy hitter, the Babe Ruth of the *Grifter,* the sultan of twat. He was Scottish, imported by Lester Moloch to ply the underhanded tricks of British tabloids in New York. Neville had cut his reporter's teeth on the mean streets of Glasgow, where he'd earned the nickname "Animal." He had evolved a uniquely effective technique of doorstopping — the practice of hunting down aggrieved relatives of victims before anyone else and keeping them quiet. He would enter their dwelling, grab the quick interview, filch photos (frames and all) from the mantelpiece, and in general act so boorish and obnoxious that he would be evicted and the door would be forever barred to all reporters.

Jude breathed deeply. "What's up?"

"I've inherited the Ratnoff story, for my sins."

Jude groaned inwardly. This could only mean trouble.

"I want to run something by you," Animal continued. "We hear Ratnoff was the kingpin of a high-class sex ring. Run out of the *Globe*'s basement. Boys, girls, women, dykes, you name it. Kinky stuff. All those conveyor belts, bundlers, puddles of ink. Guys with newspaper fetishes who want to thrash around among all that newsprint. You get the idea."

"Christ. That's the dumbest thing I ever heard. Where do you come up with this stuff?"

"We have it on good authority. Afraid I can't tell you the source — I would if I could. But it's solid. Authoritative, I would even say. We hear the sex ring was hooked in with some of those pimps and transvestites on Eighth Avenue."

"You're out of your mind. It's just not

true. It's not possible."

"So you're denying it?"

"Denying it? Who, me? I'm just a reporter here."

"So you're *not* denying it."

"I'm saying you should talk to someone else. I'm not the *Globe*'s spokesman."

"But you're working the story. I thought you'd be straight with me. For old times' sake."

"What old times? I hardly know you. I only met you last year."

"Maybe. But we always got along. It felt longer."

"Look. I don't want to talk anymore."

"C'mon. It's not like you to leave a fellow hack hanging. Can't you give me something? What angle are you working?"

"Nothing. I gotta go. Good-bye."

Jude hung up. He figured Animal was probably just fishing, but he felt he should warn someone at the paper about him. If he cornered you with an outrageous accusation and you so much as paused, he took it as instant confirmation.

He walked over to the metro desk. His friend, Clive Small, was busy on the phone, but Jude waited for him to get off. No one else had as good a head on his shoulders. The news assisstant was a lanky, sandy-haired young man who was drawn to the profession the same way Jude had been. He came from Minneapolis and still had a midwestern openness about him, though he didn't volunteer much about his upbringing. Somehow, he had talked his way onto the bottom rung at the *Globe* without having gone to journalism school. As a techie, he might have gone to work at the Web site, but it was his dream to work for the paper.

Jude figured he'd make a fine reporter one day. He was already doing legwork for some of the best — they made sure to ask for him — and he was a fast learner. Jude had taught him some tricks of the trade, including what he called the "helpless orphan" approach — that is, in certain situations, to come on as clueless and ask rudimentary questions that were apt to elicit colorful quotes. Recently, Jude had smiled when an older reporter recounted arriving in Williamsburg to cover a racial brawl between blacks and Hasidic Jews. The reporter arrived minutes after Clive left. Interviewing a rabbi at length, and presenting his own views, the reporter was surprised when the rabbi complimented him on his grasp of the situation. "Thank goodness you're not that Clive Small fellow," he had said. "He didn't seem to get things the way you do. Why, we had to explain *everything* to him."

Clive put the receiver down. "What's up, dude?"

Jude told him about Animal. He explained there was an element of self-preservation to it: He didn't want to lose man-hours knocking down Animal's phony stories. Clive said he'd be sure to contact the flak, Gulliam Toothy.

Then he said: "You know, I was on my way to see you. I noticed something just now as I was waiting in the lobby. I don't know if you've seen it. If you stand at the end of the elevator bank and face west and look up, there in the far-right-hand corner, it looks like . . . I could swear it was . . . a camera lens."

Jude scarcely thanked him. He didn't wait for the elevator, but raced down five flights of stairs. The staircase gave out on the western end of the lobby and the moment he stepped onto the marble floor and looked up, he spotted it — a camera! It was tucked away inconspicuously right above the molding, no bigger than a book, painted the same dull gray as the ceiling. He followed the line of sight of the lens. It was trained on the elevator bank! It would have recorded anyone who took an elevator to the basement on the night of the murder.

The camera had been there so long, few people remembered it. Certainly he hadn't. He felt stupid for not thinking of it. Almost every lobby was under surveillance these days, and especially newspaper lobbies, where people turned up claiming to be the queen of Romania or JFK's assassin and offering to pour out their stories for a song.

Jude walked over to the guard desk. He asked about the camera, got a shrug, and was referred to the office of the head of security, none other than James H. Engleheart. His office was on the ninth floor. Waiting for the elevator, Jude was conscious for the first time of the camera's eye, the spooky sensation of trying to act normal while being recorded.

The elevator filled up rapidly. Last to get on was Bernie Grabble. He spied Jude and squeezed over to him.

"Whatcha got?" he demanded.

"Hard to say." Jude rolled his eyes around the crowded elevator, trying to send the message: Not here.

Grabble got it, nodded enthusiastically. He stepped off at the fifth floor, swiveled around to look for Jude, and then spotted him still inside the car. Jude pointed up.

"Stop by my desk!" yelled Grabble just as the doors closed. Several of the passengers laughed.

The ninth floor was terra incognita, a warren of administrative offices. The only times Jude had gone there were to fill out requests for loans at the employees' credit union. He followed signs marked HEAD-QUARTERS, SECURITY, with arrows pointing down a long hallway, around a corner, and halfway down another corridor.

He could hear someone talking even before he got to the half-open door. He stopped and listened. It was Engleheart's voice, interspersed with silences — he was on the phone.

"I tell you . . . there're no suspects. No one's on to anything. . . ."

He paused, listening.

"Yeah. That's right."

Another pause, longer this time.

"No, I don't think so. . . . No, not at all. . . ."

Pause.

"No one knows where the fucking ice pick is. . . ."

Jude heard a sound, a chair scraping, and Engleheart's tone dropped low. "Wait a second."

He flung open the door and glared at Jude, then went back to his desk and picked up the receiver. "Gotta go. I'll call you later. . . . Never mind, I'll call you later." He hung up and turned to Jude.

"What the fuck are you doing?"

"I've come to see you."

"Were you spying on me?"

"No. I came to ask you a question. The guard downstairs referred me to you."

Engleheart's expression froze. He seemed to be trying to figure out what to do. He was silent a moment and then said, "What question?"

"It's about the camera . . . in the lobby. My question is, What did it pick up on the night of the murder? You played the tape, I'm assuming. What did you see?"

"I'm not authorized to tell you anything about that." Engleheart was staring at him now. "Or anything else, for that matter." He walked over to the door. "Now get out."

Engleheart grabbed Jude's elbow, escorting him to the hallway.

"Take your hands off me."

Jude walked down the corridor. He could feel Engleheart staring at his back.

"Don't fuck with me," he heard behind him. "I'm not somebody you want to fuck with."

Jude made a point of slowing his pace. He didn't turn around until he'd passed the corner, then walked straight to the elevators and returned to his desk. His message light was on, and as he reached for the receiver, he realized his hand was shaking slightly — out of anger, not fear. He played over in his mind what he had heard. The snatch of conversation sounded incriminating, but when you thought about it, there was nothing really specific. More than anything it was Engleheart's reaction to being over-heard — and his warning — that were suspect.

One of the messages was from Bollingsworth. Good — he was just going to call her.

She picked up the receiver herself.

"Can I come see you?" he asked.

"What a coincidence," she replied. "I was calling to ask you the same thing."

19

Bollingsworth met him at the front desk and flashed him a smile, which was certainly an improvement. She seemed less forbidding — possibly, under different circumstances, even attractive.

She guided him through the detectives' room, where the gang again stared at him as if he carried the plague, to a tiny back room that had an old television set propped on a scarred metal desk and battered venetian blinds that were drawn closed.

"Welcome to our entertainment center," she said, motioning him to a wooden chair. "Coffee?"

He shook his head. She sat next to him, facing the TV.

"I suppose congratulations are in order," she said, a touch of self-mockery in her tone. "You're in the clear."

He was surprised to find relief spreading

through his system, a sensation like a warm bath.

"How? What happened?"

"Your alibis held up."

The relief was now tempered with something that felt a lot like resentment. He pictured the cops talking to his drinking buddy, Ray, and — what really galled him — sitting down with Elaine to play back her answering machine. How would she have taken that? No big deal, ma'am; it's simply that your ex has become a murder suspect.

"I suppose an apology is out of the question."

"Not totally, no. I can do that if I put my mind to it. I'm sorry."

"What made you think I had anything to do with this in the first place? All I did was report the fucking story. I was assigned to it. I didn't ask for it."

"We'll get into that. But first I want you to do something for me."

The nerve. He felt like walking out. But there was no chance of that: His reporter's button was pressed, and whenever that happened, interesting things usually followed.

"What?"

"Look at some tapes. Help me identify people."

"From the camera in the lobby?"

She smiled again; it was disconcerting this time around. "So you finally glommed on to that."

"It took a while," he said. "A big break, huh? I guess now you can just pick out the murderer."

"Not that simple." She turned on the TV and reached down to press the play button on the VCR. "It's that old conundrum — good news, bad news. The good news is that there's a camera in the lobby. The bad news is that on the day of the murder, it hadn't been operating for two months."

Jude was aghast. "Why not?"

"Economies — that's what they told us." She shook her head. "Budget cuts. They used to keep a bunch of tapes — change them every day, store them for a week, and then recycle them. They'd eventually wear out and have to be replaced. What with the cost of storing them and changing them and buying new ones, it was easier to just junk the whole thing. Cheaper, too. I estimate they must have saved a whole sixteen dollars a month — maybe more if you count the labor." She shook her head again. "And I thought the PD was bad."

The TV screen sprang to life, a snowy black-and-white view of the lobby, which appeared elongated and oddly out of shape.

No sound. He could make out the elevators and in the background a section of the giant globe suspended by wires.

"So what tape is this?" he asked.

"The tape we put in the morning *after* the murder."

"What good is that?"

"It might tell us something."

"Like what?"

"Like who's going to the scene of the murder. Or maybe who's *returning* to the scene of the murder."

"You think he'd go back?"

"He or she. Never can tell."

Jude saw darkened figures, distorted into dwarfs because of the camera's height. They were milling around, moving slowly. The quality of the tape was poor and the faces hard to make out.

"But why would he — or *she* — do that?"

"Could be any number of reasons," she replied. "Something left undone. Something left behind."

"You think the weapon . . . the ice pick . . . is still down there?"

"No. We've gone over the place thoroughly."

"So why would the murderer return?"

"Depends. He might not — I'll say *he* for now, you take my point. Say we're dealing with someone who knows what he's doing, a real professional, as they say on *Law and Order*. He's cleaned everything up, left nothing behind. He's feeling pretty sure of himself. Then he has no reason to return. . . ."

"And so you look at the tape —"

"To exclude people. Exclusion and elimination are a big part of the game. Remember Sherlock: 'When you have eliminated the impossible, whatever remains, however improbable, must be the truth.' "

"I see."

"And believe me, in this case, excluding *anyone* is a step ahead. It leaves only about one thousand other possible suspects."

"So *you've* finally *glommed* on to that."

She ignored the remark and pointed to the TV. "Watch the tape closely, please. The down elevators are the two to the rear."

He did. At first, it was intriguing to watch people unaware that they were being observed. Everyone seemed to look suspicious. He saw a figure instantly familiar — and realized it was himself. Then a short while later, he spotted Edith Sawyer, and then Peregrin Whibbleby.

Bollingsworth checked the tape numbers against a list and fast-forwarded during the times when people took the up elevators;

the small figures scurried about and disappeared into opening doors like figurines on a Swiss weather house in overdrive. She slowed the tape and Jude watched the metro editor, Bernie Grabble — easy to identify because of his height — take the elevator to the basement. Again, the tape sped up and then slowed. And he saw O'Donnell! Again fast and slow. Then Slim Jim Cutler! And so on. At one point, he saw Skeeter Diamond. And somebody who might have been Max Schwartzbaum. And even the obit editor, Alston Wickham Howard. And many others. Jude provided the names.

The problem was, there were dozens of other people he couldn't identify. They were indistinct or stood with their backs turned. Among them was a suspicious-looking character with a beard. He wore a cap that was pulled low and dark glasses. Jude couldn't put a name to him, but something about him, the way he walked slightly stooped, was familiar.

"Bear in mind," said Bollingsworth, "some of these are printers. As you know, a few old-timers still show up and punch in. Three shifts a day and no presses. How's that for weird? For a newspaper that puts the world into perfect order every twenty-four hours, you people seem to be living in a bizarre alternate universe."

She came to the end of the tape.

"And of course these elevators are not the only way to the basement. There's the freight elevator. As you wrote so perceptively the other day, that's how the body was taken up to the fifth floor. So obviously the murderer could have used it to get to the basement to begin with."

"Meaning he knew his way around the building," said Jude.

"Right. An insider."

Like the head of security, James H. Engleheart, thought Jude. The man who, not coincidentally, had undoubtedly made the decision to stop using the recording tapes.

"Let me ask you something," he said. "Last time, you mentioned Engleheart's name. You still interested in him?"

Bollingsworth gave a barely perceptible turn of her head. "Why? You know something?"

"No, just curious."

"You said on the phone you wanted to see me. Was it about him?"

"No. I just wanted to check in, see what's new. And I wondered how interested in him you really are."

"I'm interested in him — along with other people."

"Like who?"

"Too early for names. I can't go there. It'll just mean more trouble in the long run."

Jude felt the resentment seeping back in. She was happy to use him as a spotter but reluctant to give anything in return.

"You were going to tell me why I was . . . under suspicion," he said.

"It was your fingerprints."

"My *fingerprints?*"

"On the lightbulb."

"The lightbulb?"

"Yes. If the murderer planned to ambush Ratnoff, it's possible he wanted it dark. He may have staked the place out and loosened the lightbulb. That's assuming it didn't work itself loose, which can't be totally ruled out."

"So you figure the murderer loosened the bulb before he killed him and then thought about it later and might have returned to screw it back in."

"Exactly. Using the wooden crate just as you did."

"And you found my fingerprints on the bulb."

"Right."

Jude thought back. He remembered tightening the bulb on his second visit. But on the first visit, when he went there on the day of the murder with Bollingsworth's partner, was the passageway dark? He thought so, but it was difficult to be certain.

"But there must have been a lot of other prints on the bulb."

"No, just yours."

"How's that possible? Even the person who put the bulb in . . . the janitor . . . his prints must have been on it."

"No. It was a new bulb. *We* put it in. And naturally, we made sure it was wiped clean."

"I get it. You switched lightbulbs. But that means you have the old bulb. Why not just look for the prints on that?"

She gave him a patronizing look. "We did. No luck. Too much dust and paper particles from the presses and smudge marks. It could be, of course, that the murderer wore gloves. . . . I hope not, because then we're dealing with someone who planned ahead methodically and knew what he — or she — was doing. Of course, then there's no motive to go back to the basement to begin with."

"So why did you need me to identify all those people?"

"Again — exclusion."

"Okay. Back to square one. But now you can't be sure. You don't know if you're excluding people or including them."

"That's right. But in either case, it's

information that might prove useful later. Information always helps, even if you don't know at the time how it fits in."

Half-formed thoughts nagged at Jude.

"Where did you get my prints for comparison?"

"The Feds. From the post office — you worked there one summer when you were seventeen. You were printed then."

Another thought took shape. "Wait a minute! You said I used the wooden crate to reach the bulb. How the hell did you know that?"

"We saw you. We hid a camera in the basement. So actually, we didn't need your prints. That would've been icing on the cake — had you been guilty. Juries love prints."

"Christ. Another camera. You've got enough footage for a feature film. And what did you see? Did you see anyone do anything . . . incriminating?"

"Not that I'm at liberty to talk about."

"C'mon. I helped you."

She paused. "All right. I'll tell you. Basically, no."

"Basically no?"

"That's right."

"How come you didn't ask me to identify people on that one?"

"It's police evidence. That's trickier."

They were at an impasse.

"By the way," she said, "you can't use any of this. It's all off the record."

"What! You didn't say that."

"Let me put it this way. If you use it, I'll never speak to you again."

"But all this stuff . . . cameras, lightbulbs, fingerprints. I've got to get something out of it. Give me something."

She paused again.

"Okay. Here's a fact you can use. We know how the killer got the body into the cart."

"How?"

"A forklift. A small one. We found it in the back of the basement. It had traces of blood on it. We've confiscated it."

"Any prints?"

"No. So far, no prints. Not anywhere."

"So what's that mean?"

"It means the murderer didn't have to be a Schwarzenegger. Now you see why it could have been a *she*."

He decided it was time to throw a few blind darts.

"And have you talked to Mrs. Ratnoff?" he asked.

"Of course." She gave that half smile again. "And also Peregrin Whibbleby's husband."

"And . . ."

"For obvious reasons, spouses of fornicating couples are the first line of suspects. But there's not much there, as far as we can determine."

Well, he thought, this hasn't been a total loss. He had helped her with the tape and gotten a few tidbits in return. But the whole business, the negotiation and the horse trading, grated. He knew it was often essential to swap information with the authorities, but he didn't like doing it in a murder investigation. It made him feel complicit with the police. That's why he hadn't told her about his confrontation with Engleheart.

He checked a clock on the wall and rose to leave.

"I better go," he said.

"Okay. You know the way out." She rose and shook his hand. "By the way . . . in case you were wondering . . ."

"Yes?"

"That woman you used to date . . . Elaine. She was helpful in substantiating your movements that night. She seemed concerned that you were in trouble. We told her you weren't."

She smiled as she said it, and he didn't know what to say.

20

The image of Ratnoff's body on a forklift was sufficiently compelling to get Jude more than a column of space. But he spent much of his time fending off lies and rumors from the blogosphere, including Animal's account of the sex ring in the basement. As O'Donnell often noted, "Today ninety percent of the job is playing Whac-a-Mole."

At one point, the incoming barrage got so tumultuous that Fred Bradshaw helped out by answering Jude's phone. Afterward, Jude felt honor-bound to invite him out for a drink.

The usual crowd was at Slough's: O'Donnell nursing his Guinness; Van Wessel up from the courts (did he ever leave?); Alston Wickham Howard, in a foul mood because none of his advance-obit subjects were ailing; Charlie Stengler, exhausted from dodging an assignment for four hours; and half a dozen others.

Sitting in the center, like royalty, was a surprise: Jimmy Pomegranate, the political reporter in Washington. A man of Falstaffian appetites and the self-regard of Orson Welles, whom he in some ways resembled, Pomegranate was a favorite. His expense account was bottomless, and he didn't stint on sharing the bounty of food and drink with friends, who numbered in the thousands and were sprinkled liberally around the globe.

"My boy, c'mere," he boomed out to Jude. He pulled up a seat next to him and patted Jude on the top of his head. "Wet your whistle while I tell a joke." The group had been engaged in their favorite pastime: editor bashing.

"So there's an editor and a reporter," began Pomegranate, slowing his delivery to ensure the spotlight. "And they're trapped in the Sahara. Two weeks they've been staggering along and now they're dying of thirst under the desert sun, crawling along" — here Pomegranate rotated his arms to mimic crawling — "sweat pouring down, their skin cracked and sunburned all to hell. They're just about to expire. With their last ounce of strength, they make it to the crest of a sand dune and look over" — he raised his head — "and what do they see? A beautiful oasis, crystal clear water and palm trees wafting in the soft breezes. They run down to it. The reporter dives in" — he put his hands together in a dive — "and he's happy as the proverbial clam. He's swallowing great gobs of water and splashing around and having a grand old time. Then he looks back, and what's he see? The editor's just standing there on the shore, and what's he doing? He's got his pecker out and he's *pissing* right into the goddamned water. The reporter yells out, 'Hey, what the hell you doin'?' And the editor looks up" — and here Pomegranate began to chuckle and his belly began to shake — "and he shouts back, *'I'm making it better!'*"

Guffaws all around. Van Wessel, who had made the mistake of sipping his vodka at the punch line, spewed it out in a coughing fit. Pomegranate leaned over to slap him on the back and almost knocked him off his chair.

"Another round?" The question was rhetorical. A wide-eyed young woman, a business reporter, stood up and was showered with bills as everyone tried to pay for everyone else. The conversation turned, as it invariably did whenever the Hatfield-McCoy motif of editors and reporters arose, to the legendary Virgil Bogart. They started in on stories of the correspondent's famous ripostes to unreasonable demands telexed from the foreign desk.

"One time," recalled O'Donnell, "Bogart was in Karachi. Spritzenzangler, the new night foreign editor, just took over. Brezhnev dies. So a round-robin message goes out to correspondents around the world: 'Brezhnev dead. File man-in-street reaction soonest. Spritzenzangler.' A bellboy knocks on Bogart's door, wakes him up in the middle of the night, hands him the message. He files back: 'Are no men in street in Karachi at 3:00 a.m.' "

A chorus of laughter.

"But you've forgotten the punch line," wheezed Pomegranate. "He ended it with a P.S. It said: 'What's a Spritzenzangler?' "

More hilarity.

Another story — this one about the time the foreign desk demanded Bogart file a high insert to cover a minor angle. Spelling out punctuation marks, he sent back a telex beginning "Insert high up colon . . ." and waited half an hour before sending the remainder. More laughter. The business reporter returned with a tray full of drinks and all the money intact.

"Woody says someone's opened up a tab," she said.

"Ah, Jimmy. God bless you," said O'Donnell. They drank to Pomegranate's health. He responded with a toast to them all, delivered in an indecipherable Scottish brogue — it was Burns, he said — and they demanded a translation. He obliged:

Here's to us.
Who's like us?
Damned few.
And they're all dead.

The words struck a chord in Jude. He had heard most of their stories before, all the tales about reporters outsmarting editors — in fact, he was pretty sure most of the people here had heard most of them before. It was like the old saw about the convicts who knew one another's jokes so perfectly, they told them by numbers. Curious, he mused, how many of these stories revolved around telexes; these days, foreign correspondents used satellite phones.

He looked over at O'Donnell and remembered that time about a month ago when his friend had gotten so drunk he could barely walk. Moments before staggering to a cab, he had put an arm around Jude, leaned into him with his breath reeking of scotch and stomach acid, and advised him to get out of newspapering. "The good times are gone," he had muttered, slurring his words so much that Jude caught them only the third time around. "Now it's a mug's game."

O'Donnell seemed to read Jude's disquiet. "What's the matter, Lennie. You don't want to hear about the rabbits anymore?"

"No. I'm just thinking, that's all."

"The boy's got himself a hot story," said Pomegranate. "Leave him alone." He turned toward Jude. "You know wherever I go, that's all people want to talk about. I was in Beirut day before yesterday and Walid Jumblatt, of all people, asked me who I thought the murderer was."

O'Donnell took a healthy gulp of whiskey. "So, what's cooking today?"

Jude told them about the forklift and the police theory that the killer had used the freight elevator.

"So that explains it," said O'Donnell.

"What?" asked Jude.

"Some days back, our security guy — what's his name? Eagleton, Eaglehard, something like that —"

"Engleheart," said Jude.

"Whatever. Somebody saw him monkeying with the rear elevator. He was down on his knees, examining it or doing something to it. He could have been cleaning it."

"Who saw him?"

"Dunno. The janitor or somebody. Word gets around."

"You should tell the police about that," said Van Wessel.

"Who, me?" O'Donnell seemed genuinely taken aback by the idea. "Not me. If I passed along every little tip about who killed Ratnoff, I'd do nothing else."

"Welcome to the club," said Van Wessel.

"I still can't believe the bastard is dead," said Alston Wickham Howard. "Like my granddaddy used to say: 'Time wounds all heels.' "

Van Wessel turned to Jude. "You know, you should talk to Higgle" — he was referring to Hank Higgle, the police reporter downtown. Jude had called him several days ago but he hadn't called back. "Something's up with him. He's been acting strange ever since the murder. Scared to death. Like he's convinced he's going to be next."

"That's the point," said Pomegranate. "Somebody *is* going to be next. In crimes of passion, nine times out of ten, the police nab someone within forty-eight hours. The better part of a week has passed and they haven't arrested anyone. So face it, what we're dealing with here is not some pissed-off hysterical wife or cuckolded husband. What we're dealing with is a motivated, methodical killer. A killer with some kind of agenda."

They were silent for a moment as Pomegranate's words sunk in.

"I agree," said O'Donnell. "The killer was out to prove something. Why else use a spike, unless you're trying to make some kind of statement?"

"Oh, c'mon," said Alston. "A lot of people get pissed off at the paper, a lot of people think it's been going downhill. Us, for example. But you can't tell me that's reason enough to kill one of the editors."

"I'm not sure you really need a reason to kill an editor," put in Stengler. They laughed.

"Maybe somebody on the business side did it," said the business reporter. They looked at her; it was the first time she had spoken all evening. "Those guys in advertising are rough. They play by a different set of rules."

"What I'd like to know," said Van Wessel, "is what was Ratnoff doing in the basement to begin with. What's down there anyhow?"

"All kinds of stuff," replied Pomegranate. "The morgue. The publishers' archives. Memos, personnel records."

"Even advance obits," added Alston. "I go down there to check them out. The page proofs are all made up and just waiting for the Angel of Death."

"Maybe that's what Ratnoff was doing," said Pomegranate, "checking out his advance obit."

"And that's when the killer struck."

"Maybe the killer wrote the obit. He wanted to rush it into the paper."

They laughed.

Gradually, the topic shifted away from Ratnoff and back to Virgil Bogart and how he often succeeded in slipping little jokes past the copy desk so that they exploded like land mines when the paper hit the newsstand.

"Remember that one," said Pomegranate, "when he wrote about the dentist and described his 'plaque-covered' office?"

"Or that politician," said O'Donnell, "who was heir to the Ex-Lax fortune? He called him a 'regular Republican.' "

They all laughed and sent off for another round. Jude demurred.

Deftly, Pomegranate turned the conversation to his career, which made him wax sentimental. "I've been to one hundred and eighty-two countries and interviewed one hundred and two heads of state," he said.

"King Abdullah calls me by my first name. I can call up Bob Bennett day or night. I can get a table at Rao's and courtside seats at the Knicks — I'm talking about back when people went to the Knicks."

"Big deal," said O'Donnell. "What's it all mean?"

"It means a lot," insisted Pomegranate.

"Bullshit," countered O'Donnell. "It's dross. The editors praise you to the skies. You get scoops. You work like a dog. I used to think that all added up. It was like putting money in the bank — all those canceled holidays, those late nights, those planes you jump on to fly to the latest disaster, those kids' birthdays you miss. Then the editors who praised you move on. New ones come up. They don't know what you've done. You turn around one day and the slate's clean. The bank account's vanished. You get older. People don't return your calls so much. When you get right down to it, nobody remembers any of the good stuff — nobody but you yourself."

He fixed Jude with an intense stare. "Bogart — the greatest reporter who ever lived, and what's left? A couple of anecdotes told over a couple of beers by a couple of old farts. Don't give your heart to a newspaper, kiddo. It's unrequited love."

Jude nodded to show he understood. He was feeling tired, so he excused himself. Pomegranate slapped him on the back and he made for the door. By the time he got there, the drinks had arrived and he heard Pomegranate booming out the toast once again:

Here's to us.
Who's like us?
Damned few.
And they're all dead.

Fred Bradshaw followed him outside and walked with him toward Broadway.

"That was a little depressing, wasn't it?" said Jude.

"Easy for you to say," Fred replied. "You've got a big story. You're riding high. You don't know what depressing is. Know what I heard today? They're thinking of sending me to open a bureau on Staten Island."

21

Edith Sawyer opened her eyes in panic and sat bolt upright. For a moment, she was no longer the intrepid globe-trotting reporter, but the pint-size girl growing up in Coney Island. Then she looked around at the green walls and the couch she was lying on and realized where she was: in the "relaxation room" of the women's toilet on the fifth floor. She had come here to hide and had fallen asleep.

Her Minnie Mouse watch had twisted around on her thin wrist; she straightened it and checked the time: 3:30 a.m. Perfect. The last editors had gone home half an hour ago. Now there'd be only the cleaning crew and perhaps an occasional security guard. She knew this from having pulled any number of all-nighters on big stories — takeouts on the Middle East or the intractable situation in Northern Ireland.

But of all the hellholes and trouble spots

she'd seen, nothing scared her as much as the prospect of this night at the *Globe* and what she had to do here. And nothing was as likely to mean so much, preserving her meteoric career or bringing it to an ignoble end. There were lots of people around who'd like to see the latter, she knew. She had her fans and admirers, but not among the people who worked with her day in and day out. They either feared her or hated her.

It had always been that way. You couldn't get to the top of the heap without stepping on a lot of bodies. She was born in the shadow of the amusement park, the only daughter to the manager of a rickety ride called the Human Catapult. He was a burly, jovial man with a predilection for guzzling his wages that brought out his ugly side. This soon outbalanced the free rides he gave on the contraption, which sent her, at age four, spinning through space into a net forty feet away. She had four brothers, all younger, and she had to fight their battles, beginning when taunting schoolmates made catapults out of ice-cream sticks and sent wads of chewed gum into their hair.

In junior high school, Edith took a typesetting class. Everything about it thrilled her — picking through the type tray, setting the letters in columns, pulling proofs, the smell of fresh ink. She got hooked on the comic strip *Brenda Starr — Reporter.* So it wasn't surprising that she went out for the Coney Island High School paper, *The Boardwalk,* or that she rose to top editor, or that she expanded its coverage beyond the school fence to include, among other things, the annual black riots along Mermaid Avenue. The coverage displayed a preoccupation with violence that would later stand her in good stead. At Brooklyn College, she filled in five weeks for the *Globe*'s college stringer, who came down with mononucleosis; when he returned, the job was no longer his (there were those, even back then, who whispered that she had somehow arranged for him to be infected).

Hired by the *Globe* as a copy girl, she moved up quickly. There was an episode, never fully explained, in which she allegedly ratted out a subeditor who, filling in on a Saturday for the metro editor, had rifled through his desk. She was nothing if not loyal — to which the answer, cynics said, was she was nothing. But her superiors adored her because she always brought back the goods — action-packed dispatches from disaster scenes, insider scoops from Washington, and interviews with aloof Gulf monarchs. Because the interviews were sometimes conducted in dubious places, like secluded tents in the desert, and lasted quite a while, there were those who spread rumors that she was putting out more than hard work.

At one point, she was engaged to a competitor from a Chicago paper. One evening in Morocco, the two found themselves among seven foreign correspondents given a group interview by the king; it went on for some time, the hour grew late, they were hungry, and so they all agreed to hold off until the next day and file at leisure. Edith excused herself from dinner, saying she had a headache. At the hotel breakfast table, the others found messages from their respective papers demanding that they match her exclusive interview. Her engagement was broken off.

Two years ago, Edith had hit a rough patch. She had never been made an editor — she was too contentious for that — and her legs were not only less shapely than they used to be, they also were tired. It wasn't so easy to rush off to airports and doorstop hotel lobbies. Her skin was turning pasty and her ponytail was losing its spring. She felt young reporters nipping at her heels, including young women who had graduated from Ivy League colleges and, wrapped in a cocoon of privilege, were every bit as tough as she once was. She began making mistakes and taking shortcuts and then doing things that she knew were wrong. But what the hell — the pressure to perform was unrelenting and she was a performer par excellence, the Ethel Merman of the newspaper business.

Edith briefly primped before the mirror, a vestigial reflex. Then she opened the door to the newsroom. It was unearthly quiet, the lights were dimmed, and no one was around, all of which transformed it into a place familiar and yet strange. She considered taking off her shoes and carrying them to soften her footfalls, then discarded the idea. She repeated a mantra she had often used in tight spots: You're not suspicious unless you look suspicious; you're not nervous unless you look nervous.

She went to her cubicle, turned on her computer, pulled up a half-written story onto the screen, opened a notebook, and spread some papers around, creating a stage set that could support her explanation, should anyone come by, that she was simply working late. She set out for the center of the newsroom — not far from the conference room — where the top editors had their offices, and stopped by the desk of Ellen Butterby, Ratnoff's administrative assistant.

After a quick look around to ensure that no one was in sight, she put on a pair of gloves, opened Ms. Butterby's top drawer (her observations had told her it would be unlocked), and extracted a simple metal key stamped DUPLICATION PROHIBITED. Then she marched the ten yards to Ratnoff's office, opened the door quickly, and switched on the light.

The ten-by-twelve-foot chamber was denuded. Alive, Ratnoff had been a cleanliness addict, regarding bits of paper as infiltrators in his orderly kingdom. But now that he was dead, the police had taken everything — every scrap of writing, every message, every envelope. Even his incoming mail had been confiscated, which she had intended to grab herself. There were only five things left in his office: a metal shelf filled with reference books, a lamp, a standing photo of his wife and children, a chair, and a computer.

The computer! That was one thing the police hadn't yet been able to get their hands on, because the paper was in court fighting a subpoena for it. Thank God, she thought, for the First Amendment.

She sat in his chair and flipped the on

switch. She guided the cursor through the various software-program gateways until she came to the one obstacle, the eight-letter word intended to stop intruders: PASS-WORD. And here, Edith's slippery character came into play; she had prepared for just such a moment a year ago when she had diverted the attention of a technician in systems support long enough to lift a printed list of access codes of senior editors.

Holding her breath, she typed in Ratnoff's: S-T-A-L-L-I-O-N.

Instantly, the computer complied, like an Arabian horse responding to a hint of knee pressure.

Edith quickly scrolled through the files. By mistake, she opened a file that contained stories that had not yet seen print, including one slugged *"police."* It looked intriguing, and ordinarily Edith would have read it eagerly, but now she had more important things to do. She found Ratnoff's e-mail and looked at the incoming messages. She moved the cursor down.

There it was, fifth from the top! She recognized it immediately by the return address: the managing editor of the *St. Louis Inquirer.* She opened it and started to read. It began:

Dear Teddy,
Something has arisen involving one of your reporters that, sadly, I feel compelled to bring to your attention. . . .

She couldn't go on. She didn't want to see the message laid out in black and white, and there was no need to, she thought, since she could eliminate it with a few quick strokes of the keyboard. And that's what she did, hitting DELETE. ARE YOU SURE? popped up on the screen. She hit YES.

And the screen went blank. For the first time in ten days, since she had received that horrible phone call from St. Louis, from that man she didn't even know, who used that bullying tone, she felt a modicum of relief.

She knew exactly when Ratnoff had received the e-mail — six days ago. That was when he had left her that voice mail asking her — telling her, really — to see him immediately. His tone had been soft and even a touch gentle. That was the tip-off. He had been moving in for the kill.

In any case, none of it mattered now.

She flicked off the computer, turned out the light, and closed the door. She turned the knob to ensure it was locked. Then she returned to Ms. Butterby's desk and slipped the key back into the top drawer and removed her gloves.

Nothing could have been easier.

But on the way back to her cubicle, she heard a noise, a scurrying, and almost jumped out of her skin. It was a mouse, jumping out of a wastebasket and running across her path. She laughed to herself. Who does that mouse think it is? I've covered the Middle East. I've stared down ruthless tyrants. I've been to the Paris fashion shows.

It takes more than a little mouse to frighten me.

22

On the way to the *Globe,* Bollingsworth had to admit she didn't like the way things were going. It was the fifth morning after the murder and there was not a glimmer of a break in the case. She felt her superiors were beginning to second-guess her. Last night, the chief of detectives had questioned her about the progress — or lack of it — responding only with grunts as she outlined the steps she had taken. He then asked her if she wanted "more men." Maybe it was her imagination, but something about the way he had emphasized *men* seemed to be sending a message.

Detective work was like feeling your way through a maze blindfolded. You came to a choice, went right or left, and sooner or later you came to something interesting or to a dead end, in which case you retraced your steps and took the other turn. But this time, there were dozens of choice points — and dozens of dead ends.

The fact that Ratnoff and Whibbleby had been having an affair cast immediate suspicion over their spouses, but that line of investigation hadn't panned out. Alfred, Whibbleby's husband, could account for all but an hour and ten minutes of the night of the murder. During that time, he had gone out for a video (two, actually — her partner had checked: Leni Riefenstahl's *Olympia* and a porn flick, *Boys Gone Wild*). That was hardly enough time to kill Ratnoff and get back. In any case, it would have been virtually impossible for him to plant the body at that hour, around 10:30, because the newsroom would have been occupied. After he returned home, doormen on duty all night didn't see him leave again.

Ratnoff's wife, a bitter widow who seemed to be grieving the decline in income more than the loss of her husband, had been at an upstate resort with their children and had a trail of witnesses and signed credit card receipts to prove it.

So it was reasonable to concentrate the investigation inside the paper, and it was here that Bollingsworth encountered the ever-expanding maze. Ratnoff had so many enemies, he was lucky to have lived as long as he did.

The confiscated forklift had yielded no secrets. It had no prints and, as she discovered when she took it into a garage and sat before the controls, no special training was required to run it. At first, the editor's spike looked promising. But she quickly learned that there were scores of them scattered around the newsroom and they were used interchangeably. No one even knew which one had ended up in Ratnoff's chest. The murder note wasn't much of a clue. The printing of "Nice. Who?" — all in block letters — wasn't distinctive; it could have been done by almost anyone. And the purple flow pen that was used was hardly unique. A detective had gone to six West Side stationery stores searching for the source of the pen before learning that Ratnoff had kept a box in an unlocked supply cabinet that could have been raided by any passerby. And to top it all off, the damn murder weapon was still missing!

Too many prints, too many enemies, too many people caught on the lobby tape — everything about the damn newspaper was too much. The place was a jungle teeming with snakes, and all the snakes were poisonous.

One hope for an ally to help guide her through the maze was Jude Hurley. She was cultivating him as much as he was cultivating her, but so far, she could tell, he hadn't been totally forthcoming. He seemed to have qualms about cooperating too closely with authority. In a way, she respected that position — she just wished she wasn't the authority in question.

She told her driver to park outside the *Globe* and wait for her. (It never hurt to let a field of possible suspects know you were working the case hard.) At the elevator bank, she caught a glimpse of Peregrin Whibbleby stepping into a car. Poor woman. She might have achieved a position that would impress some New Yorkers, a gossip maven and style arbiter, but she herself seemed sadly naïve and self-deluding. Even now, she didn't realize that absolutely everyone knew about her and Ratnoff. The blogs had been pumping out reams of scurrilous stuff about it. How was it possible for someone who dealt in character assassination every day not to know when she herself had been stabbed between the shoulder blades?

Bollingsworth went down to the basement. She spotted the lens of the police camera hidden in a pile of debris in a corner. The time had come to remove it, but it had at least revealed one fact of interest — that someone, an odd-looking character, actually worked in the basement morgue. That was the person she had come to interview, and she found him deep inside the complicated arrangement of tall metal filing cabinets. In an open space, at a small wooden desk illuminated by a gooseneck lamp, sat a man no more than four feet tall. He looked up from a book he was reading, unsurprised and surly. He was dressed in an immaculate white shirt, a wide tie, and gray trousers that would have fit a five-year-old. His name was Sammy Slimowitz.

Sammy was of indeterminate age, with features perfectly formed but too small by a third. For years, he had supervised the copy people in the newsroom, ruling over them with an iron fist inside an iron glove. Generations of Ivy Leaguers who had dreamed of a life in newspapering ran aground on his high-pitched, rasping voice and his hatred of the privileged class. He did them in with performance evaluations that highlighted flaws any boss would be a fool to ignore. Over time, his bitterness drove him to the bottle, then to quasi-retirement as a part-time employee.

There was a seat near him and Bollingsworth, unbidden, took it. She introduced herself. His half-lowered red-rimmed eyes gave nothing away. She thought he had been waiting for the police to show up.

"You're a contract employee, I understand."

He nodded.

"What do you do?"

He gestured around him at the filing cabinets. "I keep track of all this."

"And how often do you come here?"

He shrugged his small pointed shoulders. "Couple of times a week."

"Always the same days?"

"No. It varies."

"Your contract says you should be here every Tuesday and Thursday. Do you abide by it or not?" She spoke the question sharply.

"Mostly I do. Yes. I get my work done."

"That was not the question."

"Yes, I'm here Tuesdays and Thursdays."

"And I still do not see what your work is."

"I keep the files in order. Replace them when people use them. Make sure the clippings are in their folders."

"So your work is confined to the morgue itself?"

"Yes."

"And do you ever work outside the morgue area?"

"No." At that, he gave her a cunning grin.

She asked a number of questions about people he might have seen, but he was distinctly unhelpful. On the days following the murder, he said, he had heard any number of people walking around, but most of them stayed out of the morgue. "And I didn't feel it was my place to spy on them," he added.

"And Ratnoff . . . did he come here often?"

"Only if you consider four or five visits a day, five days a week, often."

"How do you know he was here five days if you're here only two?"

He paused. "I hear things."

"And what did he do here?"

"Research, I imagine."

"Research — on what?"

"Ah, that I can't tell you, I'm afraid." His eyes had the malevolent look of someone pleased to be uncooperative. His high, squeaky voice was irksome.

"Can't or won't?"

"It's not part of my job to interrogate people as to their purpose."

"But surely, all that time . . . you noticed what he was interested in."

"Afraid not."

"Do you have a record, any kind of record, written or in a computer, of the files he looked at?"

"Afraid not."

"*Afraid not.* There seem to be a lot of things you're *not* afraid of," she said.

Sammy's demeanor began to change.

She continued: "How about an interrogation room downtown — do you think you'd be afraid of that? Or how about a stint at the Tombs . . . awaiting trial on an obstruction of justice charge?"

She extracted her notebook and wrote something down. Sammy's eyes darted around. She reached into a pocket and pulled out her portable radio and called the driver and told him to drive to the *Globe,* cutting him off before he had a chance to reply that he was already there.

"No need for all that," Sammy said, moving off his chair with an alarming quickness that his small frame made possible. He scampered down an aisle, then returned, stuck his head around a cabinet, and beckoned her to follow him. She did. Halfway down a row, he stopped and gestured with his tiny hand at four large cabinets looming above.

"Ratnoff got files from somewhere in here — that's all I know."

She glanced up. There was drawer after drawer, all of them marked by labels beginning with the name Appleby. They were the archives of the famous publisher.

"Do you have any idea which one?"

"Afraid . . . ah . . . no, I don't."

She opened a drawer. It was crammed with hanging folders holding files. She pulled one out and flipped through it: letters, memos, documents. She returned it and closed the drawer, then stepped back and considered the cabinets. It would take weeks just to read through them, never mind trying to guess the ones that had aroused Ratnoff's interest.

"All right," she said, turning to Slimowitz and looking down at his small face. "You may go. If I need you, I know where to find you."

"I'm here. Tuesdays and Thursdays . . . And about that call you made. Shouldn't you . . . cancel it or something?"

"No need," she said. "I'm leaving."

She turned away and walked back to the vast room that had contained the presses and over to the sawhorse barricades. She looked down into the giant hole. At least, she thought, there is a faster way to home in on the research that so engaged Ratnoff. She had confiscated his computer on the night following his murder and even now her men were combing through his files. They had substituted a decoy in his office, filled with duplicates of the files. They had done this with Hagenbuckle's permission. It hadn't been a hard decision for him to come by, she mused. What publisher, faced with the choice between upholding the First Amendment or tracking down a killer who had struck at his newspaper, would hesitate longer than a millisecond?

Again a troubling thought occurred to her. If the motive for Ratnoff's killing had been outside the paper — anger over adultery, say — then his killing, horrible as it was, might be the end of it. But if the murder was founded on some twisted motive inside the paper, some psychopathology of thwarted ambition or sick hatred, then who could say what might happen?

Will the killer strike again? she wondered, peering into the seemingly bottomless pit.

23

Peregrin Whibbleby had seen that police-woman coming into the lobby and had scurried aboard the elevator to avoid her. She couldn't bear any more questions. She had just spent a trying hour with Jude Hurley. Ordinarily, she liked him . . . well, at least respected him. But this morning over coffee and bagels, he had asked the same questions that policewoman had: What had Teddy been working on lately? What had he told her? Had he seemed upset or worried?

How could she explain that their relationship wasn't concerned with such matters, that it was more intimate? How could she tell them *that* without getting into the whole sex business? She had, in fact, recently noticed that Teddy *had* appeared busy and excited. It was impossible *not* to, the way he kept chortling to himself and disappearing for hours on end in the basement. She had just thought she was getting to know the real man.

Dinah Outsalot was in the same elevator car and they said hi to each other. Peregrin didn't take to her, never had. She was so big and *unwieldy,* wearing those boots and striding around like a bronco rider and cooking those meals on TV. "Extending her brand," she had called it. She had certainly parlayed her job into face time with the public. What was she doing here this early? . . . Of course, it was her cooking day. She was heading up to the eighth floor to test-run recipes in the *Globe's* own kitchen. Ads for her show, depicting her gamely tossing an omelette into the air — with the tagline AT HOME ON THE RANGE — ran incessantly in the paper. The ad for Peregrin's gossip column, showing her holding up a bunch of grapes — I HEARD IT ON THE GRAPEVINE — had stopped running months ago.

Peregrin stepped into her glassed-in office, which was decorated with girlie artifacts that contradicted the slash-and-burn ethos of her column. On a chair sat a quaint pillow embroidered with the saying, "If friends were flowers, I'd pick you." A row of dolls stood on the windowsill, but it was so grimy, they appeared incongruously out of place — like a police lineup of It's a Small World.

At first, she didn't notice the note in the center of her desk, in front of the computer. It was lying inside a plain brown envelope, the kind used for house mail. These days, with e-mail, such envelopes were an endangered species, headed the way of the pneumatic tubes that still honeycombed the innards of the building and once carried messages and copy with bullet speed.

When she opened the brown envelope, she almost fainted. "Want to retrieve Ratnoff's diary?" asked a firm hand in block letters. A parenthetical addition followed: "(You really should, you know.)" It instructed her where to go and when and warned her not to notify anyone, including the police. The envelope also contained a hand-drawn map of how to reach the delivery room — that part of the building that had been closed off after the presses moved out. She was directed to bring the letter with her — an instruction that, had she been more focused, she might have taken as ominous.

Keeping a diary was just the kind of thing Teddy would do. Who knew what might be in there? Perhaps even — and she recoiled at the thought — descriptions of the little things she used to do to arouse him. If word of *that* got out . . . well, she wouldn't be able to set foot in the building again. No two ways about it — she had to fetch that diary. And she couldn't run the risk of telling anyone that she was going to get it.

Peregrin looked at a clock set inside a good-luck Chinese cat. Forty-five minutes until noon — the time fixed for the rendezvous. And she had to write her column by this afternoon. She decided to push ahead, the way her father had taught her. Block out the unpleasantness. She would write the damned column. She tried to concentrate and looked through her notes. The best item was about Lester Moloch. According to a blogger at dirtypervert.com, he had been spotted feeling up a twenty-three-year-old exotic dancer at a nightclub in the Meatpacking District. In the old days, the *Globe* had refused to run anonymously sourced material, but she had more latitude for her Web-based column, and besides, this was about one of Hagenbuckle's enemies. She changed "feeling up" to "canoodling," added some atmospherics about the club, which she could well imagine, and polished off the item. The second item was about a Hollywood starlet who held a fund-raiser to fight earlobe distortion in Africa (she seemed to recall that was somebody or other's crusade at the paper). She found a third one. Before she knew it, noon was upon her.

She pulled out a pocket mirror, dabbed some Trish McEvoy blush on her cheeks, fluffed up her curls, and strode briskly past her secretary's desk, which was unoccupied. That was fortunate. Her secretary was her confidante — the only person at the paper, she believed, who knew about her and Teddy — and she didn't want to say where she was going.

She took the elevator to the ground floor and, as instructed, walked through the back of the lobby toward the rear of the building. There she tugged open a thick metal door. It closed behind her with a discernible *click,* and when she tried the knob, she found it was locked from the outside, a discovery that gave her the first inkling she might be doing something foolish.

The space where she found herself was low-ceilinged and dimly lighted, like an underground parking garage. The floor was paved with foot-wide metal tiles. The thick concrete columns had numbers stenciled on them. On one side, the floor gave way to loading bays, where the trucks used to back in to take on newspapers. The huge outside doors were shuttered and sealed with padlocks. Around a corner, the space was darker — and it was here that she was directed to go. She unfolded the map and looked at it. No question, an arrow in black pointed the way. Reluctantly, she turned a corner and came to a small windowless room. Inside, it was totally dark. The map ended here. She put it in her pocket, uncertain of what to do. She knew she was to step inside, but a thin voice of caution made her hesitate.

"Don't move!" a voice suddenly commanded — a real voice, outside her head. She didn't. For the first time, she was afraid. She felt a presence behind her, hands grabbing her arms.

"But wait . . . ," she protested. "Get your hands off me. You said you were going to show me Teddy's diary."

"So you believe everything you see in print?" said the voice.

"You mean there is no diary —" Her words were cut short by a hood placed over her head. She felt a hand on her shoulder, was pushed down to sit on a stool — made of rough wood, from the feel of it. There was the click of a light switch going on, then footfalls and some muffled sounds. The unknown hands pulled her wrists behind her, cuffed them with a plastic tie. She struggled but could only bounce pathetically up and down on the stool.

Another switch was flipped, this time on some kind of a machine — she had, despite her fear, noticed something unwieldy off to one side during that moment before the hood was placed over her head. She heard a whirring sound, then a clanking.

The hands felt her pockets, extracted the map.

"You forgot the envelope," said the voice.

"You didn't . . . say to bring the envelope," she managed to squeak. "Just the note." That she was able to talk at all emboldened her. "Why are you doing this?" she demanded. "I don't even know who you are."

"So you're curious — are you?"

The hood was lifted from behind. At first, she couldn't see a thing, but her eyes rapidly adjusted. The room she was in was small and grubby.

The owner of the voice stepped around and stood in front of her with a hand-on-the-hip posture that seemed defiant. Peregrin squinted to try to make out who it was.

"You!" she gasped.

"Yes. You never expected *me* — did you?"

She couldn't speak at first. She shifted her weight on the stool and realized she could barely move. "But why are you doing this?"

Her abductor stepped back behind her and the voice was right next to her ear, a low whisper. "Because of what you write," it said. "You never think of the consequences of that, Toot Bavardez — do you?"

She didn't answer. Besides, she was now feeling practically voiceless, totally helpless. She noted that her abductor was wearing gloves, the cream-colored latex kind that proctologists use. Off to the side was the machine that was making the whirring sound, and she saw a large metal arm turning in an arc through the air.

What the hell was it? She understood finally, just as she felt herself being picked up and turned on her side, the way long, long ago her father used to carry her from the car to the house. She realized she was moving toward the machine — feetfirst. It occurred to her to scream but then she felt the cool glove across her mouth.

24

Jude decided the safest course was to abandon the newsroom for the rest of the morning. He hadn't yet come up with a decent angle on the story and that made him fair game for the metro subeditors handing out assignments. They roamed the aisles like fly fishermen casting from a riverbank. One of them had tried to get him to write about a movie star expelled from detox for throwing a cell phone during an anger-management session. At that moment, Jude's phone rang. He grabbed the receiver, paused, and yelled, "My God! I'll be right over!" The editor stalked off. Jude leaned across to Charlie Stengler's cubicle.

"Thanks, man," he said. "Perfect timing."

"No problem," replied Stengler. "You'd do the same for me. In fact, you have."

Jude took the shuttle and the number 6 train to the Brooklyn Bridge stop and entered the redbrick fortress of police headquarters, otherwise known as "the Puzzle Palace." He walked through the metal detector, flashing his yellow Day-Glo press pass, and — maybe for that reason — was frisked. Finally, he was allowed in. He was looking for Hank Higgle.

He was exasperated. The last week had been hell: dozens of questions from the copy desk, rumors flying around like gnats on a summer evening, the competition hyping the story, and, through it all, Bernie Grabble pulling him aside half a dozen times a day to get a personal briefing. The metro editor seemed to suggest that it was Jude's fault that the murderer was still at large.

Entering the pressroom at the cop shop, a labyrinth of cubicles under neon-tube lighting, he was struck by the quiet and sterility. Half a dozen young men and women sat in front of computers or talked quietly on the phone, a far cry from the chaos and anarchy that O'Donnell described so nostalgically.

Higgle's desk was in a corner and he sat at it, back to the door, his head resting in his cupped hands, almost like a reflection of the screen saver facing him, a representation of Munch's *The Scream*.

Not a good sign, thought Jude.

"Hey, Hank."

Higgle jumped an inch or two in his seat

and turned quickly, his hands gripping the armrests.

"Hurley," he observed. His eyes narrowed. "Why on earth are you here? Is there a break in the case? How come I wasn't called?"

"Calm down. I came to see you."

"Me?" He hardly sounded reassured. "Why me?"

Higgle was a slight man in his early thirties, fussy in dress and a bit fey in manner, a graduate of Vassar. Jude had discounted rumors that he was gay and had once silenced O'Donnell on the subject by observing, "If he was gay, why would he have picked a college with so many women?" Still, he was a far cry from the legendary figures of the old police shack. With his immaculate fingernails and razor haircut, it was hard to picture him as part of the lineage that one hundred years ago had included Lincoln Steffens and Jacob Riis, cub reporters and rivals, whose one-upmanship led to a phony crime wave that enraged Police Commissioner Teddy Roosevelt.

"Let's get a cup of coffee," said Jude.

They went to a diner on Broadway. Higgle was quiet on the walk over. He was one of those guys who tried to figure every angle

and ended up making things more complicated than they were. He was a short man
and he had a hair-trigger temper; he had
once covered an antiwar demonstration in
Times Square, and among the seven thousand protesters, he was the only one arrested — for mouthing off to a mounted
policeman.

When they were seated facing each other
in a booth, blowing on their coffee, Higgle
opened the conversation.

"Your story on cooping, I admit, was one
fine piece of journalism, even brilliant in
some ways. I could have wished to have
written it myself. But, I suppose you're
aware, it made our life down here one holy
hell."

"I appreciate that."

"You know what they say about the police . . ."

"What?"

"They're like the French aristocrats of the
ancien régime on the eve of the Revolution."

"How so?"

"They never learn and they never forget."

"Funny, I never heard that."

"No?"

"No."

They were silent again for a moment, then
Higgle said abruptly, "Tell me . . . between

us . . . Do you have any conceivable idea of who might have done it?"

It was a question Jude had been hearing a lot these days and he didn't have an answer, other than to shrug and shake his head. He was being honest. From what he could tell from his talks with Bollingsworth, the police still had no solid leads.

"You have any thoughts?" he replied.

Higgle looked away, a little too quickly, Jude noted.

"I might well have," Higgle said in a low voice.

"Well, this is the time to share them," said Jude.

Higgle frowned, seemed about to say something, and then turned silent. Jude could almost hear him thinking. He couldn't hear *what* he was thinking, but he could tell, from Higgle's expression and the fact that he was toying with his spoon, holding the handle between his thumb and forefinger and dangling it, that he was being ostentatiously coy — and that meant he would soon reveal what was on his mind.

"Share them with you, you undoubtedly mean?" asked Higgle.

"That's right."

"This calls for a certain amount of trust."

"Yes, perhaps."

"An arresting thought. But why? I can trust you . . . because you've been assigned to the story and so presumably you're not the murderer? That grants our editors a degree of foresight I'm not convinced they possess. Or I can trust you because you wouldn't just plop what I'm about to say into the paper without my prior agreement? Or because you're one of those reporters who would go to jail rather than reveal your sources?"

"You can trust me because you can trust me."

"I see. And I presume this is why you came down to see me — to hear what I had to say?"

"Yes."

"On a hunch, or am I to believe that someone told you something?"

"Someone told me."

"Who?"

"Van Wessel. He said you were acting scared."

Higgle took this in without comment. He seemed ready to keep shuffling the conversational deck, so Jude upped the ante — he looked at his watch with the hint of a frown.

"You have to go?" asked Higgle.

"Not yet. But soon. I'm on deadline."

Higgle glanced around the diner. There

was an old man with a grizzled chin at the counter, twenty feet away, but no one else in sight other than the waitress. Even a paranoid would feel safe here, Jude thought. Higgle lowered his voice, so much so that Jude had to lean forward to hear.

"Okay. Here it is. Perhaps it's not relevant, but I believe it is." He looked Jude square in the eyes. "For months now, I've been on a project . . . very secret. It began when I started talking to a young cop I know . . . smart guy, Princeton graduate — if you can believe it. We talked. We became friends. We began hanging out together. . . . We even went to a film at the Angelika. But that's neither here nor there. Anyway, at one point I noticed that he appeared preoccupied. He'd fall silent for long periods. I asked him about it . . . about what was troubling him. And eventually this story came tumbling out. He was being pressured to take bribes. His partner was involved. Turns out a lot of cops are. Some of it is petty stuff — fifty bucks to overlook a nightclub infraction, things like that. But some of it is big . . . drug violations and weapons possession. The Knapp Commission all over again.

"Anyway, long story short, I went to the desk. One or two other reporters had heard similar stories. So we put a team together

— me, Hancock, Blumenfield, Bryson, a few clerks. We all contributed a piece of the puzzle. It ended up thirty thousand words. It wasn't ready for publication, but it was getting there. And then word about it got out somehow. I began hearing things down here, funny looks from the information officer . . . a reporter from the *Maul* sidled up once and said, 'I hear you got a big one.' Things like that."

He paused. Jude interrupted.

"And so? What happened? Was the piece killed?"

"No, not that. It was so hot, it was going to get special editing —"

"And?"

"And so it went to Ratnoff. He got it a couple of days before he was killed."

"And you think that's why he was killed?" Jude couldn't keep the incredulity out of his voice. "To stop him from editing the piece?"

"It's a distinct possibility. Some of these people — I deal with them. I know them — they're crazy. Rogue cops . . . guys out on the edge. They're capable of anything."

"That may be. But how would killing Ratnoff stop the story? It's already in the system. It's not going to disappear."

Higgle seemed a little embarrassed, like a man told by a doctor that his illness isn't worth worrying about. "Look, *they* don't know that. They don't know how we work. And in point of fact, Ratnoff *was* crucial to the story. He was the one whipping it into shape. Each of us just knew our own little piece of the puzzle. He was the only one who knew the whole thing. I don't even know if it's going to appear now."

"Okay, I grant you — he was important to the project. But that doesn't strike me as a sufficient motive for murder. And anyway, how would these 'rogue cops' know anything about Ratnoff?"

"Simple. They've got a mole."

At that point, for the sake of argument, if someone had questioned Jude, he would have been forced to admit that Higgle's statement did cause a small blip on his reporter's radar, that a certain name did indeed worm itself into his thoughts. And that particular name made Higgle's theory less outlandish than it might otherwise have appeared.

"Maybe Ratnoff was just their first victim," Higgle said. "That's what's got me, you know . . . spooked."

Jude nodded, still deep in thought.

"And there's something else," Higgle added, his voice dropping even lower, so that Jude had to bend down with his chin only six inches above the tabletop. "Alston Wickham Howard — he called me. He asked me for some . . . you know . . . personal biographical information."

"I don't get it."

"For my . . . ah . . . obituary. In case anything happens. So even he's heard I'm in danger."

"Not at all. He heard it the same place I did. From Van Wessel. It doesn't mean a damn thing."

"I don't like it. I keep checking Wikipedia to see if I'm dead."

The conversation ended abruptly when Jude's cell phone rang.

He dug into his pocket, retrieved it, and flipped it open. Edith Sawyer was on the other end, speaking with that sense of urgency that crept into her voice when she felt she had a truly exciting story.

"Jude," she said. "You better get back here. Something's up."

"What is it?"

"Nobody knows exactly, but a number of people are getting hysterical. Peregrin Whibbleby seems to be missing."

25

Elisha Hagenbuckle and Lester Moloch usually went to great lengths to avoid each other, but this morning they found themselves seated at the same table. Each gave the other a cursory nod and then looked up in the opposite direction, as if something of interest were about to happen on the molding of a distant wall.

They were attending the annual conference of NOPE at the Hilton. The drab venue was a falling off from headier days, when the kingpins of the industry had convened in the chandeliered ballroom of the Pierre, but it was appropriate for an industry in crisis. Talk about budget cuts and circulation decline in the NDM (newspaper-designated market) ruled the day.

The two publishers were as unalike as chalk and cheese — Hagenbuckle, tall and dry, was the chalk; Moloch, short and piquant, the cheese. The one feature they shared was fortitude for a longstanding antipathy, and each seemed to reserve most of it for the other. Hagenbuckle had despised Moloch ever since the scrappy New Zealander, using his media properties in the U.K. as a bridgehead, invaded New York by buying the *Graphic* and turning it into a sensationalist rag.

Single-handedly, Moloch had brought low some of the best papers in Europe. His penchant for vulgarity and self-dramatization knew few bounds. It was reliably reported by at least three witnesses that while using the heliport on the roof of his six-story London headquarters, he had stood on the building's parapet and — in a feat worthy of a degenerate eighteenth-century monarch — urinated on passersby far below.

For his part, Moloch regarded Hagenbuckle as the epitome of the dyed-in-the-wool old-fashioned aristocratic publisher. He recoiled at the memory of his first and only luncheon in the *Globe*'s executive dining room. Hagenbuckle, seated before an arc of three-foot-tall yellowing elephant tusks, had acted the role of the big-game hunter and tried to humiliate him by serving elk. After one bite, Moloch went to the bathroom and slipped fifty bucks to a waiter to bring a ham sandwich from the Stage Door Deli.

For two hours this morning, NOPE presented PowerPoint presentations to strike fear into the most stonyhearted of publishers. The lines on the fever charts — ads, circulation, revenue — all angled downward. The only good news was that newspapers were so thin, they were saving money on the cost of newsprint.

Then came the keynote speaker, a fifteen-year-old girl who had just signed a $2.5 million contract with Bloggselvania. Her Web journal (teenage.snivel.com), detailing the day-to-day ups and downs of her life, drew close to 1.5 million hits a day. She approached the microphone, carrying a sheaf of lined white paper with scrawls on it. Less than five feet tall, she wore a clinging T-shirt, a barrette in her hair, and low-rise jeans that showed off a tanned midriff and the stud in her belly button. She had a perky attitude, as if she were used to being the most popular student in the class.

"I'm not gonna tell you my name," she began in a high-pitched voice. "Cuz nobody knows it anyhow. . . . It's not like it's on the site or anything. . . . I'm here to talk about Teenage Snivel and how I go about doing it. Like, first thing, I get up. . . . Sometimes I brush my teeth, sometimes not. . . . Whatever . . . Then I sit down . . . and like, if I had a dream, I bang it out. . . . If it's a good dream, I start with a happy face. If it's a bad dream, I draw a sad face. Then I say what it was. Sometimes there's sex in it, like I'm reaching for my boyfriend's ass in homeroom or something. . . . That's cool. . . . Then I go to breakfast. . . ."

Hagenbuckle quietly slid his chair out and left the hall for the buffet spread in an adjacent room. He felt for that reassuring bulge in his pocket; his pack of Trues was there. Cigarettes were his only consolation these days.

Things had gone from bad to worse at the paper since Ratnoff's funeral. The killer still hadn't been found. And the police had leaked the news that the murder weapon was an ice pick — the very implement he himself was missing. His was a precious family heirloom, which he used to keep in the bar adjacent to the boardroom; he had liked opening the freezer and using the pick to hack out irregular chunks of ice for scotches and gin and tonics. It was a touch of Old World class. Now, much as he tried to dismiss the thought, the fact that his ice pick was gone and the police were searching for an ice pick was too much of a co-incidence to ignore. He was torn by indecision: Should he tell the police and risk their censure for not having come forth sooner? Or just keep quiet and hope that no ice pick ever surfaced? These kinds of moral dilemmas were always so hard to sort out.

He filled his coffee cup and had just reached for two slices of ham and canta-loupe when he felt a shadow behind him and turned. It was Moloch. The Kiwi's lips were smiling but his eyes, rendered large by a pair of glasses, remained stone-cold.

"Depressing, isn't it?" ventured Moloch.

"I wouldn't know. I've never visited that particular Web site."

"I don't mean the speaker. I mean the poll data we heard. Crikey. That sixty percent of young people get their news from Jon Stewart. That when it comes to trust, the average American ranks reporters below used-car salesmen. That advertising dollars are galloping to the Internet. It all spells one thing: Newspapers are going the way of the dodo."

"I wouldn't know," muttered Hagen-buckle. "The dodo comes from your part of the world." He silently congratulated him-self on his retort and lowered himself onto a folding chair at a table where — he noticed a second too late — there was another empty chair. Sure enough, Moloch moved in to occupy it, putting down a cup of coffee and a croissant.

"Anyway," Hagenbuckle continued, "I didn't hear anything I hadn't heard before. Except for that young . . . ah . . . blogger."

"I'm obviously not worried about my own position." Moloch dipped the croissant into his coffee. "As you know, my company, Communicom Inc., diversified years ago. Cyclops Cable, BigByrd Satellite, the Vixen Network, Pudcast, DirectoMedia. Newspapers aren't even a quarter of my revenue source these days, not by a long shot. Still, they remain close to my heart. You know how it is — once you get that old printer's ink in your veins, you can't get it out."

Hagenbuckle grunted. He couldn't help noticing Moloch's necktie: Against a pale yellow background, hundreds of tiny pink typewriters, with wings, were flying in all directions. Moloch followed his eyes, looked down at his tie, and smiled again.

"One of my favorites. Had it made on Savile Row."

Hagenbuckle kept silent. He badly wanted a True. Damned Giuliani. Or was it Bloomberg? Whoever it was who pushed through that draconian antismoking law.

"And speaking of old media, how's the old *Globe* doing these days? Still the flagship of your old fleet, old boy?"

"We're holding our own," Hagenbuckle replied edgily.

"Not the way I hear it. Your stock is taking a nosedive. Your options are underwater. You've closed three foreign bureaus and cut twenty slots in the newsroom. Your board is restless. Who knows? Maybe they'll take a shot at that fancy two-tier arrangement you've worked out so that John Q. Public puts up all the money and your family gets to make all the decisions. Not many stockholders will sit still for that kind of arrangement in this climate."

Hagenbuckle kept his temper in check by imagining Moloch with a stake through his heart.

"And on top of all that," continued Moloch, "you've got a murderer on the loose. Not great for PR. Gives the impression that the lunatics have taken over the asylum, if you know what I mean."

"And your point would be . . ."

"My point is that your flagship is clearly in trouble."

"It's hardly floundering," replied Hagenbuckle. Or had he meant *foundering?* He never could get those two straight. And since he was talking about a ship, shouldn't he have used the feminine pronoun?

"In any case, she's taking on water," continued Moloch. "Maybe it's time to man the lifeboats."

"And what do you mean by that?"

"Just that we might be able to work something out. If the terms were right, I wouldn't mind taking the *Globe* off your hands. I'm prepared to make an offer. It would get you out of this jam, set you up forever — you and your entire family. All this aggravation, worry, heartache — who needs it? You could settle back, enjoy life. Go off to Africa once a year and do your big-game hunting. Know what I mean?"

Hagenbuckle felt like throttling the man. He looked across at Moloch's throat, puckered under the noose of his tie so that it showed the wrinkles and turkey wattle of old age. It would be so easy . . .

He leaned across the table and lifted the broad end of the typewriter tie. Then, slowly and carefully, as if he were dunking a croissant of his own, he plopped it into Moloch's coffee. Moloch's mouth dropped open in astonishment. He sat there as the coffee stain moved up his tie. Hagenbuckle stood up and walked away.

"Damn you! Damn you to hell!" Moloch

shouted after him. "You'll regret that. That little trick will cost you millions. I'll get my hands on your bloody paper no matter what. Then we'll see. . . ." He sputtered to a stop.

In the conference hall, Hagenbuckle retrieved his briefcase just as the teenager was finishing up.

". . . And so at the end of the day, I go home and eat. . . . Usually I eat chicken or something, but, like, sometimes we have hot dogs. . . . Then I do my homework, except for the algebra, and I talk to my friends Debby and Vicki on the phone. . . . That's the best part. We talk about boys and stuff. . . . It's cool. . . . And then I get ready for bed. . . . I pick out something sexy to wear. Then I go online and talk about everything I did since the last time. . . . And then I go to sleep. And then the next day, I wake up. Like, that's about it."

She shuffled her papers into a pile, which she carried with her as she left the podium. There was silence and then scattered applause. A number of the publishers and editors looked at one another.

Hagenbuckle left the conference, took the long escalator down to the lobby, and walked through the revolving door onto Sixth Avenue.

He felt a little skip to his step — he had to admit, it was fun getting his rocks off on Moloch like that. At times, you had to take bold action. You had to be like Hotspur and grab your fortune at its ebb. He passed a long line of limos parked on the side street, their chauffeurs catnapping behind windows of gunmetal gray. One license plate leapt out at him; it was all too familiar: MI7. Only one person had that plate: Moloch. It was the perfect avatar of his arrogance: You had your MI5, your MI6, and now, higher than them all, with longer tentacles and a deadlier suction grip, Moloch's media empire.

But who was that seated in the backseat? Hagenbuckle couldn't get a good view because the tinted window was open only a crack, but the profile looked like — could it be? — Boxby's. His own vice president? He passed the limo and halted three paces away. He would double back and take a second look. It was unlikely, impossible . . . still, worth investigating.

Abruptly, his cell phone rang. He flipped it open. It was a text message from his secretary: RETURN IMMEDIATELY. EMERGENCY.

26

The *Globe*'s newsroom was a small village, and Jude, a native, knew something big was up the moment he walked in. Disaster has its own gritty smell. Reporters and editors stood around in small knots, talking quietly, while a smattering of others were tapping on keyboards and talking on phones with a self-conscious bravado that seemed to proclaim, I'm a pro. It takes more than this to stop me!

Edith spotted him and marched over with Stengler and Fred in tow. Alston Wickham Howard followed, patting his notebook in his side pocket. Jude could read his nervousness: For once he might have to write an obit on deadline.

"I take it she hasn't turned up," Jude said.

"Nope. Gone without a trace."

"Is the thinking that she's still alive?"

"No one knows for sure," said Edith.

They filled him in on Peregrin Whibbleby's disappearance. Good reporters, they were concise and linear in their accounts. No one had noticed her absence until after lunch, when Dilly Corrigan, the online lifestyle editor, began to fret that the Toot Bavardez column was late. Dilly went to Whibbleby's office. Clearly, Peregrin had been there — her sweater, pink, with a cluster of miniature pearls on the left collar, hung on the back of her chair. Dilly found the column on Peregrin's screen and saw, to her dismay, that it was only half completed. She checked the time on the last item. It had been written at 11:57, two hours earlier.

In and of itself, that wouldn't have been cause for alarm. Dilly did what any right-thinking editor would: She sent the column to her own computer, lifted two more items about B-list celebrities off Reuters and the Associated Press, rewrote them to disguise their provenance, and put the column on the *Globe*'s Web site. She promptly went on to other things.

By this time, Peregrin's secretary, confronted with a growing in-box, began to wonder. For the past week, her boss had been secretive, even more than when she was skipping out for her trysts with Ratnoff. But for her to disappear in the middle of the day was unusual now that Ratnoff was dead, and come to think of it, she had been acting a bit peculiar all morning.

"Peculiar how?" asked Jude.

"For Christ sake, don't interrupt," said Edith. "We haven't gotten to the important stuff yet."

"Go on."

"About three o'clock, the ad department called Skeeter Diamond's office. Some new guy whose name I don't know. Apparently, according to Mickey Spritz — she listened in, as usual — he sounded flustered."

"And . . ."

"It seems a strange ad had just been submitted and he wanted to bring it to Skeeter's attention. It's one of those reader ads — you know, those four-line things in tiny type at the bottom of page one. They usually say things like 'If you're Jewish, light the Shabbat candles,' or 'Happy anniversary, Miranda. Marrying you was the best thing I ever did.' Stuff like that."

"And what did this one say?"

"Wait and listen. Skeeter asked the ad department to send it on. So they e-mailed it to his secretary, and naturally Mickey Spritz sent it around to . . . oh, about sixty people."

Edith reached into the side pocket of her pinstriped suit jacket. She pulled out a piece of paper, held it in midair, and then lowered it ceremoniously into Jude's hand.

EVERYBODY'S TALKING, N'EST-CE PAS? Are you missing a gossip columnist? Do you know where she is? We do. At supper. But indeed, if you find her not within this month . . . The Avenger — ADVT.

"What do you make of that?" demanded Edith, rocking on the balls of her feet.

" 'Everybody's Talking' — that's Toot Bavardez."

"Duh-uh."

"But 'at supper'? What's that about?"

"That's when she disappeared. Supper . . . lunch. We figure the Avenger is Continental. He takes the big meal in the afternoon."

"Christ, Edith. You sound pretty cool about this."

"No, not really."

He held up the paper. "Let me keep it."

"Sure. But I bet you've got one of your own. Just sign in."

Jude set out for Peregrin's office. He felt a buzzing in his ears, but he was thinking sharply. Peregrin Whibbleby, of all people — not the smartest woman in the world. She seemed to live through the braver people she gossiped about, the movers and shakers. In her own life, she was unassuming. Screwing Ratnoff was probably the one radical thing she had ever done. But her column could bite, no question about that. Almost like a split personality . . . Perhaps she was just missing, out for the afternoon. Perhaps the ad was a prank. But he suspected that was wishful thinking. The ad was real. The mockery in the language showed a cold contempt. That didn't bode well.

The style department was in an uproar. Nobody was doing any work. Peregrin's secretary wasn't at her desk. Jude spotted her in a far corner of the room, a stooped figure, wiping her eyes with a handkerchief. The crowd around her looked upset. One reporter — she covered the fashion shows — was weeping openly. Two others were hugging, their arms tangled protectively around each other.

He saw Slim Jim Cutler pacing back and forth and heard him mutter: "Go your ways, and pour out the vials of the wrath of God upon the earth." He had never appeared more happily agitated.

Peregrin's office was unoccupied and looked as if she had just stepped away a moment before. The pink sweater was there on the back of her chair. Jude spotted a brown interoffice envelope on her desk. The flap was open and he could tell by looking through the perforations running across it that it was empty.

He pulled out his phone and dialed the cell number that he now knew by heart. Bollingsworth picked up before the third ring.

"Yeah" was all she said. He was used to her answering that way — it meant she knew who was calling.

"I think you'd better come over to the paper. Someone's missing and —"

"I know. Ms. Whibbleby. What do you hear?"

Jude told her about the ad and she cut him off.

"I know. I'm here now on the third floor, talking to the ad people. I'll meet you up at Ms. Whibbleby's office in five minutes."

The line went dead.

When Bollingsworth arrived, she had a posse of half a dozen other cops with her. She greeted Jude with a nod and her face was expressionless.

"Got anything?" she asked.

He led her inside Peregrin's office and pointed to the envelope.

"I don't know if it's significant or not. It's

the kind of envelope we use for internal communications. You can see it's empty."

She picked it up by the edges and motioned to her sidekick, who pulled a plastic envelope from his pocket. She dropped it inside.

"Get forensics here," she ordered. "Have them go over everything. Vacuum the floor. I doubt they'll find anything. Our murderer knows what he's doing."

"So you're convinced the murderer's got her?"

She just cast him a look.

"What do you make of the ad?" he asked.

"It came in at two-twenty. Sent from an in-house computer. It's registered to a guy on the eighth floor named O'Donnell, who —"

"O'Donnell!"

"Yeah, why?"

"I know him. He's a friend. He wouldn't do anything like —"

"Well, he's got an alibi. He was having lunch with a friend on Eighth Avenue. It checks out."

"So somebody's framing him. Or picked a computer at random and it was his."

"The ad was paid for with a stolen credit card. It's on the 'Do not honor' list. The clerk who got the ad checked the list and found it. That's when the penny dropped and he figured something was wrong. Needless to say, his suspicions weren't aroused by anything in the text of the ad." She shook her head. "I get the impression you could take an ad out saying you were going to assassinate the president and nobody here would think twice."

"Speaking of the text — what do you make of that?"

"It's like the Ratnoff spike. Very public. The killer wants to make sure his or her handiwork gets maximum publicity."

"Why Peregrin?"

"That's the big question. She was Ratnoff's paramour, so that raises sexual jealousy as a motive again. But the ad emphasizes her role as a gossip columnist. And the killer takes out a gossipy kind of ad. It fits."

"But what's it mean?" asked Jude.

"What do you mean, 'mean'?"

"The words. They're enigmatic. All that business about 'supper.' "

Again, the look.

"And here I thought you were a humanities type." She tossed him a small book. "It's from your tenth-floor library."

Jude looked at it. A Yale edition of *Hamlet*.

"Act three, scene seven," she said. "I've marked it. Go ahead, read it out loud."

King: Now, Hamlet, where's Polonius?

Hamlet: At supper.

King: At supper. Where?

Hamlet: Not where he eats, but where 'a is eaten.

Jude looked up. "So that explains *supper.*" He paused. "She's been killed!"

Bollingsworth walked over and pointed to a passage lower down. "Now read this."

King: Where is Polonius?

Hamlet: In heaven. Send thither to see. If your messenger find him not there, seek him i' th'other place yourself. But, indeed, if you find him not within this month, you shall nose him as you go up the stairs into the lobby.

"The stairs! Her body's near the stairs."

"Exactly."

"So you're looking —"

"We've got ten people on it. We're searching every staircase in the building. I'd give anything to find her alive, but it's not looking good. A killer who quotes Shakespeare and who gives himself a nickname — that's a bad sign. He's really getting off on all this."

27

Five minutes later, Bollingsworth's police radio squawked and a voice came on, drowning in static. She held it near her ear, slanted the antenna outward, turned a half circle, and said, "Repeat." Jude could hear the voice, clearer now, but still couldn't make out what it was saying.

"Where?" she demanded. She was quiet for about thirty seconds, then said, "I'll be right there. Don't touch a thing."

She dashed to the elevator and Jude ran behind her. This time, by some miracle, there was no wait. She stepped into the car and Jude followed, half expecting her to order him to leave. But instead she turned to him and said, "The delivery room. First floor. Where the hell is that?"

"I'll show you."

In the lobby, he reached to open the rear door, but she held him back with a tug on his elbow. She nudged him aside, leaned down to turn the knob by its neck, and pulled the door open. Then she pulled out a plastic bag, covered the knob with it, and fixed it in place with yellow police tape.

"Never hurts," she said. "Even though I bet my apes put their mitts all over it. The door locks from the other side, I see."

The vast expanse of the delivery room was dark, a catacomb of concrete columns and shadows. She pulled out a small flashlight — Jude was impressed by the array of equipment she could fit into her pockets — and she quickly looked around, casing the place. She pointed the beam at the loading bays and then toward the back corner, where a door was open. Echoing voices came from a stairwell. They hurried over.

To one side was a small, cramped room. She shot the beam of light into it.

"What's this?" she asked.

She was staring at a machine about five feet high, with a wide metal plane three feet off the ground. It looked something like a buzz saw, but instead of a blade, it had a curved metal arm. The eye of the arm was threaded with a loop of wire that ran down to a trundle underneath.

"A bundler," said Jude. "It ties the newspapers into a tight stack. Then the mailers toss them onto the trucks. Course it's not used anymore, at least not here."

They entered the stairwell. Now the voices were loud and they could see flashes of light coming from a landing above. As they climbed the stairs, the moving beams cast shadows that lunged and darted on the walls of the boxed-in shaft.

There were half a dozen men on the landing, so at first Jude saw nothing but their legs and backs. As Bollingsworth moved toward them, they turned and one said, "Bollocks, you're not going to believe this."

"It's one for the books," said another.

"Damnedest thing I ever saw," said another.

The men parted and a path opened up. A circle of space now appeared, bathed in light, and in the middle was an extraordinary sight. At first, the apparition looked like a statue, full-size, like something encountered unexpectedly in an art gallery. It seemed to shimmer in the light beams, emitting an aura. The statue was standing all on its own, its head thrust forward on an elongated neck, one arm behind and one arm held out in front, holding something . . . a newspaper. The head was freakish, lifelike, with a mouth wide open and indentations for the eye sockets.

Bollingsworth stared, incredulous.

"Jesus," she said.

She moved closer and so did Jude. They looked at the object in the statue's hand. It was a copy of the *National Enquirer,* lurid headlines facing outward.

"This is her body?" said Bollingsworth, still almost unbelieving. "Inside there — that's her body?"

"It is," said one of the men. Jude recognized him as her sidekick on the day Ratnoff's body was found. "You get close and you can see . . . there are some spaces between the wires, especially down here. . . ." He pointed toward the statue's thighs. "You can see the clothing. She has on a dark blue dress. And down below, you can make out bits of flesh between the wires. Her legs."

"She's a mummy," said one cop. "A wire mummy."

"It was done by that machine downstairs," said Bollingsworth. "The bundler. Used to wrap newspapers." She approached the statue, touching it gently on one wrist. She tapped it with her forefinger. It was solid, like a piece of bronze.

"What a horrible way to die. I only hope she was already dead."

"I wouldn't count on that," said her partner. "Look at her mouth. It's open —

like she's screaming."

"We're dealing with one sick fuck," said another cop.

"Somehow, he fed her into that machine, wrapped her up, and then carried her up here," said her partner. "But why? Why do all that?"

"To make some kind of point," she said.

"But what point? I don't get it."

She looked at Jude. "That newspaper, the *Enquirer*. What's with that?"

He spoke for the first time. "I think it's a reproduction of a statue called *The Newsboy*. The posture looks the same. It's a statue of a boy on a street corner. He's holding up the paper and yelling 'Extra!' "

"Write that down," said Bollingsworth, turning to an assistant. "Get a copy of it. Find out where it is and get photographs of it."

"I can do that," said Jude, pulling out his cell phone.

"Don't bother," she said. "We'll research it later."

The assistant, writing on a pad, looked up. "We've got a nutcase on our hands. The first time, he uses a spike. This time, he uses this — what did you call it . . . ?"

"Bundler."

"Bundler. He's a nut with a grudge against

newspapers."

"Or this newspaper."

"Or the people who work for it," put in a third cop.

"Clearly, he's making some kind of statement," said Bollingsworth. "He went to a lot of trouble to do this. Jude, tell me. What do you think he's saying?"

Jude took a moment to consider.

"Don't think," she said. "Just say the first thing that comes to mind. What's he saying?"

"If it's a statement he's trying to make, I'd say he's attacking the paper, not just the people who work for it."

"What do you mean by that?"

"I'd say he's saying that the *Globe* is going downhill, that it's going to hell . . . that it's, you know, turning into a rag, no better than the *National Enquirer.*"

"And Ms. Whibbleby," added Bollingsworth. "What does she represent?"

"Well, she's tied in with Ratnoff, of course. We know they had an affair, and so does everyone else, courtesy of the bloggers. But she was also the paper's gossip columnist, and a lot of people here didn't approve of that. Following the comings and goings of stupid society types and airhead celebrities. A lot of people thought we should leave that to the tabloids and supermarket magazines. So I guess in the same way that Ratnoff symbolized a slippage in standards, you could say that Peregrin — God help her — epitomized the kind of gutter paparazzi journalism that people find objectionable."

"Interesting."

The cops were all staring at him. It was impossible to know what they were thinking.

"I still don't think that's enough motive for murder," continued Jude. "I mean, you might decry the direction of the paper over a couple of beers, and you might even feel bitter about it and resent it — I know a number of people who do — but you don't go out and kill because of it. Do you?"

"Who knows," said Bollingsworth. "It could go either way. Either we've got a classic revenge murder on our hands, a love triangle in which the two adulterers are now very dead, or we've got something entirely different and we've entered into the realm of psychopathology. I hope it's not that."

"Why?"

"Because then we're dealing with a serial killer. And what worries me is what we've just seen." She turned to go back downstairs. "He's clearly in love with his work. He thinks he's created a work of art. He thinks he's an artist. And that probably means he's going to keep going and try to outdo himself each time."

She turned halfway down the stairs to speak to another cop. "Stay with the body. We need shots from every angle, the more the better. Make sure forensics goes over every inch of the staircase. And that machine downstairs — I want every inch dusted. Then get it to the lab for more analysis. They can put it next to the forklift. Someday we'll probably open up a goddamned newspaper museum."

On the way downstairs, Bollingsworth and Jude heard her partner half a flight above. "Personally," he said, "I think our killer's beginning to gild the lily."

The cops around him cracked up.

28

Peregrin Whibbleby's murder unleashed a tsunami inside the *Globe*. As the news of her body's discovery whipped through the building, the state in which her corpse was displayed was the subject of endless rumors, few of them as bizarre as the reality. The bloggers, e-mailers, and twenty-four-hour cable TV stations jumped in with both feet. One report had it that she had been chopped into pieces the size of shrimp and served up at the salad bar in the cafeteria. Another said that she had been steamrolled through the presses (this despite the fact that the presses were no longer in-house), so that thousands of readers would find bits of her on their doorsteps in the morning. A third held that she had been poisoned by a Spanish freelancer in the Dining section and that the recipe — for a paella called *Periodista Perdida* — had already gone out on the Internet.

Only Bashir, manning his coffee wagon outside the building, had the accurate version of events. But few among his customers believed him. It sounded too outlandish.

The newsroom ground to a halt. People eyed one another even more suspiciously than usual and manned the rumor machine about possible suspects, sometimes throwing a name into the hopper to settle an old score. Jimmy Pomegranate, who happened to drop in on his way to Europe, stopped by Jude's desk.

"The place reminds me of Lebanon during the civil war," he said.

"More like East Germany during the Stasi witchhunts," countered Jude.

No one else appeared to be working and he was besieged on all sides. Wherever he went, people buttonholed him to get the latest details. His phone rang so often, he had to disconnect it. And just as he had gone through his notes and made a follow-up call to Bollingsworth to check the time of death and got ready to start writing, who should come running over to his cubicle but Bernie Grabble. He tripped at the last moment, so that his huge frame came barreling in and almost crashed onto Jude's keyboard.

"Son of a bitch," he shouted. "Somebody

tripped me."

He leapt up and looked over the partition, but no one was there.

"Come with me," he ordered. "Into my office. I need a fill."

"But, Bernie," protested Jude. "It's already six o'clock. I won't have time to write."

"Never mind that. This is your metro editor talking. No one's more important than me. I need to know what's going on."

"Bernie . . . our one and a half million readers?"

"Fuck 'em. I got here first."

Reluctantly, Jude gathered up his notebook and followed Grabble into his office. He took the same seat as before, facing the wall covered with metal press plates.

Grabble sat for all of three seconds. "Whatcha got?" he demanded.

He was on his feet the moment Jude began to speak, pacing up and down in his demented Groucho Marx stride. Every so often as Jude spoke, he would throw his hands into the air as if he were trying to get rid of them, exclaiming such things as "This is incredible, absolutely incredible" and "We can't have this! What's the matter with you?" When Jude described the body encased in its skintight metal casket, Grabble

293

looked at him in horror, as if Jude had done it.

"That's terrible," he said, sitting down at last. "That's disgusting. What sick mind would do a thing like that? Be careful, very careful, how you describe it. I don't like that word you used. . . . What was it again?"

"Statue."

"That's it — statue. It's not a statue. I don't want to hear any of this statue talk."

"You'll be able to judge for yourself."

"What do you mean?" Grabble looked horrified.

"I took a picture. With my cell phone. The photo desk is developing it."

"You did *what?* A picture? With your cell phone?" He paused. "Is that legal?"

"Sure. Why not? We're in our own building, for Christ sake."

"That's the *point.* Our own building. I don't think we should use it. What do you think? You think we should use it?"

"It's news, Bernie."

"I know that. I was covering news when you were in diapers. Let me think about it. I want to see it first. Then I'll decide. But I don't want you to get too graphic in your story. We don't want to pollute the reader's mind with all this statue business."

"Bernie, I'm not going to pollute the

reader's mind with anything if I don't get started."

Grabble leapt up. "What are you doing here? You better get going. Why are you wasting time?"

Jude recalled the rewrite bank's definition of *to Grabble:* "to have twenty ideas a minute, of which ten contradict those of the previous minute."

Grabble looked down at him sternly. "Did you file for the Internet? They have a deadline every minute. Just like the old wire services. This whole thing is incredible, absolutely incredible."

He led the way to the door, stopped in mid-stride, and pointed at the press plates on his wall. "I can tell you one thing: Your goddamned story's not going up there. Who would put something like that up there?"

Jude returned to his cubicle. His cell phone had been returned by the photo editor with a note: "Congrats," it said. "I think we can do something with this." He also had a voice mail. O'Donnell had called. Jude called him back and O'Donnell picked up on the first ring.

"Well, well, and here I thought, amid all the excitement, you'd abandoned me."

"Not a chance. But Grabble's driving me crazy."

"That's his job definition. His purpose in life. You're not crazy, he's not happy."

Jude explained that he was on deadline but wanted to talk to him, urgently, as soon as he filed.

"Okay, kiddo. Your place or mine?"

Jude came up with a bar, O'Kelly's on Eleventh Avenue, a place no one from the *Globe* frequented. "In two hours."

Writing the story was agony. He had banged out the lede fast enough, but no sooner had he filed it and begun work on the next page than queries began pouring in from both the backfield and the copy desk. ("Are we sure she's inside that thing?" "Could she breathe in there? Maybe she's still alive." "What's the actual composition of the metal?") Everyone wanted something placed higher up in the article.

"How about I put it all *before* the first graph," Jude finally shouted, slamming down the phone.

The same cross fire of questions and suggestions happened with subsequent pages. He was asked to provide a six-paragraph insert describing a bundler. "Maybe we should get comment from the mailers' union," suggested one editor. He was overruled.

In describing Peregrin's postmortem state,

Jude eschewed the word *statue* and tried *sculpture.* That was knocked down as "too artsy," so he tried *effigy;* when that was eliminated because it sounded "political," he reached for *relic,* which was nixed because it made her sound like a tourist spot; finally he came up with *phantasmagoric likeness,* which was blocked as being "too poetic."

A copy editor told him that Skeeter Diamond himself was following the editing step by step. "He says, let's just say *statue.*"

"Fine," said Jude. "Put it in."

Then he was asked to help out with Peregrin's obit. Alston Wickham Howard, confused by a Wikipedia entry that said Ms. Whibbleby was, in fact, a Somali nomad turned fashion model, was freezing on deadline.

"Of all people, you'd think the Angel of Death would grasp the concept of a deadline," Jude screamed into the phone.

Three hours and two thousand words later, he was done and exhausted. As he put his coat on, Fred rose in the neighboring cubicle, applauded, and held his hands up in a victory clasp. From across the aisle, Stengler was about to say something — from the look on his face, it was going to be an unpleasant quip — but he caught sight of Grabble approaching and slunk away.

The comment "Good job" actually passed Grabble's lips. "It's a horrible business, horrible," he muttered over his shoulder. "Still, you handled it tastefully. I like that description you put in, the one where you compare her to a statue."

It was after nine o'clock when Jude finally made it to O'Kelly's, but O'Donnell was still there. Jude saw him sitting with his back to the door and he could tell from the way he was leaning hunched over his glass that he was well on his way to tying one on. When he saw Jude, he lifted a shaky forefinger and started right in.

"If it isn't our little policeman."

"What do you mean by that?"

"You've been hanging around that woman cop so much, you're beginnin' to look like her."

"What the fuck got into you?"

" 'Bout five whiskeys. Six if you count the first one."

Jude went to the bar, came back with a J&B, and sat across from him. They dealt in small talk for a while and gradually O'Donnell's better nature came back from wherever he had mislaid it. Jude had been waiting for that moment.

"I want to ask you something," he began.

O'Donnell raised one eyebrow suspiciously.

"When Ratnoff was killed, you were going through his computer files."

"You already asked me about that — or don't you remember? I told you then that I was interested in what he was up to."

"But you had a whole bunch of stuff on your desk, including morgue files about him." Jude took a breath. "And some of them were dated weeks before he was killed."

"Christ, you really are a cop."

"There's more. The ad today that revealed Peregrin's whereabouts . . . it was sent from your computer."

O'Donnell sat up straight. "The cops — the *other* cops, I should say — already asked me about that. I wasn't in the office when it was sent. I was off having lunch with Van Wessel — they checked out my alibi. So somebody else sat down and used my machine. As you well know . . . sleuth that you are . . . I'm apt to leave it on when I walk away. And I have to say I'm not happy about all these questions."

"C'mon, Frank. I'm not accusing you of anything. If somebody told me you had anything to do with any of this, I'd knock their teeth in. But you have to admit some of this stuff looks bad. And if the cops get hold of it . . . shit, I don't know. You may need some help. That's all. I'm here talking to you as your friend."

The conciliatory words had an effect. O'Donnell softened. He apologized. Then he explained — up to a point.

"You see, I've been tracking Ratnoff for some time. What do you think he was doing in the basement? There's all kinds of shit down there and he was on to something. One thing I'll say for him, he was a dogged fucking researcher. You don't think he was killed just because he was boffing our Ms. Whibbleby — do you?"

"I don't know. What kind of *things* was he on to?"

"I'm still working on it. If I come up with anything — well, I can't say you'll be the first to know, but you'll be right up there. In the meantime, here's some advice. Edith Sawyer — in case you didn't realize it — has been right on your tail. I wouldn't let her get too close, if you know what I mean."

"No. What are you saying? You think she's involved?"

"I didn't say that. But I wouldn't rush to knock her off the list."

"You found something in Ratnoff's computer?"

"Maybe. And if I did . . . guess what? I uploaded it a second time today. And this time, a piece of it's no longer there."

"Frank, you've gotta tell me."

"All in good time."

"C'mon."

O'Donnell just gave a Cheshire cat smile. Jude knew he couldn't be pushed. He was enjoying his Deep Throat role too much. Years of being a reporter had taught him just how much bait to put on the hook.

They stayed and talked for another hour. And then, just as they were leaving, as O'Donnell slipped his coat on, he released a little hand grenade.

"Thanks for your little pep talk, kiddo. I appreciate your support. I may need it."

"What do you mean?"

"There's something else. Talk about looking bad."

"What?"

"That *National Enquirer* that they found in her hand. It might be mine. I had one on my desk. It's missing."

"When?"

"This morning . . . just before Peregrin disappeared."

"Christ! What were you doing with the *Enquirer*?"

"I was interested in Clinton's twin brother

being found on Mars. And now, for all I know, a critical piece of evidence has my prints on it."

"What are you going to do?"

"Nothing, for the moment. My prints aren't on file."

"Maybe you should say something. If they discover it on their own, that'll make it worse."

O'Donnell grunted.

"Wait a minute," said Jude. "How did you know about the *National Enquirer*? I didn't tell you about that." He looked at his watch. "And the paper just hit the stands five minutes ago."

O'Donnell looked at him with feigned sadness.

"You know, for a cop, you're really stupid. Your story was flying around the whole building. I read every paragraph five minutes after you wrote it. And by the way" — here he grinned — "I'm glad you finally came up with the right word to describe her in her final resting state. *Statue.*"

29

By the time Jude got home, it was close to midnight and he was feeling the worse for wear. The scotch had done its damage. His esophagus was sending out distress signals — wavelets of pain that began in his gut and rippled upward. He imagined tiny rock climbers swarming around inside, hammering their pitons and screwing in their cams. Remembering he hadn't eaten dinner, he thawed a bag of pasta in the microwave, dumped it into a pot of boiling water, and found half a bottle of tomato sauce, which he heated.

TK was bouncing around like a jumping bean, so he gave her three-quarters of a can of Alpo and they ate together, man and dog, in silence. He took her out for a walk. She pulled against the leash in all directions, excited by every pigeon and scrap of paper. It was unseasonably chilly, with wisps of mist sneaking around the corners. Avenue

B was practically deserted, except for two couples a block away. He heard a woman's laughter, full-throated, and then a man's voice, low, and more laughter.

He hadn't seen Elaine in a week. It seemed longer. He found himself thinking of her often. Images of her played in his mind's eye — that damn movie again. They had been together more than a year. At the end, they'd fought a lot, but the early times had been exciting — especially the times in the sack. She was unique. She wasn't spontaneous; she could be churlish, and she fussed about her looks in a prim sort of way. But she was quick, intelligent, sensuous, and as honest as a shiv in the ribs. He would happily spend another year with her. He just wasn't sure about the rest of his life.

He walked twice around the block, stopped in his entryway to retrieve his mail — the box was busted, so he didn't need a key — and mounted the stairs. TK ran ahead and waited at the door, her tail thumping. Inside, he poured himself another scotch, felt it burn, and then set it down. He didn't like drinking alone, but he needed something to deaden his nerves after Peregrin's murder and then that unsettling talk with O'Donnell. O'Donnell was making no bones about being secretive, which was a good feint to fend off questions and conceal something he didn't dare reveal.

Jude walked over to the window and looked out. He was tired and lonely. Thirty-five years old wasn't as young as he used to think it was. He was getting on, but was he getting up? Kids — shouldn't he have kids by now? Was his life turning out the way he had hoped? Was he living it, truly living it, or just drifting along with the tide?

Ah! The glorious career of a reporter! He could draw the recruitment poster: Travel the world on someone else's dime! Record the day's catastrophe and then dial up room service at the best hotel! Occupy a front-row seat and write the first draft of history! Maybe he should have lobbied for an overseas assignment.

Why was it that the romance of the profession he loved was always just around the corner? Was he going to become one of the many casualties, a burned-out case? Like O'Donnell, so bitter at the downturn of his career and the deterioration of the *Globe?* Or Edith Sawyer, so ambitious she'd trample her grandmother to get a good story? Or Fred Bradshaw, so meek and beaten down that he was a laughingstock? Or Charlie Stengler, so frightened of screwing up that he hid behind pillars to duck assignments?

The phone rang. Probably Chuck, the late man, with more COMAs. He sat down on the couch and answered it.

"Jude, I'm sorry to call so late . . . but I was so worried about you."

Elaine! He couldn't help it — his heart soared!

"I'm all right. What do you mean, you were worried?"

"The police came to see me. . . . I guess you know that. . . . A woman named Bollingball or something like that —"

"Bollingsworth."

"Yes. That sounds like it. And she asked me all sorts of questions. She wanted to hear my messages . . . on my answering machine. And so I played them . . . including the one from you when you were drunk. I hope that was the right thing to do. . . . I was so frightened."

Jude could picture her. When she talked on the phone, she tilted her head to one side, so that her blond hair fell straight down and covered the receiver, the little diamond stud in her ear sparkling in the light.

"That was fine. You did the right thing." He wondered what she was wearing.

"Jude, have you been drinking? You sound

like you've been drinking."

"Some. It's been a rough day."

"You shouldn't drink so much." She paused to let her admonition sink in. "Anyway, the way Bolling . . . whatever . . . was talking, I imagined that you were in some sort of trouble. I mean, the police coming here to check up on you — it's a bit much. But she said it would help you if I just answered her questions fully and truthfully and so I tried to do that. I hope she was telling the truth."

"Yes, she was. And everything's okay now."

"But what was it? What are they investigating?"

"A homicide."

"A homicide!" He could hear her gasp. "Does it have anything to do with that horrible business at the paper I've been reading about?"

"Yes. That's it."

"I saw your byline on the story. I certainly hope you weren't mixed up with anything like that. I mean, murder!"

"Yeah, it's kind of crazy. There's been a second one."

"A second one? A second murder! Who's doing it?"

"That's the big question. Nobody knows."

There was a silence.

"How are you?" he asked.

"Okay, I guess. . . . I miss you."

"I miss you, too." He couldn't keep the exhaustion out of his voice.

"Jude, you sound put out. I don't mean to make you angry. I just wanted to point out that the way you treated me . . . it left a lot to be desired. I mean, your job means so much to you . . . it takes over your life. You never really had time for me. . . ."

He heard a clicking on the line. Someone was trying to call him.

"I always had the feeling that you were just fitting me in between other things — work things, if you know what I mean."

Maybe it was just Chuck with some other dumb rumor . . . but maybe not.

"Jude, are you there? Are you listening to me?"

"I am." The clicks were lasting a long time. Chuck usually let it go five rings and then phoned back.

"Because it's important. Sometimes I think . . . you know, that breaking up was maybe a mistake. We had our problems, but when you think about it, we had a lot of good times. . . . I'm not so sure about Harry. . . ."

The clicks stopped.

"He has more time for me. And certainly

more money. We go to plays and expensive restaurants, which is nice. But I don't know. . . . He doesn't make me laugh the way you did. And he's so self-centered. Honestly, I —"

"Ah . . . Elaine, can you hold on a minute? Someone's coming in on the other line."

"Oh . . . I guess so."

The other line was dead. He retrieved a message. It was a man's voice. *"I'm not going to tell you who I am. This is to let you know that I left something for you in your mailbox. It's a tape. I don't know if it will be helpful, but I think you should listen to it."*

Jude didn't recognize the muffled voice, but it sounded familiar.

He hurried to the pile of mail on the table. A plain white envelope with no stamps and no return address was among the bills and circulars. His name — nothing else — was printed on the front. The envelope was thick. He opened it quickly, ripping it down one end and tipping it. An audiotape fell out. There was also a note, written in longhand.

I was eating dinner alone tonight seated in a booth in a restaurant on the West Side. I heard a conversation from the booth next to me and immediately recognized one of the voices. I think you will, too. I had my tape recorder with me, in preparation for an interview tomorrow, and I switched it on. I'm afraid I was not in time to record the first part of the conversation, but this may be enough, I believe, to arouse your interest. Do with it what you like. I don't want to get caught up in this whole mess, so I am handing it over in the hope, and expectation, that I shall remain anonymous.

Best regards.
A colleague.

Jude picked up the phone again. Elaine was still on the line — he could hear her agitated breathing.

"Elaine, listen. I'm going to have to call you back. Something's come up —"

"Work again? Is that it? The desk, as you always call it? Jude — that's perfect. That's just perfect."

The line went dead.

Jude fetched his recorder, inserted the tape, and pressed the play button. A voice came on instantly, low and in the distance. It was hard to make out against the background noise of dishes and conversations.

"*. . . could hardly be better. Her murder*

310

should have sealed it. Frankly, I don't see how Diamond can survive this."

Another voice replied: *"The poor jerk's in over his head."*

The first voice returned: *"It's all working out perfectly for me. I could come back, you know."*

Then the second: *"I know. Wouldn't that be sweet? . . ."* At this point, the voice was covered by noise; it sounded like a group of customers passing by. *". . . Who was it said, 'Revenge is a dish best served cold'?"*

The first: *"I dunno. I hope it wasn't the guy who cooked this tortellini!"* Jude could hear laughter.

The two talked of other things for a while, and then, at the end, they came back to the subject at hand.

First voice: *"So you know what I'm gonna do now? Nothing."*

Second voice: *"Nothing, huh."*

First: *"That's right. I'm just gonna let events take their course."*

Second: *" 'Cause they're moving in your direction."*

First: *"Damn right."*

Second: *"No need to even give them a little push."*

First: *"Nope. I already have. God helps*

those who help themselves."

The tape ended. The anonymous tipster was right: Jude didn't need help identifying one of the voices. It belonged to Max Schwartzbaum. But whose was the second voice? Unlike the first, it was blurred and indistinct, almost as if the person was trying to disguise it, though that didn't make any sense. Jude also had the sense that the second person was leading Schwartzbaum on, appealing to his vanity and drawing him out. Maybe even trying to get him to say incriminating things. Clearly, from the slurred diction, Schwartzbaum was well on the way to being drunk. No surprise there! Christ. As if this whole sorry business wasn't messy enough.

At that moment, Jude's phone rang. Maybe Elaine calling back. He needed time to think. He would let the machine pick up. When it did, another familiar voice squawked out.

"Jude, Chuck here. Pick up. This one's big. No shit."

He picked up. "What is it?"

"You're not going to believe this. A hacker got on the *Globe's* Web site. And he's posted photos of Peregrin Whibbleby — photos of her dead. She's standing there wrapped in that wire, holding the *National Enquirer.*

We're trying to get them taken off, but for now they're still on the site!"

Jude hung up and turned on his computer. And sure enough, there was that grotesque image again, Peregrin in her metal shell, reproduced half a dozen times from various angles. The last one had a headline that read WHOSE GOOSE IS COOKED? Underneath was a caption: "Shun the spawn of the press of the gossip of the hour."

It was signed "The Avenger."

Jude reached for his phone and dialed Bollingsworth.

30

"Ralph Waldo Emerson," said Bollings-worth.

"I know," said Jude, who had pulled the quote from *Bartlett's* around 1:00 a.m. "From his essay 'Books.' " He recited, " 'Be sure, then, to read no mean books. Shun the spawn of the press of the gossip of the hour.' "

"It goes on." She added: " 'Do not read what you shall learn, without asking, in the street and the train.' Strikes me as good advice for a newspaperman."

Still hungry from last night, he was half-way through two eggs sunnyside up and bacon. Bollingsworth cut into her blueberry muffin, swathed one half in butter, and took a healthy bite, followed by a swig of black coffee.

They were in Neil's Coffee Shop on Lexington and Seventieth Street, an early-morning rendezvous they had arranged on the phone last night. When he'd reached her, he could have sworn the music coming over her cell — a soulful blues — was live. She had bags under her eyes again but still looked pretty good. He liked having breakfast with her, as if they were a couple.

Neil's was decorated with black-on-white murals of dark-haired Greek beauties in chitons carrying lyres, photos of sun-bleached Aegean islands, and signed head shots of local actors and newscasters, some of whom were once known.

"Looks like our killer is showing off his erudition," she said. "Who knew he was a goddamned Transcendentalist?"

The two tabloids were lying faceup beside her in the booth, both with full-cover photos of Peregrin lifted from the Web. (It had taken *Globe* technicians forty minutes to delete them.) Both showed her metallic-molded corpse standing there, one arm outstretched like a lawn jockey, holding the *National Enquirer,* whose name was airbrushed out in the *Grifter,* apparently to deprive the supermarket tabloid of product placement. GOSSIP GODDESS A HUMAN SCULPTURE, screamed the headline. In the *Maul,* the wood was less personal: NIGHTMARE ON GRUB STREET.

Bollingsworth followed his eyes down to the headline.

"*Nightmare* is what I'm going to live today," she said. "With Peregrin's murder, this one's careering off into outer space."

"I can believe it."

"The commissioner is holding a press conference — at City Hall, no less. That means the mayor will be there as a calming presence for New Yorkers, having just exploded and reamed him out. So the PC will ream out the chief of detectives. And guess who the CD will ream out?"

"I have a feeling I'm looking at her."

"You are. And you better take a good look. . . . It might be the last one."

"Don't you have any leads?"

"He asked *disinterestedly*." She scowled at him, taking the other half of the muffin. "Nothing that amounts to much, and now, with a second victim . . . well, so far that hasn't added much."

"What do you mean?"

"A second homicide usually yields a lot more information . . . more than double the information in terms of forensics, motive, opportunity, you name it. Not to mention the serendipity factor — possible witnesses, the things that go wrong for the killer, the things he or she overlooks or leaves behind.

But so far, nothing's panned out. Either this killer is incredibly smart or incredibly lucky. Maybe both."

"But the choice of the second victim has to tell you something."

"It does. Too much and not enough."

"What do you mean?"

"I feel like I've pulled out a compass and I'm just watching the needle spin. The number of possible suspects is mind-boggling. For one thing, she was a gossip columnist. That means she wounded a lot of people . . . made a lot of enemies. People in this city carry grudges like shopping bags.

"That's outside the paper. Then we come to *inside* the paper. The two victims were lovers. Who knows how many people at the *Globe* they pissed off? You have your religious nuts — that guy Slim Jim What's-his-name comes to mind — and you have possible jilted lovers, wannabe lovers, and just plain jealous miscreants."

"What about their spouses?"

"First place we looked. Alibis for both murders." She finished her coffee. "What's odd is their being lovers doesn't narrow down the field."

"What do you mean?"

"Because you have to assume that Peregrin knew whatever Ratnoff knew. Take any

317

motive — revenge, for example. Somebody hated Ratnoff enough to kill him. Then he learns after the fact that Ratnoff was sleeping with Peregrin. He has to assume that Ratnoff probably told her about him and his grudge. So now he has to get rid of her, too. Or say Ratnoff found out something, a secret so important that someone would kill to keep him quiet. Now the murderer learns about Peregrin. He starts wondering what she knows, and he's desperate. He's already committed one murder, and so now he'll do anything, even commit a second one, to cover his tracks."

"I see what you mean." Jude waved a waiter over, pointed to their cups for a refill. He wished he could help her.

"I know you're interested in Engleheart," he said. "There's something you should know about him."

She was all ears.

"I went to his office on the ninth floor several days ago. . . . I was going to ask him about the camera in the lobby, and I overheard him talking on the phone. I could only hear his end of the conversation, but it sounded suspicious. At one point, he said, 'No one's on to anything,' and at another he said he didn't know where the ice pick was."

"This was before you wrote about the ice pick in your story, or after?"

"After."

"So he could have learned about the ice pick from your story. Did you overhear anything else?"

"No, that's pretty much it. Except that he caught me and got pissed as hell."

"Interesting, but not at all conclusive."

"There is one other thing. It turns out that a couple of reporters were working on a story about police corruption. They filed stuff and it went to Ratnoff, who was editing it, putting it all together. At least one of them — a guy called Hank Higgle, who works at your headquarters — he thinks that's why Ratnoff was killed. He's scared to death himself."

She pulled out her notebook and wrote Higgle's name in it. It occurred to Jude — who in the course of reporting had written down hundreds of names, just like that — that they were working two aisles of the same church. He had never thought of cops that way before.

He continued: "And then somebody reported seeing Engleheart messing around with the freight elevator. They said he was on his knees . . . might have been cleaning it."

"Now you've got my attention. Who told you this?"

Jude was not about to mention O'Donnell's name. "Just a rumor going around. They said it came from a janitor or someone."

She cocked an eye at him, half disbelieving, but let it pass.

"I've had my eye on Engleheart from the beginning," she said. "I told you he used to be a cop. And that he was mixed up with some bad types."

"What's his story?"

"Five years ago, he was drummed off the force for corruption. He was allowed to retire with a clean record, but that's because nothing could be proved. His partner said he was on the take and word started getting around, but then his partner freaked and refused to give evidence to the inspectors."

"And the *Globe,* with its usual all-efficient background check, took him on."

"Engleheart still keeps up with his old buddies on the force. Some of them work in my office and I hear stories about him. He's living high on the hog, as they used to say."

He waved for the check.

"Anything else? Any other angles?"

"Not much," she replied. "Other than the killer's psychological profile. It's filling out.

Putting those pictures on the Web site shows how desperate he is for attention. He wants respect. He craves it. He wants everyone to think he's brilliant."

"How about forensics? Prints? Stuff like that."

"I'm afraid I can't go into that yet. But there's no breakthrough on anything. Take my word for it." She smiled at him and her face softened. "I'm afraid that you helped me more than I helped you."

"Don't worry. It'll even out over the long run." He smiled back. "I'm chivalrous. You plucked my heartstrings. It was that line about me taking one last look at you."

"Yeah. That one works every time."

He took both checks, but she grabbed them, found hers, and handed his back.

"Corruption can run both ways, you know," she said, putting her nicely shaped legs out into the aisle and standing up.

"And here I thought it was just you corrupting me."

As he walked out of the diner, he thought that was actually true to some degree. He was cooperating with the police more than he had ever imagined he would — and it didn't bother him at all.

31

The *Globe* staff — or at least those who dared to come to work — filed morosely into the company's auditorium on the tenth floor. They had been summoned by a group e-mail sent by Hagenbuckle, who had decided only this morning to deliver what he called a "morale booster."

The hall was half full. O'Donnell sat next to Van Wessel in the third row. The two had placed a sizable wager on exactly when the publisher would compare the newspaper to an aircraft carrier. The drama critic was seated on an aisle, looking around dyspeptically, prepared to pan the show. The rewrite-bank reporters sat off to one side like vultures anticipating a feast. Style reporters and editors were together in a conclave, buzzing and still mourning their gossip columnist. Jude sat in the back, lucky to have made it; he had heard about the meeting only five minutes earlier, when he stopped off at Bashir's wagon for coffee.

Hagenbuckle sat on the stage, sweating under the glaring lights, waiting for the room to fill up. Why were newspaper people always late? he wondered. How did they ever manage to get the paper out on time? Come to think of it, more often than not, they didn't. He had once calculated the cost of a tardy press run — it had come to $1,212 for every minute after the close at 7:30 p.m. Another damned reason we're hemorrhaging money. He wanted to jot a note to himself ("Check time of closings last three weeks") but didn't dare with all those eyes staring up at him.

The idea of convening the staff had been Abby's. At first, he had agreed just to keep his wife quiet, but the more he thought about it, the more it seemed the kind of bold act one expected from a leader, the sort of anecdote you read about in *Media Moguls.* He hadn't been featured there in some time — not since his last safari gave rise to that article entitled "Bushwacker in Paradise," which he thought had been slightly snide.

Trouble was, Abby hadn't told him what to say. He had spent all morning at his desk, trying to come up with the right words, running through half a pack of Trues. His secretary, Miss Overton, had protested that smoking indoors was violating the law and he had snapped, "Goddamn it, it's my building and I'll smoke if I want to." Perhaps he had been a bit rough with her. Undoubtedly, that was why she'd been less than enthusiastic about his opening remarks. He had planned to use one of his jokes as an icebreaker (he had a stock of four, which he used in speeches around town), and she had said — rather coolly, he thought — that given the circumstances, it didn't seem right.

He looked around. There was Skeeter Diamond in the front row, damned eye twitching again. And Bernie Grabble, sitting far from Diamond, his foot bouncing. And that foreign editor, the one who kept a map of the world under his glass desktop so he could locate the countries the correspondents were phoning from. What was his name? Squire — that was it — Healey Squire. No, *Heaton* Squire. And Brisley Townsend, the Washington bureau chief. And Pomegranate, also up from Washington. He's definitely putting on weight, looks like Orson Welles. See, he said to himself, all those stupid rumors about me are way off base — I *do* know the names of my staff.

Gulliam Toothy, sitting right below, was

winking and nodding. Damned PR man thinks he's orchestrating the whole bloody event just because he was called in to brush up some of the writing. If he had been doing his job properly, maybe we wouldn't be in this fix. Next to Toothy sat Boxby, the vice president, looking officious. And next to him was the bodyguard Hagenbuckle had just hired. With a murderer on the loose, you couldn't be too safe. That, also, had been Abby's idea.

Toothy was doing something: looking to the back of the hall and to the stage and pointing to his watch, giving the thumbs-up. Must be time to start.

Hagenbuckle rose, walked to the lectern, and tapped the microphone. It thudded through the auditorium like logs crashing down a mountainside. People winced and some ducked.

"Can you hear me?" He tapped the microphone again. They winced some more.

"For crying out loud, yes!" responded one man.

"Good. I'll try to be brief. As someone once said, 'I don't mind when my audience starts looking at their watches. But it really bothers me when they start shaking them to make sure they're still running.' " (That was joke number three. It was met with a perplexed silence, which made him think perhaps his employees were more upset by the killings than they let on.)

He plunged ahead: "You're probably wondering why I've called you all here today. As you undoubtedly know, we've been through some rocky times lately. It's not every day of the week that somebody goes around killing people in the workplace. Not by a long shot. But I'm here to tell you, right now, right here, that we're not going to stand by and let that sort of thing happen. No sir. Zero tolerance for that kind of behavior."

He looked around at the audience, all those eyes staring up at him. Some were shaking their heads. They were clearly in denial. Way in the back, a young man in a brown jacket was taking notes — probably that reporter who was covering the story, Jude something. Toothy hadn't mentioned him. Wasn't this all supposed to be off the record? Another damned complication he'd have to sort out.

"Murder is totally unacceptable," he declared. "No two ways about it."

He talked about how bad murder was for quite a while, drawing from the Bible and mentioning one or two current-day examples of mayhem and slaughter. The audience appeared to be getting upset. That was good — they had to work through this. He looked at his notes. He had scribbled the word *family* in the margin and drawn a stick figure of himself, labeled "Dad." Time for some encouraging words.

"When you think about it, the *Globe* is like a family — a large, loving family with brothers and sisters and uncles and aunts and cousins all over the place. We've got our problems, like all families, our oddballs. Uncle Moe over there cracking jokes, cousin Julius provoking the twins. But we accept them. We're a family and we're all part of it. Doesn't matter what your job is, you belong. You have a place at the table. And I'm like the father. I'm very loving. But I can be a disciplinarian, too. I'm the admiral on the bridge of the aircraft carrier, and let me tell you" — at this point, a man in the third row handed another man a fistful of dollars — "when we catch the guy who's doing this, well, we'll turn him over to the authorities in an instant. Let me just say this: I wouldn't want to be in his shoes."

He had expected applause after this line and was a little disappointed that the hall remained silent. But he went on to the steps the paper was taking to ensure the safety of its employees. From now on, guards would

check the IDs of everyone coming in —
from the publisher on down — no excep-
tions! No more just watching people coming and going. James Engleheart, the head
of security, would be taking on some extra
people.

"And if anyone feels nervous or anxious,
just give him a call — Jim, stand up so
people can see you." Hagenbuckle shielded
his eyes against the lights, scanned the hall.
"There he is. Take a look, everybody. And if
you're feeling scared, just give him a call.
He'll provide an escort to see you to the
door or wherever you want to go. Hell, he
might even come himself."

Doors would be locked. And the part of
the building that was no longer used — the
basement, the delivery room, the truck bays
— all that he declared "off-limits to all
personnel," except, of course, those who
belonged there.

And finally, Hagenbuckle said, he wanted
everyone to cooperate with the police
investigation. They should be vigilant. Their
eyes and ears could be enlisted in the
campaign to hunt for the killer. "I've spoken
to the mayor," he said. (He'd been saving
this for last.) "And he assures me that
everything that can be done is being done.

And if that's not enough, more will be done."

The end of the program had come, the part that Hagenbuckle anticipated with a certain amount of trepidation — questions from the floor. A hand mike was provided. A young man in a white shirt and tie held the mike up for all to see. Index cards had been passed out at the door for those who wanted to submit their queries anonymously.

The first questions were relatively straightforward. The man in the white shirt rushed up and down the aisles, handing the mike over to people who stood and said their piece: Did the police have any solid leads? What did they think was the motive? Did they believe the killer came from the outside or — and at this point, people looked around the room nervously — was it likely to be someone on the inside?

Then a young African-American woman made an impromptu and angry speech. She said that people should be allowed to work at home "until this thing blows over," and her declaration was met with murmurs of approval. Hagenbuckle explained that if no one came to work, the *Globe* couldn't be published. The woman had the nerve to rise up and demand the mike again. She said why not at least allow those who could "telecommute" to do so. "Why should all of us be put in danger?" More murmurs. The audience was getting restive. Toothy was frowning.

A man with a goatee asked if it was true that the publisher had hired his own bodyguard. Hagenbuckle said he'd have to get back to him on that. The man shook his head and mumbled something under his breath. Then another questioner wanted to know if it was true, now that the stock had hit a new low, that someone somewhere was scooping it up? Hagenbuckle said he didn't think so.

He decided to switch to the written questions. A stack was handed up to him and he sorted through them as quickly as a card shark. Several strayed from the murders and he chose to concentrate on them. It was, after all, time to move on.

Was it true that the *Globe* was planning four magazine supplements on Hollywood to bring in more studio ads? ("No. We're planning five.") Did the paper have to cover every same-sex marriage in Massachusetts? ("I wasn't aware of that.") Why were there so many stories about hip-hop? ("Good question. We'll send a note to the culture editor and inquire.") Didn't the stories used to be longer? (Hagenbuckle tried a joke: "The stories are still long; it's the readers who're getting shorter.")

It went on and on like this for another twenty minutes and gradually the audience seemed to settle down, even to lose interest. He seemed to have calmed them, because some were leaving. Their seats popped back like rifle shots.

Hagenbuckle stuck it out bravely — all in all, he thought, it was going pretty well. But then he came to a question scrawled in heavy black ink, the loops of the letters sharp and angular. When he finished reading it to himself, he felt his chest tighten.

The card read:

UNCLE,
I bet you can't even pick me out of the audience. And by the way, when am I going to get a real piece of the action?
    Your nephew,
    who hasn't forgotten you the way you've forgotten him.

Hagenbuckle shielded his eyes again — those damned lights! — and looked up and down the rows of seats. Where was he? The boy was correct: He couldn't spot him. Of course he couldn't — he had never even

331

met him. Hagenbuckle was confused: October 1 was over a week away. The boy was not to learn the secret of his birth until then. Who had jumped the gun?

It was hard to concentrate in front of an auditorium full of people.

Not so full, actually. The employees were leaving in droves. He sighed. From the front row, Toothy was looking up at him and frowning, making some kind of sign, running his forefinger back and forth across his throat. Time to wrap it up. The publisher sighed and walked away from the lectern. It's absolutely true what the Bard said: Heavy is the head that wears the crown.

He returned to his office, sat down, and decided he was hungry. He followed his usual routine, one of the many company perks that accrued to the CEO: He would simply dial the metro desk to place his order. The drill was well established: An editor would pluck the nearest copy person and draft him as delivery boy. Derided by his peers as "the chosen one," he would traipse off to the deli with a pocketful of petty cash and return with a sandwich and soft drink to the publisher's office on the thirteenth floor.

Only this time, no copy person was around. So the editor, who turned out to be

Bridget Bates, the deputy metro editor, scanned the newsroom. She spotted a shadowy figure and ordered him over and gave him the job. He stood before her looking nervous, and as she handed him the order for a pastrami on rye, she thought he looked familiar.

32

Elmer P. Boxby walked along the Hudson piers, trying to collect his thoughts. His brain, which he liked to think of as his prime asset, was usually cold and calculating. But at times like this, it overheated.

The "plan," as it was euphemistically called, was moving ahead rapidly. Everyone was doing his part — the lawyers, the researchers, the corporation — everyone, that is, except himself. He was the one holding things up, and now the pressure had built to an excruciating level. His cell phone was ringing every half hour, and each time it was HIM on the line, demanding action.

At first, Boxby's mission had sounded so easy. Discover the identity of Hagenbuckle's mysterious nephew — find him, cultivate him, and bring him into the fold. Compared to Boxby's exploits of the past, which included a not very successful stint at the CIA, that had sounded like a cakewalk. But it hadn't turned out that way. The nephew's identity was elusive. The boy himself didn't know his lineage. Hagenbuckle was uncharacteristically closemouthed about it, saying it would be disclosed on the first of October.

Boxby had tried to shake the secret loose just a half hour ago at the publisher's "town meeting." Cleverly — or so he had thought — he had forged that provocative question from the nephew. Reading it onstage, Hagenbuckle had nearly had a heart attack. But would it force the publisher to reveal the boy's identity in some way? Boxby began to doubt it. And now just over a week remained before the *Globe*'s lawyers were to go into action and propel the young man out of obscurity by telling him of his good fortune.

Boxby walked past the gate to the Circle Line boats. He had enjoyed riding them around Manhattan when he had first arrived five years ago. He liked pondering the skyline from the harbor, feeling the cutting wind and listening to the guide's spiel ("Spuyten Duyvil — so named because an early visitor won a wager to swim across the narrows 'in spite of the devil' "). The excursions had made him feel that he could conquer New York and make it his own.

As a youngster, Boxby was about as self-confident as anyone could be who was named Elmer back in the days when Elmer Fudd's stutter and shotgun made him the laughingstock of every American child who grew up in front of a TV. He was raised in Norman, Oklahoma. His father, a nasty piece of work, toiled on the night shift at a chicken slaughterhouse, and Boxby was taught to tiptoe around the house mornings; waking his father would bring a lashing with a belt. He had one advantage: He was ambitious, which made up for what he lacked in social acuity.

In high school, he thought he'd try politics. In his freshman year, he went to a meeting of "GSA," thinking it was the General Student Association. It turned out to be the Gay Students Alliance; he was too embarrassed to leave. For the rest of the year, classmates passing him in the hall snickered and nudged one another. His father learned of the story and meted out a punishment unexpectedly creative: He dragged him to a barber and ordered the man to shave his head. Elmer reported to school the next day blushing like a red billiard ball. He grew fat, played the tuba in the band, and fantasized revenge.

He worked hard but wanted even better grades. To escape his miasmic existence, he broke into the guidance counselor's office, upped his grade point from 3.2 to 4, and won a scholarship to Yale. There he was accidentally tapped for Skull and Bones (a case of mistaken identity), which led in time to an overture from the CIA. He readily accepted; he found the duplicity attractive. After participating in various failures — to predict the end of the Soviet Union, the bomb in India, the rise of the Taliban — he was furloughed indefinitely. To get rid of him, the agency provided him with a résumé that touted him as a management whiz. He took over a limousine service, a toilet paper company, and an industrial farm, which, among other things, closed his father's chicken slaughterhouse. (The old man went on welfare, sunk into a depression, and died; Boxby did not attend his funeral.)

Leaping from one company to another like a frog on lily pads, Boxby developed a reputation as a person to hire when your business got sick. And by the late 1990s, with places like craigslist gobbling up classified ads and the country fixated on the idea that news should be a two-way street, no business was as sick as newspapers. Hagenbuckle heard about him while playing squash at the New York Racquet Club and snapped him up as his top administrative assistant and vice president.

Hagenbuckle! How Boxby despised that man, with his stuffed antelope heads, his aristocratic mien, and his mangled Shakespeare. He certainly didn't deserve to run a corporation like the *New York Globe,* a position he acquired through the simple expedient of dressing up in a tuxedo and saying "I do." Hagenbuckle would never bring the paper into the twenty-first century. His officers were relics of another age. Every week, they checked the advertising and circulation figures and scratched their heads in mystification when the figures went down.

A paper could be a cash cow if you used it right. Mark H. Willes, formerly of General Mills, had had the right idea at the *Los Angeles Times:* knock down that stupid wall between the advertising and editorial departments. What was wrong with running occasional puff pieces on major advertisers? They deserved something for their money, didn't they? How else did you get them to take out more ads? Why not position the ads next to promotional stories?

Striding around the pier, Boxby pulled out a pack of Marlboros. He extracted his old Zippo, which he liked clicking open against his thigh. He lighted up, inhaled deeply, and looked over at New Jersey. He turned and saw the *Intrepid,* which reminded him once again of Hagenbuckle and sent him into a coughing fit.

His cell phone rang. He knew who it was but had to answer — there was a price for not doing so. He flipped it open.

"Yes. . . . Yes, I know. I know we've only got a short time. . . . Yes. I will. I have a plan. It's infallible. . . . Yes, I know what's at stake. And of course I still want the job. And I —"

The line went dead.

As he closed his phone, he wondered what the hell he was going to do. In the past, he had never lied to a superior — not out of principle, but out of practicality: If you were caught, that was the end of the game. But this was different. He had never dealt with someone as vicious as Moloch. That man would eat babies for breakfast. How could he say he had no plan?

He wandered back to the *Globe,* past the drunks lining up for food at St. Luke's kitchen. On Eighth, he noticed that Puss 'N Boots had closed, its doors chained shut, its marquee denuded. He walked back up Forty-fifth Street and entered the *Globe*'s lobby. It was unusually empty for this time of day. Must be because all those employees are staying home lest they be attacked by "the Avenger," Boxby thought.

There was one other person waiting for an elevator, a young man carrying a paper bag. The car arrived, the doors opened, and the young man stepped inside. Boxby followed him and couldn't help noticing that his fellow passenger had pressed the button for thirteen — his own floor and the publisher's.

A moment later, Bernie Grabble lurched into the car, hitting the closing doors with his shoulder. The impact sent him sprawling against a wall, but he prevented a fall by grasping the shoulder of the young man, who seemed to recoil. Boxby had nothing against Grabble — the man was a dynamo — but he didn't think he'd keep him on as metro editor once he became publisher. That is, *if* he became publisher — a possibility that was beginning to recede. But then something happened, something incredible, which made the possibility revive.

Grabble looked at the young man, frowning slightly, as if he was trying to place him. The man attempted to hide the paper bag behind his back, but Grabble had already spotted it and noted that the only button illuminated was for the thirteenth floor.

"You're on your way to the top, eh?" he said.

The young man nodded.

"How's it feel to be *the chosen one?*" Grabble asked, a smile creasing his face.

The young man smiled back awkwardly and just said, "Fine."

Grabble got off at the fifth floor. Boxby and the young man rode upward. Boxby's heart was beating fast. This could be the moment of truth. Fate might have delivered his long-sought prey right into his hands.

"Tell me," he said, turning to smile at the young man. "What's your name?"

"Stengler," came the reply. "Charles Stengler."

33

Jude took the express train to City Hall for the mayor's news conference. On the front steps, the city councilman he had exposed as a crook was hemming and hawing before a bouquet of microphones. As he denounced "the jackals of the press," his eyes fell upon Jude and he pointed a shaking finger and thundered: "And there he is — King Jackal himself." The reporters looked over. Some waved and smiled and a few pointed their mikes at him just for spite.

Jude passed through the metal detector at the front door and turned right for room nine, the pressroom. Its wooden double door was plastered with more than a score of tiny brass plaques, one for each newspaper that had died over the previous five decades. Some reporter had tagged it "the door of a thousand broken hearts."

Inside, the room was hot and smelled of old sandwiches and stale beer. Unlike the police pressroom, it was a hive of activity and intrigue. The desks were squeezed in so tightly, scarcely a foot separated them. Mountains of paper were piled on each, outraged reports from watchdog groups and defensive government press releases, interspersed with banana skins, pizza boxes, and Styrofoam coffee cups. The place was like a crowded Mayan ruin littered with the detritus of sightseers.

The closets were filled with donated cases of Christmas scotch. The walls, which bore posters announcing the annual roast of politicians at the Inner Circle, were grimy and seemed freighted with a history of cabals, alliances, and conspiracies that attended the juncture of local politics and a free press. "If these walls could talk," one of the regulars used to say, "they'd be kneecapped."

Years ago, Jude had filled in at room nine but, to his relief, was never permanently assigned there. Still, he had been around long enough to learn the basic rules: Never strike a deal with a tabloid reporter, never ask a question at a news conference for a story you're secretly working on, and never score an exclusive without first informing the room's reigning monarch, stately old Joe Fitzgibbon of the Associated Press.

At first, the hubbub was disconcerting. Several reporters were shouting into their phones. Four of the regulars were over in a corner, trading information. A lobbyist was holding forth with two reporters nearby, wheezing in laughter at something one of them had said. Edmund Riddleman, the city's most notorious PR man and fixer, resplendent in a three-piece suit, was perched on a reporter's desk, leaning down and stroking the man's forearm. "You don't understand," Jude heard him purr. "He's a family man. He really loves his kids. That's why he wants to spend more time with them."

A reporter walked in behind Jude. He had been one of those attending the councilman's press conference outside. A knot of regulars closed in on him like iron filings on a magnet. They began taking notes from his dictation and stopped after about a minute. "Whaddaya think?" said a reporter from the *Grifter*. "Nothing here," responded the man from the *Maul*. They dispersed instantly.

Sam Armstrong, the *Globe*'s bureau chief, spotted Jude and shouted, "You here for the press conference?"

"Yes."

"I'm not going to be big-footed, not again. I'm sick of it."

"Sam, I don't give a shit who writes the story. I'm just here to see what I can pick up."

"Oh, I see. Okay." Armstrong walked over and put an arm around him. "So, Jude, how you doing?"

The number-two *Globe* reporter at City Hall poked her head around the door. "It's about to start." She saw Jude and smiled. "Well, if it isn't King Jackal."

Before Jude could reply, most of the reporters had grabbed notebooks and tape recorders and rushed to the door, pushing and shoving one another. They ran across the rotunda to the mayor's end of the building. The cameras and lights were already set up in the Blue Room.

The mayor marched in from his office across the aisle and stood on the wooden podium. The police commissioner, in a sparkling-clean uniform, looking grim, stood to his right. Jude saw Bollingsworth seated in the front row, along with three other detectives.

The mayor looked around the room, scowling, his customary expression for the Fourth Estate. His tan seemed to soak up the TV lights.

"We're here to discuss the situation at the *Globe,* where, as you know, a second murder

345

took place yesterday afternoon," he began. "I've asked the police commissioner to join us, so that he can bring us up-to-date on the progress of the investigation. We do not have a major announcement to make, I'm afraid; there has not been a break in the case. Nonetheless, I want to assure the people of the city of New York, and in particular the employees of the *Globe,* who have been working under horrendous conditions this past . . . week . . . that we are doing absolutely everything in our power to bring the person or persons responsible for these heinous crimes to justice.

"And now . . . if you have questions . . ."

He stood to one side and the commissioner stepped before the lectern. Hands shot up and a dozen reporters shouted. The mayor edged his way forward again and leaned down to the microphones, his voice suddenly loud. "If you're orderly, you'll all have your chance," he said crossly.

One by one now, the reporters yelled out their questions.

"Are there any suspects?" "Do you have any indication of a possible motive?" "Don't you agree that it's an inside job — that the Avenger is someone who works for the *Globe*?" (This last was from a *Maul* reporter.) "You said 'person or persons.' Do

346

you have any reason to think there is more than one killer?" "What can you say to New Yorkers who are afraid to walk around midtown? Would you advise them to keep away from the *Globe*?" "Do you see any connection to terrorism? Is the terror alert going up?"

Neville Dumpster leapt up. "Do you think," Animal asked, "there is a hit squad of readers angered over the *Globe*'s poor sports coverage who are systematically eradicating its staff?" Others continued shouting. "Have you composed a psychological profile of the murderer?" "How many detectives are working on the case?" "In view of the fact that a so-called bundler was used to kill the second victim, is the city planning to sue the manufacturer?" (This came from a reporter from the *Financial Day*.)

The police commissioner batted the questions down like badminton birds. But then came an unexpected one.

"Have you obtained the killer's fingerprints?"

To everyone's surprise, he answered with a curt "Yes." This set off a cascade of other questions: "Where were the prints found?" "Whose are they?" "Have you found a match?" "How do you know they belong to the killer?" The police spokesman, a small man in a gray suit, walked over and whispered into the commissioner's ear.

"No more questions on that," the commissioner said.

Looking at her from behind, Jude thought he saw Bollingsworth shake her head. After four more questions, he pulled out his cell phone and sent her a text message that read DRINK TONITE?

A few seconds later, he heard her phone beep. A few reporters snickered as the commissioner glared at her. She opened her phone, read the text, and left the room. A minute later, Jude met her just as she was opening the door to depart.

"I didn't mean to embarrass you like that."

"I wasn't embarrassed. I just had to get away. You provided me with a good excuse."

He walked outside with her and they went down the steps.

"I see . . . so, you want to meet?"

"Sure."

"I know a place. It's called Blues Basement, downtown —"

"I know it," she replied.

"I figured you would. Eight o'clock?"

"Okay. Maybe later."

"About those fingerprints —," Jude began, but she cut him off.

"Lord, look how the man uses me," she said over her shoulder as she strode off.

By the time Jude made it back to the Blue Room, the news conference was over. The TV lights were no longer concentrated on the podium, but shining in separate spotlights all over the room. Against the dark blue walls and blue curtains trimmed in gold, the TV reporters were doing their stand-ups.

"And so," said a broadcaster from New York 1, "we learned that the investigators into the Avenger killings at the *Globe* have come up with a crucial bit of evidence — the Avenger's fingerprints. We don't know which . . . ah . . . fingers the prints came from. . . ."

Sam Armstrong walked over, looking a little shame-faced.

"So, you want to take the story after all?" he asked.

"What you mean is, you don't see much news there — right?"

"I wouldn't put it like that. But the budget's coming out tomorrow and I gotta put something together. You know how it is — a bureau chief never sleeps."

"He just puts other people to sleep."

Sam walked away and Jude felt someone tap him on the shoulder. It was Hank

Higgle, looking wan.

Higgle beckoned to him to follow, then walked out into the rotunda and up the grand marble double stairway to the second floor, where he stood near one of the fluted Corinthian columns. He glanced around, then reached into his vest pocket and pulled out a piece of paper.

"Look at this."

In the center of the single sheet was the message "R U Nxt?" The rest of the paper was blank.

"See?" said Higgle. "*Are you next?* It's a threat. I told you I'm in danger. First Ratnoff and then me."

"No. First Ratnoff and then Whibbleby. If these murders are really because of that story on police corruption, where does she fit in?"

"I haven't figured that out yet."

"You shouldn't have handled that piece of paper. And you ought to hand it in to the police. It could be evidence."

"*Could* be? It is. I'm wondering if I should ask for police protection."

"*Protection?* But you work at police headquarters."

"Exactly. That's why."

Jude told him to contact Bollingsworth and gave him her phone number. On his way out, he looked in at room nine. The reporters were huddled in a pack, flipping through their notebooks and conferring.

"Okay, it's agreed," said one, summing up while the others nodded. "A double-barreled lede. Fingerprints found but no suspect yet."

34

The J&B felt good and Jude began to unwind. For the first time in a long while, he had left work by six o'clock, having cobbled together a halfway decent story, leading with the police commissioner's revelation and throwing in some bits and pieces of the publisher's remarks, lame as they were. He lifted his glass in a toast to the woman sitting across from him.

"Priscilla Bollingsworth — isn't that a strange name for a cop?"

"I guess a cop wasn't on the list of things my parents wanted me to be."

"So . . . what do people call you?"

She took a sip of vodka. "My parents call me 'Pril.' The other cops call me 'Bollocks,' which, if you happen to be British, means 'bullshit.' It's intended as a compliment — I think."

"What *did* your family want you to be?"

"Brain surgeon. Wall Street tycoon. Nobel

scientist. Opera diva. Something that combines prestige and money."

"And brothers . . . sisters . . . do you have any? What do they do?"

"I see. . . . We've entered the old 'time to check out the family,' have we?"

Jude smiled. She seemed different; she had from the moment they'd practically collided at the top of the staircase down to the Blues Basement — more friendly, more open. And she even appeared different — she had washed her hair, which fell in loose waves, framing her face, and put on a dress. She looked beautiful and — he couldn't help noticing — seductive.

"Just curious," he said.

"Capsule summary. Dad's a partner in a big law firm. Mom stays at home, engineering the lives of her children. Three residences — a Park Avenue apartment, a house in Palm Beach, another one in Mexico —"

"Your family isn't pressed for money, I take it."

"You could say that. Two younger brothers. One is at Goldman Sachs, the other at Union Theological Seminary. I went to Hunter, then Sarah Lawrence. I got in because my father gave a dorm. I'm not hard to place."

"Not hard to place! You're a cop. How the

hell did you choose that?"

"The challenge, I think mostly . . . and it's certainly been that. More of a challenge than I thought. Bit of rebellion, too. I think I thought we Bollingsworths were a bit too upper-crust . . . time to drag the family down a peg or two."

"That's not a real reason."

She took another sip. "You're right. I wanted the excitement. Plus, there's the element of public service. And I really like the job. Murder investigations — each one's a puzzle."

"Especially this one."

She nodded. "Especially this one."

"How come you're not married?"

"Aha! The question he was dying to ask . . ."

At this point, the manager of the club, a bohemian-looking woman in her seventies, came over, a big grin on her face. She stepped behind Bollingsworth and put both hands on her shoulders.

"Pril, honey. Been a while. You gonna sing for us tonight?"

"Not tonight, Betsy. It's been a long day. Besides, no band."

She introduced Jude. They chatted for a while and the owner moved over to a platform in the corner, where a trio was setting up. The drummer was testing the cymbals with the brushes. A tall guy was opening a bass case.

"You sing?"

"Amateur stuff."

"And play as well?"

"Piano. I'm in a band with three guys — guitar, bass, and drums. We're all cops. We call ourselves the Blue Blues. What's the matter? You look surprised."

"I am. Palm Beach . . . Sarah Lawrence . . . blues. I'm having trouble putting it all together."

"*You're* having trouble. Imagine how *I* feel." She finished her vodka and ordered another drink for them both.

"You never answered my question. Why aren't you married?"

"The question assumes you think I should be. Anyway, what makes you think I'm not?"

"No ring."

"Maybe I'm unconventional."

"I don't doubt that for a minute."

"I was — married, that is. I married a cop — that was before I became one. It lasted a spell, but it sort of ran out of steam. He turned mean. Mean and jealous. He also drank a lot. If it kept going that way, I could see the whole thing ending with some kind of accident involving a service revolver and headlines in the tabs."

"You still see him?"

"Not much. The city's a big place. . . . Of course, the PD's its own kind of village. I hear about him from time to time."

The second round of drinks came. She seized the moment to turn the tables. "And how about you — are you happy in your career and your life?"

"That's a pretty big question. Half and half, I guess."

"Where does *Jude* come from? Your parents were Beatles fanatics?"

"I guess. I'm not sure. . . . My family's from Michigan. They're pretty straight, actually. My dad's a lawyer. Good guy . . . drinks too much, or used to. He's stopped now, or so I hear. My mom works at different jobs. I went to the University of Wisconsin, then came east, tried my hand at a few jobs. . . . None of them stuck, until this one. This one's it for life. I've been thinking of trying to go abroad for the paper, but I don't know. . . . As you may have gathered, the *Globe*'s a weird place."

"I'll say."

They were silent for a moment.

"So this story means a lot to you," she said. "It could help or hurt."

"Yes."

"Same here. And so far, I have to say . . . it's not helping."

"What do you mean?"

"A high-profile case and we're not making much progress. The pressure's really coming down. You were there today, at that press conference. The PC would love nothing more than to stand there with the Avenger in leg irons. And we're far from that. By the way, do you guys always ask such inane questions?"

"Usually, not always."

"I have to say, my respect for the press isn't going up."

"You're aware that the word *press* only covers newspapers. What you're objecting to is TV. We call that 'electronic media.' "

"Well, it's enough to make one reexamine the concept of freedom of the press."

"You know what A. J. Liebling said? 'Freedom of the press is guaranteed only to those who own one.' "

"That's good. I'll remember that."

The band finished setting up. They were conferring about something — probably the playlist.

"Anything new in the investigation?"

"Very smooth — the way you segued into that."

"Don't have much time. Music's about to start."

"Not really new. We got Peregrin Whibbleby's autopsy report. Time of death is between noon and two p.m., more or less. No surprise there."

"At the news conference, the commissioner said you found prints."

"Yeah. He shouldn't have said that."

The band started in, nice light jazz. Jude moved his chair close to hers so that they wouldn't have to speak loudly.

"Where'd you find them? The prints."

Bollingsworth held up her hand in a stop sign.

"One thing I can't tolerate — talking while the band's playing."

The bass player, a light-skinned African-American, kept smiling at their table. At the intermission, he walked over, a handsome man, thin as a matchstick.

"I thought it was you," he said, leaning down to give Bollingsworth a peck on the cheek. She introduced them — Spike Giles was his name — and Jude invited him to join them. They made small talk while Spike sipped a rum and Coke. He tried to convince her to sing a song or two, but she demurred.

"Voice is hoarse," she finally said.

"Honeysuckle, you'll just sound even better."

"Spike, don't make me say *no* to you. You know how I hate that."

He gave a great big sigh, heaving his thin shoulders with a deep breath, shook hands with Jude, gave her another peck, and returned to the bandstand. The music started up again. She nodded her head ever so slightly, in perfect rhythm.

At the end of the set, she leaned across the table and said, "Thanks for sending that guy Higgle to me. He showed me the note. I owe you for that."

"Will you be able to tell who wrote it?"

"That's not a sure thing. It only consists of five letters and they're printed. Printing's easier to disguise than handwriting. Still, it's something. . . ."

"And it fits your theory — that Engleheart's responsible."

"Maybe. You can't tell. It could be a bit of opportunistic freelancing."

"You mean somebody who didn't commit the murders taking advantage of them."

"That's right."

Jude paused for just a second. "Let me ask you something. If I give you a name, can you get me his phone records?"

"Someone at the paper?"

"Yes."

"Reporter?"

"An op-ed columnist."

"In theory it's possible. We have access to all the records. The publisher, Hagenbuckle, gave them over."

"What! Without a court order?"

"Of course. When it comes to finding the murderer, he's not one to stand on ceremony. You'll have to tell me whose phone records you want and why."

"Let me think about it." Jude knew that if he told her about the anonymous tipster's tape recording of Max Schwartzbaum, she'd demand it, perhaps even subpoena it. He wasn't prepared to cooperate that far.

"Suit yourself," she said.

"Bearing in mind that you owe me, as you say you do, let me ask you about the prints you found."

"You can ask, but I can't tell you. Jude, I'm afraid on this one, I really can't. It could fuck everything up."

Before he could respond, the bandleader went to the mike and announced a song — "Ain't Misbehavin' " — and, casting a friendly look at their table, dedicated it to the two of them.

Jude raised his eyebrows. She smiled back.

Then she leaned over and placed her hand on his.

"One thing I want to say," she said. "So there's no misunderstanding. You're a young man . . . unattached as far as I can tell . . . and you're a straight shooter. But if you're looking for sex from me, forget it. It ain't gonna happen."

He was taken aback by her candor.

"I'm not saying you're right," he replied. "I'm not saying you're wrong. But just for curiosity's sake, let me ask: Why not?"

"On principle. It's a bad idea. It reminds me of that joke about the Polish soldier. He's got one bullet in his rifle and he's rushed on one side by a German and on the other by a Russian. Which one's he shoot?"

"I give up."

"The German."

"Why?"

"Business before pleasure."

35

The *Globe*'s twenty board members took, as always, the same seats around the thick mahogany conference table. The arrangement had grown over time, emanating from some primitive herd instinct. They reminded Hagenbuckle of cows. When cows leave the barn in the morning and enter in the evening, he had heard somewhere, they always file by in the same order. That's the first sign of mad cow disease — when one of them jumps the line.

As custom dictated, they had been whisked up to the thirteenth floor in an elevator set aside for them. That way, the cynics on rewrite remarked, they wouldn't mingle with the hoi polloi, lest they learn something about what was actually going on at the paper.

Hagenbuckle took his usual place at the head of the table, not far from the autographed photo of Douglas Fairbanks. He cleared his throat and looked around, mentally ticking off who would be for him and who would be against him. He did this by rote before every meeting, and it was usually an empty ritual, because the answer was always the same. But at this meeting, which he had been dreading for days, the head count could prove crucial if it came to a vote of no confidence in his leadership. He convinced himself that it was in the bag. Still, he couldn't quite stifle that nagging doubt that something could go wrong.

The only members who really counted were the ten voting members. Two of them were his twin sons, Rosen and Guilden, seated next to each other near the photos of Edgar Bergen and Charlie McCarthy. Another three were distant cousins of his wife, seated between photos of Haile Selassie and Brigitte Bardot. The five remaining voting members were lawyers appointed by the family trust. On most issues, his sons and the cousins voted on his side and the lawyers voted on the other — five for and five against. Since he was entitled to cast a deciding vote in case of a tie, he invariably won. In this manner, like a contestant in a three-legged race, the *Globe* had hobbled forward, striving for critical decisions in the brave new digital age.

So if his sons and the cousins stayed in line, he would emerge unscathed from all this murder unpleasantness.

The other ten board members, the nonvoting ones, were from the worlds of finance, arts, and philanthropy. They were there largely for decoration. They functioned as either cheerleaders or a Greek chorus of doom, depending on whether the stock was up or down. The most outspoken among them was Paul Martinet, chairman of the French luxury-goods conglomerate L'Eau Soignée Arriviste. But the real danger was Nathaniel Geyser, a vole-faced entrepreneur. Geyser had turned the Syracuse Sheetrock Company into a powerhouse of investment and insurance and viewed himself as a revolutionary gadfly. He asked tough questions and was a personal thorn in the publisher's side. At a recent meeting when an issue he raised had been voted down, he was heard to mutter, "We got the brains and they got the votes — go figure!"

Hagenbuckle called the meeting to order and stared at Geyser. Geyser stared back. Neither wanted to be the first to look away, and they might have gone on like this for quite some time, locked in a visual hammer hold, had not Boxby, seated behind the publisher and to his right, spoken up.

"Shall I read the minutes of the last meeting?" he asked.

There were murmurs of assent and Boxby pulled his chair forward a good six inches (typically, he moved up by increments, so that by the meeting's end he was sitting with his elbows on the table).

The minutes, from before the murders, seemed to Hagenbuckle to conjure up a prelapsarian era. The concerns were so simple, so ordinary. They had to do with normal business affairs that had seemed alarming at the time but now appeared almost quaint — how to arrest the falling stock, how to enforce economies, what to do to attract advertisers.

After the minutes were approved, the meeting took up new business. The first item was contentious, a vote to spend twelve million dollars for repairs at the Queens plant, the hypermodern printing facility where all mechanical functions, like transporting rolls of newsprint to the presses, were performed by robotic carts. The robots needed upgrading. The item passed, six to five.

The vote reminded Hagenbuckle of the importance of family. And this, in turn, reminded him of his orphaned nephew. In only a week the young man was to learn of his true parentage. The publisher wondered whether he should inform the board members of this development. How would his sons take it? He quickly discarded the idea, falling back on one of his favorite maxims — that ignorance is bliss.

He heard Boxby clearing his throat, an officious sound if ever there was one.

"Now we come," his administrative assistant said, "to the issue of security, which has been heightened in recent days, as you all know." He seemed to be licking his lips. "The floor is now open for observations and suggestions to deal with, ah . . . recent problems."

Martinet leaned forward. "Ze murders — she is bad for biz*ness,*" he said. He noted that by this morning, the stock had gone down by sixteen points (it sounded like "sex-teen") and that his outfit, E.S.A., which held 6 percent, had been "surly" (he meant *sorely*) tempted to sell.

The five voting lawyers nodded in agreement. Not a propitious sign, thought Hagenbuckle.

"I must say," said one, "waiting in the lobby for the elevator to arrive, I thought I detected fewer employees around than usual. It wouldn't surprise me, given the situation, if many of them were staying home."

Hagenbuckle assured him that this was not the case.

Geyser leaned back in his chair, twisting a pencil on the blank legal pad before him, and said he'd like to ask one question. "What," he said, "is being done to catch the murderer?"

Hagenbuckle ran through all the steps the *Globe* was taking: the ID checks, the extra security, the constant police presence, the talks with the mayor. After each one, Geyser gave what sounded like a tiny snort.

When the publisher was finished, Geyser swiveled his seat toward him with little ballet steps, so that the two were face-to-face. "Tell me this," Geyser said. "From all that we've seen and heard, it would appear that the murderer is on the staff of the newspaper. Would you agree?"

"I don't know that I'd go that far," replied Hagenbuckle.

"What's 'far' about that? It's a simple deduction. You've had two murders, both inside the building, both in areas closed off to the public, both apparently requiring inside knowledge of how the place functions. The killer mocks you. He leaves a body in the newsroom with a note on it! He turns another one into a piece of sculpture and takes an ad out to tell you where it is! How many more clues do you need to prove to you that you're dealing with an inside nut job?"

Hagenbuckle couldn't think of a good answer. "I don't know," he said.

"For God's sake, that was a rhetorical question!"

The publisher looked around the table. His sons looked worried, and so did the cousins. He seemed to be losing support. Damned lemmings, he thought, they leave you at the first opportunity.

"Well, big shot," he said finally. "You tell me. What would you do?"

Geyser didn't hesitate. He swiveled his chair back to face the table, stopped playing with his pencil and placed it above the leather-framed blotter pad, in perfect alignment with its upper green border.

"I'll tell you. . . . It's very simple. . . ." He was drawing out his answer for maximum effect. "If you believe that the murderer is on your staff . . . and you know that the police have obtained the murderer's fingerprints . . . then you simply order everyone on your staff to be *fingerprinted*."

He sat back, a look of triumph in his eyes.

"You can't do that," said Rosen, leaping

to his father's defense. "That's self-incrimination or something. It's in the Constitution. The Bill of Rights."

"No, it's not," said Geyser.

"We could research that," said one of the nonvoters. "See if it is or not."

"Even if it is," put in one of the cousins, "you could make it voluntary. Then whoever refuses includes the murderer. The names go on a list that you give to the police."

"Right," said another cousin, almost shouting.

Hagenbuckle realized that the moment of truth had arrived.

"It just so happens," he said grandly, "that we have already drawn up a fingerprint program. We've got the pads. We're just waiting for the ink to arrive. We'll be starting any day now."

"Bravo!" yelled Guilden.

"Zat is verie clever," remarked Martinet.

The little white lie had its intended effect. Geyser, deflated, sputtered into silence. The board mutiny was over. There had been no call for a vote of confidence.

After a few more bits of business, Boxby proposed calling the meeting to an end. Guilden seconded the motion, which passed, with three abstentions. The board members gathered up their coats and briefcases and moved onto the special elevator.

There they go, the cows, thought Hagen-buckle.

The publisher started for his office. Boxby, whose office was next door, followed.

"Want a drink?" bellowed Hagenbuckle.

Boxby, straightening his bow tie, said yes.

The publisher took two glasses from a wall cabinet, along with a bottle of single-malt scotch. From a drawer he extracted a screwdriver with a yellow handle. He opened his half fridge, pulled open a container that held a single block of ice, and chipped away at it with the screwdriver.

Boxby frowned. Wasn't that a job for an ice pick?

Hagenbuckle poured them each three fingers' worth, slid a glass over to Boxby, and sat under the trophy of a moose with a full rack. He raised his drink in a toast.

"Well, Boxby. What did you think of the meeting, eh? I think I acquitted myself pretty well." He took a generous sip. "As the Bard said: Some men are born great, some have greatness thrust upon them, and some become great by dint of their own efforts."

36

There were those who said that the *Globe* should have canceled its annual retreat at the Shallow Brook Country Club in Westchester. But Hagenbuckle insisted that to do so would be to capitulate to "the atmosphere of discomfort" brought about by the fact that a serial killer was on the loose. Indeed, he argued, if there was ever a time to hold a conference, this was it. The "staff" — he made it sound as if he were talking about household maids and butlers — needed "a little bright spot." He added, "The only thing we have to worry about is worry itself."

Shallow Brook, like the *Globe,* had seen better days. The ivy had eaten into the mortar of the main building and had been removed, so that the redbrick fortress, complete with turrets and crenellated upper walls, stood denuded on its hilltop, looking suddenly out of place among the pencil-thin firs and leafy elms. The cottages spread around the grounds were barely serviceable. The plasterboard walls in the bathrooms showed the odd water stain, seeping down like Brillo pad rust, and circles of flaking paint dotted the bedroom ceilings, often directly over the beds. The oval rag-woven rugs gave off a slight moldy smell. The place tried to paper over its deficiencies by adopting an Old West theme, on the theory that this might discourage complainers, who would be regarded as eastern tenderfoots.

The first day's session was uneventful. In the Rough Riders Room, the podcast editor, Jessica Sizzler, gave a morning talk about the *Globe*'s Web site, entitled "When the Tail Wags the Dog." To lighten up the mood, she began with color slides of a dozen different canine rumps taken in Central Park. Then the attendees were assigned to breakout groups in rooms along the Chisholm Trail: "Libel in a World Where Everyone's Famous," "Who Says Hollywood Stars Aren't Fair Game for Stalking," and "A Smaller-Size Newspaper Can Still Print Big-Size News." The Human Resources Department ran informative workshops: "Your Pension's Not Really Dwindling, It's Just Growing Less Quickly"; "Retirement at Fifty Makes Dollars and Sense"; and "A

Buyout Can Mean a Big Wet Kiss."

In the afternoon, the senior editors were forced to attend GIMIC (games intended to mold internal cohesion) in the Wranglers' Yard. These corporate games, imported from Harvard Business School, were intended to build group spirit. In "the Circle of Trust," editors were forced to stand on one leg on upended logs, able to keep their balance only by touching the outstretched hands of their colleagues. But Suzanne Preston, the culture editor, began giggling and Vickie Gimmy, the national editor, pushed her and they all fell off their logs into one big heap. Several were badly bruised.

There were cocktails at an open bar from 5:15 to 5:25. The keynoter during the dinner of chicken with rice was the witty op-ed columnist Bridget Muldoon, speaking on "From Nixon to Cheney: Why Dickheads Rule Washington." Afterward, most of the staffers withdrew to the Good Luck Saloon, the pay bar in the basement done up as a stable. Tables occupied separate stalls, hay was strewn around the floor, and bridles hung from the rafters.

Jude found O'Donnell in the Tombstone stall. He had four shots of bourbon in front of him, the glasses in a line on an upended wooden barrel — "one for each year I lived through today." Jude went to the bar and returned with a J&B. When he got back, two of O'Donnell's shot glasses were empty.

"You see the notice?" Jude asked quietly.

He didn't have to specify which one. The *Globe*'s in-house information sheet, "Longitudes and Latitudes," had been posted in the main lodge. No one was talking about anything else. At 9:00 a.m. the next day, all staffers were to report to the main ballroom, the O.K. Corral, for mandatory fingerprinting.

"Course I saw it."

"What are you going to do?"

O'Donnell shrugged. "Not much to do, kiddo. I'll let them take my prints, like everyone else."

"And then . . ."

"And then, as soon as I wipe the ink off my fingers, I'll cross them."

"You could refuse, you know. It can't be legal for an employer to fingerprint the entire staff and turn the prints over to the police."

"What would that accomplish? All that'd do is turn that big old finger of suspicion around and point it right at me."

"But I'd refuse, too. I'm sure we'd get others to join us. We could make it into an issue, maybe involve the union."

O'Donnell looked over at him, touched.

"And to think I accused you of cozying up to the cops." He downed another shot. "But thank you, no. I prefer to let things run their course. One way or another, that road of ink is going to lead to me. But don't forget" — here he blinked repeatedly and turned his face upward like a waif — "I've got the cloak of innocence to protect me."

"Still, I wish you hadn't gone around badmouthing Ratnoff all over the place."

"But I never bad-mouthed Peregrin. I may have said she was a dim-witted gossip maven who was dragging the paper into the gutter and wouldn't know a decent story if it bit her in the ass, but hell, everyone says that. It's hardly an indication I'm a murderer."

"And your — I don't mean to pry. . . . I'm just talking as your friend. . . . But your alibi for the time of her death holds up — right?"

"I'd say that depends on the time of death . . . and how long it took for the killer to turn her into *Winged Victory.* As I said, I went to the Greeks for lunch with Van Wessel, but that didn't take very long. Then I was back at my desk."

"The reader ad about Peregrin was sent from your computer shortly after two p.m. There's a chance — just a chance — that someone saw who was using your computer."

"Obviously, I've thought of that. There're two possibilities. One possible witness is none other than our very own Dinah Outsalot. She comes in about that time to rehearse her TV show —"

"I saw her there just the other day. . . ."

"Well, you can forget about her. She's about as much help as you'd expect from a Texan grande dame in love with her own shadow. She can't remember. She's not sure of the day or the time or whether she saw anybody or not. Put her on the stand and the jury'll vote to hang me."

"Who's the other?"

At that moment, Vera Slaminsky, the *Globe*'s acerbic book critic, walked by. She moved with the grace of an eel. Everyone, inside of publishing and out, was petrified of her. Her reviews were incisive — the way sharks' teeth are incisive — and they cut deep because they were so intelligent. Mortally wounded authors could only take to their beds. Slaminsky wasn't intimidated by the country's most famous writers. Quite the opposite, she seemed to set the bar even higher, and if they didn't clear it, she let them know in no uncertain terms that they had failed not only themselves and their readers but all of American culture.

"Speak of the devil," said O'Donnell.

"No!"

"Yes. As chance would have it, Ms. Slaminsky has a storage closet near my cubicle. Her habits are as regular as clockwork — more regular, in fact, since she does not require daylight savings time corrections. She writes her reviews at home, but once a week — always on the same day — she comes to my floor and goes through the locked cabinet of books sent in by publishers. She picks out the two or three that interest her, and disposes of the rest. The whole operation takes somewhere around half an hour. She must have been there that day."

"So have you asked her?"

"Ask *Vera Slaminsky?* Me? Are you kidding? I'd rather wrestle with a puff adder."

"Let's go talk to her. Right now."

"Okay, but give me a moment." O'Donnell lifted the fourth shot glass. "I need some Dutch courage." He downed it and grimaced.

By the time he and Jude looked for her, Slaminsky had disappeared. They searched in the bar stalls and asked for her in Smugglers' Gulch, the recreation room, where a dozen reporters and editors were trying to hustle one another at the pool table. No one had seen her. It was the same in the Sidewinder Room upstairs, where a small group of young reporters was gathered at the feet of Skeeter Diamond, who was telling them about the time he was jailed in Lagos, Nigeria.

". . . Fourteen hours without food," they heard him say, walking by, "and when they finally brought me something in a filthy bowl, it was awful, totally inedible. . . ."

Jude and O'Donnell stepped outside. It was a crystal-clear night, unseasonably warm. Overhead, the stars gleamed brilliantly against a black-blue sky.

"We'll find her tomorrow," Jude said.

They walked toward their rooms, passing by a cottage named Jesse James. The lights were on and they heard voices coming from inside. They drew close and looked through the open windows. Sitting in an easy chair was Max Schwartzbaum. He was talking expansively, sitting on the edge of his chair and waving his arms in tiny circles. Around him, seated on the floor and leaning against the walls, were about a dozen reporters and editors.

Schwartzbaum's words floated through the windows.

"Look, I'm not saying all this is Skeeter's

fault. He's not directly responsible for the murders. You'd have to be crazy to say that — even though some people criticize him for maybe creating the *atmosphere* that allowed them to happen. No, I've got a different bone to pick. It's the way he's *reacted* to the murders. Typically passive. Typically *do-nothing!* Where is he? What's he doing? I mean, this is a crisis, for Christ sake.

"Times like this, you need a strong leader. You're all a bunch of good reporters — the best in the business! Why hasn't he assigned every last one of you to track down this murderer? Get him once and for all . . . pin him to the wall. In three days' time, the whole mess would be solved and the *Globe* would be righted. But what's he do? Sits there in his office checking his goddamned e-mails. That's not a way for a real leader to act. Now me, I'd do it differently . . . not that I'd want to come back, of course. I've got my column and I love it, but if the place needed me, hell, I'd feel it was my duty."

Jude and O'Donnell moved away, stepping quietly onto the grass.

"If I didn't know better, I'd say that has the makings of a palace coup," said Jude.

"Yeah. Treason in the air. Nothing like a little murder to bring out the worst in people."

They came to the paved walkway to their cabins. O'Donnell reached into his inside jacket pocket and pulled out a sheaf of papers and handed them to Jude.

"Tomorrow's another day, as the philosopher put it. Meantime, here's some bedtime reading for you, if you're up to it."

Then he turned and walked off whistling, as if he hadn't a care in the world.

37

Jude poured himself a scotch from the mini-bar and sat on a lumpy sofa, his feet resting on a coffee table. The moment he finished reading the first page, he felt a sinking sensation. It was an e-mail from Ratnoff to Sol Frenchy, the managing editor of the *St. Louis Star Inquirer.*

Dear Sol,
I appreciate your bringing that grave matter to my attention. I do not know how to respond, other than to avow that we, like you, view such a possibility with horror. *Horror* is a word that I do not use lightly. We will, I assure you, under-take an immediate investigation. If our conclusion bears out your own, we will punish the reporter in question to the maximum extent of the law. Since an apology does not begin to redress the situation, or convey the depth of my

contrition should what we both fear prove true, I will dispense with one and simply promise to report back to you as soon as I have something more definitive to say.

Sincerely,
Ratnoff

The e-mail that had prompted this reply was missing — perhaps it was the very one that O'Donnell had said was gone when he rummaged a second time through Ratnoff's computer files. But it was easy to guess the nature of Frenchy's complaint. It was all too evident, laid out in the packet of articles from the *Globe* and other newspapers. The *Globe* articles were more than just similar to the others; at times, they employed *the exact same language* — not just in odd phrases here and there but in whole paragraphs. And all the *Globe* articles carried the same byline: Edith Sawyer.

At the top of the packet was the story from the *St. Louis Star Inquirer* that had brought the protest from the paper's managing editor. It was a feature on a rehab treatment center for army soldiers and Marines wounded in Iraq that appeared August 20. Four paragraphs had been expropriated and appeared almost word for word in the *Globe* story two weeks later. Among the purloined bits was a quote from a young Marine from Ohio, who had had both legs amputated and who said, dry-eyed, "The only time I don't think about it is when I dream. I dream I'm running down a football field into the end zone." The *Star Inquirer* reporter had used it in the second paragraph. Sawyer had saved it for her kicker at the end.

The breadth of Sawyer's plagiarism was stunning. It was wholesale theft. The packet included scores of articles from newspapers and wire services all across the country. Evocative descriptions, clever phrases, even ideas — all had been picked up and inserted into the pages of the *Globe.* Early on, some of the language was disguised, as if Sawyer had halfheartedly tried to cover her traces, but by the end, most were repeated verbatim.

Jude couldn't believe it. He chased his disbelief with a strong slug of scotch.

Ratnoff had done his work well. He had cast a wide net, apparently employing anti-plagiarism software to turn up stolen passages from a wide array of sources. A handsome description of palm trees in Graham Greene's Panama had found its way into a story about El Salvador and a village of huts built on stilts in André Malraux's Indochina turned up in a dispatch about a bombing in Bangkok.

Jude looked at Sawyer's dispatch from a battlefield in Afghanistan and remembered reading it at the time and being impressed.

Like wind through the leaves swept the whisper: "They're coming! They're coming!" Cries of alarm were heard as a wave of last-minute preparations ran through the troops. At the same moment, although the day was still, a light breeze rose over the army, the men's uniforms fluttered, and a flag flapped against a staff. . . .

Suddenly a shot rang out from among the Taliban, then another, and a third . . . and all through their broken ranks there was smoke and the crackle of gunfire. Several of the Marines fell . . .

Stapled to it was a fragment of text. Jude was aghast. It defied belief. But there it was: Change "the Taliban" to "the French" and "Marines" to "our men" and you were reading *War and Peace.*

He couldn't fathom such deceit. And by a seasoned correspondent! What had possessed her to ruin her career and probably those of a whole line of editors who should have caught her? Once this story got out, it would be another body blow to the credibility of the *Globe.*

Jude finished the scotch. He wondered, Had Ratnoff approached her? Had she known the ax was about to fall? Is that why the original e-mail from St. Louis was missing from the file — had she taken it? He pictured the big man calling Sawyer into his office, closing the door, asking her to sit. Ratnoff would have certainly enjoyed that part of it.

The question Jude didn't want to ask was circling around the periphery: Was the fear of exposure sufficient motive for murder?

He rose and began pacing — just like Grabble, he thought. Now he understood the compulsion to get up and stride about. His room was stifling. Without putting on a jacket, he opened the door and looked outside. The night was crisp, bracing. The stars were bright and a half-moon was up, enough to bathe the lawn in a luminescent glow. He stepped out and followed a gravel path that cut straight across the silver grass.

He walked slowly along the path as it curved around a cottage and led to the main lawn, an ellipse formed by the conjunction of all the walkways. From here, he could see the façades of most of the cottages. At the center of the ellipse, there was a small flagstone terrace. On it was a flagpole. A breeze stirred the empty lanyards and bounced the clips against the metal pole, making hollow thwacks.

He wandered along another path until he came to a bench set against a large bush that enveloped it on three sides. He sat down. There was the smell of freshly cut grass. The shock he had felt in reading Sawyer's stories turned to a calming numbness. His mind drifted.

He thought about the various contending scenarios and suspects. About Engleheart and his ties to corrupt cops and the exposé of police corruption sitting in Ratnoff's computer. About Higgle's fear down at the cop shop that he would be next and the warning note he had received. About the anonymous tipster and the taped conversation between Schwartzbaum and someone else, about the former executive editor's desperate ploy to enlist a grassroots campaign to overthrow Skeeter Diamond and take back control of the *Globe.* About O'Donnell and Van Wessel and all those countless others who were angered by the direction of the paper and who had hated Ratnoff's guts and wished him good riddance.

O'Donnell — what might happen once his fingerprints were found to match those on the *National Enquirer*? He was trying to appear cavalier about the whole thing, but Jude knew him well enough to detect the undercurrent of fear. Just how solid were his alibis, now that there were not one but two incriminating pieces of evidence against him, the prints and the fact that the reader ad was sent from his computer? That pointed to the likelihood that someone was trying to frame him. But who?

He even thought of poor old Slim Jim Cutler, with his twisted visions of the Apocalypse. Greed, fear, revenge, ambition, religious fanaticism — they were all rearing their heads at his newspaper, playing out in some combination that had proved lethal. And now, added to the list, there was still another scenario, another suspect: Edith Sawyer.

Jude looked up. Suddenly, a flicker of light in one of the cottages nearby caught his eye. He peered through the darkness. A door was opening, not thirty feet away. He could see the name above it — Roy Rogers — and he could make out a man's silhouette, standing out against the shaft of light in the doorway.

The profile looked familiar, but Jude couldn't quite place it. The man was leaning toward another silhouette, a woman. The man kissed her somewhat awkwardly. She turned toward him, as if responsive, then pivoted without a word and hurried along an adjacent path. As the moonlight caught her, Jude saw that she was wearing a red beret. He knew who she was.

He stayed on the bench a full five minutes, watching the remaining silhouette. The man stood outside smoking. His cigarette gleamed in the dark. Finally, he turned and went inside, closing the door softly.

38

Schwartzbaum waited in the kitchen, peering through the diamond-shaped window into the dining room, the Chuck Wagon. He had been there twenty-five minutes, trying to ignore the curses he was eliciting from the waiters, who wore cowboy hats and were sullenly trying to bump into him with their trays. Then he saw the person he had been waiting for: Hagenbuckle, headed for the breakfast buffet. Max bolted through the door.

Startled by the tap on his shoulder, the publisher almost dropped his melon slices speared with toothpicks bearing little chef's hats.

"Oh, it's you," he said.

He agreed to join Schwartzbaum on the veranda. His guard was up — the man hadn't said a civil word to him in months. The columnist led him to a table off by itself at the far edge of the slate-covered terrace.

Wet leaves had pressed themselves into a brown montage on the tabletop, and the moment he sat down, he felt his buttocks settling into a pool of cold dew.

"Glad I happened to run into you," began Schwartzbaum. "I've been thinking about this whole . . . murder business. I expect you have, too. Am I right or am I right?"

Hagenbuckle looked up, blinking. He hadn't expected to have to answer a question so soon and he hadn't been listening all that closely. He nodded noncommittally, a sideways flick of the head. Schwartzbaum plowed ahead.

"A couple of the reporters invited me into their cottage last night — a couple, hell! More like two dozen. They wanted to talk. Naturally, they're concerned. They turned to me for guidance. You know, I've always been sort of a father figure for most of them. All part of executive responsibility, if you know what I mean. Anyway, they seemed to have a lot of grievances about the way Skeeter's been handling this whole thing. *A lot of grievances.* They think he's been too weak — too weak and not really in charge. Maladroit. Deceitful. And pusillanimous. And cowardly."

Now the publisher was paying attention. He put on a solemn face, frowning.

"I tried defending Skeeter," Schwartzbaum continued. "For the better part of an hour. I know how hard his job is — I've been there, not through times like this, of course. We never had anything like this when I was in charge, but still, we had our moments, our little dramas. They seem small now, compared to this, but still . . . Where was I . . . ?"

"Skeeter."

"Yes. I defended him to the best of my ability. But you know what? After a while, I had to concede that they had a point. Maybe he's not the right man for the job. Maybe he doesn't have what it takes. Maybe this whole thing isn't just a horrible combination of circumstances. Maybe it comes in part from his leadership or his *lack* of leadership. Maybe" — and here he homed in on Hagenbuckle's soft spot — "maybe the fault, dear Brutus, lies not in our stars but *in ourselves.*" He was quiet for two seconds. He judged the moment to be ripe. "What do you think?"

The publisher collected his thoughts. "Think?" he replied.

"Yes. What I'm saying is . . . if I read you correctly . . . and don't forget, we go way back . . . is don't you think someone else should take over? Someone tougher."

"Someone tougher?"

"That's it!" Schwartzbaum slapped the tabletop, sending up a spray of water that struck his right collar. "You're brilliant."

"You mean someone with a firm hand!" Hagenbuckle was getting into the spirit of the conversation.

"Yes. Yes."

"I hear you. Someone prepared to be ruthless."

"Yes. Someone who knows the job, who's been there!"

Hagenbuckle paused, his mind seeming to soar over the distant firs, where turkey buzzards were riding the air currents. He asked, "You think we could get him?"

"Of course."

"Could we lure him back . . . from wherever he is?"

Schwartzbaum froze, confused. "Wherever *he* is?"

"I dunno. He left with his tail between his legs. I don't know if the staff would sit still for it."

" 'Tail between his legs'?"

"There was that whole scandal about our coverage of the run-up to Iraq. That reporter who wrote that Saddam Hussein had put missiles on a space station capable of hitting Texas and Tel Aviv simultaneously. Took us years to recover."

"You don't mean . . . you're not talking about . . ."

"Yes. Hickory Bosch."

"*Bosch!* Are you crazy? Not Bosch. Half the staff think *he* could be the murderer."

The buzzards began diving down in circles. Some animal must have perished in the woods. "I guess you're right," Hagenbuckle said. "Who did *you* have in mind?"

"Why, *me,* of course. *I* could do it. I'm happy where I am, but if pressed —"

"You?" Hagenbuckle was caught off balance. He burst out laughing. "Come on, Max. You know you're too old. That's not even in the cards."

Schwartzbaum stood up quickly and walked away, waddling with tiny steps in his fury. *Too old,* how dare he. And *Bosch,* of all people. He hadn't been talking about Bosch. It had been one of his few pleasures to watch that joker, with all his talking of improving the paper's "digestion," fall on his face so publicly. Not *Bosch — me!* No wonder the paper was doing so badly, with a dunce like Hagenbuckle in charge.

Jude slept late. By the time he took a quick shower, dressed, and made it to breakfast, the Chuck Wagon was almost deserted. The waiters had removed their cowboy hats and were clearing the tables, tossing the dishes together in hopes of chipping them. He managed to cadge a bowl of fruit and a cup of coffee, which he gulped down greedily.

He had not been able to fall asleep until 3:00 a.m. And then he had taken a pill. That was a mistake — it always took the better part of an hour to clear the cobwebs out.

He finished, left the breakfast hall, and entered the O.K. Corral, where the police were finishing up the fingerprinting. Only a dozen or so stragglers were still being printed. Bollingsworth was nowhere to be seen, but Jude spotted her partner and her driver. They were huddled over a long wooden table that contained a computer and a scanner. Stacks of thick paper, each with ten sets of prints, were being entered quickly and efficiently. The screen flashed one after another, like a conveyor belt.

The partner looked up. "We don't need yours," he said. "As you well know, we already got them."

"I'm looking for someone," said Jude. "Name's Vera Slaminsky. She's a book critic. I wonder if you can tell me if she's been through here."

"Fuck off," said the driver. Peering at the plastic replicas of bucking broncos that adorned the walls, he added: "And fuck the horse you rode in on."

Jude held up his middle finger. "You sure you printed this one?"

He took a side door that led to a long hall outside and found a small crowd reading a notice on a bulletin board. He feared the worst: Perhaps the Avenger had claimed another victim. But shoving his way to the front, he saw it was an edict enforcing new economies: Reporters on the road were told to stay at Motel 6; reimbursements for meals with sources were to be limited to $6.98 a person, and notebooks would no longer be provided gratis.

"It's not enough we're being killed at our desks," said one reporter. "Now they want to starve us out."

"Six ninety-eight," said another. "Isn't that what a Big Mac costs?"

"So now we have to buy our own notebooks," put in a third. "That's like Stalin shooting dissidents and charging their families the price of the bullets."

Jude examined the posted schedule for the half-day session, a series of panel discussions. He was assigned to one entitled "Why Not Give Readers What They Want?"

He scanned the others and found another panel at the same time as his, "When Good

Reporters Go Bad." One of the panelists was Edith Sawyer. How's that for typecasting, he thought.

A half hour remained. He passed it looking for Slaminsky. Finally, he checked with the front desk and was told the critic had checked out earlier that morning. He didn't come across O'Donnell, either.

His panel was attended by about twenty people in the Barn Dance ballroom. The panelists sat facing them behind a wooden table covered with green felt, table microphones, bottles of Evian, and cardboard nameplates.

The panel's chairman, Sydney Shivers, an op-ed columnist who had made his name as a conservative dabbling in pop sociology, kicked off the session by proposing readers' surveys as a means to boost circulation. Jude, who had probably been put on the panel as a counterbalance — people knew he sympathized with the old-timers — took the opposite tack. He argued that surveys were a way station to disaster. What readers required was not a mirror of their own preoccupations but the considered judgments of professional editors. Shivers responded with a little smile and some blather about the power of interaction.

"To hell with interaction," Jude declared.

"If people want interaction, let them go to a shrink or a ballpark or a leather bar. Let 'em stand on a soapbox or sing karaoke or write love letters. But if they want to know what's going on in the world, let them buy a newspaper. It's supposed to be information, not a conversation."

Shivers backed away, shaking his head as if to say it didn't pay to argue with a blockhead. At the end, Jude ducked out quickly and went to Bushwackers, where Edith Sawyer's panel was winding up with questions from the audience. An editor from real estate news launched into a diatribe about conflicts of interest, boondoggles, payola, and the like.

"What's your question?" asked the panel chairwoman.

The editor looked blank for a moment, then said, "Reporters who violate the public's trust — that happens maybe one time in a thousand. And yet that's all you hear about. People out there think it happens all the time."

"That's natural," replied the chairwoman. "It's in the nature of news. When planes land safely, it's not news. When one crashes, it is."

"But the paper's better than ever — the reporting, the analysis, the quality of the writing. It's higher than it's ever been. And yet every little fault we make gets magnified."

"Maybe we shouldn't have started printing corrections," cracked the chair. Everyone laughed.

Jude shot his hand up. "What steps are we taking to guard against plagiarism?" he asked. "What if we discovered that one of our reporters was stealing from other papers? Or from great novels? How would we survive that?"

The woman leaned close to the mike. "All I can say is, I trust that never happens to us." She talked about various safeguards.

But Jude had stopped listening. He was watching Edith. She reddened a bit, looked down, and poured herself a glass of water. He couldn't tell if her hand was shaking. When the panel was over, even as the audience was still clapping, she hurried down a side aisle to the coatrack. She pawed through it and extracted a camel's hair coat, and then, just before stepping outside, she added her signature red beret.

Half an hour later, Jude checked out at the front desk. He asked the longhaired young woman behind the counter if she could tell him who was staying in the Roy Rogers suite.

"Certainly." She checked her computer, moving the mouse around. "Here it is. That would be Mr. E. Boxby."

39

Driving back from Shallow Brook, Boxby handled his Lexus SUV smoothly and drove in the right lane. Usually, he swerved in and out of the fast lane, passing every car in sight, eager to get ahead. He hated being surrounded by slow drivers. As he often told himself, repeating his personal mantra, it's hard to fly like an eagle when you're surrounded by turkeys.

But today he had nothing to prove. He had already proved it, last night, in bed with Edith. Imagine! Him and Edith Sawyer! The publisher's assistant and a world-famous correspondent, together in the sack. After a couple of brandies in the Deadwood Lounge, he had seduced her. Or maybe she had seduced him — it was hard to tell. They were talking about travel and then airlines and favorite hotels and one thing led to another, and somehow she had wound up in his bedroom, standing right in front of him while he sat naked on the bed, except for his socks. She had removed every bit of her clothing in a sexy little dance that, he suspected, she had performed more than once before. No matter! This time, the dance had been for him alone. Then they had done *it,* not just once, but twice — well, maybe once and a half. That second time, he hadn't been all that excited, but she didn't seem to notice.

And then this morning, fate had unexpectedly smiled on him! He'd spied Hagenbuckle and Schwartzbaum deep in conversation on the veranda and slipped back into the main meeting room. There he spotted the publisher's briefcase. He pulled out the black book, his diary, turned to October 1, and found an entry that told him what he needed to know. "Today's the day for C.S." Confirmation! C.S. — Charles Stengler. Case closed! The young man he'd seen in the elevator was indeed the publisher's nephew.

Now he could push the plan forward. Discovering the young man's identity had turned out to be easy after all — though he wouldn't tell Moloch that — and now his reward was certain: He'd be the next publisher of the *Globe.* Dinner parties with celebrities! Visits to the White House! Meetings with world leaders! Life was good. It was exhilarating to be a Lothario, a cock of the walk.

His Lexus moved into the middle lane, began speeding up.

He lighted a cigarette, clicking his Zippo open against his thigh and then striking the flint, his practiced two-stroke motion.

He thought back to the retreat. Those old newspapermen, they just didn't get it. He had watched them during Jessica Sizzler's presentation, "When the Tail Wags the Dog." They were stuck in the Dark Ages. It all came down to a simple truth: Cutting trees in Canada, smashing them to pulp, trucking newsprint to New York City, putting printed matter on it, then trucking it to a million doorsteps across the country — all that wasn't economical. Use electronic impulses instead.

But these Neanderthals couldn't give up their sentimental attachment to the printed page. In the Q and A after Sizzler's speech, they were whining and complaining. That fellow on obits, Alston Wickham Howard, insisted that people never read more than two computer screenloads at a sitting. No problem: Limit the stories to five hundred words! And O'Donnell, the has-been, yammering on about "the serendipity factor," something about readers encountering unexpected stories that told them what they needed to know. In this day and age, people already knew what they needed to know.

Boxby's car had slipped over into the fast lane. Deadwood, that's what these so-called newspaper people were. And when he took over from Hagenbuckle, he would get rid of them. He would be the forest fire raging over the land, laying waste to the underbrush and preparing the way for new growth.

An image flashed before him: Edith's body in the half-light of the Roy Rogers suite. Had it really happened? He felt a sudden urge to talk with her. And there, right up ahead, was a service area. He took the exit and pulled into the McDonald's parking lot. Peering through the window he saw a group of reporters from the retreat eating there, so he ducked behind the dash before he took out his cell phone and turned it on.

He dialed the *Globe* and gave the automated answering system her name. There was only her voice mail.

"Hi. This is Edith. I can't take your call right now, but leave a message. I'll call you back."

She made it sound sexy.

He didn't leave a message. Up to now, he had been so careful in everything. He hung up quickly and felt a blush of shame.

His phone rang and he jumped. He looked at the dial. He had three voice mails, all from the same number. It was HIM! But he didn't feel like answering. That could bring him trouble down the line, but he didn't care. He was a cock of the walk.

Somewhere, deep down, he knew that Edith wouldn't have called him, and he believed that she probably wouldn't even have returned his call if he had left a message. That would change once he assumed his position of power. Or maybe — and this was a thought that held a certain appeal — he would get rid of her, too.

He gunned the Lexus and headed for his home in New Jersey, but he didn't make good time because the thruway was crowded with turkeys.

40

That afternoon, Jude went to the *Globe*. It was a Saturday, so only a dozen staffers were on hand, and they were hard-pressed with early deadlines and little breaking news to produce the voluminous Sunday paper. In place of its customary weekend soporific droning, the newsroom had an off-putting atmosphere of diligence.

Jude didn't normally work weekends, but he hadn't taken a day off since this roller coaster of a story began, and he wasn't about to start now. A multiple murder is not something you risk giving over to another reporter.

He went to look for O'Donnell on the eighth floor. His desk was strewn with notes and other research material, some of it undoubtedly about Ratnoff, but he was nowhere around. Jude didn't have the heart to snoop and run the risk of raising that Irish temper again.

Besides, Dinah Outsalot was less than twenty feet away, puttering around inside her test kitchen, and she could easily spy on him through the false window above the sink. She didn't usually work Saturdays.

"You seen Frank?" he asked.

She scowled at him from above — her kitchen was mounted on a platform to level the camera angle for her show. Her hand was poised over a bowl of chocolate, holding a measuring spoon, and her tongue was poking out. She was rehearsing a recipe for *Someone's in the Kitchen with Dinah.* It was a point of pride with her that the show was broadcast live.

"*Damn!* You broke my concentration."

"I didn't know you were cooking."

"This isn't cooking. This is creating. Licorice-glazed squab over mission figs, baby turnips, and *saupiquet* ravioli. I'm working on the dessert, a chocolate soufflé unlike any ever made. It contains a secret ingredient to make it swoon on the middle palate."

"Your secret ingredient looks a lot like Armagnac, judging by the bottle at your elbow."

"You may well be right. And now you'll please leave."

"One question first." He asked her if she

remembered seeing a stranger sitting at O'Donnell's computer the afternoon of Peregrin's murder. She said she had better things to do than try to remember who was sitting where. Besides, she said, the police had already asked her the same thing.

"You're double-teaming me. All I can say is I saw O'Donnell himself there at some point — before lunch, after lunch, who the hell knows? Frankly, who the hell cares?"

"The murderer might, for one. If you're a potential eyewitness, you ought to watch your step."

She said she could take care of herself. By way of proof, she hiked up her skirt to reveal, tucked into the top of her left boot, a pearl-handled revolver. "Down in Texas, we call this a 'girl's best friend' — next to a vibrator, of course. So don't you go worrying your sweet little head about me."

"You say the police asked you about this. O'Donnell did, too — right?"

"No, I can't say he did. Not that it matters."

She didn't notice Jude's frown because her thoughts were elsewhere. "Say, you want to go out to dinner tonight? You can be the fourth. I'm reviewing a place in the Meatpacking District. It's hot. Steaks beyond reproach. The atmosphere is . . . ummm, you'll just have to judge for yourself."

He was not about to be the first to decline an invitation from the food critic. It was the best freebie on the paper — the only proviso being that she ordered your meal (that way, she got to sample multiple entrées). They agreed to meet in the lobby at 7:00 p.m.

Back in the newsroom, Jude was bothered that O'Donnell had lied to him about talking to Outsalot. Why would he say he had done so if he hadn't? Or could she also have forgotten about that?

Once again, he was facing a blank computer screen that needed a story. One thing was certain: He wasn't going to try to jam in a piece about Edith Sawyer's plagiarism. That was a bombshell. The debate over how to handle it would go all the way up to the publisher, and to ensure that the story got printed, he needed to plot a strategy. Especially now that Sawyer had gotten her hooks into Boxby.

His phone rang. On the line was Neville Dumpster of the *Maul,* the voice of the deranged competition.

"C'mon, Animal. I'm on deadline. I don't have time for your shit."

"Matey, this is serious. It's confirmed, lock, stock, and barrel. I'm just calling to let you know because it's Saturday and you guys don't always staff the cop shop on Saturdays."

"Okay, let me have it."

"In a few choice words: O'Donnell. He's been arrested."

Jude's throat tightened. It could be, for once, that Dumpster was right. Jude had also tried calling O'Donnell at home, without success.

"What's the charge?" He tried to keep his voice level.

"Don't know. It's got something to do with that fingerprint gang bang up in Westchester. That must have been some scene, all the hacks lining up to get their dogs done. What was it like?"

"I wouldn't know."

"You wouldn't know. Don't tell me. What a fantastic data bank the cops are going to have. I figure it'll contain everything from shoplifters to bank robbers. Your fashion critic, for example — I never trusted her. I predict grand larceny at a minimum. Your Off-Broadway critic's kind of shifty, too. Never looks you in the eye. I'd say assault — definitely something involving violence."

"Are you going to write about O'Donnell?"

"*Going to?* I already have. It's on the Web. Top of the charts."

"Look, Animal. Thanks for the tip, but I gotta go."

"Sure you do. I understand. By the way, that cop you've been hanging out with is one foxy lady. Course, if you're hoping to get something out of her — I'm talking leaks here, not sex, matey — you're out of luck. She doesn't put out."

Jude hung up. He dialed Bollingsworth's cell. She picked it up on the third ring and must have pegged him on her caller ID, because she didn't even say hello.

"Calm down, calm down," she said. "I know you two are pals."

"But why arrest him? Believe me, Bollingsworth, he's got nothing to do with these murders."

"Yeah, well, when your prints turn up at the murder scene, that's at least a subject for discussion. And he's not under arrest — or not yet at any rate. We've just taken him into custody for a while. He's right here next to me."

"Can I talk to him?"

"Highly irregular."

Jude heard the phone being handed over and then O'Donnell's voice came on the line.

"Kiddo, how're you doing?" he asked cheerily.

"How *you're* doing is more to the point. What's happening? Are they going to charge you?"

"Who knows. They're treating me okay. . . ." On the line, Jude could almost hear O'Donnell looking up at Bollings-worth. "Slapped me around a bit, that's all —"

"You're kidding, right?"

"Right. Very much the opposite. I'm beginning to see why you've been spending so much time down here."

"She called us 'pals.' How did she know that?"

"I told her. I thought the way you de-scribed our relationship didn't do it justice. By the way, did you ever manage to reach that person we were talking about? The puff adder?"

"Slaminsky. I couldn't find her up in Westchester. Then the damned culture desk wouldn't give me her home address . . . said they weren't authorized to. Apparently, she's got too many enemies, all those writers whose careers she's snuffed out. I finally managed to wheedle it out of Suzanne Pres-ton. She lives in Chelsea. I stopped by, but there was no one home — or at least no one answered. I'm going to go back later."

"She's probably off strangling baby writers in their cribs. But keep trying — will you?"

"Sure thing," said Jude. He was relieved that O'Donnell wanted him to talk to her. "And maybe you should tell Bollingsworth about her."

"Why?"

"Could be other people are looking for her. If we figured out she might be a witness, the killer could, too."

"Okay, I will. I better go. Apparently, somebody here wants to ask me some questions."

"O'Donnell . . . before you go. I need to get into your computer. What's your password?"

There was a pause on the other end. Jude figured he was deciding whether or not he should provide it.

"Xanadu."

"Xanadu?"

"*Citizen Kane.* I always liked that movie." He covered the receiver for a moment. A bit of mumbling, then he came back on. "She likes it, too."

"Let me talk to her."

The phone shifted back.

"Bollingsworth, listen. Neville Dumpster of the *Maul* has got this all wrong. He's saying you've arrested O'Donnell. Soon he'll probably make up some charges. Can you call him and straighten him out?"

"That's asking a lot. I don't usually reach out to reporters."

"But he's got the story all wrong. It's already out on the Web."

"I thought real reporters didn't care about the Web."

"C'mon. This is serious."

"Okay," she said. "But you owe me. And I want to collect. I'll meet you tomorrow morning. Bethesda Fountain in Central Park. We'll go for a walk. Then you can buy me Sunday brunch. Ten a.m. Deal?"

"Deal."

They hung up.

Jude decided to talk to the weekend metro editor, and on his way there, he was surprised to find Fred Bradshaw in his neighboring cubicle. Fred's face darkened.

"What's that about O'Donnell? . . . I couldn't help overhearing. He's been arrested?"

"No, not really. They're just talking to him. Matter of fact, I'm on my way now to metro to warn them off the story."

Fred asked if there was any prospect of a break in the case. Jude told him that there didn't even seem to be any good leads.

"I don't think they're any closer to catching the killer than they were days ago. For some reason, as they explain it, having a second victim doesn't make it any easier."

Fred shook his head.

"I can understand that," said Charlie Stengler, popping his head above his cubicle. "If I write one news story — we're talking hypothetical here — that doesn't make it any easier to write a second one."

Jude noticed that Stengler was unusually animated. He had a large cardboard box perched on his chair and he was filling it with material from his drawers: pens, pads, files, a stapler, a box of business cards (still full), Scotch tape, stationery, the Green Book of city officials — all the right paraphernalia, as if he had been a dedicated reporter.

"What are you doing?" asked Jude.

"Moving on," he replied with a goofy smile.

"Fired?"

"Not at all. Promoted. They finally recognized quality."

"*Promoted.* To what?"

"Assistant metro editor. I'll be handing out assignments. I just heard about it ten minutes ago from some guy named Boxby."

"*Boxby!* He's up on the publisher's floor. He's Hagenbuckle's right-hand man. What's he doing handing out promotions on the metro desk?"

"I don't know, but I'm not about to question it. He's very nice, very accommodating. He said he was looking out for me . . . that he'd make sure I'd be going places."

"*Going places!* This is the first time I've seen you standing up."

"Learn to crawl before you walk — my motto in life."

"Does Grabble know?"

"I called him and told him."

"How's he taking it?"

"Pretty good, all things considered . . . especially since I'll be sitting at his elbow. He congratulated me and pretended that it was his decision. But I got the impression he didn't know who I was."

"But assignments . . . you hate assignments. You're always ducking them."

"That's what I figure. They realized it. They decided to take a poacher and turn him into a gamekeeper. Nobody'll be able to hide from me. It's brilliant when you think about it."

At the metro desk, Jude warned the weekend editor, Ellen Gaul, away from a story that said O'Donnell had been arrested. She nodded yes — glumly, observing that she had no big news. A second later, the phone rang. She listened for a moment, then leapt up in a paroxysm of joy, proclaiming, "Hot shit! Triple homicide in the Bronx! Could be a gang killing. We've got our lead!"

She sent two people to the Bronx, put a rewrite man to work the phones from the reverse phone directory, which listed numbers by addresses, and ordered up two sidebars. She assigned the main story to Vince McAdoo, rewrite's heavy hitter. In between, she could be heard singing "New York, New York." At one point, she muttered, "The city that never sleeps. Oh, I love you. You never let me down."

41

Jude found Vera Slaminsky in a coffe[
in Chelsea, where the book crit[
camped out in the one easy chair, c[
ing a latte grande and scowling at th[
Updike. "Piece of shit," she said to [
such a loud voice that six customers[
turned expectantly toward them, hop[
a fight.

"Couldn't write his way out of a[
bag to save his life," she continue[
pathetic when what emerges from a [
so-called creative artistic agony is r[
less than an abomination, a putrid [
cence, a metastasizing cancer on th[
politic."

"Doesn't sound good," said Jude. [
always amazed, those few times [
spoken to Slaminsky, at her ability t[
up with newer — and stronger — c[
nations of literary works. He orde[
espresso and sat down next to her.

417

"What are you selling?" she demanded.

He explained that he had come to see if she had happened to notice anyone at O'Donnell's workstation on the day Perrin Whibbleby was killed. Slaminsky thought for a moment. In fact, she replied, that was the one time in eleven months that she had broken her routine and stayed away. "There was a conference at Amherst on the death of the American novel," she said. "I felt I just had to go. Enjoyed every minute of it." She lifted the book up in front of her face. "Now, if you'll excuse me, let me see if I can locate the fading pulse of this dying patient."

On his way out, Jude ordered another espresso, this one to go. He nodded at Slaminsky and said, "She's paying." He finished it by the time he reached Forty-fifth Street and walked back into the *Globe.* He checked his messages, then saw Clive at the back of the room and joined him. The news assistant was trying to put together a feature story on the new video screens in the backs of taxis. Jude liked his lede.

Three days earlier, he had asked Clive to help him with research: to cull through every column written by Peregrin Whibbleby, compose a list of all boldfaced names, and feed it into the computer. There

418

it would be cross-referenced with a dozen other lists of names, ranging from politicians voted out of office to corporate executives guilty of felonies. One list was of all *Globe* employees, past and present.

"No luck," said Clive. "Nothing jumps out."

"Nothing at all?"

Clive shook his head.

Jude told him to pull up all of Peregrin's files from the *Grifter,* where her "TattleTale" column had run.

"But that was years ago," Clive protested.

"Eight years, to be exact. For a nutcase harboring a deep-seated grudge, that's the blink of an eye."

Clive agreed.

Jude returned to the eighth floor. Outsalot was gone and the rabbit warren of offices was dark. He hit the bank of light switches and watched the overhead neon tubes flash on in stages across the floor, a march of illumination that made the shadows jump.

He made his way to O'Donnell's cubicle, sat in his seat, and flicked on the computer. The screen came to life and blinked as it ran through the start-up program, then demanded: PASSWORD. He typed in X-A-N-A-D-U. It responded, seemingly grudgingly, but soon enough Jude was inside —

confronted with a long list of O'Donnell's files.

Most had nothing to do with Ratnoff. It took him half an hour to ferret out the ones he wanted, sorting them initially by date and eliminating all but those of the previous month. There were more than he'd expected.

It was a depressing dossier, for Ratnoff had functioned as the *Globe*'s J. Edgar Hoover, accumulating dirt on a multitude of employees. One deputy sports editor, whom Jude recollected fondly and who had simply dropped from sight one day, had, it turned out, inflated his expense account to finance a private S and M pad on Horatio Street. There was an entire file marked "Sexual Deviants" from the bad old days when being gay was sufficient cause to be barred from hire or promotion.

Intriguingly, Ratnoff had been accumulating reams of data about Hagenbuckle and, in particular, his wife, Abigail, and her family. There were references to letters, journal entries, and documents going all the way back to the early years of Tassius Appleby, Abigail's hard-driving father, who had wrested control of the paper and turned it into a powerhouse of journalism. Jude had heard enough about the Appleby legend to know that he had been born in Cyprus but, in terms of his early life, not much more than that. The material appeared to confirm a rumor that Ratnoff had been preparing to write a book about the paper's patriarch.

He looked at his watch: 7:10 p.m.

Outsalot was waiting for him in the lobby, drumming her long red nails on the faux-marble ledge that held the house phones. He apologized for being a few minutes late.

"I kept calling your line," she replied, making scant effort to disguise her annoyance. "By the by, something's off with your phone. There's a buzzing sound. And once I heard what sounded like a radio in the background. Do you listen to Howard Stern?"

He shook his head.

"I didn't think so. Well, somebody up there does. Typical of the newsroom. So retro."

The restaurant, Jude was surprised to learn when they arrived in the Meatpacking District, was a topless steakhouse called Lolita's. It represented, Outsalot explained, the cutting edge of a new trend — "sex and food, one-stop shopping." They were halted at a velvet rope outside by a hulking bouncer.

"Don't you know who I am?" she yelled.

She reached into her voluminous crocodile purse, pulled out a blond wig, and plopped it on her head. The bouncer recoiled in horror at his mistake, unclipped the rope, and bent so low that Jude thought he would topple over. It wasn't low enough for Outsalot.

They took a freight elevator to the second floor, which was bouncing with disco music and strobe lights. The other two guests were waiting at their table. One was a young man dressed in black, with ink black hair brushed up like a porcupine. The other, sitting there looking uncharacteristically abashed, was Edith Sawyer. Jude realized, in a flash, that she had set up the whole encounter. Maybe he should have seen it coming; she was, after all, a friend of Outsalot.

A topless waitress in lederhosen came by with the drinks menu. The others ordered cocktails whose names were unknown to him, and when he asked for a J&B, Outsalot cut in.

"Have a Cucumber Cutlass," she commanded.

The waitress reached behind and pulled four menus out from her leather-encased backside. Jude's was still warm.

"Be back in a jiffy," she said.

Jude engaged the young man in conversation. It turned out that he, too, worked for the *Globe* — in a new position, something he called "accessories critic."

Jude was confused. "You mean . . . automobiles? . . . You write for the auto section?"

His dinner partners laughed. Edith put a clammy hand on his arm.

"No, silly. Accessories, as in body adornment. It's big business."

"Oh, it is," put in the young man, touching Jude's other arm daintily. "But not, I'm afraid, as big as Howard's."

"Howard's?"

"Howard Luftsinger. He's our new perfume critic. Tomorrow he's critiquing ckIN2U — that's the new Calvin Klein fragrance — and fifty million dollars is on the line." The young man's voice dropped down a confidential notch. "But frankly, I don't think Howard's a power player. I don't think he can close a perfume."

"*Close* a perfume?" said Jude.

"That's right. He lacks the killer instinct. He can never deliver the coup de grâce. People *read* him, of course, but they don't worship at the altar. There's no blood on it."

Edith Sawyer made a point of seeming to empathize with Jude's point of view.

"Just think," she said. "We used to be a

family newspaper."

"We still are," said Outsalot. "Only now the family is under thirty and into fashion, drugs, and hooking up."

Another topless waitress came by. Jude noticed that she had one nipple pierced by a stud that was connected to a retractable pen, which she used to take their orders. Outsalot, straightening her wig, dictated them like a drill sergeant. The waitress released the pen and it snapped back into place on her bosom like a rabbit going to ground.

"Believe I need another Cutlass," said Jude.

"Switch to the Juniper Javelin," directed Outsalot. "I need to sample it."

He looked around the room, which was all abuzz. Behind the bar was an eight-foot-long water tank in which a naked woman was turning somersaults. A far cry from the carnivorous red tiger oscar in Slough's, thought Jude — or maybe not so far after all.

Scantily clad waitresses were giving lap dances to various customers, both men and women.

"That's on the menu," explained Outsalot. "But it's a big-ticket item. I don't believe my expenses will cover it."

"Darling," said the young man, "put it down as dessert."

"Don't worry," said Edith. "Who needs the hired help?" Her hand had strayed to Jude's thigh. He brushed it off.

Dinner — steak, lamb chops, pork loin, and chicken potpie (and another Javelin) — seemed interminable. It was followed by yet more drinks.

When it was over, the foursome stepped onto the cobbled street and breathed in the cool air. A mist was blowing in from the river.

"Not at all bad," said Outsalot, stuffing her wig back in her purse. "Quality meat, frisky wine, saucy decor. I'll give it two stars."

A Town Car was waiting for her and she offered to drop them off, mumbling quietly, as if she feared the offer would be taken up. Only the young man accepted.

Jude and Edith walked east, scouting the semi-deserted streets for cabs. She tried to link arms.

"Remember that night in Boston," she said. "The Democratic National Convention . . . we almost made it that night."

Jude grunted. He remembered it only too well.

"I've often wondered what it would've

been like," she continued. "A one-night stand, or do you think we would have continued — you know, gone down in the famous book of lovers at the *Globe*."

"Edith, look. I know what you're up to. You're sucking up. And it's not going to work."

"And why would I do that?"

"Because of my remark at the corporate retreat. Because you want to know what it is that I know."

"I *did* have the feeling that your remark was directed at me. Why in God's name do you think I would do something like that?"

"Because I *know* you did."

"You do?"

"Yes."

She fell strangely quiet. He waited a full thirty or forty seconds for her to break the silence.

"Maybe. Once."

"C'mon. It wasn't once. It was over and over. And Ratnoff knew about it. He was about to unmask you. It's all there . . . in his computer. Articles from other papers . . . a lot of them. Excerpts from novels. *War and Peace* — for Christ sake."

She fell silent again, and when he looked at her in the light from a streetlamp, her face looked suddenly old. He had seen that look once before in a man arrested on a murder charge. It was a look that said, It's all over.

"Why'd you do it, Edith? It was so unnecessary. I mean, you've already made it. You're respected. You're well known. Why do that?"

She considered the question earnestly.

"I did it," she said softly, "because I was tired." She paused. "Just tired. It's so difficult, this thing we do. Talking to people who don't want to talk to us. Interviewing people who've lost their families. Listening to officials lying. Jumping on airplanes to go to famines or earthquakes. Running off to places other people are trying to escape from. It's exhausting. Especially as you get older. I guess I just wanted to take a few shortcuts."

"*Shortcuts.* You took more than a shortcut. If you felt like that, you should have just quit. Gone out with honor."

"Of course. I know that now. I didn't then. It seemed . . . I don't know, almost harmless." She looked at him sideways, no longer flirting, simply uncertain. "What are you going to do?" she asked quietly.

"What I have to do. It'll come out, you know. There's no way it won't."

She didn't answer, just looked down.

"And there's something else. This whole thing could make you a suspect in the eyes of the police. I'm going to tell them about it. So maybe you should think of getting a lawyer."

"A lawyer! You're not serious."

"Yes, I am."

She took a deep breath. "I suppose you're right."

He flagged a cab, helped her in, and walked home, feeling that burning sensation once again in his esophagus.

42

"She's got the spirit of an Irish setter and the smarts of a German shepherd," said Jude. "Best of both worlds."

He threw the ratty tennis ball into the boating lake behind Bethesda Fountain and TK plunged after it, her back legs splayed awkwardly. Once in, she swam gracefully, only her head above water, bobbing.

"I envy you," said Bollingsworth. "I always wanted a dog when I was growing up, but my parents wouldn't hear of it. It would've messed up our fancy apartment."

"You're kidding."

"Nope. I used to think, First thing I'm gonna do when I'm on my own is get one. But now I can't . . . these crazy hours. It'd be cruel."

"My hours are crazy. I get a neighbor to walk her. It can be done. . . . So, you live alone?"

She gave him a hard look. "And your point is . . ."

"Nothing." He shrugged. "I just wondered."

TK jumped out, her russet coat clinging to her slender frame. She dropped the ball at Jude's feet and shook the water off, wetting both of them. They laughed.

"Let's eat," she said.

They headed up the path east of the lake, toward the Boathouse Restaurant.

"So your parents weren't exactly kid-friendly?" said Jude.

"Depends. They liked boys . . . especially my father. Both my brothers stand to get an inheritance. Not me. When I married, he was so pissed off, he wrote me out of his will."

"Jesus."

"Course, some of that might have been *who* I married. My father didn't approve of cops . . . in the family, that is. They were fine riding around in patrol cars protecting his spread in Palm Beach."

"And that's why you became one."

"Thanks."

"For what?"

"You just saved me a shitload of money. Now I don't have to go to a shrink."

Jude tied TK to the grillwork fence outside

the Boathouse. They found a table in a corner and ordered. Afterward, Bollingsworth turned squarely toward him and fixed him with an intense look that he recognized from the interrogation at the station house.

"Listen," she said. "I wanted to see you because I want to tell you something important." She said that the investigation had reached an impasse and that it was essential for him to tell her everything he knew, no matter how small or trivial it seemed. "This is serious stuff. . . . There've been two murders and there could well be another one. . . . It's not the time to play games or stand on ceremony and say that as a reporter you don't believe in cooperating with the authorities, because —"

"I never said that."

"Maybe not, but you think it. And it would be a mistake. I'm saying this now not just as a cop but as someone who wants to see this thing come to an end without more killing. You're well situated — you're inside the paper. You know a lot, or at least you're in a position to know a lot. You've got to tell me everything you can. You've got to play straight with me. It's important."

"When you say 'more killing,' you're thinking of who — possible witnesses?"

"That . . . and others. Who knows? At this

point, we still don't know if the killer eliminated Ms. Whibbleby because she was a potential witness or because she was part of some twisted agenda in his crazy brain."

"How about O'Donnell?"

"As what? Potential victim or suspect?"

"*Victim,* of course. You don't seriously think he could be the murderer."

"At this point, we're not ruling anyone out. His prints match up. That's obviously big on the minus side. On the plus side, he's got a halfway-credible alibi and you vouch for him — whatever that's worth. In any case, it won't hurt him to spend a little time in stir. He's being detained. We have another twenty-four hours before we have to either charge him or let him go."

"*Charge him?* You'd be making a big mistake."

"I understand your feelings. For obvious reasons, I can't share them."

"Did he tell you anything?"

"Not right away . . . all that crap about the 'puff adder' . . . coded messages. Honestly, he acts like a little kid. Eventually, he told us about Slaminsky. . . . I gather telling us was *your* idea. It's a good thing. We talked to Slaminsky about an hour after you did."

"How do you know I talked to her?"

"She told us. That's the point I'm trying

to make. You shouldn't be running off in all directions trying to solve this thing. That's our job, not yours. You can help us by giving us information, not by being Dick Tracy."

"Slaminsky didn't go in that day. She couldn't have seen anything. So she's got nothing to worry about."

"Only if the killer is *aware* she didn't go in. If the killer knows Slaminsky's routine, he knows there was a chance she spotted him at O'Donnell's computer. Anyone who was on that floor is vulnerable. Especially now that O'Donnell's been picked up. Until now, our hypothetical witness might have seen someone sitting at his computer and thought nothing of it. But now the witness will cop to the fact that the person he saw there was the killer. Or at least the killer might *think* he will cop to it, which comes to the same thing." She paused. "So my first question is: Did you tell anybody about Slaminsky, that she might have been there?"

Jude thought back. He had learned from O'Donnell about Slaminsky's habit of coming into the office on the same day each week. "A lot of people knew I was looking for her. We were at this corporate retreat up in Westchester — I guess you know that — and O'Donnell told me about her. He and I went looking for her at night. I tried again the next morning, so any number of people heard me asking where she was. I even asked your sidekick — what's his name, the one who was taking fingerprints?"

"Casey."

"And I asked your driver. He told me to fuck off."

"Typical. He's not a fan of yours."

"Somehow, I deduced that."

"We've put a watch on Slaminsky's apartment just to be safe. Incidentally, guess where we found her — in a movie theater, watching a rerun of *Bonfire of the Vanities*. She said she liked it a lot better than the book. Some literary critic."

A waiter brought over their food — eggs for him, a bagel and cream cheese for her. He refilled their coffees.

"You remember that morning we had breakfast at Neil's," she said. "You told me somebody saw Engleheart cleaning up the freight elevator, but you wouldn't tell me who it was."

"How do you know I knew who it was?"

"You're a bad liar. I found out, by the way. It was O'Donnell. . . . So what else are you holding back?"

Jude didn't hesitate.

"There's one other person who might

have seen the killer. Judith Outsalot, the restaurant critic. Everyone calls her 'Dinah.' But I think you've already talked to her."

"Yeah. Annie Get Your Gun. She seemed to have trouble focusing. Didn't give us anything."

She pulled out a notebook. "Another question," she said. "At the Blues Basement, you asked me if I could get phone records at the *Globe*. What was that all about?"

He remained silent for only a moment. He was bothered by the thought that he should have been more cooperative with the police. He knew this *was* more than a game. He decided to tell Bollingsworth everything he knew. So he told her about the tape he had received incriminating Schwartzbaum, which was what had led him to think of checking Schwartzbaum's phone records.

She began scribbling in the notebook. What seemed to interest her as much as Schwartzbaum's words on tape was the fact that an anonymous tipster had turned it over to Jude.

Then he told her about all the people who had it in for Ratnoff, about those who worried about the paper's declining standards, about Slim Jim Cutler's descent into religious mania, and — most significant — about Edith Sawyer's plagiarism, which Ratnoff was about to reveal at the time of his death.

Bollingsworth quietly wrote it all down, flipping pages as she went along. He suddenly understood how psychologically rewarding that gesture was: It made him want to divulge more.

"There're a number of leads here," she said. "Put together with the threat against Hank Higgle — which you were kind enough to tell us about in a timely fashion — there're a couple of new avenues to investigate."

"But are they likely to go anywhere? I was thinking just the opposite. You line up all these possible motives — ambition, quashing a story about police corruption, getting back at somebody who hurt your career, covering up plagiarism — when you look at them, none of them seems sufficient. I mean, *murder!* That's like cutting off your head to cure a headache."

"Ah, but I've seen a lot of heads fall for even more paltry motives."

"Maybe, but I don't get it. It reminds me of that old aphorism: 'Once a man commits murder, he is apt to commit robbery, which may lead to gambling, which may progress to drinking and then to telling lies and cursing and finally to Sabbath breaking. Many a man hath dated his ruin to some murder or other he thought little of at the time.' "

She laughed — a full-throated laugh. "You're full of sayings. First A. J. Liebling and now this. I may have to get that crocheted and hang it over my desk."

He finished his coffee and waved for the check.

"You mentioned Higgle. I take it you've analyzed that note he got."

"We did. The results aren't conclusive. With a small sample like that, they almost can't be. Still, we compared it to Engleheart's writing twenty years ago, when he filled out applications to join the department. Allowing for a change over time, they look pretty close. Not exact, but close enough to arouse suspicion. And of course there was plenty of suspicion about him to begin with."

"So you've got him under observation."

"Maybe. One thing I can't talk about is operational details. But I have to say I've been noticing other cops, his friends, acting strange lately. They're too friendly to me — either that or suddenly not friendly enough. They suspect something's up."

"I thought I'd write about Engleheart today — maybe not by name, but the fact that there's a story on police corruption in the hamper and that it's figuring in your investigation. That going to give you problems?"

He had never asked that question of a source before. His self-respect dropped a notch.

She thought for a moment. "I'd say that's fine. . . . So I take it you're going in to work today?"

"Yes. Why?"

"I'll call you there later." She anticipated his question. "I'll tell you why afterward. Meanwhile, if you don't have a car, I'll give you a ride home. That way, I can pick up that tape recording of your former executive editor and the note that came with it."

"Okay. I walked all the way up here with TK. I'm beat."

"And one more thing . . ."

"Yes."

"What I said about people being possibly in danger —"

"Yeah."

"That goes for you, too. And I don't think it's a good idea for you to come around the station house anymore."

The warning made him feel worse. It emphasized, in terms of cooperating with the authorities, just how wide a Rubicon he had crossed.

43

True to her word, Bollingsworth phoned Jude at his office an hour later. She issued a set of instructions: He was to call her right back at her desk, then call her from a nearby phone at the *Globe,* then call her on her cell. She refused to explain all the intrigue, but Jude had a good idea of what lay behind it. He did as she instructed.

"Good," she said after the third call. "I'll be in touch later."

"Four calls in a row. That's some kind of record. And here I thought cops didn't like talking to reporters."

"I didn't say I liked it." She hung up.

With her, he was learning, it was impossible to have the last word.

Jude checked out the other Sunday papers. For the first time since Ratnoff's killing, the *Maul* didn't run a story, but the *Grifter* was refusing to let a good thing die. It carried a speculative article quoting unnamed sources saying that an official of the mailers' union might be the killer: "Driven to distraction by a contract that paid him for not working, he wrapped up Peregrin Whibbleby in a frenzy of misdirected revenge at his own idleness." For Moloch, it was a typical double shot at two institutions he hated: the *Globe* and the union.

There was, however, an intriguing bit of news from the financial desk. After its long slide, the *Globe*'s stock was beginning to move up. That was contrary to logic. Why would the stock go up with a murderer on the loose? It appeared that someone somewhere was buying it, but who the hell would do that?

Jude began to fashion an article around the threatening note to Higgle and the fact that the police were analyzing the handwriting. He tied it to the story on police corruption Higgle and others had filed. If Engleheart and his buddies had anything to do with the murders, that would certainly smoke them out.

He was interrupted by a noise from the neighboring cubicle once occupied by Stengler and was surprised to find Fred Bradshaw there. On the floor was a large box of his belongings.

"What are you doing?" he asked.

"Moving," replied Fred, looking down shyly. "I asked if I could take over Stengler's desk now that he's been promoted. It's a little closer to the metro desk. I was thinking that might help me get some better assignments."

"You should speak to Stengler about that. It's his job now."

"I have. But you know, now that he's an editor, he's become hard to talk to. He keeps ducking my phone calls."

"He's got a lot of experience at that."

Jude started for the metro desk to run his plan by the weekend metro editor. The newsroom was deserted, even for a Sunday. It confirmed something he'd feared would happen. People were so frightened, they were staying home.

He walked by the rewrite bank. The reporters were lounging around with the Sunday sections spread around and their feet up on the desks. It was downtime. Rewrite was like a hospital emergency room — long periods of boredom punctuated by short bursts of unadulterated panic.

Vince McAdoo summoned Jude over with a nod of his head.

The dean of rewrite, Vince was old-school, a gifted reporter and writer. He played the ponies, chewed on a wooden matchstick,

441

and spoke in an unreconstructed New York accent. He had grown up only blocks away, on Eleventh Avenue and Forty-eighth Street, and he had applied for work at the *Globe* because it was the local employer. If he had lived near a slaughterhouse, he probably would have ended up swinging mallets at cows.

Vince, the last man at the paper to give up wearing a fedora, was a legend among the younger reporters. Most of them had been legmen for him at one time or other and he'd taught them, through the questions he asked when they phoned in, how to do their job. Details were everything. Once, when a woman shot her husband on Halloween and the jack-o'-lantern was still burning on their front porch, Vince sent his legman back to ascertain whether it was smiling or grimacing. Jude himself had been the subject of his grilling. In his second year, he had been assigned to a double ax murder in the Bronx, and when he phoned in to McAdoo, the first words he heard were "Give it to me, ace, the blunt end or the sharp end?"

McAdoo had not been out on the streets for two decades, and when Jude walked by, he was chewing the fat with three other reporters as if he were in his own living room. He broke off the conversation and took Jude to one side.

"Ace, I want to tell you something. The gray rat is here" — this was Vince's name for Skeeter Diamond — "which is enough to ruin anybody's Sunday. Anyway, he came by and said I should read up on the *'slay'* story in case I had to take it over for the day."

Vince was chewing his matchstick something fierce. "I like what you been doing. It's not easy writing with a dozen goddamn editors peering over your shoulder. It's a good story, but I don't want to big-foot you. I thought you should know."

Jude went directly to Diamond's office and pushed open the door. Diamond was inside, sitting at his computer. He was reading the blog Romenesko to check the mood in the newsroom. He was wearing blue jeans and a T-shirt, which made him look disconcertingly informal, as if he might have just dropped in after mowing the back forty. He looked up, surprised.

"I hear you're thinking of taking me off the story," Jude blurted out.

Diamond held up his right hand, palm outward, in a stop sign.

"Now don't jump to conclusions. I never said that. Who've you been talking to? That

443

damned McAdoo, no doubt. I didn't tell him to take over the story. I just told him to be *ready* to . . . to pitch in, in case we needed him."

"Why the hell would we need him?"

"It's at a . . . ah . . . delicate stage, winding down for a while. I was thinking of giving it a rest, just for a day or two. I notice you didn't have a story in today's paper. You know, sometimes it's as hard to phase out a running story as it is to get one going. . . . Why, once, when I was in Sierra Leone —"

"The story's not winding down. There're a lot of loose ends. It could go anywhere. We haven't gotten to the bottom of it yet."

"My point precisely. It takes experience to know where the bottom is . . . when to write something and when to hold off. We don't want to keep this droning on forever, you know, not until something . . . ah . . . new happens. Besides, it's not great for the paper."

"If you really care about the paper, you'll do one thing. You'll keep me on this story and let me pursue it wherever it goes. I'm not saying help me. I'm just saying get out of my way."

"Well, what do you have today, for example?"

Jude told him about Higgle and the note warning him that he could be next and about the exposé on police corruption. Diamond interrupted him before he was finished.

"Christ. Once you say we have a major story on police corruption in the can, we . . . ah . . . have to print it. What're you thinking?"

"That we'll print it. Especially now that it might be connected with Ratnoff's murder. It's a new angle. Everybody'll be chasing us. We'll come out looking good. Crusading journalism."

Diamond thought. "And Peregrin? Why was she killed?"

"She was involved with Ratnoff. So if the killer does him, he has to do her. The police are taking it seriously."

"The police," scoffed Diamond. "I wouldn't take *them* seriously."

"If I'm off the story, I'll lose my sources. People won't take *me* seriously."

"Oh, I wouldn't worry about that. There're a lot of stories out there. Why, in Africa —"

"And anyway, I'm working on a lot of other leads."

"Such as?"

Jude wasn't about to tell him about Edith Sawyer's plagiarism. A voice that he had learned to listen to over the years, in the same way he had learned to listen to the old-timers, told him to keep that one to himself for the time being.

"Just a lot of things. People conspiring. Maybe to bring you down and take over your job."

Now Diamond sat up.

"Names?" he asked.

"I'm not at that point yet. But as soon as I am, you'll have them."

Diamond looked pained. "Let me think about this some more. Meanwhile, you go back and keep working the story for now."

When he walked by the rewrite bank, McAdoo pulled him aside again and said he had called Grabble to come in and straighten it out. Sure enough, ten minutes later, Grabble stormed in and went right to Diamond's office. Raised voices were heard. After half an hour, Grabble came by Jude's cubicle.

"Keep it up," he said. "You're back on the story."

"What did you say to him?"

Grabble puffed up with pride.

"Oh, I just told him that if he took you off, the *Observer* would get on our case. Always works. He hates bad publicity. A murder in the newsroom or in a back

Somebody's bugging it. Watch your step. Don't stop using it — that'll just let them know you know. But use your cell for confidential conversations."

"Christ. This is all I need. You're making me paranoid."

"Better paranoia than Pollyannaoia."

"What's that?"

"The outrageous belief that one is *not* being persecuted."

44

After finishing his story, Jude decided to check out the morgue. He wanted to examine the archives of the Appleby family and see if he could discover precisely what it was that had so consumed the late, unlamented assistant managing editor.

He took the down elevator from the lobby. The door closed on the bright lights, the car rumbled, and the door reopened onto the cramped portico to the underground cave. Everything was the same — the scuffs in the concrete pillars, the time cards in their metal slots, the exposed pipes overhead. The passageway leading from the elevators, though lighted now, still seemed spooky, the way the beam from a flashlight can accentuate the surrounding darkness.

Ahead he saw the sawhorse barricade along the rim of the cavernous pit. It would hardly stop a blind man from plunging down three flights. He recalled that Bollingsworth had told him that she had installed a camera down here somewhere and had recently had it removed. Too bad. It would have been morbidly comforting to know that his movements were being recorded if anything went wrong.

He veered toward the morgue's banks of metal filing cabinets. They were seven feet high and arranged like walls in a complex maze. After several turns, he came to a central space, where there was a wooden desk, a goosenecked lamp, and an empty chair. A foot-high pile of books rested on the desk, along with a battered wooden card catalog, some pens, and a windup clock. The lamp was on.

He went to examine the spines of the books and was about to pick up the top one — *Zen and the Art of Motorcycle Maintenance* — when he heard a sound behind him. He spun around just as he heard a high-pitched voice exclaim, "Well, well, well."

It was not a friendly voice and he knew instantly whose it was.

"Sammy!" he exclaimed. "I forgot you worked here."

"So do they all," replied Slimowitz. "That's one of the fringe benefits."

"Even on a Sunday?"

"I drop in when the spirit moves me."

When he had been a copyboy, Jude was not one of Slimowitz's victims. On nights when he rode the shuttle across town to pick up the tabloids hot off the presses, with just enough money for ten papers and round-trip subway fare, he often walked instead, saving enough change to stop off for a beer. This invariably made him late, but Slimowitz did not castigate him. Perhaps he recognized that Jude had the right temperament to become a reporter, or perhaps on some level he admired his streak of rebelliousness, especially when it was directed at an assistant metro editor, a martinet who was widely despised.

Jude tried a bit of small talk, but Slimowitz, not one for social niceties, cut him off and asked him what he was doing there. He explained that he wanted to examine the files from the archives that Ratnoff had been reading.

"Welcome to the club," said Sammy.

"Others have asked you the same thing?"

"Two. One was O'Donnell. That was before Ratnoff was killed. . . . What do you think of that, by the way? You know, Ratnoff was the shitbird who busted me and consigned me to this dungeon. He finally got what was coming to him. I always say that's why the good Lord made the Earth round

— so you'd have a second shot at every motherfucker who messed you over."

"Who was the second?"

"Some policewoman. Came barging in, pushing her weight around. Even threatened me. I made sure she walked out with diddly-squat."

"Maybe you can show me what you didn't show her."

Without a word, Slimowitz marched off, his tiny arms swinging rapidly at his sides, leading Jude through a narrow aisle of cabinets.

"This is it," he said, stopping halfway down. "The Appleby family archives — all the deep, dark secrets of our overlords. Except, of course, that they've probably been vetted a hundred times to keep all those little Draculas in their coffins."

"And this is what Ratnoff was interested in?" Jude already knew the answer from his trips through the files lifted by O'Donnell.

"Yes. Especially this one." Sammy stood on tiptoe, reached up, and pointed toward a drawer. In black Magic Marker the label said "Appleby: Early Years."

"Do you know what he was looking for?"

"Not specifically. He claimed to be writing a book about old Appleby's family. He wanted every bit of background on the paper's founder. I don't know if you're aware of this, but he made two trips to Greece looking for more documents."

"Did he find anything?"

"If he did, he would have hardly confided in me. I'm too . . . *low* is probably the word for it."

Slimowitz led Jude to a large table off in a corner.

"This is where he read through the files," he said, pointing to an empty wooden chair.

This section of the basement had been the operational center for the presses. Jude saw that it still bore the marks of its former life. Above the table were metal hinges that had once held the conveyor belt that carried the printed copies upstairs to the delivery room. There was a red phone on the wall — presumably to receive the apocryphal command "Stop the presses!" from the editor in charge. Nearby was a bin that still contained the foot-long pneumatic-tube capsules that had carried messages to and from the composing room. The tubing snaked up the wall and disappeared into the ceiling.

Jude imagined Ratnoff sitting here for hours and wondered exactly what he'd been looking for.

"You don't mind if I go through the files?"

"Be my guest," Slimowitz replied, not warmly.

At first, he watched as Jude carried the files to the table and sorted through them, but eventually he got bored and returned to his Lilliputian domain. He picked up his book and began reading.

In little more than an hour, Jude discovered that something was amiss and he called Slimowitz over.

"I've gone through every file in this drawer," said Jude. "Not one of them has anything from the years Appleby spent in Cyprus. The drawer is marked 'Early Years,' but in terms of biographical information, everything begins in mid-career."

"Impossible!" said Slimowitz. He examined the card catalog on the desk, then pulled a stool over to the drawer, stood on it, and flipped through the files almost wildly.

"You're right. It's gone," he said finally. "There was an entire file on his childhood, his years in Greece, his voyage to America. It's all missing. Someone took it."

"Any idea who?"

"It could have been anybody. A whole parade of people came through after Ratnoff's body turned up. Grabble and Skeeter Diamond and Frank O'Donnell and Alston

Wickham Howard and Charlie Stengler and you, of course, and a host of others."

"How do you know that? I thought you work only two days a week."

"Word gets around. Suddenly, this place was Grand Central Station. You know who else came? You'll never guess. Wearing an old raincoat and with a cap pulled down and dark glasses. Hickory Bosch. He's grown a beard."

Hickory Bosch! Jude could hardly believe it. The former executive editor whose regime had collapsed in scandal over faulty Iraq reporting. Bosch had tried to remake the paper in his own headstrong image, promoting his acolytes and demoting those he deemed enemies. The *Globe,* he had insisted, must be "reborn" with "a new digestive tract," but the end result, the cynics on rewrite noted, was shaken baby syndrome. At the end of the debacle, Bosch was fired, and he pulled up stakes and settled in an old saltbox cottage on the shore of Cape Fear, where he indulged his passion for clamming. He had reportedly vowed never to enter the building again, a promise that seemed to sit well with the people who had served under him.

"What the hell would he have come here for?"

Slimowitz shook his head. "Who knows? Who cares?"

He closed the filing cabinet with a bang. "Shit," he said. "I hope none of the bigwigs find out that file is missing. They can't bust me any lower than this." He turned his small face up to Jude and in an unctuous voice whined, "You won't tell — will you? We were always tight, you and me. Remember how I looked out for you when you were a nothing kid?"

Jude looked down at him with pity.

"Don't worry," he said. "I'll be as good to you as you were to me."

45

Bollingsworth gave the doorman, Ernie, a big hello. Her parents — her father in particular — used to just breeze past with an imperious nod, so she had grown accustomed to overcompensating. She listened patiently as he brought her up-to-date on his family and then answered his questions, as best she could, about the *Globe* murders. She could tell, from all the red herrings, that he had been following the case closely in the tabs.

Eventually, she excused herself and went upstairs to her parents' apartment. It was a four-bedroom luxury spread on the twenty-second floor, high enough to give a view across two blocks to Central Park, from the Arsenal all the way to the Metropolitan Museum. As a teenager, standing on the open terrace, where she absented herself to sneak a cigarette, she used to stare down at the vast green rectangle and the escarpment of buildings on the West Side and feel something like respite from her parents' haranguing.

Nowadays, she went to dinner there once a month, which was enough to keep in touch but not so often that they would try to rule her life. Years ago, she had broken their hold. In fact, that had been a major reason behind her sudden marriage to Jake, the cop, and it had worked, even though the marriage hadn't. Still, it was surprising how old wounds could still hurt.

Her father refused to understand why she had chosen, as he put it, "a life consorting with killers and criminals." At the very least, he would say, usually before dessert, she might finish law school so that she could switch over to the DA's office, where his pull could assure her a good berth. Bollingsworth's mother, quiet and sweet-tempered, had a different way of expressing disappointment. Getting Pril alone in the kitchen, she might sigh and remark that it was a crime that she had wasted all those piano lessons — it had been clear, even as a little girl, that she had a gift for music. It was a shame that she had turned down Juilliard. "I suppose there's nothing to be done about it now," she would say, signing off, a slight lilt to her voice that seemed to invite contradiction.

They were having gin and tonics in the sitting room when the doorbell rang. It was Henry, her brother, the broker at Goldman Sachs. She was glad he had come. It had been months since they had seen each other. They got along and things seemed easier when he was around — his insouciance was catching. He walked in with a big stride and a grin.

"My big sister's got a helluva tiger by the tail," he said, kissing her on both cheeks and leaning back to hold her by both shoulders like a picture frame. "You solve this one and you're famous! On the other hand, if you don't —" He broke off with a laugh.

"Of course she'll solve it!" put in her father, freshening his drink at the sideboard. "You don't get to be a homicide detective in the New York City Police Department at the age of thirty-five without brains and stamina. And plenty of good old get-up-and-go."

She was pleasantly surprised: He had never talked of her profession with respect before. At the same time, his words emphasized the hard truth of just how much was riding on the case.

"You must be getting close, aren't you?"

he asked, peering over the top of his glasses at her. "It's been . . . what . . . a couple of weeks, no?"

"Yes," she said. "I mean, yes, it's almost been a couple of weeks. Not yes, we're getting close." She experienced a familiar dread low in her gut.

The doorbell rang again. While her father went to answer it, her mother sidled over to her and, holding a hand delicately over her chest, said in a low voice, "We've invited a young man from your father's firm. Now don't be upset. We're not attempting to fix you up with —"

"The hell you're not!" put in Henry, bouncing on the balls of his feet. He turned toward his sister. "Remember the old rule of thumb: Whatever they deny is true, and the more they deny it, the truer it is."

Her father rejoined them, his hand clasped on the elbow of a presentable young man, thin, with slicked-back blond hair and an open face. He grinned, as friendly as a puppy, introduced himself as Patrick Hanley, and shook hands all around, in the proper order — mother, son, then daughter. She could smell his aftershave.

"I've certainly heard a lot about *you*," he said knowingly, looking directly into her eyes, as if in fact he had taken several tutorials about her childhood. "All good," he added suavely. Her father beamed.

"You've been talking to an interested party," said Henry. "Hell, if you want the real skinny, I'll give you an earful. Sometime when you've got five or six hours."

"Oh, Henry," cooed her mother. Her father shoved a drink in the young man's hand. Bollingsworth noticed that he hadn't needed to ask Hanley what he wanted.

After small talk — the weather, the Yankees, the vicissitudes of the stock market — a woman in a black uniform appeared in the doorway and Mrs. Bollingsworth proclaimed, "Goodness. Must be time for dinner." They moved toward the dining room, the young Mr. Hanley lingering back to escort Bollingsworth. He was seated on her right. Everyone seemed to be smiling a lot.

Her father carved the roast beef, the maid came in with serving dishes, and there was a silence that went on long enough to be uncomfortable.

Henry looked at his watch. "How about that," he said. "It's twenty to. Every time there's a pause in a conversation, it's either twenty to or twenty after the hour. You ever notice that? They say it's because Lincoln died at twenty past seven."

"Is that right?" said Mr. Hanley. "I never

heard that."

"Check your watch next time it happens," said Henry. "You'll see."

Bollingsworth asked the young man exactly what he did at BlackDiamond, her father's venture-capital firm. Before he could answer, her father put down the carving knife and said, "Handles mergers and acquisitions. The engine room, let me tell you. And he's the rising star."

"Oh, I just shovel in coal along with the rest of them."

"Modest as always," said her father. "I approve of modesty."

"Unless, like Churchill said, you have much to be modest about," added her brother.

"Oh, Henry," said her mother.

The maid came to Mr. Hanley's elbow with mashed potatoes. He politely declined them.

"Now," he said, turning to Bollingsworth, as if no one else were there. "I want to hear all about your work. I understand you're on the trail of a serial killer. That sounds exciting."

"Trouble is, we haven't reached the exciting part yet. He's still at large."

"You mean you don't know who he is?"

"That's right."

"But you have some idea — right?"

"We have a couple of possible leads but nothing solid so far."

"I see. It's been a while, right? Since the first victim?"

"A while, yes."

She fell silent and shoveled food into her mouth.

"I hear homicides are up," he said.

"Nationally. That's not true for New York City," she said, swallowing.

"At least not yet."

"Not yet."

"Who's to say in the future."

"Who's to say."

Fortunately, at that moment, her cell phone rang. She pulled it out of the purse on the back of her chair, looked at the caller ID, and said, "I'm terribly sorry. I have to take this."

She rose and walked quickly out of the room, leaving her father frowning.

"Damned things," he said.

They heard her say in the hallway outside, "Oh Christ!"

Twenty seconds later, she came flying in, grabbed her purse, and headed for the front closet, saying, "I'm sorry. Have to go. Emergency."

Her mother was on her heels and reached

the front door just behind her.

"You can't go like this!" she declared.

"I have to. I really have to."

Her mother stepped into the hallway with her. "Tell me — what do you think of our young man?"

"Nice suit he's wearing."

The elevator came and she was gone. When Mrs. Bollingsworth returned to the dining room, the others were staring at one another.

"Well," said Henry. "More food for the rest of us."

46

Jude sat next to Elaine on a bench in Tompkins Square Park and realized he was facing what was arguably the most important decision in his life. And he had only this one evening in which to make it. Should he — or should he not — ask her to marry him?

He resented that he had to decide like this, with his back to the wall. He could have carried on for quite some time in that satisfying limbo, where promises of a future together were only implicit, not explicit, and where he derived the satisfaction of her company and the pleasures of sex without the lifetime commitment. The status quo was fine by him, not by her. That was why it had come to this ultimatum on her part: Fish or cut bait.

He had never been much of a fisherman.

She had called him — technically, *returned* his calls, as she had pointed out — for one last "sit-down," employing, inadvertently he was sure, Mafia terminology. She had been almost tearful when she noted that she had done a lot of thinking after their last conversation, "when you hung up on me."

"Technically, you hung up on me," he had replied, knowing as he did so that it was the wrong thing to say.

"See, that's what I mean," she said. "You're never in the wrong. You can't take responsibility for anything. You put me on hold so long, I had to disconnect. In effect, you hung up."

He thought of saying, but didn't, that he had been frantically juggling calls from the desk that night and that major news was breaking on a big story.

He had been glad she'd called this afternoon — her voice still managed to thrill him — but confused to learn she wanted to discuss where to "take their relationship." He had assumed that they had already broken up. Last he had heard, she was going out with a wealthy consultant, some guy named Harry.

Where *should* they take it? He wondered this, looking at her hair blowing gently in the breeze, at the smattering of yellow leaves falling around them, at the other people sitting on the benches nearby. Nothing gave him a clue.

"I just think," she said, "that we have to move up to the next level or we have to end it. I can't go on wondering whether we're on or off. I'm getting older and I need some solidity in my life."

Solidity. What's solidity in this world?

"I can see that," he said. Then he fell silent. Why was it that at moments of consequence in his life, which he knew to be consequential even as they were unfolding, he couldn't sort out his feelings? He seemed to step away from them, to the outside, where the emotions deadened in the cold air.

He suggested a cup of coffee. They rose and walked west on St. Marks Place. She took his hand and held it. As always, she covered his thumb with hers and he extracted it and put his on top. That had been a game when they first met. Couldn't stand to be hemmed in, he had remarked. She smiled at him. He had thought at the time that she read more into it than he did, but maybe she was right.

Clearly, he cared a lot about her. He could enumerate her strong points: She was smart, energetic, funny, committed, loyal. There were, of course, differences: She liked opera and Jane Austen and the Impressionists; he liked blues and the Beats and performance art. These were hardly insurmountable. Still, wasn't the fact that he felt compelled to list her positive attributes proof that they were insufficient?

The problem was that she resented his work. She worked in an art gallery in Chelsea. She had a leisurely lunch and left at 6:00 p.m. She couldn't imagine a job with irregular hours that you gave so much of yourself to because that was the only way you could do it. Recently, her resentments had made her shrewish. He could look ahead and envision a long line of missed dinners, forgotten appointments, apologetic calls — her resentment expanding like a hot-air balloon. The trouble with people whose work was just work was that they couldn't understand people whose work was a calling.

She stopped and looked in a store window at dresses and sweaters. Such things never interested him. He examined her and tried to imagine her getting older. She tapped the toe of her shoe impatiently, a gesture that had become a habit and that annoyed him.

The problem with asking her to marry him was that he knew with a certainty she would say yes. And that the words, once said, couldn't be retracted. They would set him on a singular course. One day, he might look back at this evening as the moment that had inexorably changed his life. Back when he had thought they had broken up, he had thought of her often. But hadn't there also been that irrepressible little cry of relief?

They entered the Starbucks on Astor Place, got their coffees, and found a small round table near a window.

He took a sip and looked out. "Maybe we should just move in together — try that, see how it goes," he said.

"Jude. We've done that. Half the time, you were at my place. Or we were at your place because of TK."

"Yeah," he agreed. He took a deep breath and told her what he was thinking — that he knew she resented his job, that working for a newspaper was like having another lover — a demanding one — and that he feared that over time her anger would vitiate her love.

She protested. She said she didn't think that would be a problem, that she could grow to understand how important his work was to him, once she had "a firm foundation of their mutual commitment" to stand on.

He wondered if that was true. She seemed more certain of him than he was of her.

"Maybe we should talk about this some more," he said. "We don't have to decide all this right now."

She began to talk, then bit her lower lip and turned away. "I think we do. I can't stand this . . . roller coaster. I can't help thinking that if you really loved me, you'd want to take the risk. All the other stuff wouldn't matter."

His cell phone rang. He ignored it and it eventually stopped. Then it rang again.

"I'm sorry," he said. "Bad timing." He answered it.

He couldn't believe the voice on the line. "No!" was all he said, breathless. He hung up and leapt to his feet.

"I've got to go," he said.

"I don't believe it. The most important discussion of our life and you want to leave."

"I can't help it. I'm sorry."

"I'm beginning to see what you mean," she replied. She had tears in her eyes. "It probably wouldn't work out. We couldn't get over all these obstacles. I could, I think. I could get used to the interruptions and the absences. But I don't think you could get over having to apologize for them."

"I'm sorry."

"You see. You just keep saying it."

"But I've really got to go. *There's been*

471

another murder."

He turned and hurried out the door.

47

Jude's cab pulled up to the *Globe.* Years of covering homicides and fires had trained him to read the body language of their bystanders. The arched shoulders. Heads leaning toward one another. The low voices. The short puffs on cigarettes.

Police were there, too, and more were arriving by the minute. Setting up the yellow tape. Stopping traffic. Red lights whirling. Excitement lending animation to their movements, giving their commands an extra edge: "Move along!" "Keep it going!" "Clear the sidewalk!"

Jude saw Bollingsworth's driver. So she was inside. He also saw her partner, Casey, who spotted him coming and threw him a dark look, shaking his head as if to say, Would you fucking believe it?

Down the street came a black SUV carrying Engleheart. Jude darted for the door to get inside before the security chief arrived and appointed himself majordomo. He knew Engleheart would like nothing better than to yank out his fingernails for the story tying Ratnoff's murder to possible police corruption.

He went up to the eighth floor. More cops were milling around the elevator banks. Toothy, the publisher's flak, was rushing about, holding his head in both hands and muttering, "My God. I can't believe this is happening to me." Jude slipped in behind him and asked, "What do you know about this?" Toothy spun around, horrified, and said, "I can't talk to you. You're from the press" and looked around frantically. Maybe he was searching for a bouncer. "You shouldn't be here," he said. "This entire murder is off the record."

Jude snorted, said "Good luck," and strode off toward the offices.

The corridors were packed with detectives and plainclothes cops. Many of them were just standing around, holding kits and cameras, waiting to apply their special skills. Some were seated in the cubicles, looking bored. One cop was talking on O'Donnell's phone. As Jude passed, he heard him say, "I swear, honey, you're not gonna believe this. I know you worshiped her. But now you can put your autographed recipe collection on eBay!"

As Jude approached, he had a good view of Outsalot's kitchen. The klieg lights were still on. They bathed the entire range in the golden glow of a TV studio. The stainless steel fridge shimmered brightly and the stove's metallic door handles sparkled. The kitchen looked as if an army had invaded during a feast: open bottles and ripped boxes, eggshells, measuring cups and bowls scattered about, knives and spoons on the floor, blotches of chocolate splattered on the wall.

Jude found his eye drawn toward the table in the vortex of the mess. On it rested a pasty brown cylinder the size of a hatbox. Jude recognized it from his previous visit: Outsalot's chocolate soufflé. Except that this one had something pressing down on the runny brown center — a heap of blond ringlets. They cascaded down the sides of the soufflé like tentacles of yellow frosting. It was Outsalot's wig. Underneath, face-down in the dessert, was Outsalot's head.

He could see, now that he was closer, that she was seated on a chair, a deadweight leaning onto the table. She was bent forward from the waist. He saw her long white neck, her arms hanging down, her dress demurely reaching to one ankle but rising up to the thigh on the other side, revealing the pearl-handled revolver in its nesting place at the top of her cowboy boot.

He pulled out his pad and started writing down everything he could see. At empty desks around him phones were ringing off the hook. It took him a moment to figure out why: Outsalot's demise had been televised; somewhere a frantic operator was forwarding calls from viewers.

A cop next to him picked up one call. "No, there's not going to be a replay," he barked into the receiver.

Police photographers appeared, shooting the scene from all angles. A chorus of clicks could be heard. He recognized a *Globe* photographer. That was good. They'd be covered for pictures. He pulled out a press card and hung it around his neck.

A voice rose above the tumult. "Don't touch anything. Nothing at all. Especially that bottle."

The voice was familiar: Bollingsworth's.

Jude joined her in front of a large screen. She barely acknowledged him. A cop grabbed him roughly by the arm. Jude pointed toward her, the cop gave her an inquiring look, and she said, "Let him stay." The grip loosened and the cop stepped reluctantly to one side.

"How was she killed?" asked Jude.

"We're about to find out."

They all huddled around a TV monitor. The tape rolled. The show's title, *Someone's in the Kitchen with Dinah,* appeared, spelled out in knives and forks. A commercial for Vita-Mix: a boy and a golden retriever scampering through a meadow. Then one for Soothe-Away antacid: Inside a cartoon stomach, a Tasmanian devil was throwing darts and was washed away by a shower of pink goo.

Then, abruptly, there she was, Outsalot, peering right at the camera with a smile as big as the Texas Panhandle. Behind her was the set of the kitchen. Amazingly, it looked authentic.

"Tonight, home rangers, we've got a special meal. Licorice-glazed squab over mission figs, baby turnips, and *saupiquet* ravioli. For dessert, a special treat — chocolate soufflé with a secret ingredient that gives it a special kick." With her right hand, she raised the bottle of Armagnac. A mischievous smile played on her face.

Jude looked at Bollingsworth as she followed every flick on the screen. She was cool and deliberate, as if it weren't beyond the bounds of everyday experience to find a restaurant critic facedown dead in a concoction of chocolate. This was her professional demeanor, a cop in control of the situation. Just as he was a reporter out for the facts.

"Let's speed it up," she said to a cop at the controls, seated below her. He hit the fast-forward button. Outsalot moved in jerky contortions, her smile appearing and disappearing. The cop shook his head. "Can you believe this was seen by thousands of people?" he said.

She touched the cop's shoulder. "Right here. Play it from here."

Outsalot slowed down, beginning to mix the soufflé. She melted a hunk of Swiss dark chocolate in a double boiler and stirred it, adding a dash dissolved instant coffee. She separated half a dozen egg yolks from the whites. Turning toward the KitchenAid mixer, she knocked a wooden spoon onto the floor. She picked it up and licked the chocolate off the back of the spoon. "What the hell," she explained in her fetching drawl. "As Julia Child would say, we're in the privacy of our own kitchen." She looked around. "For that matter . . . since we're alone and unobserved . . ." She raised the bottle of Armagnac and took a healthy swig, wiping her mouth with the back of her hand.

"That's it, right there!" exclaimed Bollingsworth. "I bet that's the moment it happened."

They watched, fascinated, as Outsalot's movements slowed and her speech became slightly slurred. She cut a ragged collar for the baking dish, then poured starch, milk, and sugar into a saucepan. She moved ataxically, drugged and confused. She rocked gently on her feet, beating the yolks unsteadily, adding them in, beating the egg whites until they were foamy and then putting them aside. She poured the Armagnac into a measuring cup, added it, and mumbled something that sounded like "seekit ingreedyent." She took another swig for good measure. Her wig sagged to the left. One leg buckled. With a sweep of the arm, she pushed all the ingredients to one side and staggered toward the oven, where a previously mixed soufflé was baking.

With two pink pot holders, she leaned down, swaying, and somehow managed to lift the soufflé dish out and heave it onto the table. She collapsed in the chair, looked foggily into the camera's eye, and raised her eyebrows in an effort to focus. Then she lifted a canister of whipped cream, sprayed the camera wildly, and fell straight down from the waist — face-first, sending goblets of chocolate into the air.

The camera hung down, broadcasting the floor tiles. Then it quickly went dark.

"Damn," said Casey, who had joined them for the finale. "This is some dramatic cooking. I bet it's already number one on YouTube."

The forensic team swarmed over the set. Everything was saved. Outsalot's revolver was handled by the barrel and placed in a plastic bag. The bottle of Armagnac was given special treatment, hoisted by tongs around the neck and placed upright in a secure box. It was rushed downstairs and off to the lab to be tested. Every ingredient was carefully packed up. The counters and floor and kitchen equipment were dusted for prints and vacuumed for fibers.

The cameraman was being questioned in a corner. Walking over to listen, Jude heard him say, "I thought she was just hamming it up . . . that it was some kind of act. You could never tell with her. Once, she cooked a rabbit without skinning it. We had to abort that show."

The soundman, his forehead resting on one hand, was giving a statement to another cop. "I had no idea what was going on. I was just trying to get a good sound reading. I never actually pay attention to the words themselves."

Bollingsworth was giving orders left and right. Jude waited until she was free, then went over to talk to her. Too bad, he said, that they had put the protection on Slaminsky instead of Outsalot.

"She had it, too. But she somehow walked out of her apartment building without the cop seeing her. My theory is she wasn't wearing the wig, so he couldn't ID her."

"The price she paid for fame," observed Casey.

Jude told them that he had seen her rehearsing for the show and had even seen the bottle.

"If it's the same one," said Bollingsworth. "Either the killer came in and added the poison or he switched bottles."

"You see anything else here worth noting?" Jude asked.

"We're waiting for our little dose of mockery. That's what our man gets off on. Each time, he goes closer to the edge. Each time, it's a little more public. It'll be hard to top this, though — murder on television."

"The public-service channel, too," added Casey.

The police by now had fanned out over the entire floor, examining every workstation and corridor and closet. As if on cue, one of them yelled out, "Hey. C'mere. I got something."

He was standing in O'Donnell's cubicle. They rushed over, to find his computer screen filled with a poem. Bollingsworth read it aloud, line by line:

> . . . as soon
> Seek roses in December — ice in June;
> Hope constancy in wind, or corn in chaff;
> Believe a woman or an epitaph,
> Or any other thing that's false, before
> You trust in critics. . . .

"That's our man, pedantic as ever," she said. "Anybody recognize the quote?"

No one did.

"Jude, when you write this up, do me a favor — leave out this part. That's the kind of nugget we like to keep to ourselves. It might lead us to the killer someday."

He said he would. As he left, the phones were still ringing. From the newsroom, he called Grabble at home and told him there had been another killing. Grabble cut him off.

"Where are you?" he demanded.

"I'm here. At the paper."

"Why the hell aren't you at the murder scene?"

"I am. This is where it happened."

"Jesus Christ! Another one in our own shop. Who was killed?"

"Outsalot."

"*Outsalot!* Who'd kill her?"

"That's the question — isn't it?"

"Don't be smart. What's she doing there?"

"She's sitting in a chair, her head facedown —"

"I don't mean what's she *doing* there. I mean what's she doing *there.*"

"She was making her broadcast. Looks like she was poisoned. She died on-camera."

"On-camera — Christ! What's this about a chair?"

"That's where her body is. Sitting in a chair facedown in a soufflé."

For once, Grabble was at a loss for words.

"Did you hear what I said?" asked Jude.

"I heard. I heard. Don't repeat it. Jesus Christ! It's the sickest thing I ever heard. What do the cops say?"

"The same thing."

"What? What?"

"That it's sick."

"Well, when are they going to figure out who the hell did it?"

"They're working on it."

"*Working on it.* Sounds like bullshit to me. We can't have this . . . this nutcase going around knocking off all our people. It's

483

perverted. An AME, a gossip columnist, and now a food critic. And Outsalot, of all people . . . who'd want to kill her? Other than chefs, of course. And restaurant owners. She could write one mean review. Still . . . *murder!* The whole thing doesn't make any sense. You better get writing. I'll call the desk, tell them to give you all the space you need. Slug it *'slay'* and let it run."

Halfway through the story, Jude got a call from the *Globe's* Web master. The paper's site had been hacked into again, this time with a photo of Outsalot, sprawled facedown in the soufflé. It had been lifted from the TV broadcast.

The headline from "The Avenger" read WHOSE BACON IS BURNT?

When Jude got home shortly after midnight, he found an e-mail from Elaine waiting for him. She said it was all over between them. She asked him not to write her, phone her, or get in touch in any way. "I need this, for my own sanity," she added at the end. "Please, *please,* keep away." She signed off with a single initial: "E."

He stared at the computer screen and lowered his head.

TK seemed to understand. She came over and licked his ankle.

Jude saw that his answering machine was blinking. Maybe Elaine had changed her mind. She had done that more than once before. He switched it on.

But the voice was not Elaine's. The Texas drawl was unmistakable: Outsalot. "Jude. I been thinking about your question. It occurs to me now that I go over it in my mind . . . yes, I did see something the afternoon Peregrin was killed. Don't know why I didn't think of it before. . . . I've got my TV gig tonight. Let's talk afterward."

The line went dead.

He reached for the bottle of J&B and started talking to his esophagus. "Okay, fella," he said out loud. "You better toughen up."

TK looked up at him, puzzled.

48

"You don't look so hot," Bashir said to Jude, handing over his morning coffee in a thin brown bag.

"Tell me something I don't know."

"Sure thing. You better rush on to your paper. There's trouble. As we say in my homeland, 'When buzzards fly over the mountain, the wise man counts the cows in the meadow.' "

Jude opened the coffee and took a quick sip to fortify himself. Another day, another news flash from Bashir. As we say in *my* homeland, "It's Yogi Berra all over again."

By the time he reached the *Globe,* pandemonium reigned. The street was cordoned off and crowded with demonstrators. They were chanting a slogan — "No Safety, No Work" — and held up hand-drawn placards: THE *GLOBE'S* A KILLING FIELD, THIS JOB'S A *DEAD* END, and HAZARD PAY FOR CRITICS. (This one was held up by

Slaminsky.)

Jude recognized most of the protesters. He saw Van Wessel standing on the sidewalk and joined him.

"What do you make of this?" he asked. "Are we on strike? Did the union get off its ass and do something?"

"No, not a *strike.* They're calling it a 'spontaneous job action.' And as far as the union actually doing something, remember: We still belong to the Newspaper Guild."

"Very funny."

"Not really."

Van Wessel asked Jude if he had heard anything more about O'Donnell — when he might get out of stir. Jude said he hadn't. He put an arm on Van Wessel's elbow and guided him away from the ruckus.

"Something I've been meaning to ask you," he said. "That afternoon Peregrin was killed, you and Frank had lunch over at the Greeks. How long did it last? Do you remember?"

Van Wessel narrowed his eyes and looked away. "Why? Who wants to know?"

"Me. I'm trying to piece this whole thing together. What's the matter?"

Van Wessel appeared fidgety. He kept turning his head toward the demonstrators as if hoping they would do something sufficiently dramatic to end the conversation. They didn't. He sighed.

"I suppose I can tell you," he said finally. "I mean, we're all friends in this together."

Jude felt a sinking sensation. "Shit," he said. "Don't tell me! You *didn't* have lunch with him!"

Van Wessel looked sheepish. "He said he really needed me to help him out. He needed an alibi. He bought a sandwich at Pret A Manger and ate alone in Bryant Park. Nobody saw him there. He said the police were hassling him . . . that he just wanted to get them off his back until they found the murderer."

"But Jesus! . . . Don't you realize . . . giving false information to the police. That's obstruction of justice, at a minimum. That's not a little thing. And the truth's bound to come out. Your lie will just hurt him in the long run."

"Why should it come out?" Van Wessel replied, looking directly at Jude for the first time. "You're not going to tell anyone, I assume. He's your friend as much as he is mine. And anyway, we know he's not the murderer. . . . Though I won't deny, this place is getting so paranoid, the thought had crossed my mind at one point. But Outsalot's death, regrettable as it may be,

488

resolves it. You must admit it does clear up that particular question. I mean, he could hardly kill her from jail — could he?"

As an old court reporter, he looked up with triumph in his eyes, as if he had just scored a point with the jury.

Jude's answer would have been drowned out at that particular moment, for the protesters turned even noisier. Engleheart had arrived on the scene, barking commands into a walkie-talkie. In his other hand, he held a bullhorn, which he waved around like a broadsword. He was wearing a blue flak jacket with matching helmet and thick gloves. He had the swagger of a general in the midst of a bloody battle — Patton, not Eisenhower.

He waded into the crowd, saw Jude, and stopped dead in his tracks. "You can't go in," he shouted. "No one enters or leaves the building. That goes double for you."

"You've got to be kidding. I'm working. I'm supposed to report to Grabble." Jude pulled out his press card and held it in the air.

"That's no good here," Engleheart said.

"*No good?* It says I can pass police lines."

"I'm not police. I'm the security chief. And this is private property. It's a newspaper office. We don't recognize press cards.

Now fuck off, before I have you arrested."

"On what charge?"

"Trespassing. And that's just for openers."

"What the hell does that mean?"

"Step closer and you'll find out."

The crowd surged and Engleheart was pushed away. He raised the bullhorn to his mouth and ordered the protesters to "MOVE AWAY FROM THE BUILDING."

One of his men shoved a middle-aged editor in a ponytail who was carrying a sign demanding ergonomic workstations. Years ago, the demonstrator had been a student activist during the sit-ins at Columbia. He fell to the ground, shouting, "Police brutality! The pigs are at it again!"

"Up against the wall, motherfucker," yelled Engleheart.

Jude sidestepped the melee, crossed the street, reached the entrance, and slipped in through the revolving door. The area near the elevator bank was empty and so a car arrived right away and carried him to the fifth floor. There, the metro desk was nearly as chaotic as the street outside. The phones were ringing incessantly, editors were barking orders into the ether, and even the rewrite reporters had been roused out of their seats.

He walked up to Clive. The news assistant

490

was dialing a number.

"What's going on?" Jude asked.

"There's a rumor the unions might shut us down. On the grounds that management can't ensure our safety. The board's supposed to meet later today. Grabble wants to talk to the publisher. . . . I'm trying to reach him now. Meanwhile, no one knows what to do. Everyone's running for the exits. It's like the *Titanic* going down."

"Only without the orchestra."

"Good thing. If we had an orchestra, it'd be playing 'Helter Skelter.' "

Clive got through on the phone line and yelled over to Grabble, who was lifting his arms to the ceiling as if in supplication, "Hagenbuckle on three."

Grabble lunged for the receiver and held it a good six inches from his mouth, yelling, "But we can't close down! This is the biggest story since . . . since I don't know what! Chappaquiddick! The fiscal crisis! Kitty Genovese and those damned thirty-eight witnesses!"

He listened a moment and his voice dropped. "No, not that big. Not the World Trade Center. Nothing's that big."

Jude figured it was all over. He walked toward his cubicle, passing Charlie Stengler on the way. Stengler had come into his own as assignment editor and seemed devastated that the paper's closure would cut him off at the top of his game. He was sitting on the carpet, leaning against the wall, like a closer knocked out in the bottom of the ninth.

"I've got a great assignment, right here in my hand," he said. "Dr. Zits . . . he's the skin doctor. I'm sure you've seen his subway ads: Dial one-eight-hundred-END-ACNE. . . . I thought it'd be fun to track him down, see just how clear *his* complexion is . . . maybe run a picture. I was going to give it to Fred. He needs a good story."

Jude patted him on the shoulder and went to his cubicle. Next door, Fred was putting a handful of belongings in his briefcase.

"They haven't said how long we're going to be out," he said. "Nor if they're going to pay us. I bet they won't. It'll be hard scraping by. And it'll be strange to go out to the newsstand and not see the *Globe* there. And you — you've lost a running story. It's not so bad for me. I haven't written anything longer than five hundred words in weeks."

"Don't worry. Cops'll crack it soon. This last murder will give them lots of clues."

"You think?"

"Sure. They'll be drowning in them."

Jude wished it were true.

He called Bollingsworth and told her it looked as if the *Globe* was going dark for a while. He asked if there had been a break yet, and she replied, "Nothing worth talking about." Then he asked her if O'Donnell had been released. She said he had.

"Oh, when?" he asked casually.

"You mean," she said, "was he released *before* Outsalot's murder. The answer to that would be yes."

"I didn't mean that," he replied weakly.

"Don't bullshit me. Remember, my nickname means 'bullshit.' "

A voice came over a loudspeaker.

"ATTENTION, ATTENTION," it boomed. "THE BUILDING IS SOON TO BE EVACUATED. GATHER YOUR BELONGINGS AND BE PREPARED TO LEAVE."

The command was repeated over and over.

"Guess I better go," he told Bollingsworth.

"I'll say. Sounds like a nuclear attack."

Jude called Clive and asked him for the latest. Clive said the evacuation was not yet official — they were waiting until the board met and decided what to do.

"Yeah, well, good luck with that. The only decisions the board's been known to make involve their own salary hikes. . . . Listen,

Clive . . . you listening? Good. If we do leave, I want you to take that computer data with you — the one tracing all the names in Whibbleby's columns. Okay?"

Clive promised he would.

Jude just had time to check his messages. There was one from Danny Devlin, the old "On the Street" columnist. That was strange — Jude scarcely knew the man. The message insisted he had to meet Jude, urgently. It said he'd be waiting in Bryant Park at noon. Jude sighed and looked at the clock. That was in twenty minutes.

He took his notes and files to Clive, asked him to safeguard them in the event of an evacuation, and left.

49

"So . . . how's the job going?" Boxby pulled a good-size plug out of his roll, slathered it with butter, and jammed it into his mouth.

"Pretty good," replied Charlie Stengler. "I've come up with some dream assignments. Like, I thought it'd be a good idea to round up some people from the projects and take them to Trump Tower . . . see what they think of it. You know, a study in contrasts."

"Sounds good." Boxby was in his conniving, cultivating mode. "Funny, I don't recall that story."

"Naw. Reporters are a strange lot. They don't always see the deeper side of things . . . the human angle. I couldn't find anyone who wasn't busy."

"I know what you mean."

"Everything looks different now that I'm an editor."

"Where you stand depends on where you sit."

"Sometimes when I walk the aisles handing out assignments, I get the impression they're avoiding me. Once or twice, I had to chase them into the bathroom. Course, it could be some horrible diarrhea is going around."

"It can be a lonely business, this thing called power."

"Tell me about it! And now . . . without a paper . . . at least for a while . . . who knows if we'll be printing. It really sucks."

Boxby tried not to frown. He didn't think the word *sucks* was appropriate to civilized discourse. Perhaps he'd have to provide lessons in social deportment to Stengler so he wouldn't feel out of place when he rose far above his current position — that is, *if* he rose. For Boxby was still not 100 percent certain that he had landed the right person. He had hired a private detective to trace Stengler's roots but with only a couple of days to do the job, the man had come up empty-handed.

Boxby continued, "Well, I expect you'll find out soon enough. . . ."

"Find out?"

"About power. What it's like when people laugh too loudly at your jokes. When they see you coming and grovel. . . ."

"I guess. But mostly, they seem to disappear."

Stengler was flattered that Boxby was treating him to lunch at the revolving restaurant on top of the Marriott Marquis. Flattered, but a little perplexed. Ever since the publisher's assistant had promoted him to the position of assistant metro editor, Stengler had been thinking kindly of him, and also of the paper. It wasn't true what people said, that it was a cold, impersonal place. Sooner or later, they recognized talent. You just shouldn't make the mistake of hiding your light under a bushel. Still, he couldn't suppress the question: Why me?

He was also fascinated by the speed at which the restaurant spun, so fast that the skyline made a 360-degree revolution every five minutes. It was a little unsettling to the stomach. Each time the roof of the *Globe,* half a block away, came into view, Boxby insisted on pointing it out. "There it is," he'd cry, and make some exultant remark. In fact, it was just drawing into view now.

"There it is," Boxby proclaimed disingenuously, "the citadel of freedom, the manor house of the Fourth Estate." His voice dropped a notch, less unctuous and more senatorial. "I can't tell you how that sight moves me." He pulled a handkerchief out of his back pocket. "It's the flywheel of capitalism. Just think — without it, demand plummets, nothing moves. Goods remain on the shelves; ships stagnate in port; trains lie stranded in the freight yard. . . . Of course, we don't do it alone. TV helps sales, too."

"And the Internet."

Boxby looked at him as if he had just farted. He frowned, stuffed his hankie back, and took a deep breath. "How 'bout a drink, heh? Who knows . . . someday soon we may have something to celebrate."

He called the waiter over and ordered two Bloody Marys.

Stengler couldn't avoid the impression that Boxby had an agenda, that he was preparing him for something, drawing him into some kind of charmed circle. At times, he spoke in a hushed, almost conspiratorial tone, and he kept signaling waiters to bring more food and drink, even after the eggs Benedict and ice cream.

It was a heady feeling. But why would somebody like Boxby, so high up on the paper that his office shared the floor with the publisher's, be so nice to him?

"Tell me something about yourself, Charles — you don't mind if I call you

Charles, do you, Charles?"

Stengler wasn't used to talking about himself. His childhood hadn't been all that illuminating. He had spent his early years in Canada, where he was born (which is why the private detective couldn't locate a birth certificate), the son of an assembly-line worker who had ten children and got pickled so often he had trouble telling them apart. His mother was a telemarketer who swindled customers from a desk in the pantry. When he was ten, he asked to be allowed to move in with his uncle Dwight.

He wasn't about to tell Boxby any of that. "You know, in a lot of ways I sort of feel I was raised an orphan," he said.

Boxby looked at him, instantly curious. "Go on," he said.

Dwight had been the captain of a ferryboat, the *Athena,* and he had plied the run up the northwest coast to Victoria and Vancouver. He often took young Charlie with him, failing to notice that the poor boy, a victim of seasickness, arrived in port covered in perspiration and unable to eat for the rest of the day. As a boy, Stengler had the fantasy, not uncommon for a lonely child, that he had been born a prince and fell into his low estate by a twist of fate.

An angel of caution settled on Stengler's

right shoulder, whispering into his ear. Skip the details, it said. Give him the big picture.

"I used to think that I was supposed to have a better life," Stengler said. "Destined for greater glory. You know, almost like I was switched in the cradle by a bad fairy or something like that."

"Yes."

Still, he had made the best of it. A middling student, he'd faked a California address and managed to attend a state university, where he mostly surfed for four years.

"I felt for a long time that I was just drifting."

Boxby nodded.

One afternoon in his sophomore year, he'd joined the college newspaper. He'd enjoyed — the few times he got a byline — that indescribable sensation of seeing his name in bold letters atop the article. He'd covered freshman soccer and rarely written more than 250 words.

"Then I ran the college paper and picked up the basics. . . . Say, these Bloody Marys are damned good."

Stengler had worked as a cub reporter for a newspaper in Seattle. Once word of his uncle's job got out, he was assigned to cover the waterfront, a beat that aroused unpleasant memories of his childhood. Luckily, he bumped into a scandal involving the smuggling of tea bags containing minute traces of cocaine from Ecuador and wrote an exposé, which won third prize in a local contest sponsored by the Lions Club.

"I won a top award. Out of the blue came a job offer from the *Globe*."

He had come to New York, wandered into the *Globe*, and lied on the application that he was a nephew of the Moscow bureau chief.

"The rest, as they say, is history."

His early years on the paper were not what would be called successful. His first job was to write the electronic news bulletins that traveled around "the zipper" on the Allied Chemical Building; he couldn't get the knack of writing in short bursts, and pedestrians remained glued to the sidewalk, trying to puzzle out the entire paragraphs that whizzed by. He developed something of a phobia about assignments and learned countless places to hide.

"I don't mind telling you that I sort of burned out in recent years. You write so many stories over a lifetime, and pretty soon they seem to repeat themselves. You walk around a corner and you meet yourself coming the other way, if you know what I mean."

"I do. I do. And yet you were always special. I had my eye on you for a long time."

"You did?" Stengler couldn't help but wonder how Boxby had managed to penetrate his cover and see him. He began to feel a deliquescent rumbling in his bowels. Maybe it was the drink.

"Yes. Lemme ask you something." The time had come, Boxby thought, to pin him down once and for all. "You said you *felt* like an orphan. Were you, in fact, an orphan?"

The angel whispered: Caution. Stengler stuttered a bit and looked down at the remnants of his Bloody Mary. He felt the lies forming over his head as natural as a cloud. "To tell you the truth, I don't really know. I never knew my parents or what happened to them so I can't say for sure."

"Who raised you?"

"A man . . . a friend of my folks." Stengler thought of a hole that needed plugging. "He's dead now, too."

"Sorry to hear that. Can you tell me anything about him — his background, his nationality?"

The picture of the *Athena* popped into Stengler's mind. Undoubtedly that was why he uttered the word that magically seemed to end the questioning. "Greek," he lied. "He was Greek."

"Aha!" Boxby settled back. He seemed to relax, reaching for the celery stalk lying in his drink saucer and biting off a piece with a resounding snap. "I'll let you in on something," he said in a confessional tone. "I happen to be an orphan myself. That's why I took you under my wing." He looked back out the window. The *Globe* building was careering into view again.

"No kidding."

"That's right. You know, as a top corporation, we may sometimes appear a little distant to our employees, a little remote," Boxby continued. "But we're not. We're a family. Sure, like any family, we've got our problems. We bicker; we fall out. But that's the bad side. The good side is we stick together. We care for one another. We — dare I say it? — love one another.

"And sometimes" — he dabbed at the tomato juice in the creases around his lips — "and I'm telling you this as a close relative, so to speak, in the great *Globe* family . . . sometimes the head of the household gets sick or slows down or can't quite hack it anymore. And that's when the rest of the family joins together and pitches in. They do whatever's required . . . even if it means knocking off . . . er . . . persuading the head to step down for his own good. I'm not saying this is going to happen. I'm just saying it pays to be ready in case it does. You get me?"

Stengler knew that he should respond favorably to this vote of confidence. But truth be told, the restaurant seemed to be turning a bit fast — in fact, it almost seemed to be spinning. He felt that old childhood churning in his stomach, the sweaty palms, the abrupt tilt in the room, which began to lurch and wobble.

And now he heard a police siren.

No, it was a cell phone. Boxby pulled it out of his jacket pocket, looked at the caller ID, and seemed to deflate.

"Excuse me," he said. "I better take this."

He listened for a moment, then replied in almost a whisper, "I'm with him now. . . . We're talking." He looked over at Stengler and smiled weakly. "A nice little chat. . . . Yes, I'll get him to the lawyers. . . ." He twisted around in his chair, turning his back to Stengler. "Don't worry, I know about the board meeting. I'm the one who has to arrange it."

Stengler wanted to pay attention, but he couldn't. The room seemed to be spinning even faster. He felt the eggs Benedict rising in his throat. He grabbed a napkin, leapt up, and bolted toward the men's room. He lost his lunch only three feet shy of the door.

Boxby watched him, shaking his head. The lad definitely required some kind of lessons.

50

Danny Devlin was waiting on a bench at the north end of the park, a Bloomingdale's shopping bag resting on the ground between his legs. The columnist was wearing a dirty raincoat and was so disheveled that Jude almost mistook him for one of the homeless people he always seemed to be writing about. When he saw Jude, he gave a wan smile and waved him over.

Jude sat next to him on the bench.

"How's it hanging?" said Danny. "I'd say not good by the look of you. Not to put too fine a point on it, but you look like shit."

Jude admitted he was tired and not a little fed up. He was impressed that Devlin noticed it and cared enough to ask.

Jude had landed in a patch of sunlight and he lifted his face to it and leaned against the back of the bench. He was feeling discouraged. For close to two weeks now he had been on the story. He had seen three colleagues murdered, viewed their bodies close-up. He had been bombarded with dozens of suspicions about people he worked with, including one who was close to him. He had followed one false trail after another.

Still, he had labored on, composing his story every day — and not just the story but also summaries, pieces for the Web site, podcasts and radio broadcasts, most of them dictated on the run. He had never worked so hard in his life. Yet through it all, there had been no praise from his bosses, no response from readers — just quibbling e-mails and the occasional "Check this out" tip from an anonymous crank. But at least he had had the consolation of seeing the fruits of his work in the paper.

No longer. If the *Globe* shut down, he wouldn't even have that. Nor would any other reporter — or, for that matter, the readers. For the first time since he'd worked there, the *Globe* wouldn't publish. Knowing that was an odd feeling. He had heard stories of how the paper had always managed to roll off the presses, how it had published even during the blackout of November 1965, using the printing plant and the typeface of the *Newark News Standard.* This time it was the *will* to publish that was lacking. That seemed perverse.

He confided all this to Devlin, who listened without comment, his chin resting on his chest as he watched a pigeon strut by.

"Guess I'm feeling sorry for myself," Jude said.

"I guess you are," Devlin said quietly. "But so what? I know how you feel. I've been there. Some things never change. You go out there. . . . You think you'll slay a few dragons. Speak up for the little guy. Go after the bosses. Rip that veil of hypocrisy and cant to shreds. You work your ass to the bone. You talk to a lot of people. You think you've got the story down, everything's clear. And you get back to the office and flip through your notebook and the fucking thing's disappeared. They start humping you for copy, so you give them what you can. They butcher it. Then you go home and your wife asks you why you're late. Dinner's burned."

He watched the pigeon fly off. "Welcome to the world of journalism."

Jude looked over at him. Something about the guy was appealing. He possessed that facility, whatever it was: that strange allure that made you want to open up a little and talk to him, out of all the people in the world. That quality was as mysterious, and natural, as magnetism.

I wonder if I have it, he thought.

He was struck by how old Devlin looked. His longish hair, looping over the temples like the cap on a toadstool, was shot through with white. Even sitting, his thick frame was stooped. Jude had never talked with him before, but of course he had heard about him. He was a reporter's reporter.

"So . . . what's the answer?" Jude asked.

"What's the answer? As Gertrude Stein said, 'What's the question?' "

Jude stared at him.

"I know," said Devlin. "You're surprised. Don't be. I read a lot."

Jude reddened.

"And don't be embarrassed, either. Excuse me while I have a cigarette." Devlin reached into his raincoat, pulled out a pack of Marlboros, and lit up.

"I guess," said Jude, "what I mean is, why do we do this?"

"At the end of the day, there's only one thing. It's not the awards — sure, they're fine, but they don't count in the long run. It's not the recognition or the fame. That doesn't last. It's not the number of page-one stories and scoops. Nobody remembers them. There's only one thing — and that's if you've earned the respect and admiration of your colleagues. Nothing else counts. Just that. Take it from me. I've been around the block."

He leaned over and patted Jude on the leg.

"So the paper's probably not going to publish. That's bad. We all feel it. But you'll still go on. It'll come back. You'll keep working. . . ." He inhaled deeply. "You know, I've worked for four papers that went under. That includes the *World Journal Tribune,* which sank in 1967. When it died, it took three newspapers with it.

"For months we had been plagued by rumors that it was on the precipice. Every day somebody'd come in with a new rumor. One day the managing editor calls everyone together, gets up on a desk, and says the paper is no more. He says we might get a little bit of severance, tells us where to pick up the last checks . . . wishes us all luck with tears streaming down his face. After he gets done, this photographer turns to me . . . you know what he says?"

"What?"

"He says, 'Holy shit. That's the strongest rumor yet.' "

Jude laughed so hard, he almost fell off the bench.

"You know," Devlin continued, "they say

you're one of the good ones." He leaned down and hoisted up the shopping bag. "Meanwhile, I've got something that'll interest you."

He said it had been given to him by an old homeless man named Barney. The guy found it on the day of Ratnoff's murder. He was foraging for soda cans in a trash container at the corner of Forty-fifth Street and Eighth, right next to the *Globe* building.

"I think you know what it is."

Jude nodded. He asked why Barney had kept it a secret all this time.

"Search me. He knew soon enough what he had found. I think he was thinking of pawning the thing, but maybe he couldn't bring himself to do that. He's got a bit of a conscience. He's the worst three-card monte player I've ever seen. Just doesn't know how to cheat, which seems to have proved a disadvantage in this city."

"And why give it to me? Why not the cops?" Jude asked.

Devlin shrugged.

"As I said, they say you're one of the good ones. Besides, I don't have all that much to do with cops these days."

"They'll want to talk to him. They'll want to know everything about how he found it."

"I know. He knows, too."

511

Devlin rose and leaned down to shake hands. He walked away toward Sixth Avenue, leaving the shopping bag on the bench. Jude leaned over and peered inside. An ordinary shoe box. He lifted it out, placed it on the bench, and removed the lid.

There, resting on a bed of cotton, was an ice pick. It was anything but an ordinary ice pick. The handle was made of ivory, hand-carved into a snake winding its way around a tree trunk, the indentations yellowed with age. The blade was covered in dried blood.

Jude replaced the lid and put the shoe box back into the shopping bag. He pulled out his cell phone and called Bollingsworth. This time, there was a long wait — six rings before she picked up.

"It better be good," she began. "I'm up to my ears in crap."

"It is," he said.

51

The board members were furious as they filed into the room on the thirteenth floor. For one thing, the emergency meeting had been hastily arranged for 3:00 p.m., an inconvenient hour. The lawyers had wanted to remain at work, since they were billing by the hour. The publisher's sons, Rosen and Guilden, had wanted to go to a movie. Paul Martinet had been in a Village love nest with his mistress, who had flown over from Paris. Nathaniel Geyser had been in the midst of a power nap at his Sheetrock company.

For another thing, they had to ride up an elevator in a semi-deserted building under police escort. Most of the *Globe's* departments had been evacuated. Ad sales, marketing, and circulation were empty, but some reporters and editors were still hanging on in the newsroom, trying to get out one last edition.

Hagenbuckle had kept his secretary, Miss Overton, at her desk. He wanted to set a good example and strike a tone of . . . not quite business as usual — that was too much to hope for — but a sort of stiff upper lip in the face of adversity. He was planning to depart the building in a calm spirit of strategic withdrawal. He rather imagined he would be the last one out, the admiral stepping off the bridge of the aircraft carrier, and he thought she might precede him, carrying his briefcase. There might be photographers.

"Zut alors," said Paul Martinet. "Zey ask us to vote to emptee ze building and it is already emptee."

"Another example of gross incompetence," muttered Nathaniel Geyser. "Putting the cart before the horse."

"What 'orse? I deed not zee any 'orse."

What happened next was unprecedented.

When Hagenbuckle went to his customary position at the head of the table and began to pull out his chair, he found a hand blocking his way. It belonged to Geyser, who fixed him with a cold smile.

"I submit," Geyser said slowly, "that given the nature of this meeting, which is bound to center upon a vote of confidence . . . or, perhaps more accurately, a vote of *no* confidence . . . in your leadership, it would be appropriate for a neutral person — such as myself — to occupy this particular seat."

Hagenbuckle was flabbergasted. No one had ever dared treat him like this. He quickly swiveled in front of the chair, managing to plant his right buttock on the seat. But Geyser, fast as a rabbit, slipped in on the other side with his left buttock. There they sat, immovable, facing in opposite directions, like Janus.

The other board members were too shocked to do more than exchange looks of alarm, until finally one of them, a lawyer, proposed taking a vote on who should occupy the chair.

"But who gets to occupy the chair during *that* vote?" queried another lawyer.

"What's going on?" asked Rosen.

"Shut up and listen," counseled Guilden.

They turned to Boxby, in his capacity as parliamentary nitpicker, to sort out the situation. But Boxby was in a bind. Much as he wanted to see Hagenbuckle dethroned, his instructions were to keep him in situ over the next few days, until everything was in place to remove him permanently.

"We haven't officially opened the meeting," he said, playing for time. "We haven't even read the minutes."

"Fuck the minutes," said Hagenbuckle. Shifting his bulk, he felt his buttocks gaining ground, and this emboldened him. "I demand an immediate vote on who sits here."

The lawyers conferred and came up with a solution to break the impasse. The chairman's chair would be retired temporarily, and the two antagonists would be seated on opposite sides of the table, so that the meeting could proceed.

They agreed. The two gave up their positions reluctantly, rising simultaneously with backsides pressed together, like Alvin Ailey dancers reaching for the stars, while the chair was extracted from underneath them. Hagenbuckle sat near the photograph of John Barrymore, and Geyser took his place next to Hirohito.

The meeting opened for new business. However, instead of engaging a proposal to close the paper until further notice, Martinet took the floor on a point of order, which he pronounced "odor." He demanded that Boxby read from the corporation's bylaws, "rule sex bee." This caused confusion until he scribbled it on a yellow legal pad: "rule 6B."

Boxby turned to a thick leather volume and eventually found the ruling and read it aloud. " 'The publisher may be removed, either temporarily or permanently, if for any reason he is deemed guilty of moral turpitude or found to be grossly incompetent. The grounds for such removal must be clear and stated —' "

"What's 'turpitude'?" asked Rosen. "Is that that stuff that goes in paint?"

"Shut up," said Guilden.

Hagenbuckle grimaced. Another mutiny, not altogether surprising. He had to nip this one in the bud. He performed his rote calculation: No matter how you diced it, he came out ahead, five for and five against, with him casting the deciding sixth.

"Let's put it to a vote," he thundered.

"Nut so fast," said the Frenchman. He requested that Boxby read "sub sex scion ate." He wrote it on the pad and with a flourish, slid it across the table: "subsection 8."

Boxby located the passage and frowned. " 'The decision on the removal of the publisher is to be taken by a simple majority of the voting members. But in the event of a tie, the publisher may not vote. Instead, that vote is to be cast by a nonvoting board member elected by all the other nonvoting board members.' "

Somewhere outside came a muffled

scream. It appeared to emanate from Miss Overton's office.

Hagenbuckle looked around the table at the lawyers. Was it his imagination, or did they exhibit that same cold smile that had been on Geyser's face? Could they all be in this together? Was he doomed?

Geyser became so excited that he stood and paced around the table, his hands gesticulating wildly. He proposed Boxby as the tie-breaking voter. The motion was seconded.

Hagenbuckle looked at Boxby, his long-time assistant, his drinking partner (that one time). He would be loyal, surely. But did he have that same reptilian smile? No, he was sweating. He wasn't enjoying this.

"Okay," said the publisher. "Let's vote on Boxby."

"I don't get it," said Rosen. "Which way do we vote?"

"Just watch Dad," said Guilden.

"But I thought Dad can't vote."

"Whatever gave you that idea?"

A lawyer leaned close to Guilden and said, "That's next time. This is this time."

"I'm confused."

"Just watch your father."

The hands went up and there was a quick count. Boxby was in. He pulled his seat all the way up to the mahogany table. He had to admit: It felt good, like graduating to the grown-up table at Thanksgiving.

"Perhaps I should now take the floor," he said, "since I am the newest voting member and the one most acquainted with *Robert's Rules of Order.* There is, as I understand it, a proposal to remove our publisher, Mr. Hagenbuckle." He looked over at Hagenbuckle as if he were a defendant on trial. "Does anyone make such a motion?"

"I do," said Geyser, smiling.

As fate would have it, he happened to be walking behind Hagenbuckle's chair. The publisher looked over his shoulder, concentrating on Geyser's neck. It would be so easy to just spring up, reach back, and get him in a headlock. He imagined the two of them landing on the table, rolling over and over, knocking water jugs, yellow pads, and pencils into the air. He could almost feel the soft flesh under his tightening grip. Go for the jugular, the air pipe — that's the way the lions brought down the gazelles.

At that moment, there was a riotous thumping at the entrance. The door seemed to bulge, straining its hinges.

Engleheart burst in, slamming the door against the wall so mightily that the photos rocked on their hooks.

Everyone froze.

"Anthrax!" he shouted. "We've got anthrax on the floor. Quick. Everybody leave."

"Where is it?" asked Hagenbuckle.

"Your secretary — she opened an envelope, found white powder."

"But where do we go?" asked Geyser.

"The room with the mainframe computer, one floor down," said Hagenbuckle. "It's the only safe place. It's hermetically sealed."

All eyes turned toward him, looking for guidance. He felt his heart soar. He paused, then said in a commanding voice, "Okay, let's all go there."

The new surroundings did the trick. The computer control room stymied the mutiny.

The board members were kept waiting outside the glass doors while Hagenbuckle, in his new role, which he likened to platoon commander, went inside to confer with the manager, a young man in a clean white shirt with a pencil guard in the breast pocket. They talked for quite a while, at times animatedly. At one point, the publisher reached into his jacket and pulled out his wallet, apparently to prove his identity. Then the young man placed a phone call, listened a moment, and hung up, visibly upset. Finally, Hagenbuckle stepped outside and said, "Here's the deal."

The mainframe computer equipment, he had been told, was expensive and extremely sensitive. The chamber was dust-free, the air purified three times before being recirculated. For insurance, the company had installed the most up-to-date fire-protection system available. Delicate smoke detectors were embedded in the ceiling in place of sprinklers, since water would ruin the computer. At the first sign of smoke, an alarm would sound. It would last for precisely two minutes, at the end of which time the doors would automatically seal and a multimillion-dollar inhalation system would be activated. It would suck every bit of oxygen out of the room within fifteen seconds. Anyone left inside would suffocate.

That sobered up the group.

For obvious reasons, Hagenbuckle said, no cigarettes, matches, or lighters were permitted inside. Nor — here he cast a telling look at Engleheart — were guns. The young man had not wanted to admit them, he added, but he had been overruled by his superiors, who believed it unwise to subject the publisher and the board to the threat of death by anthrax.

Were the rules understood? Everyone said yes. The doors were opened and they began to file in.

An elevator door abruptly parted and out popped Edith Sawyer, breathing tremulously. "What the hell's going on?" she yelled. "We hear the publisher's secretary opened a letter and found anthrax inside. I'm covering the story."

"Since you're here, you might as well come in," said Hagenbuckle. "No matches and no lighters." He looked at Edith's blouse and skirt for telltale bulges. "And no guns."

Engleheart remained outside, having taken possession of Boxby's lighter. He remained just outside the doors, with his hands on his hips and his chin up, as if he were the head of a Secret Service detail.

Inside, they glanced around as if they had found themselves on the moon. The chamber was sterile and ultramodern, everything white or metallic. It had no smell and no noise, other than a barely perceptible humming. They sat in folding metal chairs, suddenly obedient before the altar of modern technology.

The business was quickly disposed of. The vote of no confidence in Hagenbuckle was defeated, six to five. He beamed, as if he had just vanquished a Japanese pillbox. A second vote was taken to shut down the paper and close the building. A third vote required another board meeting within two days, at a place to be determined by Boxby. This item was put forward by Boxby himself, for reasons he did not feel compelled to explain. He went to a corner to draft a statement to the workers.

Edith Sawyer, who had been scribbling frantically to get all this down in a notebook, looked up, her face suddenly frozen. The ugly truth had dawned.

"Wait a goddamned minute. Here I am — I've got a story to die for. And you're telling me I don't have a fucking paper?"

Before anyone could answer, Engleheart stuck his head in the door with an announcement. The mysterious white powder had been traced to its source — a harmless box of Spic and Span in a janitor's closet. Someone had put several spoonfuls in an envelope, addressed it to look like a letter, and left it on Miss Overton's desk. She was, he added, currently in tears.

"Don't worry. I'll console her," said Hagenbuckle.

It's the least I can do, he thought to himself, after giving her such a fright. He chuckled to himself by way of congratulations. His little stratagem had brought the cows back in line.

52

"Bollocks told me to drop you off here," said Casey, pulling in front of a Greek diner on Eighth Avenue and Fifty-third Street. "She says you shouldn't come into the station house, and I concur. But watch your ass — it's only a block away."

"Does she live around here or something?"

"I'm not authorized to tell you that."

"It's not like I'm a stalker."

"You stalk her, pal, and she'll be up your ass in no time. I saw a guy try it once."

"What happened?"

"Ask him. He's in Sing Sing."

As Jude opened the car door, Casey leaned over and put a paw on his arm. "By the way, you might tell her you've got a tail."

Jude looked at him quizzically.

"A *tail*. You're being followed. I spotted the guy in the park. He pretended to be reading a newspaper, but he had one eye on you. He followed us out. When we got in my car, he got in a blue Corona. Then he took a good look and sped off. Musta realized I'm a cop."

"You sure?"

"Am I sure? For fuck's sake, of course I'm sure."

"What'd he look like?"

"He looked like a goddamned *tail* — that's what he looked like."

Jude found Bollingsworth seated in a back room, eating a salad. He handed her the Bloomingdale's shopping bag. With evident forbearance, she peered down at the shoe box but didn't open it. She just set it on the seat next to her.

"Rule of life. Never examine a murder weapon while eating," she said. "Order something."

He did, a hamburger.

He told her that Casey had spotted someone following him in the park. Without missing a beat, she pulled out her phone, speed-dialed Casey, and ordered him to the station house to look over a file of photos in her desk drawer. "You see the guy, you call me right away." She hung up.

"Four to one it's Engleheart," she said. "Casey came on after he left the force, so he doesn't know what he looks like. Maybe he'll recognize his photo. Course, it's about

525

ten years out of date. . . . Still, he hasn't changed much. Just got fatter — and meaner. That happens to cops in forced retirement."

"Why are you so sure it's Engleheart?"

"Who else could it be? He's the only person in your shop who has the capability of tapping your phone. Between you and me, he's the number-one suspect. We got the final word on the handwriting analysis of that note 'R U Nxt?' that went to your police reporter. It looks like his writing."

"I thought it wasn't conclusive. . . . You said that you couldn't be sure, since it was only five letters and they were printed, not longhand."

"True enough. It's not a hundred percent. But at this stage, I'm willing to take ninety. It's one more piece in the puzzle. And so far, the picture in the puzzle is beginning to look a lot like him."

"You got anything new?"

She shrugged, stuffing an oversize piece of iceberg lettuce into her mouth.

"It's more of an accumulation. Means, opportunity, motive — the big three, *MOM*. He rates high on all of them. . . . *Means* — he had the run of the building and knew it inside out. *Opportunity* — in his position as security chief he could have been around just about anytime. *Motive* — that's obvious. He wants to stop the exposé on police corruption because it implicates his buddies and probably himself."

"I don't know . . . stopping the exposé. It's not like killing the editor is going to prevent the story from appearing, eventually."

"Maybe not. But it'd delay it. And that's what these guys need. Especially now that they know what the story says — which they presumably do. They'll take preemptive action — cover up the traces, return evidence to the files, put money back in the narcotics fund, write postdated reports on such and such an investigation. And it might work. You'd be surprised how quickly the department jumps on exculpatory evidence when it comes to their own."

Jude's hamburger came, swaddled in french fries. He removed a thick slice of onion to pamper his esophagus.

"You got any better ideas?" she asked.

"Not really. But new things keep coming up."

He told her about Outsalot's phone message. She had him repeat it word for word.

"Christ," she said when he'd finished. "So she was a witness after all. If she hadn't been so flakey . . . if she'd only remembered . . . hell, we might have been able to save her. I'm beginning to hate everything to do with this case. So much evidence that we got two lab techs working overtime, but nobody comes up with anything definitive."

Jude asked about Outsalot's autopsy. As expected, death due to poisoning, she said. A preliminary indication was that the poison was related to curare, which causes death by asphyxia. Usually, curare works only in the blood, but this variety, favored by a tribe in Papua New Guinea that eschewed cannibalism, was effective when taken orally.

"It's not too common," she said. "Which means we may be able to trace it. Some doctors use it for muscle trauma, spasms, arthritis, even to immobilize patients during delicate surgery."

Jude told her about Hickory Bosch's visit to the basement. She stopped eating long enough to take notes, so he filled her in on the disastrous Bosch years at the paper.

"And then I've been looking through Ratnoff's files," he continued. "There's a lot of material there, and some of it's suggestive."

"You mean the plagiarism bit you talked about. Edith Sawyer."

"For openers, yes."

"You find it hard to imagine a dirty cop killing someone to keep his name out of the paper. I find it hard to imagine a reporter killing someone because she made the mistake of copying someone else's work."

"Take it from me, it's a big deal. It means she would end her career in total ignominy. Reporters around the country would be talking about nothing else. For someone who lives for her career, that's the end of the universe."

"I guess I can see that."

"And there's a lot more stuff in Ratnoff's computer. Turns out he was accumulating information about Appleby, the founder of the modern-day *Globe.* Appleby bought the paper for a song during the Depression and built it into what it is today. He passed it on through his daughter, who's married to the current publisher. Appleby's image has been airbrushed with a lot of talk about what a business genius he was — but apparently he was one tough old bastard."

Jude gestured at the diner's decor. "He came from Greece. And Ratnoff made a couple of trips to Greece."

"I know. I've read it all."

Jude was nonplussed.

"How? You went into O'Donnell's computer?"

"No. Ratnoff's."

"But I thought you couldn't get it. The

paper's refusing to hand it over. It's still sitting in Ratnoff's office."

"That's a decoy. We got the original, hard drive and all. Hagenbuckle gave it to us on day one. When it comes to defending the First Amendment or catching a murderer that's decimating his staff, what do you think a publisher's going to choose?"

"I'll be damned." Jude wondered what other secrets she was keeping from him. "So you don't think the research Ratnoff was doing is important?"

"I didn't say that. It could be. Among other things, it explains why he was in the basement. Incidentally, forensics now says he wasn't killed in the passageway. It looks like he was killed in the morgue. We found blood samples there and they match his."

The morgue! Jude thought back to his visit there. He visualized the desk where he had examined the Appleby files, the spot where the foreman of the presses used to have his command center, Sammy Slimowitz lurking around like the Phantom of the Opera.

Knowing precisely where it occurred seemed to give the murder a whole new dimension of actuality.

"You think Engleheart tracked him down there?" he asked.

"More than likely."

"You think they fought?"

"Could be."

"And what do you have to prove it was Engleheart?"

"As I say, it's not proof. It's a compelling accumulation of facts. He's plugged into a bad group of cops. Like them, he gets a lot of extra income that I suspect he's going to have trouble explaining. One of them learns about this reporter snooping around and tells Engleheart, who then gets access to Ratnoff's computer and finds the story that's going to blow the lid off. Then he kills Ratnoff. He uses the freight elevator to move the body and takes it up to the newsroom and plunges a spike into it. That's for maximum PR impact. Frighten everybody. Then he writes a note threatening the reporter who filed the story. And everyone in the group goes to ground."

"And the other murders?"

"A chain reaction. Once he learns about Ratnoff's affair with Peregrin Whibbleby, he figures she knows what Ratnoff knew, so he has to get rid of her. He tries to frame someone else for that murder. But Outsalot saw him at O'Donnell's computer, so he has to do her, too."

"It's a neat little package — I'll give you that."

"It is. And the final ribbon around it" — she leaned over the shopping bag — "might just be in this little shoe box." She lifted off the top and stared intently.

"Just what I'd hoped. This isn't your ordinary ice pick. An ivory handle, a hand-carved snake. Once seen, never forgotten. I can already hear the prosecutor preparing the jury for it."

"And you can see the blood on it."

"Where did you say the homeless guy found it?"

"In a trash can on Forty-fifth and Eighth. He was rummaging around for soda cans."

"That's the only thing I don't like. It's too close to the *Globe.* If you've got a clever killer — clever enough to plan these murders from start to finish — why would he leave the weapon nearby? It's almost as if he wanted it to be found."

"Now you're hearing the defense attorney."

"I have to. That's the name of the game. There's a lot of pressure on this case. More than anything I've experienced. I'm tempted to bring Engleheart in, but I've got to be very careful. Bringing in a cop, or a former cop, that's not something you do lightly."

Her cell rang. She answered it, listened for a minute, and snapped it closed.

"That tail following you . . . Casey says he's looked at Engleheart's photo and can't say for sure it was him. I expected as much. No cop's going to finger another cop."

She put the top back on the shoe box.

"How are you going to find out whose ice pick that is?" asked Jude.

"I already know." She pulled a black-and-white photo out of her purse and handed it to him. It was a photo of the ice pick. "It's the publisher's . . . Hagenbuckle's. He phoned me days ago to say he was missing it. I don't think he wanted to, but it's a good thing he did."

Jude felt dizzy. This story was moving so fast, it had just run out one door and in another. "So does that make Hagenbuckle a suspect?"

"Not really. What would be his motive?"

"Maybe Ratnoff was about to strike pay dirt. Some deep dark secret that would ruin the family name."

"I can't see it. Let me put it this way: If he's a suspect, he's far down the list."

"So how does this murder weapon implicate Engleheart?"

"It doesn't — not directly. Unless, of course, his prints are on it, which I doubt.

But don't forget — he's got the run of the place; he uses freight elevators. It's nothing for him to barrel up to the thirteenth floor and pocket it. Afterward, he leaves it where it'll get found. So the publisher will be implicated . . . the place will be in chaos."

"Maybe. But I'm skeptical. Much as I'd like to see Engleheart in the dock."

They got separate checks and walked to the cash register in the front.

"By the way," she said. "Too bad you can't use any of this. Sounds like you don't really have a newspaper at the moment, do you?"

Outside, standing on the sidewalk, Jude looked at her and said, "Let me ask you something. You live around here?"

"Why?"

"I dunno. First we have lunch on the Upper East Side, where you were raised. Then here, near where you work."

"Maybe you should stop trying to peg me. When cops do that, it's called 'profiling.' When reporters do it, it's just cliché."

53

Outside the *Globe,* evacuees were mingling with the demonstrators. Knots of people overflowed onto the street, not knowing where to go and seemingly reluctant to leave.

"They look dazed, don't they?" said Alston Wickham Howard to Jude, observing the crowd with a baleful eye. "I saw the same look once in a World War Two documentary about liberated concentration camp victims."

Many of the employees were reading notices they had grabbed in the lobby before spinning out the revolving doors.

Alston handed one to Jude. It was from the Human Resources Department:

The board of directors of the *Globe* met today in an atmosphere of unity and cordiality to consider the question of the safety of our workers. Nothing is as important to us as that. Profits don't even come close. Sadly, we have decided that the only recourse is to suspend publication of the newspaper. This drastic step was taken after careful consideration and a long, thoughtful discussion. It is not a reaction to today's demonstration. We remain firm in our conviction that the workplace must be free of fear and intimidation, whether from a psychopathic killer or a trade union. We regret the stoppage and we hope to resume publication after a rapid and successful police investigation. Above all, we remain committed to the well-being of the *Globe* family.

At the bottom was an addendum: "Our lawyers tell us this is not a lockout, so don't think you can file for compensation."

"Some notice, huh?" said Alston. "Brought tears to my eyes. That bit about 'thoughtful discussion' made me think that there must have been a knock-down, drag-out fight. And I haven't heard so much talk about *family* since Charles Manson's last parole hearing."

Jude spotted Bernie Grabble. The metro editor had stationed himself by the revolving door to intercept people on the way out,

536

his arms waving, his hair tousled like a weather reporter's in a hurricane.

"Don't worry! Don't worry! We'll be back!" he yelled.

Alston poked Jude in the elbow. "Say . . . did you ever get my message?"

"What message?"

"I'll take that for a no. It's not important now, I suppose. I left you a message yesterday. I thought . . . given all that's been happening around here lately . . . it might be a good idea if . . . if I were to accumulate some facts for your bio, if you know what I mean."

"I certainly do know what you mean. You're talking about my obit."

"Well, not to put too fine a point on it, but in a word, yes."

At that moment, Grabble spotted Jude and threaded his way through the crowd toward him, but Slim Jim Cutler appeared out of nowhere and grabbed his sleeve and mumbled something about the end of the world. Grabble shook him off like a bug, then came up and towered over Jude.

"I want you to keep working the story," he said. "Promise me you'll do that. They can't shut the *Globe* down for long. We'll be back in a blaze of glory."

"I will," Jude promised, touched by the

editor's faith. "I know we'll be back. Someday."

"Not just *someday*. Someday soon!"

"I just pray it happens before the world ends," put in Alston, eyeing Slim Jim, who was approaching, his eyes large and crazed above his sunken cheeks, like the ancient mariner. He fell on his knees and fastened himself onto Jude's wrist. Jude pried himself loose and attached Slim Jim's hand to Alston's coat.

"This is the man you should talk to," he said. "If what you say is true — and I don't doubt you for a minute — he's got a shit-load of obits to prepare."

He was tempted to tell Grabble the latest developments in the *"slay"* story — the discovery of the ice pick — but he restrained himself. Without a paper to put it in, that would be cruel, like dangling a steak bone two feet beyond a dog's leash.

Jude took his leave and walked toward Eighth Avenue. He had devised a plan that required entering the *Globe*, but he would have to wait until nightfall to do it. As it was, the chances of his finding what he was looking for were slim.

He admitted to himself he was a little spooked. That talk about his phone being tapped and now about being followed —

whether by Engleheart or somebody else — was unnerving. After lunch with Bollingsworth, he had walked down Eighth Avenue, stopping every so often to peer into shop windows, pretending interest in the merchandise but really using the reflection to look behind him. He saw nothing other than ordinary suspicious-looking New Yorkers.

Now he decided to try it again. He walked up Eighth, then abruptly broke his stride and stopped before a shoe store's window. He looked down, then raised his eyes to the glass. Sure enough, there *was* someone behind him, someone who seemed to be looking at him. The image was blurred. Jude couldn't make out the man, not even enough to describe him.

He set out again, this time walking more quickly. He stopped again and stood still for some time, pretending to stare into a store. He realized with a start that he had halted in front of a sex shop; he had been looking at a vast array of leather harnesses, dildos, and other sex toys. He scanned the glass for the shadow. On cue, it appeared, drawing closer, gaining on him.

He set out again. Now he really picked up speed.

"Hey," he heard someone cry out. He almost broke into a run. Again: "Hey!"

And then: "Wait up, Jude."

He spun around. It was Clive. The news assistant smiled as he drew close.

"So . . . see anything you liked back in the sex shop?"

"Very funny. I was trying to see who was behind me . . . looking at you in the reflection."

"Dude. You think quick on your feet. I'll say that for you."

"It's true." Jude asked him where he was going.

"My place. And that's what I want to talk to you about."

"You remembered to bring the computer files and my notes — that it?"

"I got them right here" — Clive held up a small gym bag — "but that's not what I want to speak to you about." He fished into his pocket, pulled out a slip of paper, and wrote something on it.

"My address," he said, handing it over. "We're having a get-together now that the paper's closed. I think you'll find it interesting."

"I'm sure I would, but —"

"A lot of people are going to be there, some you know, some you don't. Chris — the Web master, for instance. He'll be there. And Eric, his number two. A lot of people.

Geeks, mainly. Who knows what mischief we'll get up to?"

"What is it, exactly, you're planning to do?"

"You know, don't you?"

"I'm guessing."

"Dude. You should be honored. Only about a dozen reporters have been asked to join us. We don't have anyone from management. I mean, strictly speaking, we're not sure it's legal."

"Oh, I don't know. I heard the Internet was a democratic medium. It's also anonymous. Let's say, for the sake of argument, you were to activate the *Globe*'s Web site. Who's to say it was you who did it?"

"My thoughts exactly. So drop by whenever you want." Clive smiled, shook his hand, and said good-bye. "And stay away from those porn shops."

54

At 8:00 p.m., having walked twice around the block to make sure he wasn't being followed, Jude stood across the street from the *Globe.* The front doors were sure to be locked. The place was off-limits to personnel and looked to be closed tight as a tomb.

The lights in the lobby were dimmed. A shadow fell halfway across the giant globe inside, as if it were suspended in an eclipse. A patrol car was parked in front of the revolving doors and two heads lay low against the front-seat backrests. The cops are probably cooping, Jude thought. How's that for rubbing salt in the wound: They're supposed to guard the newspaper that exposed them for sleeping on the job, and what do they do? They take a nap.

He walked around the side street and turned into the back alley. Garbage was overflowing from two cans. He came to the rear door, pulled out his master key, and slipped inside. The rear stairwell was illuminated only by a pale half-light from a small diamond-shaped window on an interior door, which he opened.

He crossed a landing, followed a passageway around two corners, and came to the delivery room. It was dark and deserted. The huge retracting doors in the truck bays were closed and rays of light from streetlamps outside knifed in around the doors' edges, cutting the gloom and sending streaks on the loading platforms below. The open area made his heart race.

The worn metal floor was slippery and he trod lightly until he came to the door to the lobby. It was, he realized as he reached for it, the same door that Bollingsworth had marked with police tape the day they found Peregrin Whibbleby's body. Slowly, he unlocked it with the master key, turned the knob, and stepped into the lobby.

There, in the half-light of the elevator bank, he felt suddenly exposed. Could the cops outside see him? Not directly, certainly, since the front entrance was around a corner, but would they notice a movement of shadows? He pressed the down button, waiting. When the car arrived, it would activate a red light above the elevator door. Would they see a red glow reflected against the marble façade of the far wall?

He had to count on their ineptitude —
and their sleepiness. The car came. He
stepped inside and it plunged downward.

He entered the subterranean passageway
that led to the basement pit. Above him was
the single lightbulb that he had screwed into
the socket, believing it had come loose by
itself. A mere two weeks ago. It seemed like
two months.

The passageway opened onto the cavern,
with its metal tracks, and beyond that the
jagged line of sawhorses next to the pit. To
his left was the morgue, with its long bank
of filing cabinets. He entered the labyrinth
and followed the turns until he came to the
central area. There was Slimowitz's make-
shift office, the seat where he had been reading now vacant.

And there was the long desk Ratnoff had
used. Knowing that this was where he had
been killed gave the place a different aspect,
made it seem portentous, even frightening.
It was that knowledge that had brought Jude
here.

Then he saw what he had come to investigate.

The bin contained a dozen cylindrical
capsules. Each was about fourteen inches
long and made of thick plastic that was yel-

lowing with age. There were rubber guards around the circular ends. A cap was on one end, held in place by a leather strap stretched over a small metal knob. The capsules lay at the bottom of the bin like large pellets, left there years ago when computers supplanted this primitive but effective means of communication. Above the bin, the pneumatic tubes ascended the wall, climbing like giant vines all the way to the ceiling and then cutting through to the floor above.

Four pipe ends hung over the bin — two for sending and two for receiving. Jude looked at the labels, written in black ink in a fine hand and encased in plastic. One said "To the composing room"; the other, "To the bullpen." The composing room was another anachronism, the place where the type used to be set into pages once it emerged from the linotype machine. The bullpen was long gone too, the area in the newsroom where a cluster of top editors had presided over the paper and put it to bed.

The end of each hanging pipe was covered by a hinged metal lid with a protrusion to open it. Jude placed his thumb on the protrusion and pressed down lightly. It stayed in place, held by suction. He was surprised by its resistance. He pressed down hard and it gave way abruptly, a hissing stream of air rushing inside. He held his palm to the opening and his hand was sucked against the edge. It was like covering the draw of a vacuum cleaner pipe, only much stronger.

He decided to experiment. He picked up a capsule and inserted it in the open pipe. In an instant, with a whoosh, it was gone, flying upward inside the tube. So he was correct: The system was still operational.

The scenario he had envisioned was not impossible.

Ratnoff is sitting at the desk. He's going through Appleby's file. He discovers something of critical importance. But he's worried that someone is on to him, perhaps hacking into his computer, perhaps even shadowing him at this very moment. He hears someone coming. He must hide the file. He leaps up, grabs a capsule, stuffs the file inside, and sends it off. The killer enters, grabs him. There's a struggle. Ratnoff is murdered. The killer looks around. Where's the file? It has disappeared.

Or perhaps the scene hadn't unfolded like that. Perhaps Ratnoff wasn't surprised as he was reading the file. Maybe he had used the capsules over the course of weeks as a private courier service — a way to smuggle the files out of the archives one by one, no questions asked. Perhaps the killer came upon him just after he had dispatched his latest installment.

Either way, Jude's path was clear. He had to follow the capsules to their destinations.

He started. Did he hear something? He listened intently. Surely the sound was nothing more than his imagination.

He retraced his steps, walking back through the labyrinth and to the open area and into the passageway, listening carefully, his senses on full alert. He came to the elevator and pressed the button. From the lobby he took another car to the fifth floor.

Once there, he entered the newsroom, which was dimly lighted but at least familiar. He followed the pathways between the chest-high cubicles. The second hands on the wall clocks marched around and the computers swam with brightly colored screen savers. Still, something struck him as vaguely wrong, and he quickly realized what it was: the pervading silence. He was not accustomed to it.

He found the nook where the bullpen used to be. He remembered it from his first year on the paper. Older men in white shirts and ties had labored there, quietly reading copy and checking the wires and posting news photographs on a bulletin board to see if they merited the front page. Now, like the command center for the presses in the basement, it was just another empty corner.

He examined the wall. The pneumatic tubes were gone, but their traces were still visible under several coats of paint. They were like markings on walls adjoining a demolition site, vestigial impressions showing where staircases and floors had been. High up, where the tubes had once been attached, he could see brass fittings sticking out of the plaster.

Again — a sound! Someone stirring! Jude stood stock-still, turning his head in one direction, then another. No, there was nothing. His brain was in overdrive. He stood motionless for a moment longer, just to be sure. He walked to the back of the vast room, past scores of cubicles. His footsteps resounded in the emptiness. He reached the rear staircase. Quietly, again looking around, he opened the door and stepped onto the dimly lighted landing.

He descended two floors to the composing room, a part of the paper that had been virtually sealed off, like an old Victorian attic, for a decade. It had been closed with the advent of computer-driven pagination, which enabled specialists in the newsroom to assemble entire pages electronically.

The low-ceilinged roomed was even darker than the staircase. A blanket of dust covered everything — large racks for page assembly, machines that used to spit out page proofs, windows that led to the photo-offset room, now blacked over with dirt.

He saw trails of tiny prints left by mice in the dust on the floor. A thick book — the binding looked like a dictionary — rested on an otherwise empty desk. Cobwebs hung from the corners of the overhead lamps.

He followed the walls, looking for the bin of capsules. Finally, he came upon it, in a far corner. These capsules, too, were filthy. But the dust had been blown from the bin's center, where an empty capsule lay right in the middle. It was, he realized, the one he had launched from the basement. He filled his lungs, leaned down, and exhaled, blowing the dust away. It rose in a small cloud and he backed off, waiting for it to settle. Then he moved close and peered down.

All of the capsules were empty but one. That one, slightly off to one side, appeared to have papers inside. He picked it up, held it firmly, and opened it by stretching the leather strap and pulling it away from the small knob. He reached inside, grasping the papers between his thumb and forefinger to twist them into a tighter roll. This relieved the pressure against the capsule and so he was able to extract them. Covering them was an aged manila folder. On its tab was written "Appleby: Early Years." He opened the folder and looked quickly. Documents were inside.

Moving rapidly now, with the folder under one arm, he crossed the floor and reached the door to the staircase. He opened it and then stopped, listening. The staircase gave off a rush of echoes in the void. He strained to hear. There it was again — the noise! This time, he was certain. There was no mistaking: Someone was above him, descending the staircase. He raced to the steps, grabbed the banister, and hurried down half a flight of stairs to the next landing. He stopped and listened again, his heart throbbing. The person was chasing him from above. Now he bolted, angling his body so that he could take the steps sideways in rapid-fire succession. Another landing and another. He could hear his pursuer gaining on him.

He reached the bottom landing, then raced across it to the outside door. He slammed against the exit bar, which collapsed into the door. But it did not budge. He tried again, harder, smashing it with his hip. It opened.

He turned and looked back. A figure was descending from the half-landing above. He saw feet, then legs and waist. It was a man, carrying something. The figure stopped, appeared to see him, too, in the half-light. It froze, backed up a step, uncertain.

Jude saw the man bend at the waist, lean forward, and peer down.

Then he recognized him.

"O'Donnell! Jesus Christ! What are *you* doing here?"

O'Donnell leaned against the banister, gasping for breath.

"I could ask you the same thing," he said.

"I didn't know who the hell you were," said Jude. "I heard this noise. I thought you were chasing me."

"And I thought *you* were chasing *me,* kiddo." He put his hand over his heaving chest. "I thought you were above me. I didn't know where you were — or who."

Jude gestured toward the package O'Donnell was carrying. "What have you got there?"

O'Donnell pointed toward the folder in Jude's hand. "Again . . . I could ask you the same thing."

"I feel like I'm in a goddamned echo chamber."

"Me, too. Let's get out of here."

55

They walked up Eighth toward Columbus Circle. It was unseasonably warm, with a slight breeze blowing across the intersections from the west. Jude felt his sweat under his shirt begin to dry and his heart begin to slow.

He noticed, to his dismay, that it wasn't easy to level with O'Donnell. For a while, they beat around the bush with small talk and soon fell silent. Maybe the discomfort came because a dark corner of his brain, which he didn't want to listen to but which wouldn't shut up, was nagging him with the thought that his good friend might just be a pathological serial killer.

He thought back to that night at O'Kelly's, remembering how O'Donnell had worried about whether his fingerprints were on the *National Enquirer* found in Whibbleby's hand. At least he had had the good grace then to broach his fears. What else was he holding back? Oddly enough, he seemed more relaxed now.

"Let's put all our cards on the table," Jude blurted out.

"Good idea. Maybe that'll settle whatever ball bearing is rolling around in that pea-size brain of yours. I think I know what you're thinking, but I'd like to hear it from you."

"Okay. Here goes. Now, I don't want you to take this the wrong way. I'm not accusing you of anything. I just want to raise some points and have you clear them up."

Jude unloaded all the facts that aroused suspicion. That O'Donnell had been hacking into Ratnoff's computer files before his murder. That the ad hinting where to find Peregrin's body was sent from his computer. That his prints were found at the scene of the crime. That he had given a phony alibi, asking Van Wessel to lie and say they were having lunch together when they weren't. That Outsalot rehearsed her TV show not far from his cubicle and might well have seen him there. That the murderer had left a snatch of poetry on *his* computer. And finally that Outsalot had remembered something important, which she mentioned in a phone message, and was killed shortly *after* the police released him.

"You through?" O'Donnell asked. "You sure there's nothing else you want to throw at me?" But he said this without rancor, as if he himself recognized that the bill of particulars was compelling.

He dealt with each point in turn. He said he had noticed that Ratnoff was spending a lot of time in the archives. Observing him, he concluded that he had stumbled on a secret in old man Appleby's past, something that might conceivably affect the future of the paper. He said it was clear that someone else — who would turn out to be the killer — was tracking Ratnoff, too. In doing so, this person had undoubtedly learned about O'Donnell's sleuthing and came up with an ingenious idea. Why not frame him? It was the old "kill two birds with one stone" solution that produced most of the damning evidence — the fingerprints on the *National Enquirer,* the ad sent from his computer, and the poem on his screen.

Had he asked Van Wessel to provide a cover story? Yes, he had. But that was to give him breathing room to continue his own investigation. It was wrong and stupid. He regretted doing it. He was guilty of being an idiot — but nothing more.

He agreed that Outsalot was in all likelihood killed because she had witnessed

554

something. Initially, she couldn't recall whether she had seen O'Donnell there at the critical time. That made sense. He worked there every day. He was so much part of the landscape, his presence or absence wasn't likely to register or to be recalled later on. But she *did* remember something, something important enough for her to phone Jude and leave a message about it. It had to be something unusual. She must have remembered seeing a stranger, perhaps someone lurking about the area or doing something that in retrospect appeared significant.

Finally, there was the simple accumulation of all these negative clues. They were so glaringly obvious that it was clear he was being set up. Would he, were he in fact the killer, be so ham-fisted as to leave so many bits of self-incriminating evidence around? Unless, of course, he was doubly duplicitous, attempting to cast a cloud of suspicion upon himself in order to dispel it eventually. But surely that would be a risky proposition. To believe he was capable of it meant believing he would risk his life on a throw of the dice.

"And finally," he said, looking Jude straight in the eyes, "I must have recourse to our friendship . . . to your trust in me. I want you to take it on faith that I'm not the killer. I want you to believe it simply because I say it's true. And I want to hear you say that you believe me and mean it when you say it."

Jude readily agreed. He was convinced of O'Donnell's innocence and felt ashamed for ever doubting him. He said he would have given the testament of faith even if O'Donnell hadn't asked him to. He gave it.

Afterward, he said, "Okay, George. Now, someday soon, I want you to tell me about the rabbits again."

"You got it, Lennie."

They crossed the circle, entered Central Park, and sat down on the first bench they came to. Jude was feeling a lot better than he had ten minutes ago. It would be good to have a confederate in trying to figure the whole puzzle out. He pointed to the package that O'Donnell had placed on the bench next to him.

"What's inside?" he asked.

O'Donnell lifted the package and carefully opened one end, revealing a book binding — *Bartlett's Familiar Quotations.*

"Okay," said Jude. "I give up."

"That quotation the killer left on my computer screen — it was Byron."

"I know. I checked it, too. It's from *English*

Bards and Scotch Reviewers."

"There's a chance that the killer lifted the quote from this reference book. It was in the *Globe*'s library. I thought I'd sneak in and lift it and give it to Pril. See if she could lift the prints from it. It's a long shot, I admit."

"A *long shot?* It's not even within shooting range. Assuming the killer did use it, you figure he's smart enough not to sign the book out but dumb enough not to wipe his prints off it?"

"Like I said, it's a long shot. But anything's worth trying."

"And now, of course, you've covered it with your own prints."

O'Donnell produced a pair of latex gloves from his side pocket and shrugged. "You can't imagine the pressure she's under. They're really riding her ass to solve this thing. And I thought our place was tough on morale."

"I can't help but notice that a few days back you thought I was cooperating too closely with the cops. And now here you are, practically undercover. She must have put you under some kind of spell."

"No . . . not really."

" 'Not really'?"

"I just think she's a fine girl."

"*Girl?* She's my age."

"What can I say? She acts younger than you. She's spirited — the kind of woman who knows how to curse, play cards, and fix cars. Least I imagine she is."

"And I notice you're calling her *Pril* now?"

"Why not? It's her name. What do you call her?"

"I don't know. Bollingsworth, I guess."

"Poor boy. And here you've known her longer than I have."

Jude shook his head and fell silent. O'Donnell wrapped up the book, looked at him, and said, "What's the matter now?"

"I almost don't want to say."

"Go ahead. I won't bite your head off."

Jude said one little thing was still bothering him. Bollingsworth — Pril — had asked him not to print anything about Byron's poem. So how did he, O'Donnell, know about it?

O'Donnell looked down a moment. "Okay, I'll answer. Just this once. But promise — after this, no more questions. It's hard on our friendship, in case you hadn't noticed."

He said Pril had told him. "And I give you permission to call her and check. Though I have to say, she seems to trust me a helluva lot more than you do." He

558

switched to another topic. "Now, what's that you're carrying? I notice you don't let it out of your sight. It looks like some kind of file."

Jude said that it was the archive file on old man Appleby's early years in Cyprus and Athens, the file that had piqued Ratnoff's interest.

"Jesus. Ratnoff didn't even enter that in his computer, as far as I know. It may be the Holy Grail. I suppose you're not going to tell me where you got it."

Jude didn't want to. A voice inside his head urged caution. It wasn't that he didn't have confidence in O'Donnell, not exactly. It was that he wanted to know what the file contained before he speculated about its possible role in Ratnoff's murder.

"No matter," said O'Donnell. "You know, I'd known Ratnoff for years and I got so I could read him pretty well. I never saw him as excited as he was those last few weeks. But then I heard he and Peregrin had hooked up and I figured that accounted for it. I thought that right up until his murder."

They stood up and started walking out of the park and up Central Park West.

Jude brought him up-to-date on everything that had happened while he was in police custody. He told him about the ice pick — that it was found in a trash can, kept for two weeks, and given to Devlin, who handed it over.

"Now get this. You'll never guess who it belongs to. Old man Hagenbuckle himself. Lucky for him he told Bollingsworth — Pril — before it surfaced."

"Holy shit! I mean . . . you don't think . . . He couldn't be the killer, could he? He might have the balls for it, but I can't believe he's got the brains."

"No. Pril has her sights set on Engleheart. She's told me my phone is tapped and I'm being followed, and she's convinced he's behind it."

"I know he's her prime suspect. Because of that article on police corruption. I suppose that's possible, but somehow it doesn't do it for me. What do you think?"

"Possible. Not probable. He doesn't seem the type to leave esoteric quotes around. Then there's Edith and the whole plagiarism thing. She's guilty as hell. A couple of nights ago, she confessed it to me. . . . She said she was trying to stay on top of the profession and got tired and began taking short-cuts. . . . That night at Shallow Brook, I saw her coming out of Boxby's cottage. They'd been in the sack."

"Boxby!" He made a face. "That's a bit repulsive to the imagination, isn't it? Still,

560

you got to hand it to her. She's not going down without a fight. She's trying to circle the wagons."

Later, neither Jude nor O'Donnell could remember which one of them had had the bright idea. It had seemed to make sense. And the more they talked about it, the more urgent seemed the need to act upon it. *Somebody* had to inform senior management about the plagiarism. Of course, in the book of sins, it hardly stacked up next to murder. But for the moment, there was nothing for them to do about the murders, and meanwhile the plagiarism scandal was just waiting to crack wide open. To salvage its honor, the *Globe* had to be the one to break it — provided, of course, that it resumed publishing soon.

So there they were, at ten o'clock at night, standing across the street from Skeeter Diamond's apartment building on Central Park West. They remained in the shadow of the trees, conferring for a moment on the best way to tell him. They agreed that Jude would do most of the talking. They waited at a red light.

Just as the light changed, they saw a taxi pull up. Inside was a familiar figure — her ponytail gave her away — leaning over, counting out the fare. Edith Sawyer. She slammed the cab door and walked toward the entrance of Diamond's building with a light step. The doorman whisked the door open for her and saluted her with a familiar nod as she passed him by. He didn't even call up to announce her arrival.

"So much for that idea," said O'Donnell. "She's doing more than circling the wagons. She's banging the goddamned wagon master."

56

Jude downed his second cup of coffee and stared out the window at Avenue B. The morning traffic had subsided to the usual snarl. He was looking to see if a particular car kept turning up, or a particular person — say, someone who might look a lot like Engleheart. Jude was reasonably sure he hadn't been followed last night during his escapades with O'Donnell, but that didn't mean his tail had dropped him.

TK whined and stuck her muzzle in the crook behind his knee, her signal that it was time for a walk. He took the leash from its hook next to the door and went downstairs. The tabs were lying on the doorstep. He checked out the headlines. GLOBE SHUTS DOWN, screamed the *Maul*. LAST GASP OF A DYING RAG, enthused the *Grifter*.

Outside there was still a breeze, and Jude turned his face to it, trying to clear his head. He had gone to bed around midnight, after reading through the archive file on Appleby. The information in it fit the theory that was beginning to evolve in his mind. He'd played with it as he was falling asleep and then when he had awakened at 3:00 a.m., pondering it some more.

Now, rounding the corner on Avenue B, as TK struggled against the leash, he plotted his next moves. He hurried home and called Van Wessel, asking him to come to the pressroom at the State Supreme Courthouse in half an hour. He fed TK, grabbed his cell phone, put on his jacket, and was out the door.

Before he ducked down the subway entrance, he looked around. A sky blue Corona crawled by. Did it look familiar? He couldn't tell. He took the stairs down, waited a minute, and came back up. It was gone.

By the time he arrived at the courts, Van Wessel was already there, waiting in the Dickensian pressroom. He was nursing a hangover and complaining. "We don't have a paper," he said, stroking his goatee. "So I fail to see the point of all this."

Jude promised to explain everything — eventually. But in the meantime, he needed a favor, a bit of digging, and it had to be done quickly and quietly. Did Van Wessel have a contact in the court who might be willing to help him out, no questions asked? Even if it meant crossing the line to look through sealed records filed anonymously under John Doe?

"I haven't spent the better part of a lifetime down here for nothing," replied Van Wessel. "Or come to think of it, maybe I have."

Still, he brightened at the prospect of intrigue. "Tell me: Does this have anything to do with the murders?"

"It does." Jude ripped out a page from his notebook and wrote down a single name: Tassius Appleby. "This is what I'm looking for." He handed it over.

Van Wessel straightened up.

"Holy shit," he said.

"You see why this is important."

"I do indeed."

"What I need is the law firm that filed the John Doe. Who they represent. When it was filed. And, of course, everything in it. That's a tall order. Think you can do it?"

"You can count on me."

"Come to think of it, you should also check his original name." He took back the slip of paper and wrote it down: Appinopoulis.

Jude had the impression that it had been a long time since anyone had asked anything of Van Wessel. He had been a good reporter in his day, Jude recalled, before he developed a fondness for the grape and then moved on to higher fermentations.

Jude emphasized that he needed the material urgently and that it was important for Van Wessel to contact him the moment he came up with something. He gave him his cell phone number.

"And remember," he added. "Not a word."

Van Wessel nodded solemnly. "I may need a drink when this is over."

"I'll join you."

Jude took the subway uptown, got out at Eighty-sixth Street, walked over to West End Avenue, and found the number he was looking for. A solid prewar building with a green awning. He gave his name and business card to the doorman and said he was here to see Mrs. Ratnoff. As the doorman pressed the buzzer, Jude glanced over at the apartment listing and spotted her number: 5B. The doorman put his ear close to the intercom and listened to what sounded like an angry buzzing down the line. Abruptly, it cut off.

"She says she's not seeing anyone — especially anyone from the *Globe*." He opened the front door unceremoniously and pointed a long forefinger toward the pavement.

Jude walked down half a block, leaned against the building, and waited. After some fifteen minutes, a deliveryman arrived with a cart carrying four supermarket bags. He was escorted upstairs by the doorman. Jude entered the foyer and ran his finger down two rows of buttons, pushing six of them. A cacophony of voices responded, demanding to know who was there. Jude mumbled a few sentences. One of them bit. He heard the telltale buzz. The door was unlocked.

On the fifth floor, Mrs. Ratnoff refused to open the door. He heard a scraping sound and through the peephole he saw a bulging eyeball sizing him up.

"I said I don't want to see anyone from the *Globe*," said a high-pitched voice.

"Mrs. Ratnoff, I'm not just anyone. I'm an investigative reporter. I'm here because I need to talk to you. I think your husband was killed because he was on the verge of discovering some important information and certain people wanted to keep him quiet. I think he was a true newspaperman doing his job. . . ."

"Like I give a shit."

The eyeball blinked. He tried to look solicitous.

"He was always very kind to me," he lied.

"I could give a flying fuck."

"I think some of what I've uncovered doesn't put the *Globe* in a very good light."

A long pause. Then: "Were you friends with that Whibbleby woman?"

"Me? Friends with that slut? Not on your life."

There followed the sound of lock bolts sliding back, three of them. The door opened a foot and he squeezed through.

Mrs. Ratnoff seemed smaller than he remembered from the funeral. She was dressed in a ratty bathrobe and wore no makeup. Her hair showed gray roots.

The apartment was stifling. As a living space, it didn't jibe with his image of Ratnoff. A motley parakeet was sulking in a cage in a corner. Dirty lace doilies were spread on the arms of overstuffed chairs. The smell of old baking grease permeated the air.

Grudgingly, his hostess offered him green tea. He quickly accepted, following the reporter's dictum that you take anything that keeps you where you want to be.

While it was brewing, he kept up his patter. He asked if Ratnoff had told her anything about his work in the weeks before his death. Not much, no more than usual, she said. Which meant not a word. Had he seemed excited? As if he had discovered something? Not particularly. If he had, he wouldn't have said anything. So their relationship wasn't one in which they talked a great deal to each other? No, not a hell of a lot.

But she then began talking to him. And once she'd started, there was no stopping her. She went on and on about Ratnoff's long service to the company, the plethoric work hours, the fact that he was rarely at home, the paper's paltry death benefits, the times he was passed over for promotion, the illicit affair.

Casually, as if the request flowed naturally from their conversation, Jude asked if he might take a look at Ratnoff's study, perhaps a glance at some of his papers. By now, the widow was totally in his corner.

She led him to a windowless back room and left him there. Ratnoff's desk was spotless, with papers perfectly stacked, pencils neatly aligned, and small wooden trays filled with orderly groupings of paper clips, rubber bands, and staples. On the floor to the right of the computer was a filing cabinet. Jude dived in.

Two hours — and three cups of green tea — later, he had found nothing of interest except for a single snapshot of Peregrin in a blue polka-dot bikini. On it, Ratnoff had written her body measurements in purple ink. It was filed under "Current Affairs." (Who would have guessed he had such a wicked sense of humor?)

Jude went through all the files. Ratnoff had set up a mirror archive of the Appleby family papers from the morgue. Undoubtedly, he had used the pneumatic tubes to smuggle the files out of the basement and, once copied, to return them. But Jude had already read all that material in O'Donnell's computer.

There was only one place left to look for the document he was seeking — the two-foot-high safe at the bottom of a closet. He spun the dial. It turned easily and kept turning. How would he ever find the combination? Mrs. Ratnoff, in the kitchen, had readily given him permission to open the safe, but she had no idea of the combination. He plied her with questions and scribbled the answers in his notebook: Ratnoff's birth date, her birth date, their wedding date, the birth dates of their children, of their parakeet, and so on.

He tried them all, without success, then sat back in frustration. The more he tried to crack the combination, the more he became convinced the safe held the answer to make everything else fall into place. He tilted back in the chair, breathed deeply. He let his mind roam and it returned to the photo of Peregrin. He retrieved it. Was Ratnoff's humor *that* wicked? He entered the three numbers of her bust, waist, and hips: 39 — 28 — 41. The door clicked open.

Inside was a lifetime of documents about the Ratnoff family: birth certificates, marriage license, insurance policies, bank accounts, the mortgage. And resting on the very bottom was a plain brown envelope, the kind used at the newspaper. Carefully, Jude opened it. He saw a gray photostat of an official-looking document with seals and ribbons, written in a florid hand and indecipherable language — Greek, he assumed. He couldn't read it, but he was convinced it was what he had been searching for. He had found the key piece of the puzzle.

In deference to Mrs. Ratnoff, he gave her the family papers, had one last cup of tea, and listened patiently as she attacked the *Globe*'s spousal dental plan. Then he left with the document in his breast pocket. On the way out, he gave a tip to the doorman, who was astonished but received it with a small, practiced bow.

For the first time in what seemed like

ages, walking down the street, Jude felt the reporter's rush — that wonderful excitement that children experience in coming to the finale of a treasure hunt. But as always, it was soon followed by anxiety. What if someone else found the same information? What if — especially now that there was no paper — a competitor beat him to the punch? What if the treasure slipped from his hand?

But then, as if to prove that sometimes in life good things do follow one upon the other, he received a text message: DUE TO PUBLIC DEMAND, *GLOBE* TO PUBLISH SOONEST. REPORT EMERGENCY NEWS CENTER QUEENS PLANT TODAY 6:00 P.M. REPEAT 6:00 P.M. THE MANAGEMENT.

He dialed O'Donnell, got a recording, and yelled joyfully into the phone, "I just got the text message about the Queens plant. We're back in business!"

57

After an afternoon of running around, Jude jumped in a cab and gave the address of the Queens plant. He looked at his watch: 5:15. With luck, he'd make it by six o'clock. He wondered what the setup would be to write the story — what computers had been installed, what the deadline would be, how many other reporters would be there.

The emergency news center in the Queens plant had been constructed after 9/11, to be used in the event of a terrorist attack in mid-Manhattan. No one Jude knew had actually seen it in operation, and he looked forward to trying it out. And what a story he had to inaugurate it! Not everything had fallen into place, but he had dug up enough new information to cast the Ratnoff case in a new light.

Van Wessel had come through. He had not only gained access to the John Doe papers at the court, he had managed to photocopy them, too. That was essential. Jude would need them for backup, since no editor worth his salt would let a story like this through without unassailable documentation. It was, after all, one that would rock the *Globe* to its very foundation.

The papers cleared up the mystery of Appleby's early years in Cyprus. The final proof was the official document from Ratnoff's safe, which Jude had translated two hours ago, thanks to the help of an olive-complexioned, long-lashed secretary at the Greek consulate on East Seventy-ninth Street. The information opened up an entirely different line of possibilities in terms of a motive for murder. It was time to bring Pril into the loop. He would need her help in tracking down the participants and figuring out what role each one had played in what was shaping up as a nefarious plot to take over the newspaper.

The taxi crossed the Triborough Bridge. Jude had been able to give rudimentary directions to the driver, who, as a recent immigrant from Sri Lanka, appeared to know Queens better than Manhattan.

Jude had visited the plant once, shortly after it opened in July 2000. He went on a tour with two dozen other reporters, crammed into a bus slowed by Friday afternoon traffic. This was back in the days when management thought it advantageous for employees to know how "the product," as it was coming to be called, was "manufactured." The newsroom had been rife with stories about the supermodern technology at the plant, run almost entirely by robots, which, of course, made for endless jokes about how it was simply an extension of the newsroom's editors.

Once there, though, the jokes evaporated. For the place, almost as large as a football field, was so technologically advanced, it took their breath away. The full-color presses stood three stories high, governed by a computer console that looked as if it could guide a rocket ship — and it required only six technicians to run it. Automated racks, twenty feet high, sorted the advance Sunday sections as they ran off the presses and stored them until needed, then melded them into a million complete papers.

Most impressive of all were the robots, called "drones." They were wheeled vehicles like cut-down pickup trucks and they transported the fourteen-hundred-pound rolls of newsprint to the presses, zooming across a spotless floor at thirty miles an hour, missing one another by inches. The drones almost looked alive. Each one had an internal guidance system that told it what to do and when. After an hour or so, as its electrical charge diminished, the guidance sent it to a renewal station in a corner, where it rested, seemingly content, until able to work again. The technicians called these periods "coffee breaks," which, of course, had inspired a new round of jokes from the reporters. ("Hey, we used to get those," etc.)

The cab was delayed on the Grand Central Parkway and took side roads, skirting St. Michael's Cemetery and navigating the Whitestone Expressway. Finally, forty minutes and twenty-eight dollars later, Jude arrived at his destination on an isolated bluff overlooking the water near the Whitestone Bridge.

He was deposited at the bottom of a driveway, concrete reinforced with steel grating to carry the trailer trucks and delivery vans. There was no sidewalk leading down to the plant's entrance. Everything about the place suggested that it had been made for automatons, not humans.

The plant was surrounded by a cyclone fence topped by razor wire. A large swinging gate was open about two feet, and he slipped through it. There was a guardhouse to the left of the entrance road, but it was unoccupied. No one was in sight. That was odd. Jude hadn't expected a flood of people to be arriving, but he thought he might run into some colleagues answering the paper's summons. Perhaps the message had gone out only to a few reporters and editors, a skeleton crew to get the *Globe* up and running.

The double glass doors of the main entrance were closed and locked, but a notice taped on the inside directed all emergency employees to report to a side entrance. That was the first encouraging sign that *someone* was expecting them. He followed a cement walkway along the edge of the building and turned a corner. Forty feet ahead was a lighted globe and, underneath it, the door. He turned the knob and stepped inside.

He found himself on the main floor. The surface was as smooth as an ice-skating rink, but its white sheathing was marred by rubber tire marks crisscrossing in all directions. He remembered looking down on the floor from a catwalk during the tour, being told that it was thoroughly cleaned of all surface debris in off-hours so that the drones could speed along their computer-designated paths perfectly. He heard a distant rumbling, the presses getting ready to roll.

He looked around. He still didn't see

anyone. Thirty feet up in the air, the narrow metal catwalks hugged the walls. Off in the distance was the tower for the controlling computer console, its sheer walls rising up from the white floor like the bridge of a surfacing submarine. He remembered that the control panels were on the far side, which meant that the technicians manning them were out of sight.

Forty feet away, lined up against the wall in perfect order like Russian missiles on parade, were the drones. He looked at their four-foot-tall thick rubber tires with deep grooves. The drones were loaded with gigantic rolls of newsprint and they appeared even more immense when viewed from the same level.

Jude walked to the center of the floor, searching for a staircase that might lead to the offices. He stopped, wondering which way to go. He heard a sound, an electronic humming. At first, he thought it came from the presses, a start-up signal of some sort. But as he looked around, he caught a blur of movement off to one side. Turning, he saw one of the drones begin to move, rocking slightly. Abruptly, it lurched forward five feet, then stopped. Another nearby did the same. And a third. On a wall, a yellow light flashed. He knew what it was: a warning light!

The robots were preparing to feed the presses. Jude performed a quick calculation. If they sped across the floor, he could run either toward the control tower or back toward the door he had entered. He tried to visualize the tower he had seen years ago. If he reached it, was there a staircase there, a steel ladder, any means to escape the floor? Or would he still be exposed to the speeding drones?

He chose the door and began to run for it. Turning, he saw a drone leaving its base. It moved dead ahead with a speed that was remarkable for such a large machine. Behind it, another moved. This one seemed to be coming toward him. In a minute, the floor would be covered with them, thundering around in all directions.

He heard a crack. Ahead of him, on the floor, was a small explosion, a tiny cloud of white dust. He recognized the sound. He looked up, searching the catwalks. There it was — the unmistakable black barrel of a gun. Someone was shooting at him! Cutting off his path to the door! Another crack, another explosion. This one was closer. He turned and ran in a zigzag path toward the tower.

Out of the corner of his eye, he saw a drone moving fast. Its trajectory would cut him off. He halted, waited a few seconds. The drone passed by in front, no more than two feet ahead. He could feel the breeze and hear the whirring of its tires. He heard another sound, the smack of a bullet hitting the surface two feet away. He ran again and saw another drone coming behind him. The wall where they had been parked was empty. All of them were on the move.

He reached the base of the tower. He heard voices, shouts, running feet. He ducked out of view around the side of the tower. More shots were fired, this time above him. He leaned out cautiously, searching the catwalk high across the floor. The gun barrel was gone. No one could be seen. Then he heard more voices.

The yellow light stopped flashing. The drones slowed, then stopped. Everything seemed to be rolling in reverse. He found steps set into the metal side of the tower and started up. As he reached the top, he saw a technician pushing buttons quickly, surrounded by a knot of four or five people. One of them was Pril. She was breathing heavily. Evidently, she had just arrived. She held a gun, which she dropped in her holster, and rushed over to him. She grabbed him and held him at arm's length, as if to check him for injuries.

"Are you okay?" she asked urgently. "Are you all right?"

He said he was. But he was surprised how hard it was to talk. He was breathing so fast, he had to bend over. His voice seemed to get stuck somewhere in his throat.

"Somebody was shooting at me," he managed to say. He straightened up and pointed in the direction of the catwalk.

"We know," said Pril. "We're on it."

She took him to a canteen and led him to a chair. O'Donnell walked in and gave him a hug. He fished in his pocket, came up with four quarters, put them in a machine, and came back with a cup of steaming brown liquid that he insisted was coffee. It tasted foul. As he lifted the cup, Jude saw that his hand was shaking. He set the cup down.

"Nothing to be embarrassed about," Pril said. "It's not every day somebody tries to kill you."

He asked her how they came to be there.

"He's the one who insisted we come," she said, tilting her head toward O'Donnell. "You told him you got a text message to report to work. He became suspicious when he didn't get one and neither did anyone he knows. So he figured it might be a trap."

"The whole thing was a trap?" Jude thought of the empty guardhouse, the hand-drawn sign directing him to a side door. He should have been more alert.

"That's right."

"What happened to security?"

"Mostly off duty because of the shutdown."

"So there's no start-up of the paper?"

"No," said O'Donnell.

"And what was the idea? The killer starts up the drones and I was supposed to be run over by them? That's kind of a stretch, isn't it?"

"No, it isn't," she replied. "The technician says the drones are put through their paces every day at the same time. And the presses are run, too, even though they don't print a paper. They have to do that to keep everything in working order. I think you were supposed to be shot — probably at close range. When the drones started up, the killer probably improvised."

"It would have appealed to him," added O'Donnell. "There's a progression to the murders. First an editor's spike, then a bundler, then a TV broadcast, and finally a drone. Each one a little more ghoulish."

Jude was beginning to calm down. "Did you catch him?" he asked.

Bollingsworth's police radio came to life. She walked off and held it to her ear. In seconds, they heard her cursing.

"Shit, keep at it," she yelled. She signed off and turned toward them.

"They lost him. He ran around the back and got over the fence. Must have cut a hole in the razor wire when he first got here. He had his car right there. He took off before they even reached the fence. They've radioed ahead, but we don't know which way he's going — he could be crossing the bridge or going back to the city. Either way, he'll be gone before any other patrol cars get into the area."

"New York's finest," said O'Donnell.

Pril spun around, angry.

"If we hadn't come here, chances are your friend would be dead," she said. "So can it."

He held both hands out, palms down, in a calming gesture.

"Did they see the license plate?" asked Jude.

"No. Only a partial description of the car itself."

"Let me guess. A blue Corona."

"How'd you know?"

He explained that was the car that had been following him. "Any way to trace my

583

text message?" he asked.

"Let me see it," she said.

He handed it over.

She shook her head no. "It's been blocked."

"Shit. Of all the dumb luck. Let's get out of here."

"Fine," she said. "But you're not going home. You're not going to spend another night at your place until we catch this guy."

"I'll give you a lift," said O'Donnell.

On the way to the car, O'Donnell put his arm around him. "By the way," he said, "we got word that the *Globe*'s board has called an emergency meeting. Ten a.m. tomorrow. No idea what it's about. But if you've got any cards up your sleeve, now's the time to play them."

Jude hesitated for only a moment.

"I have a card," he said. He reached into his pocket and pulled out the slip of paper with Clive's name and address. He handed it to O'Donnell. "That is, if you don't mind a wild card."

58

Jude sat in the rear while O'Donnell drove, Pril beside him in the passenger seat. The adrenaline flowing through his system had reached high tide and was just beginning to recede. He leaned against the back of the seat, feeling both drained and elated.

The Irishman drove like a madman. Every so often, he turned around to look at Jude, taking his eyes off the road for a good four or five seconds. During one of these inspections, he said, "So, it sounds like you got a big story. What is it, kiddo?"

"About old man Appleby."

"That much, I gathered. Tell us about it — in full. Pril may have missed school that day."

"Okay." Jude thought it would be good to talk, help settle his nerves. He turned his back to the door, hoisted his legs onto the seat, and settled in.

"It goes way back — eighty-six years, in

fact, about the time Appleby arrived in New York. Of course, he wasn't Appleby then. He was Tassius Appinopoulis — a young immigrant from Greece. He was twenty-two years old, he had five hundred dollars in his pocket, and he was burning with the desire to become very rich.

"He actually came from Cyprus, from a tiny village in the mountains. He had lived there all his life and was known to everyone — and respected by everyone. Apparently, he was the most intelligent and ambitious boy they had ever seen. I saw a photo of him in the archives. He had dark brown eyes that looked like they could see into the future. He went to a crumbling old schoolhouse, where most of the pupils were barefooted, like him, and sat on wooden benches. He was so smart that the schoolmaster had to devise special lessons for him. He was put in a class all by himself.

"The boy grew up. And as he grew, the villagers noticed something else about him. He was not only smart and handsome; he was tough — not just physically but in spirit, as well. If he got in a fight in the school yard — and there were many fights because the other boys were jealous — he would always win. Sometimes he won in an underhanded way, but it didn't matter. He would do whatever it took to come out on top. Because of this, his family was not particularly popular. But the mayor and a handful of village elders had a different view. They realized they had a treasure in their midst. So one day, they came up with a plan. They entreated every family in the village to put up a certain sum. This nest egg would be given to the boy when he became a man. He would go off into the world and use it to make a fortune and come back and help his village.

"The boy was more than willing to go — he had a lust to travel. He wanted to see the world beyond his village, beyond his island, even beyond his country. But there was a catch: He had fallen in love with a young woman. And she, in turn, loved him. I imagine she was beautiful — there's a reference to a photo of her he carried with him across the ocean, but it's gone from the files. I suspect somebody found it and threw it out.

"Anyway, as you might expect, the two lovers fled one night. They ran off to the nearest large town, where they stayed in an inn. Apparently for weeks, though exactly how long is not clear. But when they eventually returned to the village, her family was dishonored by the scandal. Her father and mother wanted to punish the boy and force him to marry her and stay in Cyprus. But the elders wouldn't hear of it. They insisted that the boy live up to the agreement and go off to Athens to make a pile of money to save the village from destitution. So he left.

"On the very day that his ship arrived in Athens, fate played an ugly trick. He was mugged on the docks. Within six hours, he had lost all the money he had been given. You can imagine how distraught, ashamed, and angry he was. After several days, he happened to meet another Cypriot, someone from another part of the island, who had done well. He told his story and the man took him under his wing. For two years the man taught him everything he knew about business — he was in the olive oil trade — and the boy was a quick learner. Then his mentor bankrolled him. He gave him the five hundred dollars and sent him off to the New World.

"O'Donnell, you know the rest of this story. We all know it at the *Globe* because we've read it in any number of biographies. It's part of the newspaper's legend. But the legend doesn't tell us everything. It leaves out the most interesting parts, including the maiden lover back in Cyprus. All that comes from letters, which is what Ratnoff was working on.

"As the biographies tell us, the young immigrant prospered. He worked in the Fur District, came to own his own store, then moved on to food wholesaling and even shipping. During the Depression, he bought the *Globe* and transformed it into a powerful, profitable newspaper. Somewhere along the way, he changed his name from Appinopoulis to Appleby. He married a society doyenne in 1938 and two years later had a daughter, Abigail. He doted on her. He used to call her 'the Appleby of my eye.' Eventually, he passed the paper on to the man his daughter married, the current publisher, Elisha Hagenbuckle.

"Appleby was true to the agreement with the village elders. He sent piles of money back to Cyprus. If you go there today, you'll find shops, an olive oil refinery, a first-class hospital, and, most notably, a modern school."

Jude looked out the window at the lights of Manhattan. They were crossing the Triborough. The city had never looked so alluring.

"Go on," said O'Donnell.

"Let him catch his breath," insisted Bollingsworth. "All in good time."

"Now," said Jude, "we come to the part of

589

the story that's not known. It turns out that Appleby didn't forget his first love — far from it. When he returned to the village to check on his investments, he took up with her again, and, in fact, got her pregnant. Note the year this happened: 1938. In other words, shortly before he married the society woman. A psychologist might say it was his last spasm of freedom. Or maybe of true love.

"The child that was born from this union, another daughter, was born in 1939. He sent money to raise her in Greece. Something happened to the mother — I don't know what. She disappeared. Maybe she died. In any case, Appleby brought the daughter to America. She went to boarding school and college here and married. It's not known if Appleby saw her, probably not. But he did give her a handsome present — a large Colonial house in Greenwich, Connecticut, and a stipend to live on. The newly married woman bore a son. Tragically, a short while later, she and her husband were killed in a car accident. The son, now an orphan, was sent to the Midwest to live with a family that was compensated by Appleby. Was the boy told that the man and woman he was living with were not his real father and mother? We don't know.

"This last part of the story was pieced together by a team of private investigators who pored through records for over two years. In broad outline, it's contained in a thick file in the New York State Supreme Court. The file is sealed, but our man down at the courts managed to get it. It's the central element in a lawsuit filed by outside interests on behalf of the boy, who now is a young man nearly twenty-five years old. From the suit, we know the names of the lawyers representing the plaintiffs and we know the name of one of the plaintiffs, but not the main ones. We don't know the identity of the young man — a reference makes it sound like he works for the paper. It's not clear whether he himself knows his lineage or even knows that the lawsuit has been filed on his behalf. There's an important catch."

O'Donnell couldn't contain himself. "Who's the plaintiff we know?"

"Elmer Boxby."

"Boxby! I'll be damned. I never did care for that worm. And what's the purpose of the suit?"

"It claims, on behalf of the young man, who is, after all, the grandson of Appleby, nothing less than complete and total ownership of the *Globe*."

"But how's that possible? Even assuming everything you've said is true? Hagenbuckle has two sons already, not to mention a whole slew of his wife's cousins."

"That's the catch," said Jude. "Are you ready for this?" He paused just a moment to run up the suspense. "It turns out that the young man's mother was not illegitimate after all."

"Explain!"

"When her own mother and the young Appinopoulis ran off all those years ago, they did more than fall into the nearest bed. *They got married.* She gave her virginity to him and so he gave his name to her. The villagers probably didn't even know about it. The marriage never ended in divorce. It remained valid to the end of their lives. So you see, the marriage that's illegal — since it constituted bigamy — is Appleby's second one. It was the one that produced young Abigail, Hagenbuckle's wife. If anyone is an illegitimate child, it is she."

"Incredible! So this is the secret Ratnoff was trying to track down for his book. What a bombshell that would have been."

"Yes. And he was successful. He learned the whole story. He even went to Cyprus and managed to find the original marriage certificate and bring back a duplicate. I found it in a safe in his apartment yesterday. He wasn't the only one to do this. Another duplicate is contained in the court papers.

"For Ratnoff, as you suspected, was not the only one on the trail. Others were ahead of him, and they learned the story, too. They filed the information under the name John Doe to keep the names secret, and they planned to get a court decision at the proper time. Meanwhile, their goal, presumably, was to discover the identity of Appleby's grandson. Once he was in pocket, maybe even contractually bound to them, they were going to use him to take over the *Globe.*"

"So Ratnoff was a threat to them," said Pril. "He would have revealed their plans prematurely, and that's why they had to get rid of him."

"That's certainly likely."

"Sounds like a motive for murder to me," she said. "But, Jude, you weren't going to write this, were you? When you went to the Queens plant tonight?"

"I was thinking of it."

"But with Boxby's name and the name of the law firm, we can identify everyone who's involved in this. We have phone records and access to phone records. You've got to hold off just a little longer. You don't want to tip our hand."

"I don't know," he said, sitting up and lowering his feet to the car floor. "I don't much like the idea of using phone records taken from the paper." But he knew, even as he spoke the words, that her argument made sense.

"Oh, you and your damn First Amendment," she said.

"The one thing I don't know is when the plaintiffs are planning to come out of the woodwork. When are they going to reveal the name of the true heir and take over the paper?"

"I know that," said O'Donnell. "Tomorrow. As I mentioned, Boxby's scheduled an emergency board meeting, and I'll bet my bottom dollar that's the reason. So if the *Globe* doesn't start publishing tomorrow, we're screwed. The only way we can get the story out is to give it to the *Maul* or the *Grifter*. I'd rather piss glass."

"Not necessarily," said Jude. "There may be another way."

59

"Dude. Welcome to the *Globe* newsroom in exile!" Clive exclaimed as Jude and O'Donnell walked in.

"I believe you," said O'Donnell. "It's messy enough."

He and Jude had dropped Pril off near the station house to follow up the investigation. They had no trouble finding Clive's home, a fourth-floor apartment in a ratty building on West 116th Street, near Columbia University. When they had parked out front, they'd seen so many young people ducking in and out the front door, they'd thought it could pass for a poker club.

Inside, it looked like a student apartment. Dishes overflowed the kitchen sink, and grease-stained pizza boxes and empty cans of Bud littered the shelves and windowsills. Posters of Che, Bart Simpson, and Mick Jagger hung on the walls. Two frayed couches, one purple, the other green, sat side by side. Books were everywhere — lying on tables, used as doorstops, and jammed willy-nilly in a ten-foot-long set of shelves that lined the entrance hallway.

The apartment was crowded. About ten young men and women were busy in a living room and an adjacent dining room, most of them clustered around three wooden desks that had been pushed together. Four computers were on the desks, all of them up and running. Chris, the Web master, sat before one of them, leaning forward in his chair like a jockey on the home stretch.

Jude recognized four or five others from the *Globe* but didn't know their names. They had worked in the digital end of the operation, which to him was a foreign country, where he didn't speak the language and wasn't especially fond of the culture. But this place, he admitted quietly to himself, had the frenetic feel of a genuine newsroom.

The news, Clive explained, was being piped out to the *Globe*'s Web site, which they had activated with secret computer commands and codes. A few chosen reporters had been cooperating, dropping by to send off stories. Some of the Web people were cribbing articles from the wires or going off to cover things themselves — their first taste of street reporting, which they found exciting.

The articles were posted anonymously because the paper's management hadn't given them permission to use the site. In fact, Clive added, if you wanted to be a stickler, you might say the entire operation was technically outside the law.

"I see," said Jude. "My friend here works closely with a policewoman. Maybe you shouldn't let him participate."

"Don't worry," O'Donnell said. "She's strictly homicide. If you haven't killed anyone, you don't have anything to worry about."

Clive introduced them to the others. He was clearly proud of the setup.

"The quality of the report's pretty good so far," he said. "We had an exclusive earlier today on a proposed bill in Albany that would deny dental treatment to illegal immigrants. If they're apprehended after they've had cavities fixed, they have to give the silver fillings back. We wrote about the Republican senator found giving a blow job to a pilot in the janitor's closet in the Orlando airport — both claimed they weren't gay and it was just an accident. And we've even got a big shot in Washington writing a column for us. I can't tell you who he is, but I can give you a clue: He's as rotund as Orson Welles."

"You seem cut out to be an editor," said Jude. He noticed that a quote from Adlai Stevenson had been attached to Clive's computer: "An editor is someone who separates the wheat from the chaff and then prints the chaff."

"And I see you still remember who the white hats are."

He had always liked Clive and thought him talented, but for some reason the young man hadn't been able to catch the eye of people who mattered when it came to bumping news assistants up to reporters. Usually, that grueling process of menial servitude took two years. Clive was already in his third year, and if he didn't make it soon, he would have to move along to some other organization.

Clive brought over a chair for O'Donnell and sat the two of them in front of his computer. He cleared the screen, typed in a few commands, and opened a blank page.

"Okay," he said, "whatcha got?"

Jude and O'Donnell stared at each other. "Jesus Christ," said O'Donnell, "he's been hanging around Grabble too much. Doesn't he sound just like him now?"

They decided, as discussed with Pril, to hold off on the story of the lawsuit and the shooting at the Queens plant. Instead, they would unload the whole sad saga of Edith Sawyer's plagiarism.

Chris came over with brief instructions: "No bylines and nothing traceable. That's the rule. Other than that, anything goes."

"How about a dateline?" asked Jude. "What's the date anyway?"

"October first. But on the Web, you leave that off. It's on the site itself."

O'Donnell tapped into his own computer at the *Globe* and was able to extract the files detailing her theft. Together they shaped the story, Jude at the keyboard and O'Donnell sometimes dictating. The others came over to watch, astounded and shocked at what Sawyer had done. In black and white, with a number of examples, Sawyer's transgression looked even more brazen.

When they were finished, Clive came over and took Jude's seat. He said he thought that the story was tough but important and had to be put before the public. Shaking his head sadly, he struck the keys to speed it to the Web site.

"Anything more?" he asked.

O'Donnell looked over at Jude tentatively. "What do you think?" he asked, beginning to relish the idea that had struck him. "The ice pick — who it belongs to and all that. It's a significant advance in the case, finding the murder weapon. And look at it this way: How often does a hack get a chance to write that the vile instrument that struck down a senior editor belongs to none other than *the publisher?* That's something to tell your grandchildren."

Jude smiled and told him to go ahead. He himself was exhausted. His day had been one for the books: running down to the courthouse, dealing with Ratnoff's widow, getting shot at in the Queens plant, and then writing the story about Sawyer. They all agreed that it would be foolhardy for him to return home, given that somebody out there was trying to kill him. Clive readily showed him to a cot in a back room. Jude called his neighbor on Avenue B to look after TK. Then he took off his clothes, got in bed, and was about to drop off to sleep, when there was a soft knock on the door.

Clive came in, apologizing profusely for keeping him up a few minutes longer.

"I need to talk to you," he said. "Or to somebody, and I'm glad you're here, because I think you're the best person."

He sat down on the floor with a beer and slowly, as if he still didn't believe it, said that something had happened to him that day, something he could scarcely fathom. Out of the blue, he had received a phone call. He was invited to a meeting at an attorney's office and he was strongly urged to attend. He said yes. A black limousine fetched him and took him to a skyscraper on Wall Street. When he arrived, he was ushered into the plush office of a senior partner, where two elderly attorneys awaited him. They smiled at him kindly, offered him a seat, and had a secretary bring in an excellent cup of coffee. And then they told him an incredible tale.

Jude knew what the story was, but he heard Clive out. The young man recounted everything he had been told: Appleby's youthful transgression, his rise to power, his will, and the secret of his own birth.

"I still can't take it in," he said. "I grew up in Minneapolis in a foster family named Small. I used to pester my parents . . . my foster parents . . . with questions about how I got there. They never talked about it fully, and so after a while, I gave up. I stopped thinking about it. This — it's a lot to assimilate all at once."

"I can appreciate that," said Jude. "You realize, of course, that it means you'll assume a position of prominence at the paper.

Perhaps even run it." He filled him in on the John Doe lawsuit and the attempt to wrest control of the *Globe* away from Hagenbuckle. Clive was amazed.

"Welcome to the dog-eat-dog world of New York media," Jude said. The advice he gave was simple: "For the time being, until everything shakes down, tell no one, no one at all.

"And promise me one thing," he added. "When you get to the top of the mountain, you'll stop saying 'dude.' And now, I've got to go to sleep."

In the morning, Jude slept late. Clive was gone — to a meeting somewhere downtown, said one of his roommates. O'Donnell had stayed over also, so the two went to the West End Bar and Grill for breakfast. On the street, they passed a newsstand and looked down at the tabloids.

"Guess they picked up our stories," O'Donnell said.

The headlines were so triumphant, you could almost feel the delight in the hands that had crafted them. GLOBE SCRIBE NABBED RED-HANDED, shrieked the *Maul,* above a file photo of a bleached-out-looking Edith Sawyer. The *Grifter* had gone one better: MURDER ICE PICK POINTS TO GLOBE

PUBLISHER.

"You know," said O'Donnell. "Writing those stories was painless. No editors, no second-guessing, no rewrites. I'm beginning to think this thing called the Internet has something to recommend it."

60

With the *Globe* closed, the board needed a place to assemble, and so Boxby had rented a banquet room at the Hotel Edison on West Forty-seventh Street. He knew the hotel well because he often ate lunch in its cafeteria, dubbed by regulars "the Polish Tea Room." He was able to secure a good rate, which he thought would impress the members and — more important — Moloch, soon to be his new boss.

A long table surrounded by folding chairs dominated the room. The board members traipsed in and looked around suspiciously. Hagenbuckle performed his automatic count and quickly realized he was shy two votes. Guilden and Rosen were missing. That was odd — he had arrived with them in a taxi. Boxby went to fetch them, found them in a video arcade, and returned with them in tow. Behind him came a dirty-looking man in a wrinkled raincoat, who went to a closet, hung up his coat, and began rummaging around the cleaning equipment. A janitor, thought Hagenbuckle. No matter.

He sat at the head of the table — unchallenged this time, he noted gratefully — and called the meeting to order. Boxby read the minutes of the last meeting, which halted at the anthrax scare and then resumed only for the final vote in the computer control room. Geyser, Hagenbuckle noted, was barely listening. He sat there unusually quiet and composed, a smile playing upon his face.

Why became apparent a few moments later, when the floor was opened for "new business." Geyser rose. Calmly, he said he would like to poll the board members on a point of information. He asked how many had read that morning's story in the *New York Graphic.* A smattering of hands went up.

"For those of you who have not read it, let me summarize it," Geyser offered. "It said that the police have located what is believed to be the murder weapon in the killing of the late Mr. Ratnoff. And said weapon — the famous ice pick — belongs to none other than our publisher here, Mr. Hagenbuckle. I would venture to say that suspicion of murder is ipso facto a qualification for moral turpitude."

"Back to that damn paint thinner," said Rosen.

"Shut up," said Guilden. "But who's Ibsen Fatso?"

Geyser glared them into silence. Hagenbuckle stared balefully at Geyser. He had wondered if anyone would bring up that damned story. He himself had been bowled over when he read it over his breakfast tray. He hadn't had time to prepare a strong line of defense.

"You can hardly put any stock in that," he said. "It's a tabloid."

"But the story itself cited the *Globe*'s Web site as a source."

Shit. He must have skipped over that part. He had to think quickly.

"But that's hardly possible, is it? We've shut down the entire operation. There is no *Globe* Web site that's up and running."

"Then who is writing all these stories, and how are they posting them?"

Hagenbuckle hadn't realized the Web site was up. He was getting hot under the collar and looked over at Geyser's neck. He noticed that the other board members were sliding their chairs back from the table. And what was that damned janitor doing in the back of the room? It looked like he had pulled out a mop.

Boxby's voice cut through the air. He sounded unusually assertive. What was that he was saying? In the general atmosphere of confusion, it took a moment for Boxby's words to make themselves heard. He had to repeat himself three times, each time a bit louder.

"I've an announcement to make," he said. "An important announcement. It is essential that you all be absolutely quiet and listen to me." Finally, he gave a piercing whistle and shouted, "Listen up!"

And they did. He launched into what seemed to be a prepared speech.

"We need a change at the helm of this company. We need new leadership. Never mind the murders — they're just a symbol of deeper problems. The whole company is dying. Circulation is stagnant; advertising revenue is plummeting; readers are fleeing to the Internet. In short, the *Globe* — which for some reason the publisher here keeps calling an aircraft carrier — is sinking. And we've no compass! No life preservers! No lifeboats!

"We need someone who can turn this situation around, someone responsive to the concerns of stockholders, someone willing to make the tough decisions — close more bureaus, let more reporters go, cut back on health plans, take on more freelancers."

Boxby appeared to be gaining strength, and conviction, the more he talked. He got out of his chair and walked around the table. "So we add a little more water to the soup. No one will notice. And so what if they do — they're not going to give up soup!"

"Soup! What soup?" yelled Hagenbuckle. "We're talking about a newspaper here — not some goddamned soup!"

He jumped to his feet, his face crimson, the veins at his temples throbbing visibly. The others moved their seats back still farther. Boxby came to a halt at the far end of the table. He did not, however, look cowed. Far from it, he looked eager and challenging, as if a force that had been bottled inside was finally free.

"I'm not through," he said. "Sit down and listen,"

Unaccountably, Hagenbuckle did.

What happened next proved so astounding that multiple accounts of it later surfaced. The most reliable would come from Danny Devlin, who observed the proceedings while mopping the floor in the back of the room. He had been tipped off about the meeting by the owner of the Polish Tea Room and had agreed to keep tabs on it for Jude.

As Devlin later related, Boxby pulled out a cell phone and rather grandly made a show of dialing a number. The call had been prearranged. Within minutes, while the board members sat there bewildered, they heard several limousines pull up outside. Footsteps — heavy footsteps — resounded at the door. In came a parade of lawyers, each more impressive in dress and manner than the one before.

Behind them, smiling wickedly, was none other than Lester Moloch. And behind Moloch, grinning sheepishly and looking a bit confused himself, a lawyer on either side of him, as if to protect him from either a wayward bullet or from the urge to flee, was Charles Stengler.

Hagenbuckle collapsed in confusion, his mouth as wide open as the stuffed lion in his office. Moloch took over the meeting. With a flourish, his nasal Kiwi accent growing more irritating as he proceeded, he narrated the story that Jude had told O'Donnell and Pril the night before. He spoke of old man Appleby's liaison decades ago in Cyprus, his rise to prominence and power, the woman left behind who was later impregnated, and, finally, their daughter's untimely death and the plight of the orphan boy.

Talking a bit more slowly, as if to savor the moment, he then let loose the explosive fact that Appinopoulis had taken the hand of his first love in marriage. Which, he pointed out, meant that Appleby's second marriage was not worth the paper it was written on. Which further meant, he noted, that the issue of that marriage, Hagenbuckle's wife, had less of a claim on his property than the legitimate grandson, who, in the ways of this wonderful topsy-turvy world, would now be poor no longer. Especially since he had a battery of lawyers and outside parties to protect his interests. For that very day, a lawsuit down in the New York State Supreme Court would substantiate all this and in so doing install the heir to the *Globe* and all its properties in his rightful place. And it just so happened that the heir was so grateful that he had already signed a significant proportion of the newspaper over to Moloch's Communicom, which would run it for the public good.

Like a prestidigitator waving a cape to reveal a white bunny, Moloch pushed Stengler forward. The skinny assistant metro editor was as hesitant as a stage-shy performer at the Apollo. He still wore that odd grin.

Not knowing what else to do, he lifted his right hand and waved weakly to the room.

"And this is the new rightful owner," said Moloch. He turned to Stengler. "Say something," he commanded.

Stengler opened his mouth to speak, but at that very moment he was cut off by Hagenbuckle, who thundered, "You don't mean to tell me that this is my nephew by marriage!"

"Yes," replied Moloch in a voice oozing with rancor. "That is exactly what I *do* mean!"

Hagenbuckle stood erect, his face beaming. He then collapsed in laughter and fell back down on his chair, pulling out a handkerchief and wiping his eyes.

"But, Lester," he said, his laughter ringing with vituperation and genuine jocularity, "you've got the wrong man!"

Moloch looked disbelievingly at Boxby. The longer he looked, and the more nervous Boxby appeared, the more his disbelief began to waiver. It turned, slowly but firmly, into furious belief.

"But . . . but . . . ," Boxby stammered. "He was 'the chosen one.' . . . He told me. . . . He has the right initials. He said he was . . . The Greek man who raised him . . . the struggle."

Boxby looked over at Stengler, who had regained the power of speech.

"Oh, that," said Stengler. "I was maybe exaggerating a little there. It's what we in the newspaper business call 'piping.'"

"At this very moment," put in Hagenbuckle, "my real nephew is conferring with my lawyers. He learned his identity only yesterday and he has consented — so I've been told — to take a place on this very board and help us chart the course for the USS *Globe*."

Moloch, surrounded by his legal entourage, stalked out. They heard his angry footfalls along the corridor outside.

The board session might have gone on longer, since the members wanted to discuss the sensational news they had just heard and relive the intensity of it. But at that point, Devlin dropped the mop, Boxby ran out, and Rosen and Guilden demanded to know what had happened.

Still laughing, Hagenbuckle adjourned the meeting. But the moment he found himself alone, his laughter broke off faster than a snake bite. For he himself had not known about Appleby's bigamy.

The horny old goat. . . . He's probably laughing at me from wherever the hell he is, he thought. Thank heaven I haven't lost the

Globe to Moloch. But must I now relinquish it to some goddamned nephew I don't even know?

61

Boxby rushed across Forty-sixth Street, so preoccupied that he didn't notice he was crossing against the light. A golden Hummer bore down on him, swerving at the last moment. As it whizzed by, he saw the silhouette of the driver's middle finger extended upward.

Ordinarily, such a sight would have pushed him close to the edge. But he paid it no mind. It was the least of his worries.

What could have gone wrong? How could he have been so far off base? He who prided himself on being right, who took such delight in the mistakes of others. He had been certain that Stengler was Hagenbuckle's nephew. Hadn't Stengler confirmed it? Stengler — that idiot — he had just stood there grinning when he was trotted out. Boxby thought back, tried to re-create their conversation at the Marriott Marquis. Usually, he secretly taped important meetings, but that time he had decided to dispense with it — why go to the bother, since everything had seemed so straightforward. His instructions to himself had been simple: Doublecheck Stengler's credentials, make sure he is who you think he is, and then begin to rope him in.

He didn't dare wonder what Moloch was thinking now. The Kiwi hated to lose. Worse, he particularly hated to lose to people he despised, and Hagenbuckle headed the list. Even worse, he hated to lose *in public* to people he despised. Representatives of the prestigious law firm of Howe, Ballentine and Grisby certainly constituted the public. Those guys lived to dish gossip. Right now, the story was probably rippling uptown like a backwash of fetid water.

Boxby's hopes of taking over the *Globe* were dashed. And not only that; he was out of a job. He'd get no severance. He'd be expected to just disappear, probably without even cleaning out his desk and taking home his knickknacks. It wasn't fair. He thought of the photo of his wife, Millicent, on the windowsill, the three framed newspaper clippings that mentioned him, and the picture of him and Vice President Spiro Agnew at the Gwynn Oak Amusement Park in Baltimore County.

He walked south a block, passing by a deli, a souvenir shop, and a video store — places he had seen a hundred times. He didn't lift up his head to look. Instead, he went directly to the back alley that led to the paper, extracted his master key, and let himself in. The building was empty. But what if there was some kind of guard? He decided against taking an elevator and instead walked up the stairs, thirteen grueling flights. By the time he reached his office, his white shirt had a half-moon of sweat under each armpit. He sat down at his desk and looked around. There was Millicent. There was Spiro. And there were the newspaper articles. But they suddenly struck him as ephemera. The office seemed indifferent, cold, as if it no longer belonged to him.

Everything had turned to dross.

His cell phone rang loudly, making him flinch. He pulled it out, looked at the display. HIM. So soon. He was surely calling to berate him, to tell him he was a moron, to fire him. Why answer? Why subject himself to such abuse any longer? He tossed the phone into the wastebasket.

He opened a drawer and pulled out a piece of paper. He dated the top in a steady hand, then wrote, "To Millicent." He thought for a long time, looking out the window. Two pigeons flew by and one landed on the outer sill, ruffling its feathers and walking with high, nervous steps. Why don't you ever see baby pigeons? he wondered. He crossed out "To Millicent," threw the paper into the wastebasket, and took another sheet. On it he wrote, "My Darling Millicent." He thought for a long time and then wrote quickly, "Please forgive me for what I'm about to do. I never should have gone to work for a newspaper."

That pretty much said it all.

He left the note on the center of the blotter, walked to the window, and looked out at the buildings next door and the wooden water towers. In the distance he could see a slice of the Hudson, a band of gray at the end of a ravine of glass and steel. He left his office and took the stairs one flight down and came to the glass doors of the computer room. The lights were dimmed inside. For a moment, he feared that the doors were locked. He slipped his right hand behind the metal bar on the right door and pulled gently. It was open. His heart beat faster, but from what — relief? fear? foreboding? — he couldn't tell.

No one was inside. The humming from the computers provided a steady background noise. The sound was almost comforting.

He sat at a central desk, right under a small metallic eye embedded in the ceiling. He leaned back in the chair and put his feet up. Then he pulled out a pack of Marlboros, thrust it up so that the blond filter tips popped up like tiny organ pipes. He caught one in his lips and pulled it out. That's the way they did it in the ads, back in the old days, when the Marlboro man played on TV.

With his other hand, he reached deep into his front pocket and pulled out his redoubtable Zippo. He clicked it open against his thigh, struck the wheel with his thumb, and raised the flame high. He lighted the cigarette and inhaled. The smoke rushing into his lungs made him dizzy, then light-headed.

The alarm sounded, a piercing metallic clanging. It was so insistent, it intruded on everything and made it impossible to think. How long had they said it would last? . . . Two minutes.

Two minutes can be a long time if you're watching the clock doing nothing, a short time if you're waiting to die.

62

Jude and O'Donnell approached the glass doors of the computer room but found the way blocked by Pril's partner.

"Tweedledee and Tweedledum," said Casey. "Hey, how the hell did you get in? The building's supposed to be sealed."

"It is," said O'Donnell. "But it's about as effective as Homeland Security on the Mexican border."

"We heard the sirens and were told there was an accident up here," explained Jude. He didn't feel a need to enlighten Casey about their master keys.

"Jesus!" he suddenly exclaimed, straightening up. He had just looked through the doors and caught sight of Boxby's corpse lying on the floor near the desk. The dead man's skin was blue and his chest cavity looked sunken. A cigarette with a blackened tip and a lighter lay on the floor next to him.

"I've never seen a body look like that,"

said O'Donnell.

"No one has," Casey replied. "The medical examiner just called. He can't wait to get his hands on it."

"What happened?"

"The emergency fire system went off. It sucked the air out of him so violently, his chest collapsed. Looks like his ribs are broken."

"Was he murdered, or did he commit suicide?" asked Jude, pulling out a notebook.

"Suicide."

"How do you know?"

"He left a note."

"What's it say?"

"Afraid I can't tell you that."

"Just one thing. Does he take responsibility for the murders?"

"No. He regrets only one thing — working for a newspaper."

"I can relate to that," said O'Donnell.

"How'd he do it?" asked Jude.

"He sits at the desk and lights up a cigarette, which sets off the alarm. Then he just stays there, waiting."

"Damn. That takes sangfroid."

"Yeah, whatever that is. You guys better leave now."

They went downstairs and over to the

Greek place on Eighth Avenue. Devlin had called Jude half an hour earlier on his cell to tell about the confrontation at the Edison, but he wanted to provide the play-by-play, and so they had agreed to meet here.

A TV was bolted to the wall. O'Donnell nudged Jude to look. The screen showed a tear-stained Edith Sawyer, who was turning away from the camera. RESIGNS IN COPY-CAT CONTROVERSY flashed above the crawl at the bottom.

She blocked her face by holding up a folded newspaper. Around her was a scrum of cameras and microphones. It reminded Jude of the dozens of perp walks he had covered as a cub reporter. Years ago, she had covered them, too. In fact, she had always gotten a kick out of them, savoring the chance to look directly into the eyes of a killer or count the worry lines on the brow of a kingpin going down.

O'Donnell read his face. "Don't feel sorry for her. What she did was inexcusable. She deserves whatever she gets. She'll be lucky if the paper doesn't sue her ass."

"It *was* inexcusable," Jude agreed. "But I can still feel sorry for her."

Devlin walked in, ordered a double espresso, and sat down. He was still riding high from the scene he had witnessed in the hotel banquet room.

"I couldn't believe it when Moloch walked in. I've worked on two of his newspapers, so I know what he's done to them. You could tell he thought he had the *Globe* in his pocket. He gets this little smile and a glint in the eye. If you dangled a rabbit in front of a rattler, you'd get that same glint. . . . Anyway, he just about wanted to kill that little guy, whatever his name was . . . Bartleby . . . the one who was supposed to have fixed the whole deal —"

"Boxby," said Jude.

"That's it. Boxby. He looked like the bottom just dropped out of his world."

"It did," said O'Donnell. "He just committed suicide."

Devlin whistled. "Man, this is the most dangerous newspaper I ever worked for. How'd he do it?"

"Smoking. He activated the oxygen-suppression system."

"I knew the place was trying to discourage smoking. But still . . . isn't that kind of extreme?"

"It's only in the main computer room. To save the computers, not to safeguard the health of the employees."

"Clearly not. . . . Anyway, tell me about that other guy there. Stengler. The one

Moloch thought was the publisher's nephew but wasn't. He was flopping around like the proverbial rag doll."

"He was a metro reporter until Boxby, thinking he was dealing with a soon-to-be VIP, promoted him to a desk editor."

"So is he part of this?"

"I don't think so," replied Jude. "This seems a little too ambitious for him. He's a slacker. I can see him drifting into it by accident and then sort of staying the course to see what would happen."

"So if Stengler isn't the new long-lost relative of Appleby, who is?" asked O'Donnell.

Jude knew the news was already out, or soon would be; Clive had probably wrapped up the second meeting with the lawyers by now. He said the name out loud.

O'Donnell's jaw dropped. He started to speak, then stopped.

"What's the matter?" Jude asked.

"I'm trying to remember — was I nice to the guy, or did I treat him like shit? I don't think I had much to do with him, not until last night. He was pretty impressive then. But he's young."

"I've never heard of him," put in Devlin. "But he can't be as bad as most of the publishers I've worked for."

"Anyway," said O'Donnell. "It makes for

a good ending. The whole thing's wrapped up now. We got our killer. The excitement's over. The rubberneckers can go home. And the *Globe* can reopen."

Jude remained silent for a second. He wasn't convinced. "It doesn't bother you that Boxby didn't confess anything in his note?"

"Why should he? It's obvious. His suicide is an implicit confession."

"Maybe he committed suicide because the plan to take over the *Globe* failed and because Hagenbuckle or Moloch, or both, would skin him alive. Not because he was the murderer."

"But doesn't it all fit?" protested O'Donnell. "He wanted to take over the paper in league with Moloch. Ratnoff got in their way because he learned their plan. They had to eliminate him. The others were killed because they were witnesses. And then the whole plot crumbled, thanks to Boxby's mistake in thinking Stengler was the mysterious nephew."

"I don't know," Jude said. "It seems to me if you want to wrest control of a major corporation, you'd do it on the sly. You'd try to sneak it through. Why blast everything to pieces with a murder?"

"They *wanted* to do it on the sly. That's

what the plan was with the John Doe filing. But then along came Ratnoff, following the trail like a bloodhound. He would have exposed it. They had no choice but to get rid of him. He would have messed everything up."

"Do we know for a fact that Ratnoff actually knew the whole plan? That he knew the true identity of Hagenbuckle's nephew? Or, for that matter, that he knew that Boxby and Moloch had filed their John Doe suit?"

Now O'Donnell was the quiet one.

"Imagine if Boxby were still alive and standing trial," Jude continued. "Is there any strong evidence against him? The murder weapon — the ice pick — hasn't been traced to him. Originally, it belonged to someone else. Pril tells me there're no prints on it. It's been wiped clean. I imagine Hagenbuckle's prints were on it to begin with, but it would have been hard to use it as a weapon without obliterating them. Boxby could have stolen the ice pick — his office is right next to Hagenbuckle's, so he had ample opportunity. But so could anybody else.

"It was picked up in the trash can on the corner, right near the building. Why leave it there? Whoever did that expected it to be found immediately. He didn't expect it to take almost two weeks to turn up. So why would he want to implicate the publisher right off the bat, turn him into a suspect, if a plan was under way to remove the publisher later through the courts?"

"I don't know," replied O'Donnell. "Maybe extra insurance. You have him removed for murder and in the meantime you install your puppet."

"Maybe. But then there's the second murder. And this time the killer implicates someone else — *you.* Why do that?"

"You can't go around trying to implicate the publisher in all the murders. That's a tough sell."

"Okay. But if you implicate one person, you might make it stick. You implicate two and right away you raise questions. The more I think about it, the more I don't get it. I think once they started out in the courts and tried to change the line of succession at the paper, they'd have wanted to keep it in the courts. Why run the risk of gumming everything up by committing the ultimate felony?"

"So how do you explain it?" Devlin asked.

Before Jude could answer, O'Donnell stood up and pointed out the window. "Hey," he said brusquely. "Why don't you ask *him?*"

Stengler was strolling down the sidewalk, looking dazed, as if he had been run over by a pedicab. They quickly ran out and trundled him inside and sat him down. He smiled weakly.

They insisted he recount his role in the corporate shakedown. He laid out the whole sad story, and they listened, transfixed, until he finished.

"Why'd Boxby think *you* were the heir apparent anyway?" asked O'Donnell.

"I have no idea. Maybe it was my natural bearing." Stengler took a sip of water and added, "I guess my days as an editor are over. I hate to go back to writing."

"What do you mean, *back* to writing?" said O'Donnell.

"Don't be stupid," Jude said. "You don't have to. Nobody who was in that room knows who the hell you are . . . certainly not Hagenbuckle. The only one who did was Boxby, and he's dead. He committed suicide."

"Boxby . . . dead?" Stengler brightened. "So you think I have a chance?"

"All you have to do is help us — us and the police."

"What do you want to know?"

"I'd like to know exactly when Boxby made his first move . . . when did he first

627

contact you?"

"He first called me nine or ten days ago. Then he promoted me that Saturday — you remember."

"Right. And did he talk to you more recently?"

"Yeah. A couple of days ago. He took me out to a revolving restaurant."

"What does that prove?" O'Donnell asked Jude.

"Nothing definitive. But consider this. Ratnoff was killed two weeks ago. I figure if Boxby didn't suspect the identity of the nephew until nine or ten days ago — getting it wrong in the process — then probably Ratnoff didn't know it, either. They would have picked it up from his computer. So in what way was Ratnoff a threat? What could he have exposed if he didn't have the name? At most, that some lawsuit had been filed. That's hardly a major threat to someone like Moloch."

"Speak of the devil," said Devlin. He pointed toward the TV.

The screen showed a quick parade of images, then split in two. On one side was the *Globe* building and on the other the headquarters of Communicom Inc. A caption read "Breaking news." And there was Moloch, glaring in front of the cameras. He was on the sidewalk, reading a statement. By the time they turned up the sound, most of it was over. But they caught the gist from the last two lines: "These rumors that I have attempted to take control of the *Globe* are absolutely false and unfounded. I deny them categorically." He turned and walked away.

The anchor's voice-over intoned, "We're still not sure what's going on here . . . but it seems . . . I mean, Mr. Moloch is the owner of our network . . . but it appears that Mr. Moloch — you can see him there on your screen — it appears someone accused him of trying to wrest control of the *Globe* . . . an absolutely ridiculous accusation, as will be obvious to anyone who knows him . . . and his lovely family. . . ."

"Turn that off," O'Donnell commanded. The restaurant owner did.

"They missed the lede," said Devlin. "That shot of the *Globe* building was live. Didn't you see it? People were going in. It looks like the paper is back in business."

Jude's spirits lifted. "Maybe people missed us," he said. "People bitch about us all the time, but maybe now, after a couple of days without us, they'll appreciate us. They've seen what it's like to get the sum total of their news from TV and the blogs."

O'Donnell grunted again.

"Maybe it's a blessing in disguise," Jude offered.

"In that case, to quote Churchill, 'the disguise is very effective.' The horrible truth is, a couple of days, yes — they'd miss us. A week, they'd still miss us. Two weeks, a little less. And after a month, they'd forget we ever existed. That's life."

"Jesus," said Jude. "I forgot how upbeat you can be when you put your mind to it."

63

Reporters and editors rushed back to the *Globe,* spinning through the revolving doors like lotto balls. The mood in the lobby was a mix of anticipation and dread, as if they were a bunch of ninth graders on the first day of school.

Grabble was wound so tight, he looked ready to pop a spring. His long arms reached out to hug anyone in the lobby not quick enough to duck away. Minutes later, he was in the newsroom, roaming the aisles, handing out assignments off the top of his head, sending reporters all over the city, muttering, "Got to fill the tank . . . get this old jalopy back on the road."

When he saw Clive Small, whose ascension to power as the new scion of the Appleby line was now widely known, he reacted as if he had just encountered the Sun King, all but prostrating himself on the floor. Clive, to his credit, offered to help out by resuming his old duties, at least for the day, but Grabble wouldn't hear of it. He made him deputy metro editor on the spot, pulling Bridget Bates out of her chair and banishing her to the picture desk. Clive's presence on the desk made things awkward, since Grabble and everyone else insisted on running every decision by him and even answering his phone.

Stengler took his editor's chair and sat there, hands folded, with a meek expression, waiting to see what would happen. Nothing did. No one challenged him. Soon he, too, got in the swing of things. He went looking for Fred Bradshaw with an assignment that had occurred to him during the hiatus: He thought it might be fun for a reporter to make the rounds with an elevator inspector in Co-Op City and ask him about the ups and downs of his job.

Clive called Jude on the sly to say that Chris was back to using the Web site in an official capacity.

"I'd just as soon you didn't mention that pirating episode to anyone," Clive said. "And by the way, I'm still going to finish cross-referencing all the names that appeared in Peregrin Whibbleby's gossip column over the years. Our number-one priority is to catch the killer. I don't believe it was Boxby."

Jude thought he detected a new maturity in Clive. How much came from within him and how much was conferred upon him by those aware of his new station was impossible to determine. But he seemed to have turned from a private first class into a three-star general overnight.

Grabble called Jude up to the desk and informed him that someone had been posting exclusives on the paper's Web site. Now, he ordered, Jude would have to chase down all those stories to see if they held up, in addition to providing a multicolumn wrap-up on Moloch's failed attempt to take over the *Globe.* Clive overheard him and cast Jude a conspiratorial smile.

Jude returned to his cubicle. The phone rang. It was Grabble again, this time wanting to know if Jude thought he could handle all that. Jude said he could. There were only six hours to deadline. Did he need help, maybe a legman? Jude said he didn't. Fred rushed over with a plea: Could he get Stengler and his asinine "day in the life of an elevator inspector" assignment off his back? Jude called back Grabble and requested Fred's help. He got it.

"Thanks," said Fred. "I owe you."

Jude pulled out his notebooks and spread

them on his desk, along with the John Doe legal file, the duplicate of the marriage certificate, and other documents. Grabble had given him three thousand words for his story. It would take some doing to construct a flowing narrative, beginning with Appleby's early years as a young boy in Cyprus and ending with today's corporate showdown at the Edison.

At least Fred was there to help him. From his neighboring cubicle, he volunteered to track down the exact quotes of Emerson and Byron that the Avenger had left behind. He dug up background on the law firm, found a short bio of Appleby, and came up with a detailed description of Moloch's business empire.

An hour into the story, Jude was wrestling with a passage about Ratnoff's research in the basement archives. He found it difficult to describe the murder site. How many rows of filing cabinets were there, five or six? Exactly how large was the table where Ratnoff had been sitting? How far away were the pneumatic tubes? He tried to visualize it. Two minutes passed, five minutes, more. His fingers cramped. He began to feel the cold finger of the looming deadline tapping him on the shoulder.

Fred peeked around the corner. "What's

wrong?"

Jude told him.

"No problem. I'll check it out for you."
Fred opened his desk drawer and returned
with a metal tape measure dangling from
his fingers. "I can even take exact measurements."

Jude resumed writing. He left some blank
spaces in his copy, sprinkling it with TKs,
to be filled in later. When would Fred get
back to him? Where was he? He checked his
watch. More than twenty minutes had
passed.

His phone rang. It was Fred, calling from
the basement, speaking indistinctly. Apparently, something was wrong. Jude couldn't
make out what he was saying, but he seemed
to want to show him something. Jude sprang
up, hurried to the elevators, and took a car
to the lobby, where he transferred to one
going to the basement. As it descended,
something nagged at him. Maybe it was the
voice, vaguely familiar. Or maybe something
Fred had said earlier, something he had
been too busy to pay attention to.

The doors opened and he stepped out into
the passageway. It was dark. The lightbulb
was extinguished. The doors began to close
behind him. It came to him in a burst, the
thing that had been nagging at him. Fred

had offered to look up the quotes of Emerson and Byron. *Byron!* The fact that the Avenger had left a quotation from Byron was a secret. It was a potential snare to catch the murderer. And Fred had stepped right into it!

Jude stepped back into the elevator, deflecting the doors. They opened and began to close again, but this time they were stopped by a man's shoe. By the light of the elevator, Jude saw a gun barrel appear, aimed at his chest. A command followed: "Step out!" It was Fred's voice, but it sounded different — no longer downtrodden and self-effacing, but hard and confident.

Jude obeyed. The doors closed behind him. It was dark again, with only a distant gleam of light from the vast pressroom chamber.

"Over there!" said Fred. His eyes beginning to adjust to the darkness, Jude saw the gun barrel wag angrily toward the end of the passageway. He walked in that direction.

"What are you doing?" he asked, not really anxious to know.

"What do you think I'm doing?" said Fred.

"I don't know."

"You can imagine. You have an imagination, don't you?" His voice softened a little around the edges. "I wasn't sure you'd come. I know how busy it gets on deadline. Not from personal experience, of course. It's been quite a while since I've had to write a long piece on deadline."

He was being sarcastic. Jude decided to take his words at face value.

"I know," he said. "But you can never tell. Things turn around. You might get a big one."

The laugh that came was bitter. "It's a little late for that now — don't you think?"

They stepped onto the metal floor tiles lined by tracks. The pressroom was vast and cold. Fred motioned him over to the lineup of wooden sawhorses, poking the gun barrel in his back to keep him moving.

"A few months ago, I might have believed you," Fred continued. "All those years, I was waiting and hoping. But it'll never happen now. We both know that."

Jude stopped six feet from the sawhorses. "How can you be so sure?"

"C'mon, Jude." The tone of anger was back. "Don't play games with me. We both know why not."

Jude turned enough to see the gun was still pointing at him. "You mean because you're the Avenger."

"Yes." Fred told him he could turn around and they faced each other. "It was Byron that gave me away, wasn't it?"

"Yes."

Fred sighed. His anger seemed to slip away. "I knew it the moment I said it. I wasn't thinking, I just blurted it out. I really wanted to help you. . . . Incidentally, there were so many quotations attacking critics I could have used. They really inspire venom. You should look that up sometime."

"I will." Jude stood motionless. "Can I ask you something?"

"Try me."

"Why did you do it?"

Fred stood there, thinking. Five, ten, twenty seconds passed. "Did you ever read John le Carré? *Tinker, Tailor, Soldier, Spy?*" he said finally. Jude nodded. "In it, when the mole is finally unmasked, someone asks him why he did it. And you know what he replies? He replies by citing a piece of his résumé. He says, 'I spent four years in Wroclaw. You ever been to Wroclaw?' Well, I spent four years in shipping news — *shipping.* This in a city where the ports have moved to Brooklyn and everything comes in containers. You ever been in shipping news?"

Jude shook his head. He had to keep him

talking. Fred was moving closer.

"If you had, you would understand. And to think it all went bad because of one story. . . ."

"The story you wrote about that fire in Brooklyn."

"Yes. My lede. It wasn't really that bad. Not enough to wreck my career. I know people make fun of it. I know they keep it in their drawers. But still . . . one damn story. That shouldn't be enough to change your whole life." The anger was back now.

"Fucking people. They think they're so smart. They don't know anything. I could have been a great reporter. I studied literature at Princeton. I graduated with honors. I chose this profession because I believed in it. And look what they've done to me."

He told Jude to back up and stand next to the sawhorses. Jude did. Behind him was the pit. He could feel the cool air from it on the hairs on the back of his neck.

"Incidentally," said Fred, "I don't think it'd be a good idea for you to try to grab the gun. It's likely to go off right in your belly. Or you might plunge backward. Either case, you're gone. The Avenger's last victim."

His voice softened. "I'm sorry it's you, Jude. I always liked you. You were one of the few who were good to me." He was swinging like a pendulum between rage and remorse.

Jude held on to the sawhorse. He was playing for time and looking around, searching for a way out. "Let me ask you a question."

"Go ahead. Shoot — if you don't mind the expression."

"It was you who left me the tape of Schwartzbaum talking to someone and called me at home to tell me about it, wasn't it?"

"Yes. And you know who he was talking to? Me. He only condescended to talk to me because he was smashed. I kept feeding him vodkas."

"Why'd you do that?"

"To help you out. Give you other clues to follow. Of course, they were all wrong."

"The publisher's ice pick?"

"The same. Another red herring. I pocketed it at the farewell party on the thirteenth floor for the Paris bureau chief."

"Those pornographic images on Stengler's computer?"

"Ditto. And now that I've answered your questions, I want you to do something for me. Move that sawhorse aside."

Jude did. There was nothing between him

and a plunge into the pit three stories deep — only a single step. But he thought he heard something — the distant rumble of the elevator. He was sure of it. He had to keep talking, keep Fred's attention on him.

"But why kill Ratnoff? What did he ever do to you?"

"Ratnoff! He's the shit who busted me. The worst of the lot. Plus, he drove the paper downhill — everyone knows that."

"But Peregrin?"

"Peregrin Whibbleby! Don't get me started. Gossip columnist. A bitch in sheep's clothing if ever there was one."

"Outsalot?"

"Oh, come on. She was a total media slut."

The elevator door opened. Jude saw five or six cops behind Fred.

"And O'Donnell? Why place the ad from his computer? Why plant his fingerprints? Why frame him? What did he ever do to you?"

"Did you ever hear how he'd rag me? He was a real shit. Never let me forget that one goddamned bad lede. You find him charming . . . all that lace-curtain Irish bullshit —"

"Now see — that's why you'll never be a good reporter," shouted Jude. He kept shouting to cover the sound of the cops.

641

"You can't write. *Bitch in sheep's clothing! Media slut! Lace-curtain Irish bullshit!* You just spout clichés!"

Fred, shocked, took a step toward him but heard something behind him, turned, and saw the cops. His gun spun around toward them. Jude lunged. He tackled Fred around the legs and held on tightly. Fred kept his gun aimed at the police and raised his other hand, swinging it down hard. The metal tape measure crashed against Jude's temple. He held on and felt Fred fall to the floor. The cops came running toward them.

"Let me go," screamed Fred. "Let me go."

They struggled. Fred smashed Jude's cheek with the tape measure. They rolled toward the edge of the pit. Fred dropped the gun. Jude released his grip around Fred's legs and reached up to grab his waist, but Fred wriggled free and kicked him hard in the shoulder. Jude fell back. Two cops finally came and held Jude from behind as Fred, his eyes wild, looked up at them. Lying on his back, he dug his heels into the floor and lunged backward in a somersault, falling into the void, his shoes kicking at the air. He disappeared out of sight and made not a sound as he plunged downward.

"Jesus Christ," said one of the cops. It was Casey.

Jude glanced up. Pril was looking down at him, concerned.

"I'm okay," he said. "But I'm glad you got here when you did. Second time you saved me."

"You saved us, too. He was ready to shoot. So call it even."

Casey went over to the edge and peered down. "Well, well, well," was all he said. He sounded heartless, especially when he followed it with a laugh.

Two other cops joined him, looking down.

"Holy shit," said one.

"Perfect landing," said another.

A third cop joined them, then motioned to Pril to come over. She helped Jude up, and together they walked to the edge and peered down. Three stories below, Fred was lying impaled on a newspaper conveyor. The weight of his body had caused it to move down a gradual slope, so he advanced, head-first and arms dangling on either side, like a stuck pig on an assembly line.

"Wonder if it'll carry him back up," said Casey.

The conveyor hit the bottom corner and stopped.

"Shit," said Casey. "We better go down and get the poor bastard."

The first cop sighed. "Guess that's the

reporter's equivalent of dying with your boots on."

"Get a ladder," said Casey. "And a net. Go down and put him in it and we'll haul him up."

Jude and Pril began walking toward the elevator.

"How did you know where I was?" he asked.

A high-pitched voice piped up from behind a cabinet in the morgue and Sammy Slimowitz stepped out. "I called the guard. We can't keep on having people killed in the morgue." He looked over at Pril. "Course I didn't know *she'd* show up."

"The guard alerted us. We were on our way into the building," she said.

Pril went upstairs with Jude to the newsroom. He sat at his desk and rubbed his head.

"Maybe you should have that looked at," she said.

"No, it's nothing."

O'Donnell joined them, and then a circle of other reporters gathered around the three of them. Pril explained that they had been on their way to arrest Fred. She had tried to call Jude on his cell minutes earlier when she had established Bradshaw as the likely killer. Using applications at the time of hiring, the police had been comparing all employees' handwriting with the note from the tipster that accompanied Schwartzbaum's tape. Finally, they found a match — his.

"I figured that the killer was laying down a false trail," Pril said. "And the fact that Fred sat next to you meant he could eavesdrop on your conversations. When he feared you were getting close — because you had ordered up a computer search that might lead to him — he felt he had to eliminate you. So he sent you the text message to report to the Queens plant, where he planned to shoot you."

"So he killed Ratnoff because Ratnoff was the one who busted him for that horrible lede?" O'Donnell asked.

"Busted him and kept him busted," said Jude.

"And then he killed the others because they were witnesses?"

"Not at all," said Clive, walking over with a piece of paper in his hand. "Not according to the results of the computer research. It seems that Peregrin Whibbleby, ten years ago, when she was doing her gossip column for another paper, wrote an item about the bad lede that caused a scandal here. She mentioned that just before that lede was filed, Dinah Outsalot had written a two-thousand-word story on the proper way to fry bacon. Outsalot took personal affront at Bradshaw's lede and demanded that Ratnoff punish the writer. And because the whole thing was public, Ratnoff's hand was forced. He had to come down hard on the guy. So from Fred Bradshaw's point of view, all three of them played a role in crushing his career."

"This is beginning to stretch credulity," Pril observed. "All these murders because of a newspaper lede?"

"You don't understand," said O'Donnell. "It was a really bad lede."

He walked over to the rewrite bank, opened a drawer, and returned with a yellowed, coffee-stained piece of paper. He held the paper high and read it aloud with theatrical flourish: " 'A baby was burnt to an almost unrecognizable crisp today as a three-alarm fire swept through a dwelling that was once home to a happy family in the Park Slope section of Brooklyn. Early this morning, with the alacrity of grease going through a goose, flames broke out . . .' "

"No need to go on," he said. "It doesn't get any better. Some people thought it was the mixed metaphor that did him in — the juxtaposition of animals, the implicit reference to bacon combined only a sentence

646

later with the goose. Others — and I count myself among them — feel that it was the use of the word *almost* before *unrecognizable* that went beyond the pale."

"I'm beginning to see what you mean," said Pril.

"That explains the Avenger's taunting notes about 'bacon' and 'goose,' " said Jude.

Grabble came sprinting down the aisle, creating a downdraft that swept papers off the desks behind him.

"What's going on?" he yelled. "This man's got a story to write and you're all standing around talking." He looked at Pril. "You there, get back to your desk."

64

Slough's was packed.

"Just like the old days," proclaimed Woody happily. To celebrate the occasion, he announced to everyone that the first drink was on the house. That may have been a mistake. For the rest of the evening, many customers, even those who could barely stand, swore they had just walked in the door.

Jude was exhausted. He had never come that close to death. But even more trying, he had never written so much on deadline. It filled more than six columns. And he had assisted with four sidebars that took up another two pages. So much had happened at the *Globe* during the recent hours, he and everyone else felt dizzy.

The board, barely recovered from the confusion of its session at the Edison, managed to quickly reconvene on the thirteenth floor and name Clive Small as a voting member. His first words upon entering the august chamber were, "What is with all those ancient photos on the walls?" In a subsequent vote, which was so confusing that Rosen and Guilden split their votes for the first time, the board decided to allow Hagenbuckle to remain on as publisher for a period, though it seemed clear his days were numbered. After the meeting, he slunk away to his trophy-stuffed office and was heard to remark, "Let's away. We'll talk of court news. Who loses and who wins, who's in, who's out, who's up and who's down, and all that kind of stuff about promotions and demotions."

Skeeter Diamond was in disgrace because of his affair with Edith; it contradicted not only company sexual harassment policy but also, as the cynics on rewrite remarked, the higher ordinance of good taste. He was bumped as executive editor but allowed to remain on the paper as a roving correspondent in Africa, based in Lagos, Nigeria. He took the reassignment like a man, though his tic started acting up.

James H. Engleheart was fired as chief of security after the police department officially notified the paper that it was he who had tapped Jude's phone, enlisted a confederate to tail him, and sent the threatening note to Hank Higgle. Engleheart was facing indictment on a range of charges.

The board voted to expel Nathaniel Geyser when it was discovered that he, too, was sleeping with Edith.

As for Edith, she was told to pack up immediately and leave. The national desk planned to run a complete account of her fabrications and plagiarism but hoped to do so with a modicum of restraint. It was thought that a planned series on the paper's serial killer — ten parts, entitled "Death Stalks the Newsroom" — would completely overshadow the story of her crimes. Edith herself was said by a friend to be negotiating a six-figure book contract that could well lead to a movie deal.

The odd thing was that the *Globe*'s stock was up. Apparently, Moloch had started the buying spree two weeks ago, building a foundation to support his own takeover, but now it was continuing. People were calling in from all over, glad that the paper was about to reappear at the newsstands and on their doorsteps.

The bloggers had been going crazy all day. Not all of them got the story of Fred Bradshaw's one-man murder spree straight. One attributed the killings to Moloch and said it was part of a right-wing conspiracy; the blogger asserted this was borne out by the fact that Moloch's cable station had abruptly switched to a feature on sheep-herding dogs in Scotland. Another thought Bradshaw was implicated in the assassination of JFK. A third speculated the serial killings had something to do with aliens landing at Roswell, New Mexico.

Jude told Woody to pour him a J&B and then carried it over to join the riotous group in the back. O'Donnell was there and so were Van Wessel, Alston Wickham Howard, Hank Higgle, and Danny Devlin. Pomegranate came up from Washington, on his way to Baghdad. Stengler was buying a round; he was puffed up because he had actually assigned himself to a story. But the center of attention was, naturally, Clive Small. Everyone seemed to want to sit next to him and they all laughed uproariously at his jokes.

After an hour or so, Clive signaled for quiet and said he had a purely theoretical proposition to put before them. "Let's say, for the sake of discussion only, there's a top editorial position to be filled." The room seemed instantly sober. "Who would you like to see occupy it?"

The whole bar fell silent.

Clive fixed O'Donnell with a dead stare and said, "How about you?"

"Oh, I don't know who I'd put there."

"No. I mean how about *you* going there."

O'Donnell looked as if the wind had been knocked out of him. For a while, he couldn't speak, and when he could, he told a tale.

"You know, I tried that once. I came back from abroad and I filled in as assistant foreign editor. On my first day, I had to call Pomegranate, who was at the Commodore Hotel in Beirut. Something big had happened. . . . I forget what. He wasn't in his room, so they transferred the call to the bar. The barman answered, called out Jimmy's name, and put the receiver down on the bar. And I could feel the energy coming through that line. I could hear the hacks in the background laughing and talking all at once, telling lies, probably. I swear I could almost smell the drinks. I felt that adrenaline rush of a big story. And I thought to myself, O'Donnell, you're on the wrong end of this goddamned telephone line. And that day, I quit being an editor."

The room erupted in applause. When it died down, Clive turned to Jude and said, "And how about you?"

Jude smiled and thanked him for the compliment but said he didn't think he could do it. When he was asked why not, his answer was shorter than O'Donnell's.

"A wise man once said the world is divided into two groups: those who are the doers and those who order the doers around. I guess it's my nature to remain a doer."

More applause.

Names were tossed around. None stuck. None seemed quite right — except one, and when it was offered, by Van Wessel of all people, everyone knew instantly that this was the right man for the job.

"Grabble. He may be crazy. He may have a hundred ideas a minute. He may drive us all insane. But it'll be a helluva ride and the goddamned paper will go in the right direction."

There were cheers, which set off a round of inebriated, hopelessly optimistic proposals.

"Let's get back to our roots, get back to the basics. Afflict the comfortable and comfort the afflicted, that's the motto."

"Let's be who we are. Let's stop trying to be everything to everybody and just tell it straight."

"Let's get back to hard news, do hard-hitting investigations."

"Let's swagger a little. Let's be brave again."

"Let's dump the ombudsman!"

"By Christ, print's not dead yet!"

Jude watched Clive's face. At one point, he heard him mutter, almost to himself, "Some of that, yes. But not all. We can't go back. The Internet is here to stay and we have to adjust to it."

At that moment, who should walk in the door but Pril, who had been tying up loose ends. She had dressed up for the evening and she was all smiles. Finally, the case was solved and the PC had gotten his slice of the glory cake.

"Jesus, and I thought cops got stupid when they drank," she said.

She sat down between Jude and O'Donnell.

O'Donnell asked her how strong the case against Fred had been. She said, "We got him dead to rights. We got his DNA on the envelope left on Peregrin's desk. A log of the phone call to Jude's apartment. Plus, he confessed to Jude moments before he jumped."

"I don't remember," said Jude. "Did he show up on that tape from the lobby camera? The one of the people who went to the basement the day after the murder?"

"No," she replied. "He used the rear elevator coming and going and never returned to the scene of the crime. He might have loosened that lightbulb, though — to throw us off the track. He wasn't stupid."

"There's something else I've got to clear up," said Jude. "I told you some time back that Hickory Bosch, our former executive editor, went down there disguised with a beard and wearing a hat pulled down over his face. Did he have anything to do with this?"

Pril laughed.

"No, we interviewed him. Casey did. He spent a pleasant afternoon down at Cape Fear, hanging out with the guy. Found him charming. Bosch went to the basement to look up his own advance obit. Wanted to see how long it was and what it said. He's got a good alibi for the night Ratnoff was killed — he was at a shooting range in Maryland. He spends most of his time working on his book. It's a four-volume series weaving his experiences in the newspaper business with anecdotes about clamming."

They answered questions, laughed, told stories, and exaggerated well up to midnight. Gradually, Slough's cleared and the noise died down so low, people could hear one another talk. Woody's free drinks policy had pretty much decimated them. After several rounds, Clive excused himself, said good night, and shook hands all around.

Jude was feeling none the worse for wear. Then Pril had one of those brainstorms people get when they're three sheets to the wind.

"Let's go to the Blues Basement," she said. "I feel like singing."

Five minutes later, she and Jude and O'Donnell were outside, linking arms, walking to the subway. Jude noticed someone up ahead, coming toward them — a woman, a familiar figure. He saw who it was. He felt the recognition hit him in the gut.

"Elaine!" He didn't know what to say. This moment was one he had dreamed of, and dreaded, for so long. "What are you doing here?"

"I was looking for you," she said. She cocked her head to one side in that old charming way. Her blond hair brushed one shoulder. She was dressed in a figure-hugging rose-colored outfit and, he had to admit, she looked good.

"I heard the news. I thought you'd be celebrating. I'm happy for you — the paper's back. I know how much that means to you."

"Yes," he said. "It's good news."

She looked hesitant, glanced over at O'Donnell and Pril. Jude introduced them. Elaine said that of course she had heard a lot about O'Donnell. She remembered Pril from the time she had been interviewed by her, and she had seen her on the news earlier that evening.

"Yeah," said Jude. "She's the cop who broke the case."

"Bullshit," said Pril, slightly slurring her words. "You broke it. I cracked it. I mean, I only put a crack in it . . . a little crack. You *broke* it."

Elaine looked around uncertainly, gave a little shiver, and patted her skirt with one hand. She looked at Jude.

"You want to get a cup of coffee?"

"I thought you were coming with us," said O'Donnell. He didn't try to disguise his annoyance.

Jude was silent.

"Don't you want to hear Pril sing?" O'Donnell persisted.

Pril remained quiet. Jude looked over at her and she looked away. A lifetime passed.

Jude thought, I never know how to make the right decision — until I make it, and only then do I realize it's the wrong one.

Elaine tapped the toe of her shoe impatiently. That's what did it.

"I'm sorry, Elaine," he said. "I promised these two drunks I'd go with them."

She stopped tapping. Her face fell.

"I understand. I really do. I'll call you . . .

sometime, maybe."

"Okay."

She continued past them and they kept walking toward the subway. The three of them felt they had just done something significant together. They didn't turn around to see if Elaine was watching them. O'Donnell could tell, even in his drunken haze — or maybe because of it — that Jude still wasn't sure he had made the right choice.

"C'mon, Lennie," he said. "I'll tell you about the rabbits."

Pril looked up.

"Rabbits? What the hell are you talking about?"

"You know," said Jude. "Rabbits. Lennie and George. *Of Mice and Men.* And here I thought you were a humanities type."

"Ah, the boy never forgets," said she.

"You always have to have the last word — don't you."

"No, I don't."

"Yes, you do."

"Don't."

They laughed.

Since it was so late, they decided to grab a cab, and they made it to the Blues Basement in no time. The place was still crowded. The owner greeted Pril with a hug and then shook hands with Jude and O'Donnell and showed them to a cozy table on the side with a good view of the band. They ordered drinks, which arrived right away. The owner came by and whispered something in Pril's ear. She smiled and nodded, then stood up and walked to the microphone.

The band started the beat, a good, slow, bluesy sound. She took the mike off the stand and introduced herself. There was some applause.

"Here's one you all know, from Billie Holiday." She nodded toward Jude's table. "I'd like to dedicate it to that young man over there."

She opened her arms wide, lifted her head, and began to sing.

AUTHOR'S NOTE

This book is a work of fiction. The characters in it do not represent real people, either living or dead. However, to lend the work an air of verisimilitude, I have drawn upon various incidents and anecdotes that have made the rounds of newsrooms. In particular, the witticisms of the character Virgil Bogart were actually said to have been uttered by the famous reporter and foreign correspondent Homer Bigart. Two events — an account (somewhat changed) of a police reporter who went AWOL and the murder by Charles E. Chapin (city editor of the *Evening World*) of his wife — are true and were taken from Stanley Walker's *City Editor.* The story about Big Bill McGee's interview with a deaf-mute is also said to have happened, but I changed some details, including the name of the reporter. It may fall into that category, "too good to check."

ACKNOWLEDGMENTS

I wish to thank my agent, Kathy Robbins, and my editors, Phyllis Grann and Sonny Mehta, for their help in shaping the idea for a novel about a newspaper and for their reservoirs of patience in seeing it through to the end. I am also grateful for the assistance of Kate Rizzo and David Halpern in the Robbins Office; Karyn Marcus, formerly at Doubleday, and now at Thomas Dunne; Jackeline Montalvo at Doubleday; and the superb copy-editing work of Carol Edwards. Among my friends who helped, I want to single out Nicholas and Elena Delbanco, who vetted the manuscript at an early stage; Richard Cohen, a former publisher and now a writer, who made valuable suggestions; and Peter Osnos, who reminisced about various newspaper characters he has known. For information on the NYPD, I relied on Bill Clark, a former homicide detective. And above all, I am once again indebted to my wife, Nina, who read every word multiple times and made many suggestions and saves, and to my children — Kyra, Liza, and Jamie — for their help and forbearance.

ABOUT THE AUTHOR

John Darnton has worked for nearly forty years as a reporter, editor, and foreign correspondent for the *New York Times.* He won the George Polk Award for his coverage of Africa and Eastern Europe, and the Pulitzer Prize for his stories smuggled out of Poland during a period of martial law. He is the best-selling author of *Neanderthal* and *The Darwin Conspiracy.*

The employees of Thorndike Press hope you have enjoyed this Large Print book. All our Thorndike and Wheeler Large Print titles are designed for easy reading, and all our books are made to last. Other Thorndike Press Large Print books are available at your library, through selected bookstores, or directly from us.

For information about titles, please call:
(800) 223-1244

or visit our Web site at:
http://gale.cengage.com/thorndike

To share your comments, please write:
Publisher
Thorndike Press
295 Kennedy Memorial Drive
Waterville, ME 04901